KT-450-942

# In Praise of Hatred

## Khaled Khalifa

*Translated from the Arabic by Leri Price*

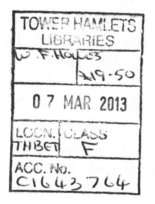

TOWER HAMLETS
LIBRARIES
W. F. Howes
19.50
0 7 MAR 2013
LOCN. CLASS
THBET F
ACC. No.
C1643764

W F HOWES LTD

This large print edition published in 2013 by
W F Howes Ltd
Unit 4, Rearsby Business Park, Gaddesby Lane,
Rearsby, Leicester LE7 4YH

1 3 5 7 9 10 8 6 4 2

First published in the United Kingdom in 2012
by Doubleday

Copyright © Khaled Khalifa, 2008
Translation copyright © Leri Price, 2012

The right of Khaled Khalifa to be identified as
the author of this work has been asserted by him
in accordance with the Copyright, Designs and
Patents Act, 1988.

All rights reserved

A CIP catalogue record for this book is available
from the British Library

ISBN 978 1 47122 785 1

Typeset by Palimpsest Book Production Limited,
Falkirk, Stirlingshire
Printed and bound in Great Britain
by MPG Books Ltd, Bodmin, Cornwall

MIX
Paper from
responsible sources
FSC    FSC® C018575
www.fsc.org

For Amina Muhammad Ali

# CONTENTS

# CONTENTS

# FOREWORD

This novel's main locus is Aleppo, a city surrounded by olive orchards and pistachio fields, ancient enough to vie with Damascus for the title of the oldest continuously inhabited city on Earth. The wider setting is the urban Levant, with its markets, mosques, caravanserais and luxury consumer goods, and the social networks and carefully guarded reputations of the traditional bourgeoisie.

Our nameless narrator is the youngest of a house of women who live suspended – like embalmed butterflies, to use one of the novel's recurring motifs – waiting for men to act, and often suffering from their actions. Hers is an emotional, conflicted, self-contradicting voice, at once passionate, sensuous and austere. She is 'the shy girl who used to stand on the doorsill afraid of loneliness and orphanhood'. She is also, by force of her context, capable of formulas like this: 'We need hatred to give our lives meaning.'

Part of the problem is self-loathing and sexual repression. As she grows, the increasing weight of her breasts causes the narrator to talk less. She wears cruel bras. Her school friend Dalal tells her that women are 'animated dirt'. And the narrator is trapped in this dirt: 'I felt my body to be a dark vault, damp and crawling with spiders.'

*In Praise of Hatred* is full of images of vaults, cloisters, enclosures. This is because imprisonment – by ideology, by history, by hatred – is the novel's most persistent theme.

The values in the narrator's home are sometimes harsh and unforgiving, but they are real and true nevertheless. Wrapped up with them are perfumes and carpets, music and plays, a rich Islamic and poetic heritage, precious mystical experiences.

But beyond the walls there's a non-conservative Aleppo, too: the dominant secular world. At school the uncovered girls call the veiled girls 'the Penguin Club'. The *mukhabarat* (secret police) sympathizers write reports on the indiscretions of their peers. These students, like Mao's cultural revolutionaries, are able to terrorize their teachers and trample on the moral code. A girl called Nada, in her 'suits of commando camouflage', is kept by a much older lover who works for 'the death squad'. Political and sexual transgression are closely associated in the narrator's mind, and she is outraged when her friend Ghada gives up modest dress to enjoy an affair with a regime figure. 'Hatred bewildered me,' she confides, 'just as powerful love bewilders a lover.'

She praises hatred because she perceives it to be, like the struggle for sterile purity, a means to power. She calls on it to save her from the 'absurd compassion that threatened my inner strength'. She calls on hatred religiously; indeed there is a suggestion here that hatred is the common religious impulse linking up Syrian society. The regime, too, conflates compassion with weakness and violence with strength, as does the Islamist organization the narrator approaches first through women's study circles. Her guide urges the girls 'to hate all the other Islamic sects'.

The dictatorship in Syria gave secularism a bad name, because it was a forced and sectarian secularism, to fit with the general Middle Eastern postcolonial dispensation, in which minority groups ruled over majorities. The French had established an 'army of minorities' which took control of the state shortly after independence. In 1963 the military wing of the Ba'ath Party reached top position, and by 1970 Hafez al-Assad and his generals – from the Alawi community, an esoteric Shia offshoot – had reduced the Party to an instrument of absolute power.

At first the Assad regime was perceived as a popular nationalist, modernizing alliance between Alawi and Sunni peasants against the urban Sunni bourgeoisie. By the late seventies, however, unrest was bubbling in a population outraged by over-representation of Alawis in the security services, a corruption-crippled economy and, most of all, the regime's 1976 intervention in Lebanon to aid Phalangist forces against the Palestinian-Muslim-Leftist alliance.

Syrian leftists and Islamists organized against the regime, which responded with savage repression. Soon opposition activity degenerated into an assassination campaign run by the Muslim Brotherhood's armed wing. At the June 1979 Artillery School massacre, Alawi cadets – 'the ones', in Khalifa's words, 'who had descended from the mountains with limitless ambition and vitality' – were separated from their Sunni fellows and shot in cold blood. The regime's savagery culminated in the February 1982 massacre at Hama, where tens of thousands were killed, and in the slaughter of hundreds at Tadmor prison.

The poet Hassan al-Khayyer, an Alawi from the president's village, summed up the tragedy:

> *There are two gangs: one is ruling in the name of patriotism but has none of it.*
> *Another gang claims good faith; and religion forbids their sayings and acts.*
> *Two gangs. My people, be aware of both! Both drink from the same evil waters.*

The regime murdered al-Khayyer in prison.

From the eighties until 2011, Syrian society was effectively depoliticized. It became a state of fear, a kingdom of silence. Discussion of the *'ahdath'* ('events') publicly was taboo. Stories were transported by whisper, in private.

So how brave and necessary it was to write a

fiction of these 'events'. In our narrator's harsh euphemism, Alawis are 'the other sect' and the Ba'ath Party is 'the atheist party', but the historical references are unmistakeable. Khalifa plays one of the noblest roles available to a writer: he breaks a taboo in order to hold a mirror to a traumatized society, to force exploration of the trauma and therefore, perhaps, to promote acceptance and learning. He offers a way to digest the tragedy, or at least to chew on its cud. In this respect he stands in the company of such contemporary chroniclers of political transformation and social breakdown as Günter Grass and J. M. Coetzee.

The regime, which we now know hasn't changed mentality since the eighties, didn't recognize Khalifa's achievement. *In Praise of Hatred* was published secretly in Damascus, where it remained available for forty days until the regime discovered its existence. Next it was published in Lebanon by Dar al-Adab, and was shortlisted for the International Prize for Arabic Fiction, otherwise known as the Arab Booker, in 2008.

In purely literary terms as well as politically, the novel rises to a daunting challenge: how to represent recent Syrian history, which has often been stranger and more terrible than fiction.

For a start, it's a perceptive study of radicalization understood in human rather than academic terms. It accurately portrays violent Islamism as a modernist phenomenon, a response to physical and cultural aggression which draws upon Trotsky, Che and Regis Debray as much as the Quran, and contrasts it with the more representative Sufism of Syrian Sunnis.

Next, it examines the dramatic transformations of character undergone by people living under such strain: the bucklings and reformations, the varieties of madness. The characters here are fully realized and entirely flexible – even our bitter narrator – and their stories are told in a powerful prose which is elegant, complex, and rich in image and emotion. There is musicality too in the rhythm of the episodes, the subtle unfolding of the plot.

If readers are imprisoned by the narrator's perspective, they can escape into the many lesser stories within the frame. The detailed backgrounds and narratives of the characters met weave a realist fabric dense enough to rival that of Naguib Mahfouz. The range is broad: Turkish inn-keepers, English archaeologists, a Yemeni ex-Communist and a CIA officer who together enthuse over a future Islamic State, and a Saudi prince who wants a palace 'that looks like his mother's womb'. During the 'events' we meet death-squad members with skulls tattooed on their chests, kicking volumes of Shakespeare, and fugitives who evaporate into the night sky, and death becomes 'as commonplace as a crate of rotten peaches flung out on to the pavement'.

Just a few days before sitting down to write this, I was lucky enough to meet Khaled Khalifa in Beirut. He was calm and effortlessly cheery, despite the fact that his arm was still in a sling, broken five weeks earlier when regime thugs attacked a funeral procession for the murdered musician Rabi Ghazzy.

Glancing from Khalifa's novel to internet updates, it seems that nothing has changed since the eighties; the same massacres, tortures and battles unfold. It's as if Syria is locked in a recurrent curse. But this twenty-first-century uprising is a popular revolution on a far greater scale than the one in the eighties; its revolutionaries arise from a far broader social spectrum. Instead of assassins and secret cells, there are grassroots organizers and defected soldiers. In the early months at least, the slogans on the streets focussed on freedom, dignity and national unity. Yet violence and the regime's instrumentalization of sectarianism has reopened deep and rarely examined wounds. Khalifa's plea for 'absurd compassion' is more necessary now than ever.

So this is a work of immediate importance, but Khalifa is keen to escape stereotypes. 'I don't want people to read my book because I'm an "oppressed writer" or a "writer who lives under dictatorship",' he told me. 'I want them to read it because they're interested in the story, and because they enjoy it.'

Both for its style (translated here beautifully) and for its human truth, *In Praise of Hatred* is a supremely enjoyable book.

Robin Yassin-Kassab
July 2012

# THE MAIN CHARACTERS

The nameless narrator, a teenage girl and member of an old Sunni family in Aleppo

Her mother and father, a fish trader

Her brothers: Hossam and Humam

Her three maternal aunts: Maryam, Safaa and Marwa

Her maternal grandmother and grandfather, a carpet trader

Her three maternal uncles: Selim, Bakr and Omar

Radwan, an old blind family retainer

Khalil, the grandfather's driver

Hajja Radia and Hajja Souad, leaders of local prayer circles

The narrator's classmates at middle school:
Fatima
Dalal

In Nazdaly, Turkey: Esmat Ajqabash, the owner of a khan in a remote part of the country

Wasal, his wife

Zahra, the daughter of Khalil and Wasal, later Bakr's wife

Wasal's lovers in Mosul, Iraq: Khalil, the grandfather's driver; Mister John, an English expat; in London, a Pakistani cab driver; Abdel Ghany Bilany, a Syrian trader; a Spanish sailor

The narrator's fellow students at secondary school:
Hala
Nada, who has a lover, Abu Ramy, in the death squad
Ghada, who has a middle-aged lover, an officer in the Mukhabarat
Layla
Hana, a member of the same religious circle
Hiba

Rima, Omar's wife

Abdullah, a Yemeni man, Bakr's friend and associate, later to marry Safaa as his second wife

Zeina, Abdullah's first wife

Prince Shebab El Din, a Saudi prince, schoolfriend of Abdullah, and later a close associate of Abdullah and Bakr

Alya, a member of the religious organization and mentor of the narrator

Nadhir Mansoury, a death squad officer who later marries Marwa

Jalal, Selim's son

Philip Anderson, a CIA operative

Saleh, a former Communist protégé of Abdullah

Um Jalal, Selim's wife

The narrator's cellmates in the desert prison, including:
Sulafa
Suhayr
Rasha

Sheikh Nadim Al Salaty, an associate of Abdullah's in driving the Soviets out of Afghanistan

# PART I

# WOMEN LED BY THE BLIND

The smell of the ancient cupboard made me a woman obsessed with bolting doors and exploring drawers, looking for the old photographs I had carefully placed there myself one day. A picture of my mother shaking the single lemon tree in the courtyard, with me standing beside her with shining eyes; of my father in military dress, smooth-chinned and sharp-eyed; of my brother Hossam wearing his school uniform and laughing, holding our younger brother Humam who was swathed in a blue blanket; of me in my long black clothes, my face circular in the middle of the black sheet and my body completely concealed, in front of a faded picture of hunters and their dogs in pursuit of a fleeing gazelle.

The picture had been placed there by the photographer to whose studio my father had accompanied me. The photographer took me by the hand and sat me down on a cold wooden chair, cajoling me kindly, and directed me to look towards his thumb near the camera shutter. 'Laugh,' he said to me. I didn't know how. I looked at my father, seeking permission, then back to the thumb of the photographer; I grimaced as if I really was laughing. I can still remember the click of the camera and the solemnity of that moment with total clarity, as if I had only just left the studio that smelled heavily of mothballs and on whose clothes hooks were hung faded outfits of army officers and peasants, Mexican hats and cowboy costumes, like the one Terence Hill wore in *Trinity is Still My Name*. My small hand was weak in my father's palm which clutched mine in fear of losing me amongst the crowds on Telal Street.

I am still searching for the smell of that ancient cupboard, placed in the room that the eldest of my aunts, Maryam, had designated for me after she sat facing my father and convinced him to let her take me to live with her and Safaa, my middle aunt. She told him that they were lonely after the death of my grandparents and the marriage of my youngest aunt, Marwa. My father nodded his head in agreement and then laid down some conditions which I didn't hear. After Maryam agreed to them, she and my mother began to gather up my clothes, my books and my other personal belongings. They were strewn all over the small room my father had built for me in the open space close to the kitchen after two small, firm mounds rose on my chest, their increasing weight causing me to speak less and less.

In my grandfather's house I was very pleased with my high-ceilinged room, the strictly observed mealtimes, and the regular visits to the hammam

4

every Thursday, and to Hajja Radia's house every Friday evening, like rituals whose necessity I didn't understand. The first thing that worried me was the cacophonous chanting of the women behind Hajja Radia. They made me nervous – I almost suffocated in the crowded room, but I didn't dare flee. But on later visits the smell of sweat mixed with women's perfume began to relax me, like a woman whose desires are inflamed by chanting.

During the first year I lived in the large house I found the enormous spaces bewildering. I was half lost among stairs of stone and banisters of iron, the wide rooms, the high, decorated ceilings delicately coloured by a Samarkandi artist. My grandfather had brought him back from Samarkand after one of his journeys there to look for Persian carpets, and my grandmother assigned him the best quarters during his six-month stay in their house. Every morning, he would wake up at five o'clock, perform the ritual ablutions with my grandfather, and then both of them would go to Aleppo's Umayyad Mosque, after eating the breakfast my grandmother had already prepared and laid out for them on the low table close to the large pool.

The Samarkandi wasn't known to have a name. He used to return from the mosque and enter his small room to mix his colours and clean his brushes, and then he would close his eyes and withdraw into an ecstasy of painting like a devout worshipper. He transformed the ceilings of the

5

three large rooms into everlasting masterpieces. His fame spread among the rich families who vied with each other in the decoration of their homes, but the Samarkandi continued to live in the house in silence, with the exception of a few words to my grandfather, until he left for Paris with his Aleppan wife and child. He left with a French officer who had been bewitched by the hands of this Samarkandi who 'created masterpieces out of thin air'. His ceilings bore perpetual witness that he had, at one time, lived in the city of Aleppo. His leaving was like a death for my grandfather, who had discovered the Samarkandi's talents and interceded on his behalf in his marriage to Bint Aboud Samadi.

Before his departure, the Samarkandi had come to the house in clean clothes, his small eyes laughing. My grandfather embraced him warmly and kissed him goodbye; the artist said, 'You are my father.' Afterwards, he sent a letter with his address in Paris and a photograph, an unheard-of miracle, showing himself, his wife and his child standing in a park. His wife was wearing brightly coloured clothes; her large white breasts were on display and she wore a stylish beret instead of a proper head covering. My grandfather laughed and gave the picture to my grandmother, who sneered at the unveiled face and threw it into the fireplace. She never again mentioned the bare face of Bint Aboud Samadi, even when she came to visit twenty years later together with her son. He wore a suit which was overpowering in its elegance, and there wafted from him a strong fragrance which disconcerted Maryam.

The Samarkandi's son was astonished by our spacious house, by its stone arches and its vaulted doorway, and by the two pillars decorated in Corinthian style and added by my grandfather, thereby turning what was supposed to be an entrance hall into his own room. The son scrutinized the house, then took out his camera to meticulously record every detail of the house's angles and his father's ceilings, while his mother (a true Parisienne) sipped coffee quietly and composedly with my grandfather. He was expansive, beaming with joy at hearing news of his Samarkandi son, who still recalled him as the saviour who had lifted him from a corner of the ancient souk into the welcoming space of the world, and he repeated as much to his visitors, students and teachers of decorative art. My grandfather was delighted with this Aleppan woman who had removed her black clothes and consistently demonstrated astonishing adaptability, having swiftly learned French to be of assistance to her husband, who declared her to be his world. Husband and wife worked as determined as tortoises climbing rugged mountains.

Maryam remained alone, struck with confusion by the perfume which embedded itself deep within her pores, and then within her heart. She stole glances at the Samarkandi's son and examined him furtively, frightened that someone would notice her ever-longer, stupefied stares as he leaned over to focus the camera on a corner and record in minute detail the care taken in the harmonious composition of stone, walnut and coloured lines; much of it remained a riddle whose meaning no one could understand. After they left, my grandmother, without looking into my grandfather's eyes, said that he had been too indulgent towards Bint Aboud Samadi. Maryam was distraught that the son had gone, and she reflected on her sin. She was unaware, even then, of how it had happened.

Like all the women of my grandfather's family, of whom my mother was one, Maryam had a round face with a high forehead and clear green eyes; her fingers were long and soft like those of all women in old aristocratic Syrian families; her figure was tall and sensual, but her unexceptional chest was formed by two unappetizing breasts, above which was a neck of average length. This all created an impression of ugliness which green eyes could not hide.

Meanwhile, in the large house, I would lose myself in the galleries and the three generously proportioned rooms. I was captivated by a large mirror hanging at the back of Maryam's room that had a wide walnut frame carved with creepers and damask roses. I took advantage of any of her absences to enter her room and stand in front of

8

the mirror, engrossed in the details of my face and body whose weight I would palpate. I remained sleepless without knowing that I had begun to change and enter through the gates of young womanhood. Safaa noticed my transformation, treated me kindly and alluded to certain matters, in contrast to Maryam, who I knew was worried that I stood so often in front of a mirror, inspecting my figure and my chest and indifferent to other exciting things in her room. She wrote down a charm for me, observed me cruelly and closely, hung a hijab on me, and ordered me never to take it off because Satan was lurking in my body. My sternness increased and my silences lengthened.

The only man who was not related to us and who was still allowed to enter the courtyard and wander throughout was Blind Radwan, who lived in a small room in one of its corners. Blind Radwan was tall and gaunt, clean-clothed, and his hands always smelled of the perfumes he traded in. He mixed them in large glasses whose capacity he was familiar with, then decanted them into small medicine bottles, sealed them tightly, and sold them to private customers who were drawn chiefly from the women of the district of Jalloum and visitors to the Umayyad Mosque. He promoted his small trade using pleasant songs, overlaid with *dhikr* and verses from the Quran. He claimed that his brand, under the name of 'Blind Radwan', was known in every corner of the Arab world, and boasted that foreign traders had tried various means of obtaining the secret of a certain mixture which made women compliant, amorous and delicious in bed. Another blend made men overflow with charm and virility that no woman could resist. In front of Maryam, he claimed that this particular scent was the one with which the Prophet had perfumed his Companions and forged them into rare flowers which he planted in the Levant, never to be uprooted.

Radwan had been used to sleep, eat and drink with his blind companions from the mosque, who would disperse around the area of Sayyidna Zakaria to read *mawalid* and infiltrate various houses of Aleppo in the evenings. No one had known about Radwan other than those in the mosque, as if he had been born, lived, and would die there, silently; his eyes, with their lost sight, would trace circles in their sockets, sniffing the colours and richness of the clothes of the worshippers.

My grandfather brought Radwan to the house and gave him the room which had at one time belonged to my great-grandfather's groom and carriage driver. Maryam cleaned it out and my oldest uncle, Selim, moved in a squeaky iron bedstead which had long been overlooked in the cellar, along with a woollen mattress. My grandfather refused to listen to protests from my grandmother who considered this to be a violation of the sanctity of the house, although she worked to make up the deficiencies of an unmarried man's room.

Blind Radwan lived happily like a servant with special privileges, entering into the fabric of the family to become one of its permanent features. I couldn't imagine the house without Radwan; when I was much younger he used to sit me on his knee and take out sweets and cloth toys from his small closet. He would sing to me in his sweet voice and I would paw his chest sleepily. When I moved into the house permanently, I avoided him and treated him the way a lady would a servant. He neither protested nor overstepped the boundaries – he would eat at the kitchen table and move on. Maryam never forgot his meal times, and he was never far away from her. He accompanied us to the hammam every Thursday carrying a large bag, waited for us by the door until we had finished, and accompanied us back the same way, his crudely made cane never misleading him. He would walk in front of us, head raised, with stable and evenly spaced steps. For Jalloum, this scene became a symbol of the little that remained to my aunts of the bygone glory of their forefathers, which they had created out of their permanence, and their refusal to submit to the transformations which the city and its families had not escaped.

Every Thursday I went to my parents' house after school to eat with them and my two younger brothers, Hossam and Humam. They were like strangers, and greeted me politely like an unexpected guest. My mother would kiss me without warmth, and as I helped her to prepare the food she would ask coldly about my news and about my aunts without waiting for a reply – she was confident that nothing would change in her old family home. She had left it as a young girl twenty-five years earlier after my father's return from Alexandria, where he had gone to work as a fish vendor directly after the 1958 union with Egypt. Many people doubted the truth of this tale, and declared that my father was an agent of Abdel Hamid Sarraj. Two years after Syria's secession from the United Arab Republic, my father returned to Aleppo and, without any preamble, asked my grandfather for my mother's hand. My mother had vague memories of him back then as a young man with a big head, who walked haughtily and unhurriedly buckled down to work, never deviating from his chosen course.

My mother stayed in her father's house after the wedding, while my father embarked on his compulsory military service, which lasted three and a half years, and it was during this time that I was born. They didn't rejoice at my arrival; a leaden atmosphere was hanging over the large house as my grandmother was gravely ill, as if she were insisting on catching up with my grandfather who had died a couple of years earlier, in the tragic manner of men who choose their lives and the manner of their death. These men would not brook anyone's

12

mockery, despite the infirmity of their old age, which my grandfather described as the other face of God's love.

My grandfather resigned from his three businesses and gathered my three uncles in the house's reception room. Maryam and my grandmother sat beside them as my grandfather briefly explained that he was no longer capable of overseeing his business affairs, and turned their management over to his sons. To mitigate against any unforeseen difficulties, he bequeathed his wealth according to Islamic law and the house was to become the property of his daughters, who would retain the right to make use of it until the end of their lives. Uncle Selim protested against this defeatist tone, trying to dissuade his father from his resolution. My grandfather laughed and leaned on his cane; he ordered my grandmother and Maryam to prepare the table in the dining room reserved for guests, and to take out the best silver dinner service.

My uncles didn't understand their father's intentions until a week had passed, during which my grandfather exerted all his efforts to retain the ability to stand and walk like a military leader inspecting his troops. He accepted only Blind Radwan's help, leaning on him like a crutch when going to the mosque on Friday or when relieving himself. He wouldn't allow my grandmother to treat him like an old man; he used to say to Maryam, as he leaned on Radwan, 'A woman must not see how low her man sinks in old age, so she

13

can remember him with love.' For four years, Radwan left him only at night. Sometimes he would even sleep nearby on a mattress prepared especially for him in the corner. One evening, my grandfather asked my uncles to come the following morning, as he wanted to visit the Citadel. They debated the matter between themselves, but not one of them dared to venture an opinion.

At nine the next morning the three men were confounded. My grandfather had asked them to help him up but when they rushed over to carry him, he stopped them with a gesture. Confusion reigned over everyone as he directed them outside, and asked for Radwan to accompany him. The folk of Jalloum couldn't believe the scene: my grandfather in the lead with Radwan beside him, smiling as if he were the only one to have understood what had happened. Leaning on his companion's arm, my grandfather stood in front of the gate to the Citadel, contemplating the high walls and sniffing the stones as if he were settling his debt with time. He descended to the gate of the covered market and plunged into its crowds, savouring the smell of clothing, textiles and sackcloth; of gold; of the crowding of women's bodies; of the souk, blazing with lights; of abayas embroidered with silver and gold and spread out over shop fronts; of strips of rugs and dappled carpets. He entered the customs house and stood in the entrance to his shop where Khalil got to his feet smiling, and kissed him before returning to his place. My grandfather looked for a long while at the pile of carpets in the shop. He said, in a voice barely audible to my uncles and looking at Radwan, 'This blind man has an equal share in all your wealth. If he comes to be in need one day, you will all be held responsible before God . . .'

Selim murmured and Radwan raised his head, smiling. He pressed my grandfather's palm whose face lit up like the dawn in delight at meeting the other traders and his former clients. He opened his pores to the breezes and sounds to chase away the ignominy of previous years. My grandfather directed his footsteps home after praying in the mosque with my uncles. Radwan bore the sarcasm of his blind associates who, in a salute to their smiling friend, chanted a *mawlid* without taking a penny.

That afternoon, my grandfather returned to his house in state. He briefly teased my grandmother and lavished praise on my aunts for the delicious food which had been laid out on a table near the fountain. Everyone sat down and savoured the overlapping conversations while a chaos of inter-weaving hands stretched out towards the lamb stuffed with almonds and laid on a mound of *freekeh* fried in butter. My uncles had brought their children who were longing to see their grandfather, and their wives who disbelieved the marvel which was embellished with every retelling. After washing his hands, my grandfather got up, entered his room, took off his woollen robe, lay down on the bed, and died.

That evening, my uncles recalled that my grandfather had hobbled to the family tomb, contemplated the gravestones for a while, then pointed with his cane and said, 'Bury me here.' He had sketched out a rectangle, adding, 'Here I'll be close to my ancestors and friends.'

Radwan disappeared for four days, during which no one laid eyes on him. It was understood that my grandfather had chosen the manner of his death, and with Radwan's help he was able to determine precisely when would be his last moment.

Within this house, incomplete tales of men, women and miracles were narrated, and they fascinated me. They made me a captive of the light reflected off the water in the stone pool, the focus of the circle we formed when we gathered around it. In summer we clung to its moisture and moved all our everyday effects into the courtyard: the dinner table, the comfortable cane chairs, and the radio from which Safaa was never parted. During summer days she was a victim of bouts of deep depression, and sometimes even of a gaiety whose secret no one knew. She wore diaphanous clothes cut above the knee and hurled water over the plants and stones, which would release a fresh scent thanks to the invigorating moisture. She would bring coffee and sit on the edge of the pool, slowly and deliberately drinking from her cup in the early afternoon breezes. Maryam objected to her nakedness, her voice becoming increasingly strident with an accent of stern rebuke. The affable Safaa made no reply, other than to refute Maryam's argument that Radwan would soon be back by saying, 'He's blind. He can't see.' When Maryam retorted that God in Heaven could see us, Safaa replied that God saw us naked, and in all forms and situations. The argument always ended when Maryam stood up from behind her Singer sewing machine and sat by the pool, quietly drinking coffee and rereading Sura Yusuf. I noticed the premature wrinkles on her forehead and the harshness in her eyes. She tried to hide her tenderness, which was noticeable only when it exploded all at once and drowned me. She had tried to kill something with her black clothes and her severity, but she couldn't. She never spoke of her softer, affectionate side to anyone; she never allowed any trace of its existence or even attempted to make it appear, but hid it in a deep and abandoned well. I tried to question her, and gathered up my strength and the words necessary for marshalling a sentence, but I stuttered, and the words fled. She raised her eyes and fixed them on mine, waiting for me to speak; I kept quiet and looked elsewhere, wary of meeting her gaze again.

The Samarkandi's son returned with his mother so he could bid my grandfather goodbye before their return to Paris, and my grandfather welcomed them as honoured guests. Maryam was afraid, foggy with the scent that had lingered since the Samarkandi's son's first visit. He asked everyone to pose for a souvenir picture which would make his father happy, and my grandfather agreed. Everyone gazed perplexedly at the camera shutter, holding their breath; Uncle Omar looked afraid, Maryam lost. The son of the Samarkandi took another picture of my grandfather standing alone near the lemon tree, and another of him sitting on a cane chair next to the pool, then yet another of everyone with Bint Aboud Samadi. A festive atmosphere animated everyone apart from Maryam; she was numb, and couldn't shake off her torpor. Before mother and son left, my grandfather went into his room and came out carrying a skilfully decorated carpet, a portrait of Omar Khayyam surrounded by cupbearers and Persian phrases. The Samarkandi's son was taken aback by this treasure, which my grandfather said was one of the original carpets he had bought from the auctions in Istanbul, and which befitted the success of his own Samarkandi son. Bursting with happiness, my grandfather led his guests to the door. When the Samarkandi's son stood in front of Maryam and put out a hand to bid her goodbye, she had reached the end of her trance. Her lips murmured almost inaudibly, 'You have slaughtered me . . .' No one noticed the alteration in her except my grandmother, who knew that her daughter was wretched, the prisoner of a concealed adoration she could never express. There was no need to guess who the person might be; since coming of age, Maryam had seen no other eligible man's face. My grandmother tried to get closer to her daughter to have this acknowledged, but Maryam's silence hardened. Her secret remained confined to her sisters, who tried every means of convincing her to relinquish this hollow pride.

Two months after this visit, a letter came from Paris bearing the signature of the Samarkandi, who called my grandfather 'my dear father'. He thanked him for his warm hospitality to his wife and son and conveyed his inability to thank him adequately for the carpet, the significance of which he cherished. He had enclosed four cards from his son: for my grandfather, a representation of Notre-Dame; for Maryam, a view of green lawns, water fountains, and red, yellow and lilac flowers; a third for my uncles Omar and Bakr. The final card was for Radwan, who had convinced him that he was the most important purveyor of perfumes in Aleppo. To him, the Samarkandi's son sent a general view of Paris and the addresses of several important *parfumeries* so that Radwan could get in touch with them. In addition to the cards, he sent the photographs he had taken, printed on postcards, which everyone passed around. Radwan touched the pictures and said that he would write to the French manufacturers to offer them his inventions and his secret blends. He searched for someone to write his letters and who wouldn't betray his secrets. The pictures eventually came round to Maryam and everyone soon forgot about them. They never appeared again until after my grandfather had died.

After his death, Maryam appropriated my grandfather's room and rearranged it. She embroidered a new bedcover with a brightly coloured peacock in the centre, restoring happiness to the wool, and spread out new azure, flower-strewn sheets. She left other things where they were, such as the cane chair, the bedside table and the large mirror (after wiping the dust off it). She brought out the photograph in which my grandfather, mother, aunts and uncles were gathered, and placed it on a small table in front of her so she would see it every morning. Next to the picture she placed the postcard from the Samarkandi's son. At Maryam's insistence, Radwan had taken both the photograph and the card to a carpenter far away from Jalloum who made frames for them out of dark brown wood. I used to see Maryam dusting them carefully; Maryam who never woke up from her stupor. She exploited Radwan's need for someone to write to the French perfume companies. Sworn to total secrecy, they conspired together without reaching any agreement. Maryam wrote a letter for him in Arabic and read it out to him while he remained silent, raising his face to the sky and shaking his head in dissatisfaction, adding a sentence here and cutting a sentence there. Then he would dictate a letter to Maryam, who wrote it down with fierce enthusiasm. Anyone watching them sitting together, arguing and raising their voices, would not have believed that this woman was Maryam and this man Radwan who shouted that this was his international career, that it was impossible to treat the letter lightly, and concluded by saying the French loved refinement in all things. Maryam tore up the paper and waited expectantly for Radwan's next words. He calmed down, after remembering that he was the servant. He apologized and brooded for a while, then began to recite a poem from one of the *mawalid* still lodged in his mind; she reminded him that that wasn't a letter to the French company. Radwan laughed and told her a story about the French man he had accompanied home in order to recite poetry to French women, as they sat half-naked on walnut sofas carved with the ninety-nine names of God. The man was openhanded and generous before returning Radwan to his bed in the Umayyad Mosque, with more than the requisite respect.

Radwan resumed his consideration of the letter, and formulated the perfume Maryam requested of him in return. They swore an oath that his letter and her perfume would remain their greatest secret. They called on God to witness their agreement and even named it the Maryam–Radwan Accord, which Radwan shortened to the Man Accord. Maryam disliked this abbreviation, which drew attention to phrases she dreaded thinking about or referring to. She always insisted to me that the body was filthy and rebellious, and these words embedded themselves in me like an irrefutable truth. I began to guard myself against this rebellion named 'body'; I obdurately hated my incipient breasts, their two brown nipples beginning to blossom. I hid them beneath cruel bras made for me by Maryam out of satin box-linings. Whenever my breasts broke free, I would touch them and feel their strange delectability.

When I saw uninhibited girls undoing their bras and showing off their cleavage to the breeze and the sun in the small square, or for the titillation of the young men crowding around the entrances of the girls' schools, I felt rage at their filth. I avoided looking at their gestures or listening to their conversations describing sexual positions both for men and women; girls would relate these tales with ardent enthusiasm, sometimes explicitly naming the body parts. Fatima was the boldest of these girls. She tried to be nice to me, but I shunned her obscene conversations and the smell of sweat emanating from her pores. I turned to the group surrounding another girl named Dalal and exchanged books with them.

Dalal was sober and grave; she seemed, in her black clothes, to be our leader. Her orders were final, and delivered tersely and in a coarse voice. She dominated us, and we were happy to have a leader who wouldn't hesitate to pull the hair of any girl who ridiculed our silence and our black clothes. Dalal said that women were animated dirt. Her own thoughts never came to her briefly or concisely, so she gabbled incoherently instead. I would nod, agreeing with everything in order to reach Paradise.

I arranged the room Maryam gave me in a style I will always try to recreate: the iron bedstead in the Mamluk style and the woollen mattress; the perfumed, snowy-white sheets; the small, ancient wooden table on which I placed an embroidered cloth to hide its battered scars; the chair carved with snakes and butterflies (I don't know why its maker decided on such a combination). I would sit on the comfortable chair, lost in thought for hours at a time, alongside a wardrobe and a small shelf for my books. The most valuable of the furnishings was a small Persian carpet from my great-great-grandmother's trousseau: it was my share of the valuable carpets that belonged to the women of the family. I loved the patterns on the carpet; I was so afraid of dragging my feet through it that I stretched it out and hung it on the wall. Maryam was pleased when she saw it hanging there. My room opened directly on to the courtyard and from the window I could see the radiant silver moonlight on the surface of the pool as I felt a chill seize me. I was powerfully drawn to this scene, and clung to every detail; it became my little world. I decorated the walls with the paintings I made during my period of silence, which continued until I lost any desire to speak at all.

After we returned from the hammam, my aunt Safaa would enter her room and bring out a bottle of perfume wrapped up in a gauzy nightshirt. She would take off her clothes, smear flowery cream all over her body and sprinkle it with perfume, before putting on the nightshirt and a Moroccan abaya over that to cover all traces of her charms, and returning to the living room. She didn't help Maryam with dinner on Thursdays. We sat at the table in silence as Safaa got up and entered her room, not to emerge until morning. Maryam would open the Quran at Sura Yusuf and continue with her daily recitation until she rose with strict punctuality at ten o'clock and crept into bed. I never understood Safaa's withdrawal every Thursday night until some years later, when we began to speak unreservedly about the men whom we had never seen, and the sweetness we had never tasted.

My grandmother abandoned the project of marrying off Maryam after she refused three suitors whose suitability and good looks my grandmother had spared no effort in talking up. Maryam would always enumerate their non-existent faults, grow resentful at these 'suitors' and then return to her room. As she took off her clothes a strange perfume would envelop her; the perfume which had settled in her pores. Every day, it emanated from her dreams and her body, while she lay in bed like a cold corpse waiting for salvation and the fever of a man. She tried to grasp its features in an attempt to describe the scent to Blind Radwan, who would listen in silence. He would go to his room and return bearing a blend of essences: camomile, anise, damask rose. He would mix them again the following day and present the blend to Maryam who would sniff it and then either hand it back or throw it into the bin, with no regard for his anger as he gibbered that what she had done was a denigration of his experience and perfumes. After this, recalling that she had written his letters to the French company and kept his secrets, and that she was in charge, he lowered his voice and listened to her description. Very slowly, word by word, she once again described the perfume that calmed her.

After years of discussion and failed experiments, Maryam finally forgot about the perfume when Blind Radwan, with great daring and drawing heavily on the patience which it had taken him seven years to acquire, told her, 'This is the scent of a man you love, not a perfume.' Radwan also forgot about the French company after their curt reply asking him not to embarrass their public relations department, and declaring that what he had sent them was not a proper perfume at all, but a mere essence.

Maryam read the letter out slowly and with conspicuous relish; she dwelled on certain words more than once, but she was saddened when she saw the betrayal etched on his face as if tears were about to gush from his eyes. She took his cold hand and nursed him with tactful words, trailing behind him when he went to his room, letter in hand and stumbling over the tiles, as if he had forgotten the position of the objects on the floor – his memories of a place he usually remembered by heart and in which he had never been mistaken had become confused. The letter, which no one other than Maryam read, remained as proof of the infidel West's perfidy with respect to genius, as Radwan angrily complained to his blind companions when he went to visit them in the Umayyad Mosque. He would bring them food and sweets which Maryam had made, walking confidently to the door of Sheikh Abdel Jaber who welcomed his friend and invited him to sit on the bed. In the courtyard of the mosque he cried out in a way that all the blind men recognized, and they all came to throng the room. They caught the scent of food and sweets, and did not mistake Radwan's own scent – Radwan who, as a response to their singing an ode to the Prophet in welcome, thanked them for their princely reception and lauded them one after the other, replying to their sarcasm and jibes with great forbearance. They all crowded into the streets of the city, oblivious to the glances of passers-by fascinated by the scene of nine blind men whispering in eloquent Arabic, laughing loudly, or reciting love poetry and describing the faces of unknown women drawn from among the many worlds of humanity.

Something I didn't know how to describe grew inside me and granted me a calm I had never known before. After paroxysms of anxiety and fears that caused me physical pain, and Maryam's lessons about virginity and a body which must be braced for Hell on account of its sins, I felt that I was drawing ever nearer to a luminous image. Its features became clearer every day for a virgin believer who remained undefiled by any man other than the halal one who would arrive one day. I would sit by his side as an obedient servant, and acknowledge his guardianship over me. I would serve him as a slave and worship my lord so he would inspire me to be a virtuous captive. It was an image drawn for me by Maryam with painful precision as she quoted verses from the Quran, the Hadith of the Prophet and biographies of those pious Muslims whom she adored to the point of infatuation. I would sit on my chair opposite her and near the fountain once the summer evenings grew refreshingly cool, or close to her on the sofa during the winter nights, or clinging to her during Hajja Radia's gatherings when her sweet voice responded to the beat of the tambourines and she sang about the life of Rabia Al Adawiya. Deep emotion would take hold of me and the rest of the women; tears would pour down our cheeks and we would sway like the slender branches of a poplar tree, embarking on a long journey whose roads opened up on to rivers of milk and honey, and the pleasure of absolute certainty. Hajja Radia would sing a *nashid* and the sound of the tambourines would embed itself in my pores.

I flew over cities and houses; I performed my ablutions and swooped over the walls of Paradise. I saw the best Muslims fluttering in their white abayas like seagulls over the azure ocean. I was absorbed with the sweetness of the sounds, with the singing of the women, with the journey into the trance whose secrets I had learned. I ascended step by step, slowly, gradually, before reaching the peak where the plains opened up before me far in the distance. I joined them, the most pious and believing of all Muslims, and I saw their glad, smiling faces. What sweetness was taking possession of me, cleansing me, baring me, making me captive to the long dream which sought to seduce me throughout my life? The Prophet came from far away in a snow-white abaya, walking over the water in quiet contemplation. He came nearer and I retreated. I saw him reach out his arms to me, surrounded by colourful birds whose sound reminded me of the peal of golden bells. The Prophet was coming . . . his footsteps were splashing in the water . . . I drew back to reach the other side of the water . . . I sat down cross-legged, waiting for his glorious arrival . . . I heard his sweet voice and its echo submerged me: 'Come closer, my daughter, O Believer.' I came closer and he was flying.

Maryam told me joyfully, 'There are the gates of Heaven.'

I said to her, 'But he was flying!'

'Yes; he flew and rose to Heaven.' Maryam blessed me. Tears flowed from her eyes as she advised me, 'Guard your secrets.'

I perfected this advice and began hiding my secrets. I would avoid the long sessions with Safaa; I couldn't look into her eyes without being possessed by a desire to confess everything.

Safaa warned me about plunging too deeply into Hajja Radia's trances, without really explaining what she meant in plain language. She would come into my room at night and stretch out on the bed, grab a book and then return it to its place. She would pick up another and become bored with it just as quickly. I saw she was distracted, her eyes clinging to the ceiling as her body relaxed on the bed. With a curse on silence and renunciation, she would open the door and go out into the courtyard where she would sit on the large wicker chair close to the pool, waiting for something.

Sometimes, in the mornings, she went out alone to visit her sister Marwa. I would hear her violent disputes with Maryam who refused to allow her outside on her own, censuring her and charging her with immorality. Safaa would reply brusquely, cruelly, letting her veil drop over her face as she left. Maryam would dress hurriedly and rush after her, and Blind Radwan would join them as soon as Maryam called to him. He completed the scene, so familiar to the residents of Jalloum: my aunts in their long black clothes hiding the whiteness of their bodies all the way to the tips of their long fingers, and Radwan in front, silent. No one saw Safaa's tears under her black veil as Maryam walked upright, without turning around or moving her gaze away from a fixed point on the horizon. Radwan would return to his room and I would be left alone in the dreary house.

I was overwhelmed with a curiosity to explore the place calmly and thoroughly; to examine my face and the details of my squalid body. I hated my leering breasts, so like antlers. I wished they wouldn't stand out so much. I wondered: how does the body die? How do nipples, pores, desires die? How will I walk that luminous path leading to the expanse of water where Rabia Al Adawiya, just outside His kingdom, searches for the face of God? I reach out to her, I anticipate her fragrance, I ask her to take me with her along the path of light. She reaches out for me, I touch her fingertips. I am struck with a tremor that shakes me to my depths. The standing waters begin to move. I tell her to baptize me with holy water and leave me on God's shore, alone. I look into her golden eyes beyond the limits of spoken language, and a deep silence extends between us. I hear the sound of distant tambourines gradually drawing nearer, the sound rising on all sides; soft, with precise rhythms. From far away, the faces of ghosts appear to me, human in structure; faces without features, with smooth contours. I didn't understand the *nashid*; Rabia's hand became even warmer and softer. My fingers sweated and desire rose in me like sap through a tree. The caravan approached our stopping-place and Rabia's face was still submerged in its silence. Black horses, featureless beings, tambourines; I raised my gaze to Rabia's face, looking for an explanation for this gathering. She was absorbed in her murmuring. I didn't understand the imperfect words. She took me by the hand and led me outside. I hadn't realized that we had flown, nor that we had crossed the streets of Jalloum, and that the scents of thyme and spices scattered within the narrow confines of the alleyways had become embedded within us.

The land was vast, its meadows as lush as brocade, and the desert sand sparkled like silver confetti, as did the houses made of white stone which we entered. I heard people's voices, but never saw a single one: I heard women's laughter, children's screams, the clamour of musical instruments. We went out into a narrow alley which became still narrower the further along it we walked, until we reached the point where we could no longer walk side by side. Rabia took my hand and I followed her, panting, trying to cling to the rustle of her white gown and her braided hair. She didn't turn towards me, but continued walking behind the mass of horses, *nashid* singers and tambourine players. At the end of the alley the space narrowed and prevented me from passing while Rabia slipped through easily, as if the walls had been drawn aside to admit her. She looked behind, smiled at me, and left as the barrier opened up on to infinite water. The tambourines drew off and the horses departed.

Only I remained. Everything around me, stones, water and sky, was silent. I was alone. My grandfather took my hand with a chuckle, my three aunts walked behind us at a measured pace in their usual clothing. At the first bend I saw Radwan leading our caravan to the gate of the huge house, leaving us in the vast outdoor space and taking himself off to his room without a word, as ever. There were plants surrounding me and water in front of me. I was sure that Rabia would never descend from the ceiling to take me by the hand again and lead me back to the water, which was unlike any water I had ever known. Whenever I tried to recreate the whole image, that water at the end bubbled in my memory, honey-coloured and shot through with green.

I felt very tired and went into my room shivering, crept into bed and slept deeply. I tried to recall the details of Rabia's face and eyes. Features, voices, scents: all fled as if I were in a faint or turning delirious. I only woke up because of the clamour made by my aunts. I heard Marwa's voice and got up wearily from my bed, quickly washed my face and went into the living room where she was wailing. I hugged her and buried my face in her hair, and I felt the last of her sobs as she drew back to examine my face; its wheatish complexion hadn't regained its purity yet. I didn't understand what had happened. My aunts were speaking all at once and then suddenly falling quiet. After a short while, Radwan entered and said, 'Selim is coming.' He left and my aunts were silent.

My aunt Marwa had a beauty spot on her cheek, an old family legacy which had been interrupted for two generations. When my grandmother saw it for the first time she said, 'She will return the family to its true path. The women who come after her will enjoy their lives and they will have many children. Isolation will never enter their hearts.' My grandfather, desperate, didn't much care. He was convinced that his daughters would never break the bonds of spinsterhood and believed that fate, despite erring once, would doubtless return everything back to its natural course. For this reason he didn't care about the charm hanging around the neck of his youngest daughter, nor the blue beads my grandmother used to make colourful necklaces in order to adorn Marwa when she accompanied her to family councils. These sessions roused a wish in Maryam to curse these perverted women, who gathered as if in a bazaar to inspect the value of the girls, the suppleness of their bodies, the size and firmness of their breasts. There were interviews and hidden deals between the women who enjoyed buying and selling and enlarging upon the qualities of their absent sons, and the mothers of those girls strutting around in long gowns, laden with fake jewels, their faces coated with creams, as strange blends of perfume wafted from their bodies and weighed down their breath. The expert old women would reach out for hair and teeth and breasts, exposing chests to palpate the tender-skinned bodies, only just blooming with coloured desires.

My uncles Selim and Bakr arrived and Marwa cried in front of them. She said she could no longer bear life with her husband, who came home only when he was drunk or high, and who would beat and kick her. When her family cursed her and accused her of destroying his life, she uncovered her white back in front of us. Maryam pointed to the blue and ruby-red bruises that resembled whiplashes. Selim concealed his fury while Bakr angrily looked back and forth from his brother to my aunt's bare back; I was haunted by the blotchy colours of her skin, like scorched earth. Marwa calmed down after Selim assured her he would put an immediate end to this brutality of her husband, and she would not leave this house unless his behaviour changed. Bakr swore to smash his head in with the hammer hanging in our cellar; this last was spoken to his uncles, who had intervened more than once to curb his violent conduct.

My uncles left at the end of the night, their presence having rendered appropriate a long conversation about how everyone was. Among those present was Radwan, who informed his friend Bakr that he had created a new perfume that he was taking to the markets, and which he would release under the name 'Attar of Secrets'. Bakr spoke about his increasingly frequent trips to various places all over the world, which were necessary for the expansion of his business.

Maryam was overjoyed at this reunion of the whole family. She forgot to grumble about Safaa's behaviour, and pretended to forget Marwa's problems after she went into Safaa's room. Marwa took off her black outer clothing, and in her light clothes she appeared effortlessly beautiful when I saw her throat and her hair reaching out from underneath the thin head covering tied around her neck.

Selim asked me if I needed anything, and Bakr complimented me on my upstanding morals, which had become proverbial among all the members of the family. He kept proudly repeating, 'Leave this one to me, she's like a daughter to me.' I was gladdened by Uncle Bakr's attention; for me, he represented the pinnacle of vigour and brilliance on account of his tall figure, his powerful body, and his features that hinted at cruelty yet were lined with a fervent tenderness and deep sadness which no one discerned. His eyes rolled ceaselessly in their sockets as if a fire were burning deep within him. I didn't understand the anxiety and reticence in his movements, which could quickly grow suspicious and agitated. He was absent for days at a time without informing anyone of his whereabouts. His wife complained to Maryam, who told her that my grandfather had often said that business had its secrets.

I would have liked to tell Maryam that the city was secret, the streets were secret, so were the stones and people, houses, rooms, hearts . . . even laughter was secret in a city that celebrated secrecy and where everything was enacted far from others' eyes. Recently, I had started feeling that everyone was conspiring against everyone else. It was conspiracy that I saw in Marwa's eyes as she prepared a bed in Safaa's room, both of them absorbed in asides they were trying to hide from me. I tried to come closer to them to listen in on their whispered conversation as they were weaving.

I could feel from Marwa's eyes that she was flooding me with love. She would wake me up for school and make my bed while I washed my face, and then she would prepare breakfast for me and coffee for herself. Her light, tender conversation swamped me with a deluge of hidden affection; I felt that I needed it more than at any time in the past. Questions blazed inside me. In school, with Dalal and the other girls muffled in black clothing, I plunged into descriptions of Hell and the torment of the grave; these images terrified me, and the girls excelled in their sober narrations. I felt that the black Angel of Death was waiting for me on the other side of the street. He would open the ground to me and I would wander with him among the risen corpses. I would wait my turn to walk on that path, no features on my face, a flat being without scars. If I fell before reaching the gates of milk and honey and the sweet rivers where the believers were gathered, I would perish in the midst of the sins from which I no longer knew how to distance myself.

In school, I became hostile to Fatima and her lithe body. She jumped about in the courtyard during breaks and sports classes, revealing her chest without caring. She enjoyed loosening her pink, lacy bra; it formed a total contrast to the one which grasped my own breasts. I didn't dare touch them, so I wouldn't awaken the desire that Dalal warned us against.

Hajja Radia wept when she reached Rabia. I told her, 'Help me.' The black veil covered my hair and face so I resembled a fish swimming in black tar. She reached for it and plucked it away, and she said, 'Walk with me.' For the first time, I saw the face of Rabia glowing with the brilliance radiating above the trees along the road. Tambourines welcomed us, the horsemen dismounted and lights shone from their faces, overflowing with joy. I tried to touch them; I reached out a hand and stretched up but Rabia drew me back and said, 'Stop that. The sun illuminates everything.'

I asked, 'What about these men?' She laughed. I saw her lips part in a sweet smile and her teeth gleamed with a shade of white I had never seen before, like dazzling quartz or a multi-faceted crystal. She told me, 'They are not men.'

We crossed the fields of palms and pistachio trees, shaded by their branches, and a special perfume I had never smelled before permeated the air. Rabia walked beside me, or I walked beside her, and she beckoned to me and said, 'Have you seen the face of God?' I raised my head as if I were seeing the azure heavens for the first time. 'Where is the face of God, Rabia?' Alone in the fields of palms and pistachios, the earth closed up in front of my feet. I felt increasingly desolate and oppressed as I neared the end of the fields. I was struck with fear and an obscure feeling like the one that penetrated me whenever I sat close to Hajja Radia, who was indulgent with me and tried to respond to my anxious questioning. When I told her that I had seen Rabia, she asked me, 'Do you go to her, or does she come to you?' I couldn't understand the point of her question. It wasn't important if I went to her or if she came to me; it was only important that we had walked together through the fields and crossed the rivers. After this, whenever I saw girls washing in this water, I was no longer afraid that the river would damage their chastity. Hajja Radia added, 'They are rivers of Paradise, not rivers of this world.' I left the fields of palm and pistachio trees, depressed. The sun which had shaded us had turned sullen, announcing its ire at the heavy veils we lowered over our faces.

★   ★   ★

I left school that day weighed down by heavy dreams which put me on my guard. I entered the narrow alleyway, and asked Maryam, 'Are there any forbidden smells?' Without slowing down she said, 'Yes: the smell of men who aren't related to you.' I remained vigilant against this forbidden smell, against glances and the accidental meetings of eyes which sent tremors through my limbs, and for which I punished myself cruelly. Maryam gave animation to, and Safaa alleviated, the feelings of affliction that made me a slave to a delusion that I was polluted. I felt as if these glances had robbed me of my chastity and penetrated the depths of my femininity, despite the heavy protection afforded by the hijab, prayers and the bonds of the path I walked along towards the gates of Paradise. From there, I would walk up the steep steps to sit in the presence of God.

The forbidden smells persecuted me. I no longer approached Radwan so I wouldn't smell the forbidden scent; I almost convinced Maryam to forbid Radwan from entering the living room without permission, and to order him to stand at a distance when he spoke to us. I would have succeeded were it not for Safaa's violent intervention, which I had never seen before, as she said, 'Do you want to turn this house into an asylum?' Maryam recalled her great need for Radwan as a servant; she was still describing the scent of the Samarkandi's son to him. She never despaired, and exaggerated and heaped praise on Radwan's genius at composing perfumes, even though he had failed and no longer took Maryam's descriptions seriously. Every month, he used to bring her a vial he had chosen at random, enlarging on its special properties, and ending with a prayer to the Prophet which Maryam would repeat after him and then thank him for.

Marwa spread out her clothes and arranged her few possessions in the wardrobe, listening very quietly to Uncle Selim's information that her husband had persevered in threatening her if she didn't return to their house unconditionally. Marwa laughed and said that she would never return, and that she would prepare herself for life without a man. She took out her bright clothes and arranged them next to Safaa's, the two of them immersed in endless conversations, interrupted by suppressed sobs or brazen laughter which irritated Maryam, but she concealed her ire. She raised her eyes to me, as if willing me to be deaf so I wouldn't hear them.

I longed to join Safaa and Marwa in their nightly talks on the wide bed as they reclined in their delicate, soft, colourful night clothes. I would enter their room and Safaa would make space for me close to them, but I sat on the edge of the bed, and didn't know what to say. I contemplated Safaa's brown chest which looked like mine. I saw her breasts which had retained their firmness even though she was thirty. I sensed them quiver within the silkiness of the fabric; breasts deprived of pleasure.

Marwa would relax quietly, sneering at women's perfumes or their inane conversations about their absent children. One day, Nishany's mother had accompanied her to the hammam along with women of the extended family, who didn't know the importance of a fleshy hip creasing slightly over a generous thigh; or of a chest with a texture like pleats of sand in the desert, untouched by the wind; nor of two breasts equal in grandeur, like tagines of polished marble. They reached out their hands for her hair and Abdullah's sister almost tore it out by the roots. Marwa screamed, 'These are original goods!' Playing with the snaking locks of her hair she said to us, 'They lose it in Nishany's house.' Marwa concluded her lampoon of Abdullah's mother, whose mouth had the fragrance of sorrel, by saying, 'I don't know how I could bear her.' And she added, 'I don't know how I bore her for three years!' It was my grandmother who had wanted this marriage, whatever the cost.

Marwa told me that the scent of men was delicious if they were really men, but I didn't understand what she meant. She got up slowly and went into the kitchen to prepare tea, not forgetting the sprigs of mint and the cinnamon sticks. She didn't much care that the noise might disturb Maryam, who was fast asleep in her spacious bed. Next to the bed was a small chest of drawers, and hidden in one of the drawers were

41

three pictures of a young man of medium height and average build, brown-skinned, with clever eyes. Other pictures smelled of the fragrance whose secrets Radwan was unable to attain. Marwa still remembered that she had heard him assert, protesting against Maryam's yell that he was a failed perfumier, that this woman wanted to sleep with a man's scent. Marwa came into the room carrying the silver tray with three large cups on it, and poured the tea. By the weak light, I saw her figure swaying with delicious malice. She offered me my cup lazily, with a 'There you go, my little one.' Safaa winked and reached a hand under the bed. She took out a box of cigarettes, which I was seeing for the first time. My aunts smoked with relish. Marwa turned towards me and, on seeing my aversion, told me, 'It's horrible, but it's not *haram*.' I was embarrassed, and felt a huge rush of love for Marwa and Safaa, whose eyes roamed over the ceiling. I would have them round to my room after Maryam fell asleep, and I clung to Marwa as her sweet voice rose in songs of the Prophet's flight to Mecca, and occasionally the even sweeter songs of Um Kulthoum who entered the fabric of our daily lives. Marwa dusted off our asceticism with music and we withdrew from Hajja Radia's *nashid*. Maryam never interrupted her attendance at these Friday sessions, even after Safaa stopped going, having announced that she was bored with repeating *nashid* and episodes from the Prophet's *sira*.

Maryam observed us silently as we all practised deceit and clung to the rituals set precisely according to the Scottish clock purchased by my grandfather from a Jewish trader. He hung it on the wall of the living room and its position never changed; nor did its ticking, which resembled frogs croaking at night in a bog. We mended the stone fountain in the pool and the sound as it scattered droplets over the expanse of calm, unmoving water stirred up those nightly rituals of ours which I will never forget.

As Marwa sang 'First He Entangled Me' or 'They Reminded Me About You', her soft, deep, melodious voice flooded me, and created openings that I found frightening. A real shudder ran through me when I heard her voice in the deep of the night. Marwa stood like a professional singer and closed her eyes, surrendering to the movements of her hands as if they were clutching something precious or beloved. Safaa, distracted, smoked silently. Radwan sat beside his room, and I heard his suppressed sighs, born out of the ecstasy we had been missing before our discovery that Marwa had such gentleness and nobility in dealing with the night. Her presence made me acknowledge that I was a young woman, groping towards new tastes. During these nights I told her the meanings of the things accumulating around me, rising up like an imaginary barrier no one could see but me, or like a snare calling me to overcome it. Marwa was deeply affected

43

by my words. In her eyes, I read deep satisfaction accompanied by the doubt that afflicted me, and from which I fled to the deep, warm moments by Hajja Radia's side.

Blind Radwan would arrive at Hajja Radia's house and stand by the door without ringing the bell. He waited for us without speaking to anyone and when we came out he could sense our footsteps. He walked in front of us as if he were clearing the way, and I surrendered to Maryam who clasped my arm without uttering a word as we crossed the streets. People were used to watching us every Friday and, at the same time, didn't care. Our footsteps were full of fear, and we slunk like silent lizards over the stones of Jalloum's alleys. Radwan reached the door of the house and his hand did not fumble with the key. We would enter the courtyard silently and Maryam would raise her black abaya. I saw the creases in her face, and her skin appeared to be curling a little. She still retained the powerful effect which accompanied her every Friday, when she didn't care what was happening in the house. She went to bed early: she rose from her chair without excusing herself, she entered her room, she closed the door behind her. After a little while she would put out the light. She made an effort to bring the copper brazier closer to her, to scatter the shadows with the weak light of its flames. On Fridays, Safaa's disposition changed and she was sunken in silence, staying up late by herself. She would

44

pay no attention to me if I brought my books and sat at the table close to her; she would offer me a cup of tea and run her fingers through my hair, stroking it tenderly, and then she would return to her chair by the radio, turning the dial to find songs she loved.

Marwa believed that the house had a soul; I didn't understand what she meant until long afterward. My attempts to look for the soul of the place bore no fruit and I was afforded no assistance by my strong attachment to my room. The ancient cupboard hadn't lost its shine; whenever I opened the door, there wafted the scent of old walnut. In its creak I could hear cries from a bygone era. The Persian carpet hanging on the wall seemed like the fragment of a scattered dream which craftsmen had carefully restored. I began to think: had a woman or girl made it, had a man specified the colours? Were the grandchildren of these craftsmen still reconstructing this crumbled dream, or had their descendants been annihilated? Perhaps they had died in a war, or a torrential flood had descended unexpectedly, tearing away their looms and scattering the threads and the dyes. Yes – the place had a soul. How often I searched for it, scattered between Maryam (whose silence and severity kept increasing) and Safaa and Marwa. It was as if my younger aunts were stepping in to save me, to return me to the path of a female who exposed her nipples to the licentious water, to air replete with ethereal hands which caressed and awoke them and caused them to rise, standing haughty and majestic.

I was this female in need of air and water. I felt my body to be a dark vault, damp and crawling with spiders. I would wait for Thursday, the day we went to the hammam in the souk. After Marwa joined us, the scene which I had thought was changeless became thrilling: four women wrapped in black, Radwan walking in front of them carrying a bundle on his shoulders. We crossed the same streets from Jalloum to Bab Al Ahmar and as I heard our footsteps on the pavement, I had some sympathy for Radwan's masculinity. Before we reached the door to the hammam he held out the bundle, which Maryam took wordlessly, granting him a short break. We bent our heads to enter the low doorway. I was engrossed in the details of the stone crown painted with an eagle with wings outstretched, and underneath it were some obliterated words and a history of the flight to Mecca, which I couldn't decipher. I would linger at the entrance and look into the eyes of the eagle which gazed with such disdain and hauteur. I was enamoured of the tales of the grandeur of my ancestors which Maryam related, and I believed them to resemble the eagle carved into the wall. The sanctity of this past kept me awake at nights.

I didn't realize where the anxiety rising within me would lead. It began to prevent me sleeping properly. I would toss and turn in bed before taking the pillow to the windowsill and observing the silence and the expanse of calm water in the pool. Something in my chest hurt me, and the pain spread out to the ends of every limb. I could feel it in my pores, in my fingertips, and between my thighs. I didn't dare to approach or even touch my own limbs – I would disappear silently into the darkness. I felt my shame and nakedness in front of people, their eyes goggling and their lips slackening in horror at the scene. 'Something needs to die,' I would repeat to myself, but I didn't know what exactly: my sensitivity to the place and the vast expanse of my room; my body which I feared would explode like a pane of glass; or the desire of my pores. 'Yes – desire must die.' *Desire* . . . that word burdened with thousands of meanings had to die. It quietened down a little, allowing me to sleep as I hadn't done for years. If I could touch it and see it and therefore determine its size, colour and smell, then I could kill desire and scatter it, disperse it in the gale.

Our entrance into the hammam was regulated according to a tacit agreement. Maryam went first, then Safaa, and then Marwa. I would dawdle behind them at the door for a few moments. Nazima usually came out from behind her reception desk to welcome Maryam and joke with us. She would conclude her short speech with an acknowledgement of the beneficence of God and the might of His majesty until she seemed to me, at that moment, to be angling for an empty role

47

in the family's history, fortresses and shadows: that of my grandmother, whose compartment was still reserved for us every Thursday, even if we didn't come.

I was very young when I first went to the hammam. I saw bodies shadowed by steam, women of different ages stretching out naked on old yellow stones and releasing faint, insolent laughter, moisture infusing their pores as they opened up with a lust for water. The place choked me. I left our compartment as my aunts and my mother washed and listened to my grandmother's voluble indignation at the early onset of flabbiness in her daughters' bodies. She took herbal infusions out of her bag along with *bilun*, the special clay from Aleppo, and many other things I didn't know the use of. After setting out some basins she distributed the oils and infusions to her daughters. Silently they reached out their hands and applied it to their bodies according to her instructions, and none of them dared to utter a single word.

Suddenly, I felt very short of breath. I was afraid of my grandmother's gaze, her body swathed in a wrapper and her hair spread out between Maryam's hands for an application of henna. She looked like a wicked witch escaped from a story with her white hair caked in black all the way to its ends; when she removed her false teeth, it was as if she were shattering her body into pieces. Her flabby skin was repugnant . . . I fled from them and sat down in order to observe other compartments. Naked women were talking, others were scrubbing each other's back. At a distance women were singing and swaying, one of them dancing with a hysteria I couldn't understand, then. Her tongue protruded from between her lips; she winked at me and smiled. I loved the swaying of women's bodies and the intrusion of their nakedness. The fragrance of the stone rooms enfolded me. I entered vaults although I didn't know where they might lead. I surrendered to the labyrinth, as if the hammam were a citadel and the women who moved freely within its interior were warriors, forgotten prisoners of war with tokens of servitude dangling from their ears and their masters' tattoos on their breasts. The labyrinth still shines in my memory whenever I go into the hammam.

In an exaggeration of femininity, I would walk quietly and remove my clothes slowly. With my aunts I wore a wrapper and never left the compartment, behaving like a respectable woman. Marwa and Safaa exchanged basins of hot water, trying to grasp the steam in order to cram it into their pores. Sometimes I would join them in their ribald jokes, but at the same time I noticed Maryam's angry eyes roaming with silent indignation at them, and with satisfaction at my silence. She didn't notice my smiles, which were reciprocated by Marwa, murmuring incomprehensibly to Safaa as she scrubbed her back until it was red. She would liberally spread foam from the hammam's soap on it until it shone beneath the yellow light, ignoring the herb infusions which Maryam had given her in keeping with my grandmother's traditions. Maryam had inherited everything from her, from her severity to her usual seat in the grandest of the compartments in the Red Door hammam.

We would leave the hammam at eight in the evening. Radwan would be standing by the door and when he heard our footsteps he would move off silently towards home, after taking the bundle from Maryam. Safaa would tease him briefly, igniting Maryam's suppressed anger. The water made Safaa and Marwa into different women; they would chatter all the way home while Radwan followed the well-known road in silence. I would be engrossed in the black basalt-paved streets and the windows which looked like extinguished lamps from beneath my veil. I couldn't see a thing; black shrouded all. I could only guess at the change of expression in men's faces when they came near us and were assailed by the scent of Safaa and Marwa's perfumed bodies. These bodies were fragrant in the narrow alleys; it was the only indulgence to which Maryam didn't seem to object. I couldn't have guessed how delighted she was when she saw men wheeling round to scrutinize the scene: women led by the blind, and for each of his footsteps moving according to an invisible, long-agreed order.

Sunk in silence, Maryam entered her room: Marwa and Safaa took off their black clothes and chatted. I would go into my room, using the mirror to search for eyes looking at me. I would try to overcome my shyness and imitate Marwa when she strutted in front of the mirror in light, silken clothing, as Safaa sat brushing her hair, but it was as if I could see Hajja Radia and Maryam's faces drawn on to its surface. I would wait for ten o'clock, when I would return to Safaa and Marwa's room in the thick cotton clothes which hid my body. Shy at first, I would sit next to Safaa as Marwa sat in front of the mirror finishing off her make-up: expensive red lipstick which Radwan had bought from one of the classier shops in Azizieh, kohl and a touch of light cream. They seemed to be waiting for a man, or a shade, or an illusion; at the time, I didn't understand what they were waiting for. After a long while, the image ripened in my mind and I carried it with me always: two women adorning themselves to sip tea and listen to Um Kulthoum and Abdel Halim Hafez on the radio. I didn't wonder at any great length about their secrets; I thought it was a joke they liked sharing. But their gravity and their exaggerated insistence on the details; their strict observance of the silence which dominated when Um Kulthoum began to sing; their posture, like spectators in an invisible theatre; the sips of tea and the crystal fruit bowl; the dishes of roasted spices and the cigarette smoke; brief murmurs and long, silent sighs . . . it all suggested that the wait wouldn't be a long one, and that the arrival of those who were still absent was assured. I tried to find a name worthy of the scene, but it was enough to watch

51

Marwa's lips as she murmured along with Um Kulthoum, smiled, and reached out a hand for Safaa who was ensconced in a nearby sofa as tears slid silently down her face.

Waiting for something which never came was better than having nothing at all to wait for. I recalled the image and coloured it in: after the songs, the two of them would rearrange the sitting room, desperately, for an arrival – I didn't know what kind, or even if it was all nonsense. Then they would go back into their room and stretch out on Marwa's bed, looking from the window at the calm sheet of water in the pool and the gleam of the yellow stone paving, which was almost an enchanting shade of blue when the light lost its intensity. From the window it seemed an apparition, hiding shadows and muffling footsteps. Once, I asked Safaa sharply, 'Are you expecting someone?' They laughed, and as they exchanged a quick glance, she said, 'We're expecting expectation.'

I lay down on the bed next to them, and I tried to relax and reply concisely to Marwa's teasing banter. I shared the boredom which rose from the fragrance of their perfumed clothes. They would sink into their beds, and I hadn't even approached the depths of that moment which still echoes in front of me.

I was reminded that we were women who had been abandoned the more I tried to hold back the images of one particular journey of my grandfather's. He would ride in an oak carriage pulled by two light-skinned mules, hybrids he had bought at a khan in Nazdaly in Turkey. He would arrive in Nazdaly in the evening, at a carefully calculated time he only rarely deviated from – such as on that winter evening in 1945. My grandfather would narrate the story every time he saw a rainbow, although this wouldn't help him remember the details in full. I became suspicious of the story in the form in which it reached me – and Maryam couldn't conceal its second part, concerning as it did Khalil (my grandfather's driver) and Wasal Khanim, the wife of the owner of Khan Cordoba.

That evening, the owner, Esmat Ajqabash, was roused from his sleep in his private quarters, which were separate from the guest rooms at the khan and the stables. My grandfather's voice was weak, and Esmat didn't recognize it at first. This call for help was different from that of men who had lost their way, or hunters who had unexpectedly come across Khan Cordoba in its secluded part of the country. From the main road, it took more than half an hour to reach it on foot. Esmat rose from his bed and his wife, Wasal, pleaded with him not to open the door – it was late, it wasn't safe. Esmat carried a lantern and tried to recognize the man who was coughing heavily and whose fist beat violently against the wooden door. Esmat knew my grandfather's voice after he called out his name, and quickly opened up. My grandfather was standing there, marks of exhaustion on his face that looked more like illness. Khalil stood next to him; his face was cruel, and his sharp gaze penetrated Wasal's body as she stood half-naked behind her husband, pressing down on her breasts revealed by the opening in her flimsy nightgown. My grandfather collapsed on to Esmat's chest, who embraced him and brought him inside. Khalil remained standing at the door, shivering in the biting cold. Confusion overcame Wasal and she tried to find something with which to shield her nakedness. Everyone went into the bedroom and my grandfather sat on the edge of the tall iron bed. Esmat asked with his eyes what had happened; my grandfather couldn't pronounce a single word, and Khalil was engrossed with Wasal. She began to feel a pleasure she had never known before, and lingered over warming the soup and pouring it into the bowls made from Constantine crystal.

My grandfather responded with some difficulty to Esmat's urgent requests to pull himself together a little. He brought the bowl to his lips and slowly raised his eyes, glancing at the shadows on the face of Esmat, who was anxious for his dear friend, as he always liked to call him. For ten years, my grandfather had been accustomed to stopping at this khan, after he decided to alter the previous caravan route set by his father; this used to cross Iraq, halting at its cities and villages, until it arrived at Isfahan and went on from there to Samarkand.

Wasal brought a second bowl of soup and

offered it to Khalil, who was slow to reach out for it as his eyes sought out her breasts now concealed beneath a long veil of wine-coloured velvet, shimmering and dotted with yellow flowers. He took the bowl, touching her fingers and sending a very clear message to a woman who received it just as clearly. She didn't withdraw her fingers when he folded them inside his own, seeking their warmth, but she seemed numb. She didn't remain standing in front of him for long, and didn't stay silent either. She returned to her husband who was preoccupied with my grandfather; he seemed to be dying. Warm blankets and hot lemon juice calmed his delirium, and he desperately wanted the deep sleep he hadn't enjoyed for two nights. Esmat got up, reassured of my grandfather's health, and when he saw Khalil standing in the corner of the room he seemed to be seeing him for the first time. He enquired from Khalil what had happened, but soon realized from the movement of his lips that he did not speak Turkish. He put on his coat, went outside into the khan's courtyard and unlocked the door to a small room with an ancient wooden bed in the middle, fit for a short stay. Wasal helped him make up the bed with clean sheets and pillows embroidered with peacocks and roosters. The men began lifting my grandfather under the arms but, in the twilight before dawn, he came to and walked beside Esmat without assistance as Wasal followed behind, arranging a blanket over his shoulders. They laid him on the bed and covered him well.

Marks of contentment were inscribed on the faces of Esmat and Wasal when their guest surrendered to deep sleep, judging from his snores. Esmat closed the door behind him and beckoned to Khalil to follow; my grandfather would not have liked to wake up and find one of his servants lying in the same room as him. Wasal made up a clean bed in the corner of the kitchen and motioned to the driver that he should sleep there. Before closing the door she looked at him and saw him still standing there, watching her with unmasked desire. He took note of her happiness and her coquetry as she withdrew to her husband's bed.

Esmat only understood what had happened to the travellers when he saw the mud-stained carriage; its sides had been crushed and the axles had collapsed. In the morning, my grandfather told them how one of his mules had died when a torrential stream surprised them and almost claimed their lives and their goods; he was fulsome in his praise of Khalil's strength which had saved their lives, and which inflamed Wasal still further.

The rain poured without stopping for ten consecutive days. During this time, Khalil repaired the carriage and my grandfather went with Esmat to a nearby church where they bought a new mule from a priest who was passionate about horse breeding. They were away for a few hours, which was enough to weave the story of Wasal and Khalil. (My grandfather tried to hide it from everyone although, really, he was pleased with the few moments of their mad courage and let slip many details that Khalil neither denied nor confirmed. He limited himself to a smile, and sometimes ignored the subject altogether.)

When Khalil saw that my grandfather and Esmat had left for a while he didn't dawdle, or think overmuch. He entered the house and walked firmly towards Wasal's bedroom. He opened the door without knocking and stood on the threshold. Wasal was still in bed. She looked at him, and saw the strength of the desire which she had tried to stir up over the preceding days with coquetry and gestures which were unrestrained to the point of almost compromising her. She spoke a word which he didn't understand; it was enough for him to be silent and look at her closely, lingeringly, examining hair, eyes, white marble chest, firm breasts. When she removed the cover from her body and rose from her bed, Khalil lost his head and he boiled over like an engine furnace. She closed the curtain behind her and the shadows lengthened.

He came close to her, quietly, and his breath seared her. She heard his heartbeat quickening as if she were in a trance or facing a test that might destroy her. He enfolded her waist in his powerful arms, covered her mouth with his strong, roughened palm, and tore off her clothes until she seemed to be a victim enjoying her abduction.

57

He laid her down on the carpet, and thrust himself and all his craving inside her; one moment, and it was finished. He got off her and left. Wasal rose in a daze, afraid of someone bursting in. After half an hour, she came downstairs and saw him sitting there; the old serving woman was offering him and other travellers bowls of strong-smelling lentil and onion soup. Her breathing calmed when the serving woman told her that her husband and my grandfather had gone to the church. Wasal calculated the distance and the time necessary for their return, and desire rose in her again. She lured Khalil into the storage cellar away from the house and on top of the sacks of split lentils, she lay down quietly and began to unfold the secrets of womanhood. In the weak light she toyed with the hair on his chest and gazed at his naked body; she prattled in Turkish in a voice which resembled that of a squirrel in a sleeping forest. Those few hours on top of the lentils in the dark cellar and four more days were enough to make them climb on to my grandfather's carriage, still full of carpets, and ride away on roads known only to them. They wrote their own ruin, and left stupefaction scrawled on the faces of all the guests, and my grandfather. Madness took hold of Esmat and he saw no alternative to seeking them out, accompanied by his loaded rifle.

Esmat returned to his khan on the evening of the third day, raving like a broken man. He wouldn't listen to the advice of his elderly serving woman, who had confided to him more than once that Wasal bedded certain customers on the split lentils; she swore that she had once heard Wasal ask an eccentric Iranian man to hit her on the behind and stroke his long beard over her chest; and she told Esmat how she had seen Wasal writhing like a snake in the arms of a Turkish effeminate who sang at weddings.

Ten years later Khalil, defeated, walked into the souk, dragging his feet heavily as if lugging a lead weight behind him. Bewildered, my grandfather stood up and watched him. They exchanged a long glance of mutual understanding filled with sorrow, and Khalil returned to the roofed arcade. He ran his hands through the carpet fringes as if nothing had ever happened. The weight of the subdued opulence in the shop and the smell of the silks and mothballs bestowed on him this silence, these faded eyes.

I sat next to Khalil once as he tried repeatedly to describe the taste of that dawn which enfolded him and Wasal in mist on the edge of Mosul, where they arrived after the long journey had exhausted them both; they had crossed the mountain routes, and afterwards the plains opened up before them. Mosul's houses appeared in the distance, wanly lit, and Khalil and Wasal were like people sensing the power of salvation. They got down from the carriage and stretched out on a carpet underneath a tree, and they slept until the afternoon like two murder victims hurrying to be buried together so they could rest their agitated limbs. Wasal didn't burden him with words; she perfected the role of a mute woman to avoid replying to the many questions which poured over them in Mosul's souk when Khalil displayed the first carpet under the eyes of traders eager for pictures of Iranian peacocks. Khalil was convincing as an expert, speaking about contracts and colours and wool types, naming traders in Syria and Iran, and he soon convinced everyone that he was a wandering trader and a skilful craftsman. They succeeded in selling the carpets for a good price and winning people's trust. Wasal's presence, which had been a burden at first, became much sought after; her smile banished doubt and silenced questions. Before they flung themselves on to their bed at the Nahrein Hotel and left their mules with the groom, they hurried to the mosque and sat with the sheikh, who saw no objection to writing out a marriage document. He gave Wasal his ring as her dowry after Khalil claimed that he was escaping from the brutality of the French, and that Wasal was a distant relative of his whose *entire* family – every single last one of them – had died of cholera. The five dinars Khalil paid was an adequate guarantee for the oath the sheikh pondered as he gazed at Wasal's lips, drawn carefully like ripe, red berries.

They left the souk as man and wife, and dreams of life, love and the accumulation of memories opened up in front of them. The evening air was cool and refreshing as they found a restaurant and ate some grilled meat. They hurried back to their room and shared a bed, away from the dangers they had avoided successfully on their journey across the mountains, villages and plains thanks to Khalil's sharp wits, honed on his travels to Samarkand and Iran with my grandfather. There, the roads were swarming with armed men and the cities were embroiled in chaos, forcing traders to travel in large caravans protected by hired gunmen and guides who knew the safe routes.

On their first night, Wasal had no regrets about forsaking the odour of other men clinging to the lentil sacks in the dark cellar, itself permeated with the smells of fried aubergines and decaying rats. She washed in the rose water which she had brought with her, and put on a wedding dress which Khalil tore off her before carrying her like a butterfly to the bed; she was insensible to the strength of his arms and the blaze of his kisses as if it were the first time she had been to bed with a man. Her voice rose without shame, and in Turkish she prattled words of surrender to a hidden fate. Afterwards, she became quiet and buried her head in his chest, savouring the scent which penetrated her heart and captivated her. She taught him to speak Turkish and clip his nails, and insisted that he wore cactus-blossom perfume which would waft from his clothes when he walked confidently through Mosul's souk.

Khalil began to deal in cigarettes with the other traders, guiding them to the best makes, and he exchanged for coloured silks the carpets he designed and produced himself on his own loom, and which looked like icons. These astonished the people of Mosul, the passing traders and the foreign antiques collectors who all trusted Khalil's imagination and his skill, as well as his sympathy for amateurs' lack of knowledge in the wild and varied field of carpets.

He craved the security and protection he felt in Wasal, who gave birth to a daughter called Zahra. Zahra resembled her mother completely with the exception of her black eyes; they brought to mind a mixture of racial origins that might have been nearer to those of Nubians than Wasal and Khalil's own particular combination.

Back in Aleppo, my grandfather touched a carpet, on which was this line of Mutanabbi's:

Homes! There are homes for you in our
    hearts
You are now deserted, yet you are inhabiting
    them.

He knew that Khalil had made it and included the verse on purpose: the speaker is calling out to the empty home of his beloved; although the home is now abandoned, it provides the memories that still live on in his heart. My grandfather had heard that Khalil missed Aleppo, after a trader from

Mosul had discussed his skilful workmanship and the beauty of his wife, who would interfere in the colouring of the carpets. The colours seemed strange at first, although foreign clients were enticed by Abyssinian roosters, the arms of women whose swelling chests were like those of Sumerian goddesses, and winking eyes which always resembled those of a woman Khalil had once known. He was immersed in the warmth of the delights renewed every night, which seemed to the couple never-ending.

What is it worth to live through a spell of happiness, even if it will never return? The depression which had clung to Khalil throughout his life lifted completely. He became cheerful at gatherings, especially at the house of a certain Mister John, whom he used to visit every day. He would drink coffee with him, and show him paintings from the Nahda era, and even accompanied him several times to excavation sites in Babel where an archaeological mission was encamped.

What Khalil didn't know was that Wasal was beginning to feel bored. She missed other men, and she no longer came to him wearing perfume and insisting that he washed his hands. Her days finally became dull; he was a man certain of his success, and she a woman no longer seduced by the resplendent colours of carpets. She quietly withdrew and fell silent. She didn't care when the kitchen shelves collapsed, shattering the Kashmiri-porcelain bowls and scattering shards everywhere, and it was days before she gathered up the pieces and coldly tossed them in the dustbin. She regretted the ten years she had spent in this city invaded by mosquitoes and silence, where the smell of roasting meat seeped from every alleyway like an inescapable fate. Wasal listened, stunned, to John enlarging on vulgar descriptions of his nights out in London. She was enamoured of the sordidness in the mid-fifties bars which John felt considerable nostalgia for whenever he remembered the smell of those long nights. He saw her astonishment, listened to her never-ending questions and answered them in a low, steady voice. He complimented her taste in serving coffee; and he compared her to the princesses whose amorous exploits were sung of in the romances that had once been so popular in castles all over Europe.

'This arrogant Englishman is making me dream,' she said to herself as she gazed at the dawn through her bedroom window. Insomnia tyrannized her and she lost weight. She would wait for the evenings when John came round, accompanied by members of the dig, antiquities collectors both amateur and professional, spies, and horse traders passing through on their way to Bedouin camps. They would swarm all over Khalil's house, demanding to have tea according to their own traditions and jabbering away in English, displaying their amazement at the interweaving of colours and lines in the carpets spread out before them.

John moved amongst them like an expert guide and interpreter, and he laid a trap for Wasal, who immediately felt that the circular motion of her breasts had seduced him from under their veil. She enjoyed his ravenous greed at seeing them when they stood out through her abaya for a moment, the nipples showing clearly underneath the long cotton garment. It was a game that both John and Wasal loved at the beginning, before it became a burden and the cause of sleepless nights.

Khalil wasn't quite aware of what was going on – he was in thrall to the security of the little money he had saved and hidden inside the small ebony case at the bottom of the clothes box, and he thought fondly of his young daughter, who had begun to lisp in both Arabic and Turkish, and of his wife, Wasal. (Unnoticed by him, she now performed her duties coldly and without enthusiasm.) These blessings were all sufficient reasons to set him thinking about making a pilgrimage to Mecca, and returning from there to Aleppo to live in that city in complete bliss. His eyes shone when he told Wasal, convinced that this happy ending would delight her also. Wasal listened to him and was distracted for a long time: she didn't know why she became jittery when Khalil enlarged on his wish that she become pregnant once more in order to have a boy, to replace the one whose body had broken out in buboes short of his second year. Before they had agreed on a name for him, he had died and they had buried him in a small grave close to their house. The two of them dreamed of different worlds, linked by a house whose future seemed only half-assured, and from which wafted the smell of beans and the sound of sad Iraqi songs. Wasal was devoted to these songs, which spoke about falling in love with young men and waxed eloquent about infatuation, but John was articulate in explaining the odes as stilted and affected. As their sessions lengthened, John realized how much he longed to be in London after being absent for so long.

Wasal's story affected me greatly; I knew, afterwards, that she had caused my grandfather sleepless nights. When she lived at the khan in Nazdaly, she used to make him bring henna, perfumes and expensive fabrics from Aleppo, seemingly just presents from a generous friend that would not cast suspicion on him; the gifts were in exchange for special services she offered him as a regular client of an inn on a little-used road.

My grandmother was implacable in her hostility towards Wasal's daughter, Zahra, whom my uncle Bakr had determined upon marrying. My grandfather was silent in the face of everyone's supplications, in an effort to persuade his wife to renounce her oath that she would never allow *her* into the house, and that she would never see Bakr again *as long as she lived*. We all loved Zahra's beautiful face, whose complexion changed and became luminous when evening fell. Through her asceticism and her faith, she won our hearts. She and Bakr formed a married couple whose outer quietness and timidity hid a storm of passionate adoration which they revelled in and drank of right to the dregs, wrapping their secrets within it. Many envied Bakr for his life, piety and clean house, and for the wife whose clothes did not smell of onion and fried cauliflower, and who remained patient in the face of catastrophe, which was a revelation to him. As my grandfather said, Bakr saw Zahra's face and felt her kindness, and cast everything else aside; in this way, she resembled her mother, who had made Khalil into a man haunted by yearning. Khalil drowned in tears and nightmares, especially when the rain poured down. He spoke quickly and angrily, cursing the English, and whorish women, and debauched men. His disconnected sentences didn't shed any light on the past; no one understood them other than my grandfather, and my uncle Bakr after he was alone with his bride. She walked like an orphan in the small procession Aunt Maryam insisted on holding so Hajja Radia wouldn't be angry after Radia had spoken highly of Zahra and her piety.

My grandmother kept her oath, and Zahra paid no heed to the goings-on in my grandfather's house. I became used to Bakr's visits and my grandmother's refusals to receive him, despite all his entreaties and intervention from my mother. She said that my grandmother loved Zahra but couldn't find the right time to relinquish her unjustified obstinacy, especially after the death of my grandfather and in view of Zahra's lack of defence of her own mother – it was widely said that Wasal had made a living from prostitution after she abandoned the Englishman, John.

Wasal had run away to London with John, and there she attached herself to a Pakistani man, a taxi driver who picked her up one night outside a bar when she was exhausted, fatigue and intoxication all over her face, and only half conscious. In his suburban bedsit, she gave him her body coldly in exchange for spending a night in a narrow bed and a bowl of hot soup, which reminded her of that cellar which she never yearned for, and never regretted leaving.

Wasal woke up late the next morning. All that remained in her memory of the previous night was the taste of pepper from the soup. When she found herself alone in a shabby room, she got up wearily and washed. She heard Pakistani music and snooped through the man's pictures, which showed him with a corpulent English girl, doltish and flaccid as a dead fish. She realized that he was a strange and lonely man, for all his soft features and thick black eyebrows.

She rather enjoyed being away from John's affections and his calls for her to respect English traditions. She went back to sleep for a while and, on waking again, made a light dinner of wilted parsley, cabbage heads and a few morsels of potato. She spontaneously started to behave as if she were the mistress of this mean room, rearranging the sweaters and books strewn at random over the only sofa. She made the Pakistani laugh in an attempt to combat his bewilderment at the continued presence of this transient woman in his room. She surrendered to him coldly as the night elapsed, despite his attempts to get her to explain her past.

The two quickly came to an understanding. She liked his oddness, and the unambiguously dirty jokes he made when, on the third day, he took her to the apartment of a Syrian trader called Abdel Ghany Bilany, in exchange for twenty pounds. The Syrian had a predilection for visiting Madame Tussaud's, reading biographies of famous politicians, and memorizing quotations. Abdel Ghany Bilany was an entertaining host, at first; but he was in collusion with the Pakistani, who soon left them alone. Stifling a sarcastic smile, Wasal practised the role of a professional whore, but she wasn't vulgar. She praised his cologne and his taste in the colours of the bed linen in the spacious room. She almost expressed an opinion about Churchill and Abdel Ghany was restored to his earlier enthusiasm as he summarized the history of the man who taught politics to Europe.

Wasal conspired many times with the Pakistani, whom she began to invite to her house. She introduced him to John's guests and laughed with him in the street. Sometimes she went to stay in his room for a day or two when she felt she was on the verge of putting poison in John's food, leaving him to his dog whose smell got on her nerves, to his fat books and archaeological journals, to his boring conversations about digging seasons and his endless reminiscences – of diving into the dust with friends and colleagues, who boasted of being burned by the Iraqi sun, eating canned food with the Bedouin, and trying to ride horses – 'their stupid stories about falling on to their backs', as Wasal used to describe them.

'This Pakistani understands me,' she said to herself as she observed his repeated depravities, which entertained her at times and exasperated her at others. She often went to Abdel Ghany's flat when he was in London, and after several months she convinced the Syrian to take her with him to Aleppo. She spoke captivatingly of the splendour of Palmyra, the markets in Aleppo, the gentle kindness of Syrians. She knew that she had enticed him when he took her picture next to the statue of Spartacus in the waxwork museum, and she surprised him by baring her chest, smiling with lust and thrilling ambiguity. She made an eccentric out of Abdel Ghany, a lover who expressed his innermost secrets all at once. He lunged at her and instead of catching at her breasts hanging like ripe apples, he bowed at her feet. He recited some lines by an Aleppan poet who had left behind him a *diwan* of poetry entitled *Songs of the Dome*, a huge encyclopaedia of Aleppan customs, tastes and jokes which boasted of Aleppo's uniqueness. Abdel Ghany recited some lines, treating them like a religious singer keen on making the beauty of the vowels appear clearly.

He took her to Aleppo and she breathed deeply when she walked in the souk. She saw the domes and minarets of the mosques, and she looked for a messenger to convey a brief note to Zahra, informing her of her room number at the Baron Hotel.

Zahra was unsurprised. It was as if she had been expecting this appointment, confirming her constant feeling that Wasal would one day appear in front of her, her last friend, who had made out her mother's story through snippets of contradictory conversations between the men she knew, and from memories fixed in her mind as a young child. Nothing remained of her image of her mother other than the features of a grumbling woman who would coquettishly flutter her reliable eyelashes when giving instructions to the reluctant latest of a long succession of unfortunate servants. Zahra kept the impressions of that meeting at the hotel to herself for a long time. She told me about it only in her darkest moments, when she was lying in her bed and death had settled over the city like a vampire we could see but couldn't touch.

Zahra sat opposite her mother in the salon of the Baron, ignoring the courteous gestures of the foreign men who had come looking for the primitive place Agatha Christie had once passed through, leaving the dust from her shoes on the floor. Zahra raised the black veil from her glowing, pure face, her dark eyes full of forgiveness. Both of them knew that there was not enough time for long reproaches, so they made do with crying and quickly came to understand one another. They left the hotel and went out into the crowded streets, bewildered, wrapped up in their eternal kinship.

'We both needed a companion,' Zahra explained to me, recollecting the few, tedious hours which had passed like heavy-footed ghosts on their way to the *barzakh*. Zahra told her mother that she was both a stranger, to the extent that she didn't know her at all, and a close relative, to the extent that it was as if they had never been separated and the years that had passed were like a lie, a dream which had lasted only a few seconds. Any moment now Wasal would get up and go to the kitchen to add salt to the peas and then return to gather up the balls of coloured wool with which Zahra had been playing, just like any mother absorbed in her family. Dispassionately, Zahra formed cold, disciplined sentences, which she did not use to describe her sadness and excruciating pain at being a motherless child with a depressed father. She sketched for her mother a picture of Bakr as a loving husband and father. She talked at great length about my grandfather in order to defeat Wasal's desire to see her grandchildren. She fielded questions cautiously and, before leaving her mother, she asked her to swear that she wouldn't die in a brothel; an odd request, to which Wasal duly acceded. Zahra ended the conversation where it was supposed to begin. They exchanged addresses and hugged warmly in the manner of lovers who would never meet again.

Wasal understood that everything between them had come to an end. A series of disclosures began across the cruel letters that Zahra would write in reply to Wasal's repeated petitions for her to pronounce the word 'mother' just once, in any language she wanted. Zahra was troubled during that time. She sat beside Hajja Radia and didn't care about the drumming tambourines, nor the religious lessons illustrating the influence of the mothers of the believers and the wisdom of the Prophet. They made us weep, amazed at Hajja Radia's eloquence and the river of knowledge that engulfed our hearts, returning us once more to the certainty that filtered into our souls. Hajja Radia didn't understand Zahra's insistence on spending the equivalent value of her favourite expensive bracelet on food for poor families – until the letters started arriving punctually every Saturday. She handed them over without asking their origin after she made out the name of Zahra's mother.

A strange relationship had already sprung up between them. Hajja Radia was mother, sister and companion to Zahra, and their closeness frequently caused envy within their circle. This was especially true among those who considered their own powerful family connections with the most pious inhabitants of Aleppo as sufficient to warrant occupying the most exalted positions in their sessions, despite their chattering away without restraint about the price of gold, the fatwas issued by Ibn Malik, and women's problems. The relationship between Zahra and Hajja Radia was the subject of much speculation. Khalil accepted it without objection and Bakr sanctioned it, especially as he had started staying abroad for weeks at a time.

Zahra was forbidden from entering my grandfather's house. She was marked by the sins of her mother – these the envious tackled first, before accusing Zahra of having a sexual relationship with Hajja Radia, who had a well-known penchant for beautiful women and their perfumes. This penchant stopped at passionately smelling those women's necks, praising their soft skin and pinching them, as they generally let out an 'Aah . . .' tinged with hidden lust.

Zahra memorized the Quran, the principles of its recitation, and the tambourine beats in Hajja Radia's house; the latter did not hide her pleasure at Zahra's long face, with its complexion tending towards fair, and her slender body which grew before her eyes. She watched its transformation as Zahra fled from the chaos of banging crockery and children's runny noses in Khalil's house to the calm of Hajja Radia's house, which was respected by all the families of Aleppo. The silence, the clean smell wafting from sofas and pillows, the incense, all enveloped Zahra and she fell into a trance, unaware of why the afternoon breezes affected her so. She stretched her legs out into a pool and relaxed under the pampering of Hajja Radia, who was looking for a daughter whose fingers tasted of *ghariba*. Khalil's refusal did not last long in the face of Hajja Radia's insistence on sharing Zahra's upbringing between them. As a motherless child, Zahra found a new mother who, during two consecutive marriages over four years, had given birth to two sons. The elder was a drug addict; the second was mad and tried to swallow his nose and his toes, roaming through alleyways covered in their grime, his body lined with poison. Two husbands, two sons – but it was as if they had never existed in her life; as if they were lies, or a pot of ink spilled on to a dusty pavement. Hajja Radia took a job singing *nashid* at *mawalid* and weddings, and giving recitations of Rabia Adawiya, trying to forget her past all in one go. I asked her once what men tasted like, and without any hesitation she replied, 'Just like shit.'

My grandmother died and Zahra entered my grandfather's house for the first time, accompanied by Hajja Radia, who had insisted on preparing my grandmother for burial herself, and mourning her with dignity. The two of them had shared a lifetime of frying spices, eating apricot jam, gossiping, singing and going to the resplendent hammams, where they fell asleep together in a

75

private compartment. She bantered with the body and teased it about the years of estrangement due to Bakr's marriage to Zahra, which my grandmother had believed to be Zahra's plan all along. We stood in the courtyard and waited for the body as Zahra wandered through the house, examining paintings and doorways. She smiled at me and hugged me, then quickly reached a state of harmony with my aunts. Hajja Radia came outside and asked us to clear the way so the men could carry my grandmother's body to the grave. Her sharp gaze couldn't prevent the sound of weeping from breaking out. Men buried the dead woman and the women wailed and waved at a distance from the coffin.

I once asked Hajja Radia, 'Why don't women bury the dead?' She seemed distracted, as if she were remembering that all the squalor of the world, and all its purity, could be found within us. I told her once, 'I dream sometimes that I am burying a dead person.' I carried on, 'I didn't recognize his face, but he looked like a lot of men I know.' She hung my hijab over my face and ordered me to recite the Sura Al Baqara ten times. I was happy with my veil and closed my eyes, recited the Sura Al Anfal and Sura Yusuf from memory, and never told anyone my strange dreams ever again. I was no longer afraid of the scenes in my dreams of the pilgrims circling the Kaaba, nor the scenes of women carrying biers, praying and then burying them with laughter and drinking iced berry juice.

One of them looked like Maryam, dancing to the rhythm of a strange love song which resembled Syriac music I had heard once as I was passing in front of a record shop. I had steeled myself, gone in, and bought a cassette. I convinced Safaa that we should listen to it together, taking advantage of her gaiety one evening.

I tried to capture whatever I could remember, and having decided to write it down, I bought a pink notebook and coloured pens. The writing changed into drawings. I found the pictures to be a way of confessing what no one could unravel, even when the notebook fell into my aunts' hands. The most beautiful of these dreams I had drawn as a tree with a squirrel standing on one of its branches, laughing as it looked at the clouds. It was a dream that a man ripped off Fatima's bra and was raping her in the school courtyard under the gaze of her schoolmates who were clapping with glee. It was the revenge of the companions in black for her immorality and her shamelessness in using obscene words only spoken by criminals. I didn't want to wonder if the man's member was visible or hidden in the dream, afraid of touching upon an image I didn't know anything about. It was a major source of confusion in my life; I imagined it to look like a corncob, which was how Fatima had described it to her friends as I listened in astonishment at her daring in recounting an entire porn film, as unconcerned as if she were peeling an apple. In another picture, I drew a cornfield and then blotted it out with black, afraid that desire might possess me and destroy my dignity, blowing me away like grains of sand from the steps of an ancient house.

My first days in secondary school made me depressed and irritable. Something bit into me and made me cry when it wouldn't die; female desire, which I couldn't run from, rose inside me and drove me almost to madness, and I began to understand the meaning of women's lust for men. I sympathized with Safaa who was struck down by chronic migraines and long periods of distraction, during one of which she shattered a bowl and scattered its pieces as a reminder that they were all condemned to a fate Maryam had surrendered to, and from which Safaa tried to distance me by inciting me to wear pretty dresses, light and open-necked, when going to the markets. She would kick me affectionately, and she would explode with anger at the books Bakr brought for me, putting them on the table as he left us. Maryam would examine them and leave them for me, lying like dead bodies. Her eyes shone with pride at her 'little scholar', as she liked to call me, amidst Safaa's sarcasm and Marwa's rebukes – she reminded me constantly, 'Women are not entitled to be muftis.' She would follow this up by leaning towards me and saying, 'Decree many marriages for me.' We would all laugh. Maryam would be confused and ask us for a clue, then she would return to the Quran and leave me to the fatwas of Ibn Baz.

I was wearied by the yellow books but I couldn't leave them alone. I devoured their pages to escape my anxiety and my fear of something I was ignorant of but which I could sense, squatting on my chest and trying to smother me. I would study each fatwa of Ibn Baz and feel the pleasure of renunciation. I would look pityingly at the girls around me, certain that they were going to Hell. I imagined how Fatima would broil before prostrating herself, weeping and regretful, seeking succour from our generous Prophet.

My journey to the secondary school was long, and it went through Jalloum to the copper market. I went on foot, and it became more familiar every morning. I would be brave and dawdle a little bit to look at the shop owners who lowered their gaze when I passed. I didn't think what my passing at the same time each morning for three years might mean to them; that I, to the men yawning in their shops and drowning in the smell of cheese, was a black bag carrying a satchel: featureless, scentless, without even a single bump.

My otherness came to an end when I got close to the girls who were like me in many respects. Some of them removed their veils as soon as they arrived at school and took off their heavy outer coats to fit in with the other schoolgirls, who were frank about their hostility to us. They gave us nicknames such as the Penguin Club, or sometimes the Zuzu Club, an ironic reference to our refusal to see the film *Beware of Zuzu*. It starred Souad Hosny, who danced her famous dance. The girls at school imitated her by resting a finger on one cheek, pretending to be meditating on their conquests and famous lovers they regretted, and sighing for imaginary bridges to faraway cities which Hala described as if she were describing a brothel; she also said that everything here was nauseating, and that I would leave one day.

There was an unwritten pact between us and those girls. We openly exchanged spiteful glances and hatred as we sat in school like respectable classmates suffering the same oppression and burdened spirits in that depressing building. We also concurred tacitly in our hatred of the Mukhabarat sympathizers, who wrote reports for their branches expressing their loyalty to the Party and their pride in the word 'comrade', which the headmistress pronounced with the same deliberation, heavy meaning and veneration. We hated Nada who wore suits of commando camouflage and marched around, shouting in high-pitched masculine accents, the very image of the officer from the death squad who brought her to school with his car stereo turned up and the *misbaha* of wine-coloured amber beads clattering away. He sang along cheerfully to Fuad Ghazi, a singer famous for her frequent appearances on state radio and television. As the girls came out of school, the officer almost blocked the gate with his car door.

We saw how handsome he was, while the head-mistress averted her eyes as he stared shamelessly at our chests. Nada climbed in beside him with a military showmanship that made her terrifying. She would walk in halfway through a lesson and leave whenever she felt like it. The teachers all ignored her slam of the classroom door – with the exception of the chemistry teacher; on one occasion she wouldn't allow Nada to leave and threatened to expel her. Nada left with a derisive glance, and we all waited for the next chemistry lesson with the ardency of someone desperate for the next instalment of an exciting TV serial. The chemistry teacher curtly asked Nada to leave. Nada laughed sardonically. The teacher came up to her and grabbed her by the hair and flung her out of the classroom. She closed the door and calmly returned to the blackboard, to the sound of Nada's threats. The headmistress tried and failed to prevent the teacher's transfer to Izaz, a small town north of Aleppo. Quietly, the chemistry teacher gathered up her papers, stood in front of us and said, 'This is a pigsty. Not a school.'

With her taut brown face and strong features, Nada looked like a professional handball player. Her hair was long and curly, her breasts large, her movements swift, and she spoke authoritatively as if she came from a place we knew nothing of. The girls tried to curry favour with her, but she fled from them and went off on her own. She was candid about her lover, Abu Ramy. She revealed

81

some of their secrets to impress some of the girls, who didn't hide their pleasure in his bulging muscles when he drove off at excessive speed. They talked about his officer friends, discussing their names, their salaries, and the brands and colours of their cars. The girls asked her to take them to the restaurants and hotels in Aleppo where the death squad officers went, where they would place their guns on the tables and guffaw as they saw other patrons avoiding their gaze before leaving quickly. The girls accompanying the officers felt arrogant, and repeatedly changed their orders, enjoying the servility of the restaurant owners who complied with their requests and apologized for the bad service.

Hatred bewildered me, just as powerful love bewilders a lover. I would fumble for my salvation by sitting alone for hours at a time, reading my yellow books and ignoring Marwa and Safaa's calls to join them in making stuffed vine leaves and listening to songs, and torturing Radwan with nonsensical requests. He would try to fulfil them, and then they would ignore the bags of ground bird bones and dove beaks which he had gone round several markets looking for.

'I hate school,' I told Hajja Radia, choking back my tears. I told her about the chemistry teacher and Nada, and Hala and her hatred for our veils and our lowered voices, and her sarcastic comments about the rulings of Islamic jurors. She listened so intently I almost told her about my friend

Ghada who kept singing lewd Maha Abdel Wahhab songs quite audibly during our morning assemblies where we saluted the flag and sang the Party anthem. Then we would parade in front of Nada and the Al Futuwa leader, who would both review us as if we were a herd of donkeys.

Ghada suddenly shone in the school firmament like a star. She removed her veil and no longer shared our silent falafel sandwiches in the breaks. After the summer holiday she shook hands with us coldly; I couldn't believe my eyes when I saw her dancing to Boney M, or linking arms with Nada, who had forced the teachers to disclose the answers to the exam so she would pass. The teachers were repulsed, but whenever they thought of protesting they remembered the chemistry teacher, and the skinny geography teacher who was taken from her house by a Mukhabarat patrol under the eyes of her neighbours. They tore at her clothes as her young children sobbed – all because she had given a zero to a student whose father worked as an interrogator for the military Mukhabarat. The father described the teacher as a whore and threatened her with torture and death in the darkness of the Mukhabarat detention cells. The geography teacher was silent, stupefied. Afterwards she lost the ability to look her students in the eye. Like a ghost, she drew on the blackboard and spoke distractedly about capital cities.

I couldn't bear Ghada's desertion of me. I couldn't admit to myself that I loved kissing her every morning and inhaling her scent; sometimes my hand would inadvertently slip to her breast and I would press it warmly with unbounded desire. This fact alarmed me. I asked Layla insistently to try and convert her back to us, but she didn't care very much about the matter. So I stood in the courtyard and confronted Ghada; I asked her to stop this blasphemy and to stop going around with Nada, and showed her the veil I had brought her on behalf of one of our venerable sheikhs. She took it from me and kissed me gently, and then put it in the pocket of her clean khaki shirt and said, 'You haven't tasted happiness yet.' I didn't understand what she meant. Hala interrupted and called her a bitch. I couldn't bear her insult; before I knew what I was doing, I had lost my head. I grabbed Hala's hair and began to hit her in the face with a strength I didn't know was in me, repeating over and over, '*You're* the bitch, not Ghada.'

Hala was shocked, but forgave me when I cried in the headmistress's room. I couldn't utter a single word; the scene moved Hala and we embraced and returned to class as friends. I felt suffocated. In the following days I felt everyone's eyes boring into me: students, teachers, the headmistress, my aunts and my mother when I went to her and cried for no reason, then wiped my tears and left without saying goodbye. Ghada asked me affectionately not to defend her, adding gently that she was powerful and fully capable of burning down the school. Then she ignored me completely. I stopped going out into the schoolyard. Layla tried to convince me that no one remembered a stupid fight between classmates; anyway, the school was preoccupied with more serious matters after a blue Mercedes had begun waiting for Ghada every day – inside it was a man whom even Nada's death squad officer was afraid of and made sure to greet when they met at the school gate. I started going back out into the yard, but I was exhausted, and inattentive in class, to the astonishment of the teachers, who knew the extent of my intelligence. Whenever I spotted Ghada climbing in beside that fifty-year-old man whom I saw as mysterious and coarse, I felt that my knees wouldn't support me any longer.

Safaa ignored the incidents with Ghada, and my tears when I hugged my mother and left like a fugitive. She suggested that I help Radwan formulate a new perfume, and write the song he would sing at the Prophet's *mawlid* in front of Bakr and the other guests who were soon to congregate at my grandfather's house. She added, 'Men . . . forbidden men will be coming to this tomb; we'll cook for them and have a look at them through our windows.' She was gleeful when she pronounced the word 'men' and she took me by the hand, trying to impose a smile on me which soon turned to brazen laughter. It disturbed Maryam who came out of her room and stood, watching us from afar.

I wrote down Radwan's dictation. Safaa deliberately mixed the quantities wrongly but he didn't protest, and occasionally even praised her dexterity in carrying out his instructions. He had returned to the status of a wandering poet who wrote odes in praise of the Prophet. Safaa egged me on not to stick to what he said, but to write down its opposite. I didn't possess Safaa's courage in teasing her servant; I considered him to be an uncle whose ancestry I had forgotten. I pretended not to notice his frequent plundering of the *Peak of Eloquence* by Ali ibn Abi Talib, his breaking of the poetic metre, and his descent into cruder regional dialect when describing his perfumes and praising my grandfather, uncles and some notable sheikhs. I laughed from my belly when he gave himself free rein and cursed French colonialism in two lines. He smiled sourly and said, 'Write. Write! Aleppo will remember this, and the musicians will come running.'

Maryam didn't approve of how close we were to Radwan. She sat by Marwa and the two of them began loudly discussing preparations for the party. Marwa wrote down a list of requests which they would send in the morning to my grandfather's shops; Selim would spend three days dispatching his workers, laden with bags, to fulfil my aunts' requests, causing the larder to overflow. Safaa was roused to anger and Maryam to contentment by this – now Maryam had the chance to declare proudly that no guest had ever gone wanting in this house; and if ever the larder were found empty, then its inhabitants would no longer have the right to hang the family tree on the wall, and its daughters would be little better than passing beggars.

At night I read over Radwan's dictation of his ode. I was pleased with the game, and added on a couplet of beautiful love poetry which no one knew was my monologue to Ghada. I described her beautiful face and my heartbreak at her departure from me. Radwan never acknowledged that it was an addition to his ode; his *mu'allaqa*, as he termed it. I told him, 'It will be your legacy.' His voice rose in defence of his talents as he reminded Maryam of the odes he used to sing to my grandfather and his guests.

I didn't know why Bakr summoned me urgently for a matter of the utmost importance. He came to the house late one night, spoke with Maryam for a few minutes, and then came into my room. He didn't wait around for me to ask after his wife Zahra, but demanded to know what had happened at school. He listened intently and questioned me closely about Nada, Hala, Ghada and other girls. He reassured me and said, 'Keep away from Ghada and don't clash with Nada, whatever happens.' He said this in a commanding tone, and I didn't understand why he thought it was so necessary. He asked me to call another friend, Hana, whose authoritativeness I used to hate, despite her constant attempts to initiate conversations on purification literature and examine every detail of each school of jurisprudence. I said to Layla, 'I don't like her,' and finished by saying, 'She thinks she's Fatima Al Zahra.' Layla laughed, and fell silent for a few minutes. Then she changed the subject, afraid of plunging into a biography of the Prophet's daughter.

There was a hidden rebuke in Bakr's tone. This was no time for trivialities, he said. I felt his worry and his enthusiasm at the same time. He stopped in Marwa and Safaa's room and drank coffee with them, listening to them as a close, beloved brother and confidant, despite his deep religious devotion. He soon began talking neutrally and eloquently on more intimate and interesting topics, but the reason for his presence at that time was a mystery to me.

My uncle Bakr had a scar that distinguished him from the rest of the family: it looked like a coin in the middle of his cheek. Everyone who saw it thought the plague which had struck the city had passed through him but not taken him, so they regarded him as an omen of good luck. He was always clean-shaven. He seemed destined for a greater role than that of a carpet dealer, a trade which he had inherited from his father. Whoever saw him from afar thought him to be resigned to his fate, his limited ambitions, his happiness with Zahra, an eternally contented woman. Those close to him numbered no more than a few friends whom he saw intermittently and briefly, doing no more than reassure himself of their welfare. He left all the financial and accounting details of the business to my oldest uncle, Selim. With his steadiness and patience, Uncle Selim was the image of his father. He woke early, prayed in the Ottoman Mosque, carefully ate breakfast and then went to the shop. He and Khalil drank coffee like two old men worried that the Day of Judgement would arrive too soon for them to arrange their coffins and mend the carpets in the attic of the shop. With great difficulty, Selim learned some English phrases necessary for talking tourists into buying carpets as souvenirs of the oldest Eastern cities. He left the discussions with experts and syndicate owners to my youngest uncle, Omar, who had perfected his English and French at a sharia college. Although he had chosen to attend this college wholeheartedly, he soon grew bored with the opinions of legal jurists and baulked at my grandmother's wish that he complete his education at Al Azhar so he could return with a doctorate, qualified to dispense fatwas to the women and men who flocked to their sheikhs and broadcast their secrets with great gusto.

After Omar returned from military service he went into his room, packed his religious books in a wooden box and carried it to the cellar, resolute in his refusal to go to Al Azhar. He began to work in the business with great enthusiasm. In his house, my grandmother sat waiting for his return. She waited for two whole days, and when he finally returned and saw her sitting with Maryam and his wife, Rima, absorbed in chopping quince, he leaned over and kissed her head. He laughed as his mother told him everything she knew about the fallen women he wasted his money on, and praised the fortitude and elevated morals of his wife. She only quietened down when he swore on the Quran that he wouldn't fall into bad company again. Before my grandmother died, Omar had timorously sworn on the Quran nine times; afterwards he returned to his hellraising as if what had been said was nothing more than a puff of air. Anyone looking into his cunning eyes and his yellow, emaciated face might have thought he had come down with jaundice. As a child he wanted to become an actor; he left school and spent most of his time in the cinema, or following news of actors and imitating their gestures and Egyptian accents in front of the large mirror.

'He was wonderful, and so kind,' Safaa said, recalling Omar's never-ending attempts to be a renegade who scorned tradition. The most idiotic of his actions caused consternation in the family, which gathered a number of times to admonish him; he would listen calmly and quickly burst into remorseful tears, only to surprise them the following morning with further follies. Once, he brought a flock of geese to the house. Omar straightaway began opening the doors, upon which the geese spread out and began ravaging Maryam's flowers. He tossed them a slice of bread and began herding them like a cowboy. He almost put my grandmother into a swoon and Maryam felt hysteria coming on when she saw her delicate plants trampled and scattered over the ground like there had been a frivolous and unexpected festival. Safaa smothered her laughter and she and Maryam confronted Omar who looked at them, perplexed, and then stormed out of the house. His dream of being a gooseherd came to an end. He herded his flock to the Bedouin, greatly enjoying the open air and the cane in his hand, which he raised to hush the beaks of his flock. My grandfather and uncles returned in the evening to turn out the remnants of this flock, which had strutted through rooms and cellars and left its excrement and footprints on bedspreads and flowered sofas. My grandfather was more tolerant of Omar's odd jokes, and he was astounded at his son's talent for generating profits when he began to work in the family shops, despite Selim's fear that his flippancy would ruin everything. It was as if he had found certainty at last in the pleasure of dividends, which he used to philosophize about, explaining ideas that occasionally shook the market; they also made him into a much-sought-after partner in risk avoidance.

My grandfather and other uncles ignored Omar's levity because of his boosting of their trade, which had become rather lacklustre at a time when Persian and Kashmiri carpets were no longer a source of pride for Syrian families. Also, there were certain telegrams that allowed Omar to put important families in touch with some powerful officers who had taken over the rule of law after the army entered Lebanon. These men were transformed from officers, warriors strutting about in their uniforms, into smugglers of ceramics and electronic equipment, and they had connections to foreign tobacco barons. They became a familiar presence in upmarket restaurants, praising Aleppan vine leaves and kebab, dividing up their profits, and raising their voices in arguments that sometimes escalated to the point where they were on the verge of ordering their own men to shoot each other. Echoes probably reached the government in the Republican Palace, which intervened with a curt judgement that everyone accepted. After that, these officers went back to taking girls to restaurants and country estates, delighting in their great power, giving themselves free rein in plundering the country's riches, and imposing their rule on all the institutions that became their targets. The staff of these institutions trembled when they saw military vehicles stopping in front of their buildings. Soldiers in pretend uniforms would get out carrying weapons, and when they entered the premises they would be offered cold drinks and petit fours and any orders they gave were implemented immediately. The city, which used to boast of being compared to Vienna, became a ruin populated by frightened ghosts grieving for their glorious past. The great families lost their money and their sons were forced to ally themselves with farmers with whom they now played backgammon, ignoring their boorishness and praising them, even offering their daughters in marriage.

Selim considered Omar's partnership with the smugglers to be mad, stupidity that would consign the entire family and its wealth to oblivion. He didn't expect Omar's cold defence of this partnership, the way he reeled off the details of their father's willingness to bend to the prevailing wind, and their grandfather before him, who delivered Sheikh Daghstani's grandfather to the Ottomans to be summarily executed in front of Bal El Hadid. Omar reminded Selim of how the four wings of Yildiz Palace in Istanbul had been furnished with splendid carpets as the reward for his betrayal, which my grandfather tried repeatedly to rewrite to make it seem more of a coincidence than a conspiracy.

Bakr didn't object to Omar's strategy, and offered advice which the other two didn't hear. Omar became like a Mafioso, totally preoccupied; he didn't know the taste of relaxation. He no longer came to us at the end of the evening as he used to – just drunk enough to be contented and cheerful, to fight with Maryam over the principles of *fiqh*, to drink coffee with Safaa and Marwa, to joke with me and leave me a considerable amount of cash. Maryam would put it away in my special box – as if she wanted to distance me from the overpowering, disgusting smell of fish that wafted from my father's clothes and hands, which, to her, had been transformed into putrescent gills.

Omar's public infamy and shamelessness worried my aunts, who raced to write a charm for him, which was stitched, wrapped in elegant, colourful material, and hung around his neck as he sat between them with the meekness of a mouse. Afterwards he was struck with the idea of making copies and selling them to other dervishes.

Safaa's eyes sparkled happily when news of his fight with an important official who raised objections to Omar's lover was circulated around the city. She was a married woman who boasted of her relationship with Omar; she went out to restaurants with him in public, travelled with him to Beirut for a few days, and returned to show off to her friends the evidence of his generosity. After a long conversation in which Omar complained of his attachment to his lover and her exploitation of his fierce tenderness, Safaa advised him to get her divorced and then marry her, adding sarcastically that a wife was cheaper than a mistress.

We couldn't understand Omar's ambition, nor his anxiety and fear; we couldn't find sufficient reason for Omar's mad withdrawal into his pleasures and his being hell-bent on provoking scandal. Whenever Maryam looked at his sharia qualification hanging on her bedroom wall, her eyes swam with tears and she muttered a prayer – we stopped joining in after a conversation we'd had about the enormous funds he had accrued in the short months he had spent as an arms dealer. He was now devoting himself almost entirely to this trade, at the expense of the patterned carpets and the smell of silk and wool. He became wary at the growing number of assassinations of civil service employees and lower-ranking officers, lauded by most people who were astonished at the cold-blooded murders.

Rumours circulated madly that certain groups had taken it upon themselves to cleanse official circles, were organizing and arming, and were intent on targeting the most venal and corrupt. They had no compunction about using violence and some even viewed it as essential; but others feared that their actions would create a spiral of unstoppable brutality, as the government forces were sure to retaliate in kind.

Apprehensive silence began to dominate the city, along with a fear of what ruin the future might bring. Omar couldn't easily withdraw from this business; he was trapped by his knowledge of suppliers and the names of Palestinian, Syrian and Iraqi politicians embroiled in the trade, and their connections to the dried-up wells and concealed passages of houses that acted as hidden warehouses. He felt suffocated, and one night he entered Maryam's room, took off his clothes and put on some blue silk pyjamas. He didn't speak to us for three days; he read the Quran piously, his voice hoarse whenever he raised it to recite Sura Al Ahzab. We all felt his tiredness and his need for the old image of our family, as if he missed that awkward adolescent who had once thrown flour in the air, watching the motes land on the edges of the pool, the flowers and the branches of the trees. He had opened his arms and whirled like a dervish in a Sufi ring, wondering quite seriously why the sky didn't rain flour.

Three days was enough for my aunts to celebrate Omar's apparent reformation, and it was long enough for me to get closer to my uncle and draw his attention to my erudition and demonstrate my knowledge of *fiqh*. It was a festival of food the likes of which I had never witnessed before, and Maryam gave herself up to it wholeheartedly. She ordered us to clean the neglected, dusty walnut table, and took out a crimson silk cloth whose borders were decorated with pictures of Chinese musical instruments and blossoms. She unrolled it and rebuked Safaa, though quietly and tenderly, for her aversion to making stuffed *kibbeh*. She turned to me with her observations about how messy the stuffed vine leaves were, and praised Marwa, who had inherited all the Aleppan know-how in preparing food. Marwa would add her own touches, and caused disputes with other Aleppan women until they became convinced of her talent to innovate.

Radwan was one of the most enthusiastic partici-pants in the feast, and found justification for sitting for hours by the stove, stretching his legs out on the sofa and delightedly chatting to Omar, whom he loved. He shared the same frivolous temperament and used to intercede with my grandfather to spare Omar his wrath. The array of dishes laid out in rows inspired an appetite that did not respect table manners, avenging the coldness of the table at which we women had sat in silence, eating with exaggerated etiquette. Omar insisted that Radwan should eat his meals with us, and Maryam didn't object. His conversations and his jester's clowning made us laugh, and we laughed without fear of uncovering our shame or being held to account for it.

In the evening, Maryam recounted stories from Omar's childhood. Her enthusiasm astonished him, and her face appeared loving as she tried to imitate my grandmother's desperation to reform her youngest son's errant behaviour; for the first time, I knew that he had thought about renouncing Islam, inspiring such real panic and confusion that it almost drove my grandmother to hysteria. She pronounced him to be mad and in need of special care, cried for entire nights and took him to the sheikhs of Aleppo. Omar surrendered to their recitations and charms, which bored him in no time at all. He would open the charms and read the names of devils and symbols of entry into Paradise, and then throw them down without any semblance of reverence in front of my grandmother, who gathered them together and burned them so as not to insult the honour of the best of the Muslims.

The tales of his adolescent years affected me greatly, and I tried several times to write it down and redraw his past; he was as close to me as if he were my own son. After his departure I began to understand the secret of Safaa's depression and Marwa's sadness, which made them complain so much of the exhaustion of our isolation and at the requests to uphold our honour – 'as if we walked naked through the city,' Safaa would retort irritably. Marwa was resigned, seemingly expecting nothing other than death; she agreed with everything, lost the will to talk. Safaa would carry her pillow and come to share the bed with me, and there would follow a never-ending conversation about the families who visited us, whose receptions we attended and whose wedding invitations we accepted. In the end, her conversation always sang the praises of women's strengths and mocked their weaknesses. She mocked Rima's coldness and declared that Omar had to divorce her; whereas Zahra, Bakr's wife, she described as a friend, reviewing the details of her long neck, the size of her breasts and their provocative bouncing. Safaa made me laugh. I felt her breath beside me when she dozed off, and as I looked at her face I believed she would be wretched as long as her pores were empty of the smell of men.

Omar left our house to wander in the mountains; he spent three weeks there alone, and his behaviour was more like that of an ascetic than a hellraiser. He slept in cheap hotels and savoured the smell of the pine trees in the Kurd-Dagh Forest. He avoided direct contact with the hotel owners, who were overwhelmed with his generosity. They thought he was on the run, or that he was cursed to silence and loneliness. He needed to reconsider everything: his relationships, funds, projects and dreams, his relationships with Rima and his friends, whom he had told he was going abroad. The pure mountain air of Salnafa and Kasab and his abstinence from alcohol brought freshness to his face and vitality to his feet. He rediscovered his connection to nature, climbing for hours in the mountains and avoiding the main roads, walking briskly through small country estates which led him to places that he thought, for the first time, were blessed. Oak branches twisted among the pine trees, and the scent of white cedar wafted from the forests after the fleeting night rains. His losses gained meaning. When the forested plains stretched out before him, it occurred to him to jump. He wished he were a paper aeroplane which could float over the country. His childhood came back to him in ever-accumulating images, the dust dislodged from them; he began to arrange them, mixing up their order and recalling their anxious taste, like a peach bitter despite its ripeness.

'I was closer to God,' he said to Maryam on his return, assailed by feelings of purity and lightness. Losing no time and allowing no one to venture an opinion, he informed Maryam of his decision to divorce Rima and grant her the right to live with his children in their sumptuous apartment – which was a hell to him because of the smell of pickles constantly emanating from the kitchen. His allergy to pickles made him irritable and unable to blow his nose. Quietly and as expected, their marriage came to an end, destroyed by her passion for cold meats and pickles – she would spend hours arranging the jars in the attic and on the tops of the kitchen cabinets. She had been made desperate by Omar's strange requests, unworthy of the daughter of a sheikh whose honour and asceticism were known throughout the city. 'He wants to turn me into a whore,' she would wail, before getting up and going to the kitchen to put salt on the pickled beans.

Safaa sympathized with Omar and praised his divorce, cursing Rima's idiocy and criticizing the smell of cheap talcum powder that came from her children. Maryam arranged the divorce, aided by Selim, who was forced to curse Omar more than once while at the same time blessing the memory of my grandmother, who had been the one to choose Rima over many other girls on account of her decency, her obedience and her family's fragrant reputation.

In the following days, Omar began to take his revenge on a history of decency, obedience and fragrant reputations. After his silence and isolation (which failed to last even a month) he returned to his profligate ways, causing ever-increasing mayhem. He sought out trouble, and provoked scandals in cold blood and with the utmost confidence: he harassed married women and adolescent girls, and openly accompanied prostitutes to restaurants; he would live in their attics for days at a time without any discretion, swapping joints and obscene photographs with them. He took them to the markets and listened to what was said about him without caring. He repeated to my aunts, 'Nothing will save me but love.' These few words of his awoke our desire for seclusion and silence. The silent house was gloomy and abandoned; Radwan roamed around it freely, relishing the temporary absence of Maryam's demands, Safaa's sarcasm or my pleas.

'Nothing will save any of us but love,' Safaa said to Marwa, who had begun to design a carpet whose borders were to be decorated with images of goddesses. I was terrified when I discovered that they were pagan deities I had seen once in an illustrated book about the Ancient Greeks. Maryam sank even deeper into her isolation and moved only between her bed and the cane chair by the window. At one point she took her photograph album out of her closet drawer, drew the curtains and locked the door as if getting ready to commit a sin. She stayed lost in a few photographs, then got up suddenly. She sat on the ground and recited the Sura Al Qasar. Her voice rose as if she were singing *nashid* for a celebration, or trying to drive out the demons which would descend from the chandelier hanging from the ceiling.

On the fourth day of our festival of silence and seclusion, we all went to one of Hajja Radia's sessions. My aunts joined in the singing of the women beseeching the Beloved Prophet. At that moment, I said to myself, 'It is so difficult for a woman to reveal her secrets.' I envied Omar for a moment, and then threw off my suspicion and depression. Later, on my bed, I conjured up an image of Ghada and then her scent. I pushed deeper into the daydream, and after reassuring myself of my solitude and the shadows in the room, I penetrated deeper and surrendered to my desire which plunged headlong like a train through green plains. I reached out my fingers for the buttons of her blue dress I knew so well, unfastened them and gazed at the pink bra which held her smouldering nipples and delicious breasts.

Then I got up, locked the door and drew the curtains and got completely naked in order to sink into the softness of her stomach. I panted like a dog and kissed her navel with the voracity of a woman abandoned to her own debauchery.

In the morning, I deeply regretted this. I was terrified of going to school, afraid of the familiar sounds. I hated Ghada when I saw her in the line-up, laughing with other girls and dawdling on the stairs. When I came close to her I felt as nauseous as if a corpse's stench were wafting from her, but

I missed her in the last lesson and almost left my classroom to find her. I needed to see her. I was distracted and couldn't hear the maths teacher despite my love of equations and geometry. I looked for Ghada at the end of the day and lingered in the exit. The car of the fifty-year-old man passed in front of the school and Ghada calmly waved at me from it, in complete command of herself. I smiled at her as my agonies increased; I wished she would die along with that man.

I said to myself that I must drown in onion fumes, piles of *molokhiyya* and bulgur wheat soaked in stone pots. This was the day before that offer that was to confuse Safaa and create a past impossible to erase, like a dishonour which no blood could wash away. Zahra came to the house with her two children, and she unpacked her clothes in my room. I needed someone to share the space with, to help me calm down a little. I decided to tell Zahra about Ghada and the cruelty of her abandonment, about my hatred and resentment which increased whenever I saw that middle-aged man picking her up outside school. I became completely engrossed in preparing the food for the important guests Bakr was shortly to bring to the house. I felt Maryam's contented gaze watching me as I seasoned fish and stuffed it with pepper, tasted it, and added some sticks of parsley. Marwa encouraged my daring in breaking with long-established cooking traditions, while Safaa whispered with Zahra briefly and appeared grave and bewildered. She took on the role of mother to both Zahra's and Omar's children – Maryam had invited them over so they could see their grandfather's house, which everyone felt was falling away.

Maryam's efforts to re-align our present according to the rhythm of the past would be of no use; it would only increase our delusions of belonging. We didn't know how we would one day throw off its weight from our shoulders and free ourselves from the tyranny of the framed pictures of our ancestors hanging on Maryam's wall, from the brass bedsteads and silver table service our grandparents had used, along with the ornate ancient mirrors, the walnut chests, the locked boxes and the hundreds of other fragments scattered all over a house whose sanctity increased every morning. The ropes wound around our necks and turned us all into slaves. We cleaned it all, polished it, reassured it; we didn't dare smash so much as a vase, even accidentally.

Maryam saw, as if for the first time, that I had grown to look like any woman who wore loose clothing and whose breasts drooped. I was no longer a little schoolgirl. I was allowed to approach Zahra, and to correct tacitly Maryam's errors in cooking the mince or using it as stuffing for the *kibbeh*. In all my life I had never seen such a huge parade of food as on that day. Maryam wanted Bakr's guests to relay their impressions to their womenfolk, so they would talk once more about our affairs and our skills as women; our absence from their gossip disturbed her as much as if we had somehow been tarnished.

Zahra was divided between us that night; at first, in the early evening, the conversation revolved gravely between Marwa, Safaa and Zahra, whom I saw from afar talking confidently and sipping from a cup of tea. Marwa was silent, watching Safaa as she asked a question, flinging up her hand in desperation. I was absorbed in bathing; my body needed to relax and waste some time. I felt that they had chosen to exchange secrets they wanted to keep from me, leaving me with Bakr's young son. We bathed together and I was delighted with him, and with his tears when the soap burned his eyes. I sang to him; I hadn't realized before that I hadn't learned anything other than Hajja Radia's *nashid*, which he didn't like. I immediately discarded the question of how boys grow up to become men. I remembered the pain of the previous night and laughed at my misgivings. I wondered how I could reduce their power and make them into a silly, transient idea which wouldn't corrupt the innocence of the first male I had washed with, as I pelted him with hot water and laughter.

At the end of the night, I told Zahra coldly about the perfidy of friends; about Ghada and my fear that she would get entangled in irresponsible adventures that would turn her into a woman of ill repute. I abandoned myself to describing my pain and Zahra was silent. She didn't agree with my stern opinions, but she didn't raise any objections to them. That was what I loved about her; she listened so intently to whoever needed it that the other half of the truth, which had always been concealed, came to light. I felt my predicament when she looked at me as if she were saying, 'How miserable you are,' and relief because I had let her into my stagnant world, like a lake forsaken by breezes, ducks and fishing hooks.

My mother came the next morning, early as usual. We were woken by the clamour and uproar of the copper saucepans she and Maryam had fetched to prepare the *freekeh*; my mother excelled at sweetening it with saffron to give it a special, indescribable flavour. She seemed decrepit to me when she complained of my father's indifference and extolled my brother Hossam's superlative grades and devoutness, singing the praises of his light moustache and slender frame. She was devoted to her first-born son, and loved him to a degree approaching madness. She believed that he would pluck our family from out of its wretchedness and, like all mothers, she wanted him to be a doctor and a philosopher. I became like a younger sister or companion to her; after four years away from her I had grown distant. I was no longer a part of her daily vocabulary. She received my news with unconcern, afraid only that I would be afflicted with the same curse of spinsterhood as my aunts, but when she returned home she would remember that my father had sold fish at the entrance to the souk at Bab Jenein. This was enough to ensure that the door to our house would be knocked on only by a poor bridegroom, or by one of the cousins whose faces remained unclear to me even after the few times I had met them. She only stayed a few hours, and when she left I saw Maryam slip some money into her handbag which earlier she had refused to take.

We were surprised at the group of thirty guests Bakr had invited, and I couldn't understand the secret of my brother Hossam's presence next to Bakr, nor his clear authority when he kissed the assembled men. I knew some of them, and Maryam pointed out who some of the others were as we sat in the kitchen. We watched them eating greedily, and Maryam was overjoyed that Sheikh Daghstani was there; for her, his acceptance of our invitation was a public exoneration of Omar. She praised his forbearance and piety; she enumerated some instances of his generosity and described him with exaggerated emphasis as a man of God. How had all these diverse people come together? I asked myself. They included important traders, manufacturers, a retired politician (who played a dubious role in independent governments), sheikhs (some of whom were involved in politics), men who were known to belong to the Muslim Brotherhood, an army officer I didn't know, a Saudi man and a Yemeni man of about forty-five. Maryam said he was a carpet trader who was friendly with Bakr. The Yemeni sat in the middle of the gathering.

From his seat he could see the window of Safaa's room.

My brother and Selim's children served the guests silently and Radwan tried to convince them that dinner was the ideal time for listening to his ode in praise of the Prophet. Hossam dismissed him resolutely, upsetting Radwan, who complained to me. I was astonished at my brother's coldness and indifference when I asked him to allow Radwan to recite; he didn't hear me when I insisted on what this gathering meant to Radwan. I was surprised at the hidden joy on Maryam's face when she explained at length that the family was gaining new men. We crept from the kitchen behind the curtain we had prepared so we could return to our rooms without the strangers seeing us. I went into Safaa's room and flung myself on her bed, exhausted, and was astonished to see her wearing an embroidered Arabic abaya and a head covering. I fell asleep and when I woke up two hours later, the siege was still going on. My aunts had gathered with Zahra in Maryam's room and although their voices were raised in excitement, they fell quiet when I entered.

Bakr stayed on with the remaining guests; we knew there were five of them when he asked us to prepare ginger tea for six. The Saudi and the Yemeni were no longer there, and neither was Sheikh Daghstani, all of whom Safaa had seen leave. I was overjoyed that Zahra had stayed and was delighted she would be sharing my room. I felt how lonely I was, how afraid of something unknown. My dreams had transformed into nightmares in which I discerned bad omens. In my notebook I drew huge snakes devouring children, bats cooing like doves in the sky over the city, and wolves devouring a woman. 'How hard it is to listen freely to your inner voice,' I said to myself. I informed Zahra of my desire to swim in the sea naked. I looked at her face; she was in utter disbelief that such a desire could have taken hold of me. I laughed and reassured her that my dreams sometimes broke loose.

Three days later, Bakr was still hosting the same five men we didn't know. They sat in a room in the attic for hours, spreading out papers, and he left with them after whispering a little with Zahra, who nodded her head and returned to us to complete a conversation which had become tedious. We listened, distracted, as Maryam quoted what the local women had said about the food we had spent the previous Friday preparing for their men.

Bakr was worried and confused. He suffered from insomnia, which was evident from his drooping eyelids. On the Wednesday, as usual, we prepared the light dinner and fresh berry juice he always asked for and hid in our rooms so the guests could leave at a certain time. After the evening prayer Bakr entered, and with him was the Yemeni man. In our presence, he asked Safaa to consider marrying this man, called Abdullah. He told her frankly that he was asking her to be a second wife and left her the freedom to come to a decision and become acquainted with him according to the principles of sharia. Safaa agreed without hesitation after Bakr praised his morals, with the only stipulation that the marriage should happen within days.

Zahra was the sponsor of this marriage, which Safaa had determined upon without love. Maryam tried to defer it for a while. Safaa surprised everyone with her serious, sad tone when she shouted, 'I want to become a woman. I don't want to die a virgin.' She concluded quietly, 'I want a child.' Maryam had no time to praise the morals, piety or wealth of her sister's prospective Yemeni husband at any women's gatherings. My uncles blessed the marriage as they usually did, as if our remaining without menfolk had made them expect a future scandal. Omar dismissed Maryam's irritation and presented Safaa with a gold belt and a ring set with precious diamonds. Laughing, he informed us that he had bought it for one of his girlfriends in Beirut. Omar's libertine words seemed alien to the dictionary of decency that Maryam was intent on reviving, reminding us of its vocabulary all the more frequently as she advanced in years.

In hastily prepared sumptuous white clothing, and with a small trousseau filling no more than two bags, Safaa left our house as a bride to the sound of Hajja Radia's tambourines. A few women had been invited to the *mawlid* which lasted no more than two hours, and their extemporizing swiftly angered Maryam, who wept as Safaa stepped outside the house to be welcomed by Abdullah. He was accompanied by four men: two Yemenis, an Aleppan trader famous for his friendships with men of religion, and Sheikh Daghstani. We closed the door and an awful silence settled as if we were at a funeral. Maryam's tears bewildered us and made me, Marwa and Zahra cry as well, while my mother told her beads next to Hajja Radia as she gathered up her tambourines. She waited for Maryam to calm down so she could talk to her cruelly about her portion of the inheritance, and ask her to stop adhering to such stringent requirements for her own marriage, which simply wouldn't ever take place, despite our lineage and the reputations of my grandfather and uncles. I suddenly remembered that I hadn't seen Radwan for three days, after Maryam prevented him from leading as usual our procession to the hammam. I knocked at his door and heard the sound of sobbing. I opened the door and saw him eating dried figs and weeping for his 'devoted friend, Safaa' as he described her on our first visit to her new home. He gave her a bottle of perfume, with what seemed like a secret understanding. He laughed like a child when she promised to name her second son Radwan and bring him over so the original Radwan could help him memorize the Quran and teach him how to make perfumes.

Safaa reassured Maryam that she felt optimistic about her marriage to the Yemeni, and whispered companionably with Zahra, as if expressing her gratitude to her. Safaa's new house in Jamiliyya was composed of two rooms and a living room. Maryam almost suffocated in the narrowness of the reception room, which she said resembled a tomb. For the first time, I saw Safaa's spirit expressed in a place of her very own; she shook off her lethargy and fiercely defended her new life. The house was arranged in a manner that revealed her hatred for my grandfather's house filled with its old furniture. There were a couple of sofas in the living room in the American style, elsewhere was a soft bed beside a gleaming black chest of drawers topped by a candlestick with three branches. There were not many pots and pans in the kitchen, as if the owners of the house were spending a short holiday there and would be leaving it soon. Safaa didn't listen to Maryam's suggestion to move some things from my grandfather's house, which she offered up as if it were Safaa's greatest right to have them. Safaa stroked her hand and informed her that her carpet would be enough, relinquishing her portion of the inheritance; it was as if she didn't trust that this small house or the unknown places where she would join her husband were really a long-term arrangement. Marwa kept Safaa's wardrobe filled with dresses, some of which became gifts, along with her bedding, her pillows and all her small effects.

Marwa seemed unconvinced that Safaa had broken free from their fate and would not be returning to the house a lonely woman.

Our monotonous evenings began to herald a long isolation from which I didn't know how to escape. Marwa embroidered handkerchiefs. I didn't know who she would give them to; she piled them in her wardrobe and postponed her death a day at a time. She offered to teach me how to embroider and I told her seriously, and to her astonishment, 'I don't want to wait for death.'

I went to a daily meeting at Hajja Souad's – I had recently begun to frequent her house despite the feeling of estrangement that attended me as I sat with the other girls. I had met most of them the day Hana took me there, in accordance with Bakr's orders and his insistence that I would only understand his purpose when Hajja Souad began to divide us into smaller groups and meet us at fixed times. We spoke gravely about the group and its ideology of establishing an Islamic state, and enthusiastically conveyed news from school, and our aims to include other girls in our gatherings, which had started to expand.

Secrecy, silence and zeal were on the rise in our state, in which the knowledge of the Prophet would soon stir. 'We will punish the blasphemies of the unbelievers,' Hajja Souad repeated with full conviction, as if she could see that very day. We, the sisters, the believers, would sit in Paradise next to the Prophet and the mothers of the believers.

I didn't grasp from where came the conviction that the path to Paradise was open before me. All I now wanted was to become a martyr borne up by white birds, pure, sins forgiven, to that paradise which Hajja Souad drew for us patiently and confidently. My sufferings were calmed. I found that my belief was encouraged through my relationship with Bakr who, I now saw, had been created to realize the dream of eradicating dissolution and debauchery, and to re-glorify the Islamic Caliphate.

I couldn't find a better interlocutor than Safaa's new husband, Abdullah, especially as Bakr was always busy; he never spent two nights in a row in his own house. Maryam didn't object to my sitting with Abdullah for hours at a time, and we would discuss and exchange information about Islamic clans and stories of martyrs who had died in prison cells and on battlefields. Safaa was astonished by the speed at which I became involved, and my stubbornness in the face of her attempts to dissuade me from this path. She praised my femininity and my promising academic future, trying to save me from the path of destructive politics and, more particularly, from all the details of her husband's past I could gather. I extolled the strength of conviction that had made Abdullah relinquish the path of error, and how his heart used faith to illuminate a segment of

114

his tortuous journey which had continued for more than twenty years. He had spent them in anxiety, in a search for answers to the questions his heart had been repeating since being opened for the first time at the English School in Cairo, a building surrounded by giant cypress trees in the district of Abdeen. He had been one of its most distinguished students, and his teachers had great confidence in his subtle analyses of William Blake; the awe and accent with which he recited the verses reminded his teachers of Welsh farmers, overcome with emotion at an Eisteddfod. Abdullah would reread long sections of 'The Tyger' for me, which he had never forgotten, despite the years separating him from that student who had dreamed of his home in Yemen. He stood up suddenly, raised his hands and, with considerable feeling, began to recite the poem in English.

To me, he seemed like a first-rate actor, and more joyful than usual. Safaa was fixed on his gleaming eyes as if she were noticing their dark colour for the first time. I smiled shyly and laughed when I heard Radwan insist on reciting the ode that Hossam hadn't allowed him to recite the day of Bakr's banquet. I thought that he had forgotten about it, but he got carried away and recited it without waiting for permission. Politely, but with increasing boredom, Abdullah listened as Radwan attempted to imitate his style of recitation. We clapped for a long time, and Maryam slapped her palms together, saying, 'You've all gone mad.'

Then she left us to express our need for strangers to talk to, even if only politely and shyly.

Abdullah's father decided to send his son away from Aden on the basis of advice from an Indian sailor who entered his old shop in the souk one day. He was looking for a copper Umayyad-style lamp which he described in minute detail – a wandering Englishman he had met in Alexandria had convinced him that he would never find it anywhere but Yemen. The Indian sailor seemed bewildered as he explained this in English to a man who understood only a few words of the language. The father called over his son, Abdullah, and asked him to translate this strange foreigner's request. The two quickly understood each other, and the Indian expressed his delight at this student who was no more than four years old and who could describe a lamp and speak about imaginary worlds that the sailor admired. Abdullah listened attentively to the Indian's tales of adventure, and the long conversation between the boy and sailor pleased the father, who wondered about the secret behind their effusiveness, and their enjoyment of a conversation neither wanted to finish. He was proud of the eloquence of his young son, who made the sailor laugh and keep returning to the shop to teach magic tricks to Abdullah. He was a fast learner and after a week, he could produce a rose from his shirt sleeve. Before the sailor's ship left Aden, he had bought a multitude of lamps, copper goblets and silver-plated narghiles to sell at other ports, or to give to the directors of shipping companies in Athens. The sailor advised the father that his son must complete his studies at the English School in Cairo, if he wanted him to have a different future from the rest of his generation – which wandered the streets, waiting to avenge tribal blood feuds or to carry out the whims of Imam Yahya's men.

It was a dream that was closer to a fantasy than reality, but eventually Abdullah took his first steps into a school that made him afraid, then lonely, then a leader to his classmates, comprised of the sons of kings, petty princelings and families known for their vast wealth. 'The stuff of legends,' Abdullah would often say to us as he described for us his first months. The oddness of his never-ending stories always astonished us.

In Cairo, he felt a strange taste he still yearned for. He was forced to work in a printing shop during the holidays to reduce the burden of the exorbitant fees on his father, who wasn't a prince. His father was determined that his son should stand in graduation robes next to the sons of kings, and enumerated their names for everyone who asked him about Abdullah and his studies. He clung to this image even if it meant he might be forced to sell his shop, spend all his savings and sell what remained of his large camel herd. Whenever he saw a picture of his son with royalty, he remembered the Indian sailor and blessed him.

He would, yet again, narrate the story of how the sailor had come into the shop, of his long conversation with Abdullah, and then of their friendship, which shaped and transformed the young Abdullah into a guide who led his friend through the alleys of Aden, where he had become immersed in dreams of travel and destinations which the sailor talked about simply and thrillingly. All the sons of Abdullah's tribe came to know the story, right to its very end, and they would often repeat it – an echo of a legend that rectified much in their own fates, which were mostly left to chance.

At the age of eighteen, in the cellar of the printing shop, Abdullah met Selim Dessouki – a genius, according to Abdullah's affectionate description. He was a man who always lingered over choosing his words, always smiled, and who guided Abdullah to Marxism and led him by the hand through some of Cairo's poorest districts. They visited artists and journalists who dreamed of a world ruled by justice, and hung pictures of Lenin and Marx on the wall. Abdullah smuggled the leftist books into his school and spent the night turning their pages, heedless of the danger created simply by having them in his possession. 'I became a fanatical Marxist,' he said bitterly as he recalled his frankly expressed atheism, when he believed that the hungry would overrun the world and institute a reign of justice.

His father's dreams collapsed when he received a telegram informing him that Abdullah had been arrested on the charge of being a Communist; he was expelled from Cairo after enduring the torture that left scars on his back and in his soul. He fled to Damascus and from there to Moscow with a forged Syrian passport given to him by his comrades. When he came out of Moscow airport, he breathed in deeply. He remembered the Indian sailor, and his father who had searched for him in Cairo, full of regret for the savings spent on a now fugitive son. Abdullah had left the company of princes and their retinues loaded down with gifts, and had gone instead to the mob which smelled of excrement. The school administration ignored its previously star student and now considered him non-existent, effacing his records as if ridding themselves of an oppressive nightmare.

His father's feet led him to Selim Dessouki, who tried to reassure him by saying that his son's future would liberate Yemen from the Imam's rule. His father was horrified; the coming days would destroy everything he had spent years building. He sold his shop in Aden and returned to his tribal lands, which were bound by strong alliances to the Imam's men after years of bitter dispute.

Abdullah spent ten years in Moscow fighting on all battlefronts and, with his few Yemeni comrades, laying the foundations of their impossible dream which they felt drew ever closer. They created a picture of their happy Yemen where children wore resplendent clothes and cheered the non-existent 'proletarian class'. His nights of sleeplessness were over when he came off the steamer in Yemen with his comrades. He examined the faces of the people who were welcoming them but couldn't find his father or any of his brothers or sisters. He returned to the tribal grounds to search for them, and found his father stretched out in a mud room surrounded by Abdullah's seven siblings who had grown up and become shepherds and warriors cheering for the glory of the clan. He felt remorseful whenever his father looked at him. The clan told him about the days his father spent in the Imam's prison because of him, Abdullah, after news of his preparations to oppose the Imam and end his rule had reached Yemen. 'One of the cruellest things he bore, other than you, was the torture of being related to you.' Time passed heavily between father and son. Abdullah tried to share breakfast with him, and reassure him that he would be compensated for all his frustrations and the dreams that had turned into a mirage.

The politician soon became absorbed in his own dreams, dealing with delegates from Damascus, Cairo and Moscow who brought alliances which didn't last long. Dividing the country became the only solution to stop the massacres and preserve the dreams of two sides that never met: the pan-Arabists and the Communists couldn't even sit together on one rug to sip green tea, chew *gat* and take a nap in the afternoon.

Maryam's face changed colour when she heard Abdullah's admission that he had been an infidel who didn't believe in God. Despite his power as a storyteller, he narrated a strange tale we couldn't possibly believe: his suffering, his pain, his dreams, his discoveries which opened unnamed doors. He leapt in without hesitation, always risking sudden death. Death was so close to him, he could feel it seeping from his skin.

This path of torment and doubt brought Abdullah to a state of absolute certainty a few years before he reached forty. He entered his fortieth year cleansed of agonizing questions, never to return to insomnia or addiction to the Russian vodka brought in special boxes from Moscow which bore the signatures of senior Communist Party members. They described him as a brother in arms when he decided, along with his comrades, to divide up Yemen and 'sit on the throne' of Aden. His comrades' dreams of revolution, justice and progress didn't prevent them from strolling along Aden's beaches like devoted citizens, accompanied by their wives and girlfriends who had removed their tribal markings, which they considered folklore from a bygone era. They dreamed of the flurry of Moscow snow, where they could wallow without fear of their cousins' pistols.

Abdullah married Zeina, dumbstruck at her ability to memorize the story of Abu Zeid El Helaly and then repeat it by heart at Sheikh Zaal El Tamimi's council; the sheikh had adopted her after her father was killed in the camel market as part of an old blood feud. Abdullah approached her and asked, 'What's your name?' She answered softly, with an orphan's timidity, 'Zeina.' She was sixteen and still held company with men, so she had acquired their coarseness and habits. He encouraged her to raise her voice while the sheikh, whose house she lived in, pretended not to notice. He had married Zeina's mother, who was famous for her strength, her aversion to specifically Bedouin habits, and her perpetual longing for the oases of the Najd, her childhood playground.

Zeina had inherited her mother's strength, long black hair and indigo eyes. She was consumed with bewilderment and worried by the uncertainty of her future with this man – news of his follies filled the tribe's houses until they grew into a complicated story narrated by many people, with concurrent beginnings and contradictory endings.

He asked her to marry him in a few words, without negotiating a dowry or giving her much time to think his proposal over. Her mother agreed and informed Sheikh Zaal El Tamimi of her preparations. She had wanted a marriage such as this for her daughter, who had begun to think seriously of avenging the murder of her father, even though the tribe had agreed to abandon this course of action in exchange for ten she-camels which subsequently died in mysterious circumstances. Everyone knew that Zeina had slipped poison into their fodder, refusing to accept them as the price, which she considered far too low, for her father's death. Zeina became used to riding horses and going hunting, a reincarnation of Al Zeir Salim in his moments of worry when he thought of his revenge on Jassas. The air of Aden weighed heavily on her chest, as did the air of the small house constantly filled with company and books. Abdullah told her about the lives of other men, who weren't Al Zeir Salim or tribesmen. He showed her pictures, and movingly rendered the story of Lenin's return to Russia to lead the Bolshevik Revolution and found an empire of workers and peasants capable of defeating imperialism.

Zeina longed for the stories of Abu Zeid El Helaly and Al Zeir Salim and their sad odes in Sheikh Zaal El Tamimi's council, instead of the biography of Lenin which bored this typical teenager. She couldn't find any common ground between them, and refused to go to Abdullah's comrades' parties. She suffered from chronic headaches and her dream of avenging her father's blood receded, and then faded away altogether. She spent her time with their baby which had arrived in the meantime, and took no notice of the comrades' conflicts, the news of which had spread to every house in Aden.

Aden was quiet, and walked alongside these men into an uncertain future. Arguments escalated; Abdullah felt threatened by the pointed discussions of who might be unfortunate enough to succumb to a stray bullet, or which route would be suitable for the grand funeral of a statesman. Close friends advised him to move abroad, and Zeina and her child rapidly moved to Beirut. Abdullah followed them, sighing with regret, after three years of trying to convince his comrades to put their differences aside and re-build the Communist Party. He reminded them of their dreams, of their years of fighting, of the taste of exile and prison. In Beirut he was depressed, and seemed to have no future; when an old comrade, now ambassador to Lebanon, refused to see him, he realized that everything had come to an end. Abdullah started wandering around the country, writing articles in Lebanese periodicals about his experience of the Party and accusing Abdel Mohsen of taking power in a coup in which he executed old comrades. He heard that his siblings had been arrested and that their interrogations had lasted for hours, in locked rooms filled with foul smells.

His successive crises ended only when he wept in front of the Kaaba in Mecca after arriving there with Prince Shehab El Din, a childhood friend who still remembered his genius at solving geometry problems at the English School in Cairo. With the prince's help, Abdullah was granted a pardon and royal permission to enter Mecca on the Haj and stay in the prince's palace as a long-term guest, where he enjoyed generous hospitality. In the prince's private quarters they would play chess and reminisce about their erstwhile companions, most of whom Abdullah met again when they passed through old friends' houses. They went out hunting together for a few days and made plans to meet up soon in other cities.

'I saw God in Mecca,' said Abdullah with the faith of the ascetic; I envied him these visions that had changed his life. Zeina exulted when she saw him raving at night in prayer, beseeching for his soul to be saved, now hovering like a hawk who has been pursued by the hunters' guns and who is, at last, exhausted, returning to his nest in the mountains. His friendship with Prince Shehab El Din opened doors to him. Zeina narrated the story of Al Zeir Salim once again, reciting his grief-stricken elegies for Kulaib bin Wael in the salon of the prince's wife, who loved Zeina's magic and the power of her words. The audience listened intently to her and to her wide-ranging learning, gleaned from mixing with men in various capital cities and from her uncles who were famous in the Najd for their Nabataean poetry and their cunning. Most important was her knowledge of the secrets of pleasure; she spoke fluently about horse-riding positions, glancing lewdly at the men. Zeina brought to mind the story of Scheherazade, whom I always liked to recall; I traced her image in my dreams many times, and I always drew her as a frightened woman, seeking help from words in order to be saved from tyranny. Words drew never-ending, chaotically intersecting lines that led to futility; I was frightened of becoming entangled in them, in case their shifting sands swept me away.

Abdullah met Bakr at one of Prince Shehab El Din's councils. They became close after a long conversation in the palace garden, which began with the merits of Kashmiri carpets and ended in politics. Bakr didn't hide his pleasure at Abdullah's metamorphoses. He paused for a while at the point in the story where Abdullah described holding a position of authority and explained (with a great deal of verbosity and confidence) its arrangements, ambitions, secrets and connections. Then in a quiet voice Abdullah reviewed his childhood and studies at the English School as if he were throwing a heavy weight into the shadowy depths of the ocean; he joyfully recalled the Indian sailor who had led him to a fate he didn't regret. He remembered the cruelty of those moments that had haunted him during the cold Moscow nights when he longed to run barefoot behind a herd of camels, heedless of the wild thorns.

They weren't parted for three days. They accompanied one of the prince's hunting expeditions into the desert, content to praise the precision of his aim and spend the rest of the time chatting. The friendship that grew between them delighted the prince. Abdullah didn't hesitate to support Bakr in obtaining a contract to furnish the prince's new palace with rich carpets, in order to realize the building the prince had dreamed of one night. When the dream was repeated another night, the prince considered it to be an order from the world of spirits to erect this palace to honour the memory of his mother, who was praying on a small carpet in the dream. The prince described the structure minutely and enthusiastically, and Bakr listened attentively to his account of coloured peacocks, birds of paradise and basil plants surrounding fountains, all reminiscent of the small palace of Abi Abdullah, last of the Andalusian kings. The prince, exhausted after abandoning himself to the remembrance of his dream, concluded his speech by saying briefly, 'I want a palace which looks like my mother's womb.'

Abdullah obtained the prince's permission to accompany Bakr as he fulfilled the prince's dream, which he had sworn zealously to do. They left the palace on uncharted roads, and became semi-vagrants in the alleys of Iran, Iraq, Afghanistan and Central Asia. They used an old Jeep Bakr had chosen so as not to arouse the cupidity of the owners of what they sought – such as five-hundred-year-old carpets upon which famous globetrotters and sultans had once sat; or boxes made from rare wood and inlaid with silver, once given to women in their youth by famous men who adored them – women who, in their old age, were forced to sell them in public auctions for less money than the cost of a few glass bottles.

Bakr and Abdullah both enjoyed the subterfuge, and enjoyed discovering all these deserts, cities, villages and houses, all the while recalling in the depths of their souls the story of the Prophet, who blessed legitimately acquired profit and trade; fully and unreservedly, Bakr would praise the hidden talents of his friend Abdullah, whom he hadn't thought possessed such ingenuity. Sixteen shipments were unloaded in the warehouses of the new palace; the six decorators and the two hundred and fifty craftsmen and labourers, who specialized in polishing antique lamps and renovating furniture, were at work for more than six consecutive months under Bakr's supervision, who came down with a fever twice. The doctors advised him to avoid inhaling the fumes of molten gold when it was poured into the mould created by a young drug addict from Iran. He had convinced Bakr and Abdullah that it was a faithful rendition of the taps in the palace of Haroun El Rashid, over whose paving stones Abu Nuwas used to roll with his beautiful young boys. (As the price for his totally fraudulent design, he asked for no more than a small sum which would buy less than a week's supply of heroin.) Both Abdullah and Bakr liked the strange design: a tap suspended over a butterfly which laughed and spread its wings when the water ran.

Prince Shehab El Din objected to nothing, and almost wept with joy at the strange palace when he entered it for the first time and wandered through its twenty rooms together with his brother and cousin princes. Abdullah was their guide and explained the story of each piece of furniture and the place where he had bought it, while his friend Bakr remained under his protection, anticipating the fruits of his adventures in realizing the prince's dream. When the prince approached the outstretched carpet, he confirmed that it was the same one his mother had been praying on in the dream and whispered to Abdullah, 'This is what I've been looking for.' He commended Bakr's genius and cursed the freeloaders who came flocking in, smiling biliously and offering a captivating Italian girl the prince had often watched in the porn films he had been addicted to, before being afflicted with longing for his mother's womb.

Long before Abdullah married Safaa, he and Bakr had become friends with shared memories and ambitions; not many knew that, for a considerable period, Abdullah smuggled money to Syria for Bakr and his brotherhood so they could buy arms and plan what they had dreamed of for a long time. They calculated that the general resentment at the allocation of the principal army posts to supporters of the regime had reached such a degree that people were prepared to die for God. (I used to think: if people die as martyrs for God, how do both the killers and killed enter Paradise?) Bakr used all his wiles to convince traditional community leaders that they needed to fight. But he couldn't counter their protests as they related the history of their struggles, reminding him that politics couldn't be conducted on the basis of an unchanging formula, like following a fixed list of ingredients in a recipe. The nights that Bakr spent in discussion with Abdullah in the palace garden in Mecca had made him into a man who believed his own goals were clear, confirming to himself deep down that it was Abdullah who had been betrayed by his comrades in Yemen, because he had believed that words were enough to solve arguments and distribute positions of power. Abdullah directed Bakr's reading towards Régis Debray and Che Guevara, who had dreamed of liberating an entire continent with a few men, believers in the piercing vision of the Commandante. After reading the works of Trotsky, accounts of revolutions and *The Communist Manifesto*, Bakr quietly responded, 'Enemies always have something to teach us.' Abdullah agreed and in his soft voice, generously endowed with his usual refinement and dignity, outlined everything he had learned from his enemies.

I was in raptures about this man who wasn't forbidden to me, and called him my uncle. I listened to him ardently and paraded my reading material in front of him. Once, I showed him my drawings. He looked over them quickly and paused at the drawing of Ghada, who appeared as a wounded gazelle surrounded by brindled hunting dogs.

Two months after their marriage, Safaa returned to our house so that she wouldn't be alone when Abdullah travelled to Mecca again. She was quiet and spoke with the slow deliberation of someone who knew the secrets of Bakr's meetings with men we hadn't seen. We felt, from their dawdling and their shouts which occasionally continued until the dawn call to prayer, that real danger was imminent. The assassinations of civil service employees continued unabated, responsibility for which was attributed to the young men whom Bakr, along with another senior member of the organization, Sheikh Abdel Jaber, had taken into the forests by the sea to be trained in marksmanship, judo and karate. We used to see them gathering in front of the Umayyad Mosque as if they were friends going on a trip, looking forward to shouting in meadows and forests.

Hajja Souad invited me to her house to meet a girl I had never seen before. She greeted me cordially and said, 'I'm Alya.' I looked at her and her cold eyes, and almost laughed out loud at her nose which resembled a goose's beak. She added foolishly that she was to be my mentor and baffled me when she told me, passionately and precisely, that she couldn't bear any other principles of the Quran than self-discipline and fighting the moral decay which was spreading among the daughters of Islam. I joined her cell without discussion, and she named a contact who would tell me the dates and locations of the meetings I had begun to dream of. She hinted that our group was just one of many across the city, and had links with others in the organization even as far away as Hama.

Summer came, and it was depressing. I spent some of it in my parents' home, thus avoiding

Maryam who complained of imaginary kidney ailments and neglected to drink the cold, thick liquorice Marwa made in large batches and whose taste remained on the tongue for days afterwards. Hossam was engrossed in new secrets which worried my father; I sensed his anxiety when Hossam ignored his questions about his repeated absences from the house, and added that the civil engineering college he was going to attend meant nothing to him. My mother's dreams for Hossam went unheeded. He spent days at a time with Bakr and the rest of his companions in the Kurd-Dagh forests, where they used the North Star and compasses to orient themselves when lost in the mountains; in this way they were shaken from any monotony. After two weeks, eagerness carried them back, filled with even more ferocity, and ardently desiring the beginning of the battle. Hossam banned me from his room. I felt coldness and loneliness, which didn't match the usual warmth of his presence; it wasn't like us to avoid each other.

I thought how painful it was that places can settle in you and you can't extricate yourself from them: I returned to my grandfather's house and chose once more to be an occasional and impromptu guest at my parents'. Suddenly, without any preamble, Hossam gave me his textbooks for the baccalaureate. He wanted me to be privy to his dreams. I read his writings and saw his drawings that filled the margins with guns, hand grenades, strange, cold faces with pop-eyes and thin upper lips like Alya's – to whom I had begun to listen anxiously during her lectures on hatred.

A girl I didn't know led me to the first meeting of Alya's group. She waited for me in front of a coffee stand at Bab Al Nasr, and we kissed each other like any friends who were meeting to go to the cinema without permission from their families. She smiled and informed me that the house wasn't far. We were the last to arrive, and I sat by the door and watched the seven other girls. The only one I knew was Hiba, the daughter of the timid schoolteacher; she soon acted as a sort of secretary at our meetings. The girls listened respectfully to Alya as she urged us to hate all the other Islamic sects and praised ours for being closest to the Prophet, quoting the doctrines of certain imams and from the biographies of sheikhs and mujahideen. In another meeting, she distributed papers to us and asked us to keep them safe. I read them carefully in my room and hid them when Safaa came in to complain about her perpetual headache, and how much she missed Abdullah whose return had been delayed until the end of August. I wished he would come.

I hated the scorching summer heat which drenched me every time I walked outside in my thick black robes. 'I wish my pores would die,' I said to myself as beads of sweat gave off that sour smell I hated. I remembered the sunflowers Safaa had brought from a nearby village. She had picked them before sunrise so they would retain their dew. She gave them to Radwan and persuaded him that their extract, when brewed, released a scent no words could describe, adding carelessly, 'It helps pregnant women with an easy childbirth.' Radwan was enthusiastic; he always liked Safaa's strange ideas, particularly when she asked him to keep their conversations to himself. It allowed him the secrecy he needed to make perfumes, which he would insist on whenever we asked him about the vials carefully arranged in rows in the wooden box tucked away in a corner of his room.

By the end of that summer, hatred had taken possession of me. I was enthused by it; I felt that it was saving me. Hatred gave me the feeling of superiority I was searching for. I carefully read the pamphlets distributed at every meeting with the other girls and memorized whole sections of them, particularly the fatwas charging other sects with heresy. I became closer to my seven companions and grew to love them. We exchanged secrets and books describing the horrific agonies of the grave. My integration with them saved me from my desires for Ghada, who had in my mind become wretched; she was still far from the power and severity I possessed when asked my opinion on punishing those who showed contempt for religion's doctrines. I astonished them by requesting to make a list of such girls at my school and seeking permission to disfigure them with acid for wearing tight shirts that clearly showed their breasts. Alya's eyes shone as she asked me to be patient, as if she already knew the date we would do it.

'We need hatred to give our lives meaning,' I thought as I celebrated my seventeenth birthday alone. It is hard when no one celebrates with you, or gives you flowers and presents. Safaa returned to her house with Abdullah for a while, after which they would be leaving for Saudi Arabia. Marwa packed a small bag and went to stay with Zahra. Maryam considered birthdays to be a foreign heresy whose merrymaking was not appropriate for the daughters of the family God had settled within the corners of our house. I sat alone and stretched my feet along the edge of the pool. I relaxed and enjoyed the September breezes. While I drank juice, I began to anticipate the next school year and my revenge on the girls who had made me feel that I was gloomy, unsuited for such relaxation in the sunlight. I loved how the spray coming off the sleepy fountain tickled my feet and my soft fingers. I needed hatred to reach love, to leave behind all the ashes, the twilight of objects and faces.

I read the margins of Hossam's textbooks and inspected the drawings scrawled over the chemistry volume; I burst out laughing at the picture of a donkey with a Roman letter 'N' on it. (I guessed that it was meant to be Najwa, our neighbour's daughter – she had married a wood merchant and had never noticed Hossam's confusion. He loved her and would write her love poetry praising her chastity and virtue.) All this was a letter Hossam had written to me, replacing the years of silence and estrangement with confidences as between friends. He had left me his notes so I could read them and know how tormented he was; how he longed to achieve martyrdom in God's service; how his skinny body could no longer contain his soul, hidden behind fiery words and pledges to the infidels that their Day of Judgement was near. There were also *nashid* I had never heard before, which incited mujahideen to the death. I missed him; we were as harsh to each other as if we were strangers. When we passed each other, neither of us lingered to exchange a confidence, or relate some trivial moment which was given value by being shared. I missed him, but didn't seek him out.

I observed him silently the day when he rushed into my grandfather's house, all agitated, with a black-speckled shawl on his shoulders. There were bloodstains on his shirt, and Maryam didn't believe that they came from a sacrifice a friend of Hossam had made to his mother's memory. My brother entered the cellar and I saw him hide a gun in a sack of bulgur wheat. I knew that he had killed our neighbour Abbas, a pilot whose green eyes Safaa used to be infatuated with. Hossam washed and assured us that everything would be fine. He sipped his coffee in silence and avoided looking at me; he wanted everything to seem normal. I left silently for school and saw people crowding around the pilot's body, now covered

136

with a woollen blanket. I didn't stop, but I glimpsed his huge corpse's hand lying there limply, between the armed men who were surrounding the body and closing off the street. I felt nauseous and dizzy in the second class of the day. Ghada brought me a cup of tea and put her hand on my forehead, reviving all my desires for her. I cried, and as I told her I'd just seen someone murdered, Hiba and Hana moved away from me. They observed me, and there was contempt in their eyes for my weakness. I was allowed to go home, accompanied by Ghada who squeezed my arm affectionately as I cried in silence.

Members of the Mukhabarat were searching houses in the alley, ours among them, after having carried the body away and cleaned up the blood. The corpse evaporated: his smile no longer beamed. I fell asleep and was haunted by nightmares. I saw his smiling face. In the early evening, I heard Bakr whispering as he listened to Maryam describe how the Mukhabarat had searched the house and rummaged through the sacks of bulgur wheat, adding that she had taken the precaution of hiding Hossam's gun in the hole where my grandfather used to hide his money and his rifle, and thanking God that Hossam had left a few minutes before.

Bakr's face was exhausted and worried, showing everything he couldn't speak about, and he stayed in bed for three days. Different images merged and all my memories of Hossam caved in all at once, from when he was a silent child, skinny and mad about mathematics. No one then could have predicted his future; he was silent and distracted for hours at a time, oblivious to the din surrounding him – we thought he was going to become a poet. His odd ideas had reminded my mother and aunts of Omar's strange and contradictory childhood. When we were young children, Hossam would prepare a seat on the branches of the only tree in our courtyard and stay there for hours. When he was a teenager, he never went to the cinema with schoolfriends, or chased cheerfully after girls with the idiocy typical of that age; he hid and suppressed his violent feelings. I used to see him get up from his bed during the night, sit on the step to his room, and cry unrestrainedly. I didn't know why he would pace around like a madman in the Sufi circles Bakr took him to, without even listening to the rhythm. Bakr effectively adopted him, and assessed the fullest extent of his intelligence. Hatred and cruelty slept in his nephew's heart. Finally, Hossam saw a light in the shadowy tunnel of his life. He spent a long time with Bakr, until he became almost like a secretary or bodyguard to him. He joined a gym and his body began to develop. His muscles grew and his movements quickened, like those of a runner training for a marathon.

Hossam and I didn't talk properly like siblings, or conspire together; moving to my grandfather's house made me a stranger to him. My infrequent visits to my parents' house made his image fade in my mind. When I saw him, I felt he was a stranger at first, but I loved him, and objected to his constant observations that made me out to be a woman who must be controlled, and who must obey the orders she's given. My father had initially blessed his son's relationship with Bakr, reassured that the smell of fish would never emanate from his clothes. For a short time, he wanted Hossam to become a carpet trader, while my mother wanted her precious boy to be a doctor and reminded us that his soft fingers and piercing eyes would suit a skilled surgeon. His image as the murderer of our neighbour the pilot held sway over me: the coldness as he hid the gun after throwing his bloodstained shirt in the bathroom stove, his quiet slumber – it all made me wonder about the power of the hatred in his heart. I liked it, setting aside the moments of sympathy that had afflicted me when I'd seen the dead body.

While I was off school, Ghada visited me and brought me flowers. We spoke like close friends; I loved her sympathy for me, and I sensed her worry when she spoke to me about her relationship with the fifty-year-old man. We no longer saw him as much, as he was overworked and had grown wary in his movements following the assassinations. They seemed to herald a serious confrontation that would drag the country into a cycle of violence, and no one knew how it would end. Ghada told me of her difficulties with her family who refused to acknowledge the relationship but kept silent out of fear of violent recrimination from her lover, over thirty years her senior. She denied that he brutally tortured prisoners, describing him as a magnificent man.

Her lips were full, like ripe figs which dripped honey as they were devoured. I briefly envied her her daring and asked her forgiveness. Haunted with longing for her, I sank wearily into her arms and wept. I felt wonder as her fingers combed through my hair like a plough through earth; the air she breathed out had a smell of decay which clung to my black hair, which I didn't look after any more, and to the *malbad* under my thick hijab, which I rarely took off even in my own room. I was afraid of being spied on by the unfamiliar men I saw in dreams.

Later that day Safaa and Abdullah came and drank tea in my room, happy and lively; they were travelling abroad that same evening. Safaa wept as she said goodbye to us. I went out of the door with her and craned my head to see her leaning on Abdullah's arm as they disappeared around a bend, fearing I would never see them again. I was afraid of losing the people I loved, and I clung to whatever they left behind them.

I slackened in my hatred, and openly expressed my sympathy for the murdered pilot. Alya scolded me for this; the other girls in our group mocked me and reminded me of how our sect had been persecuted, and of the corruption of the officers who had turned the country into a private money-making farm for themselves and their own sect. I suddenly felt a secret pride that it was my brother Hossam who they now described as a mujahid, declaring that God loved him. I scolded myself for my weakness; I saw the girls, even as they mocked me, as illuminated icons, and I envied Alya for the powerful hatred that lived in her heart. I almost kissed her hand so she would forgive me and return that essence to me which had given my life meaning in the midst of turmoil. I felt that the tranquillity I had known in our group was rotting away, like my hair which Ghada had stroked with her affectionate hands.

I scolded Marwa vehemently for her sympathy for the murdered Abbas's family; I was astonished when she retorted that I wanted to destroy the country. I didn't answer her or explain my feelings, but I reread entire sections of the pamphlets, which dwelled on descriptions of the unbelievers, in a low voice in front of Hana and my companions. I became much closer to Ghada and, obviously, I learned more about her assignations with her lover and their secret meeting-place. I went with her to cake shops; we laughed on the streets and we whispered girls' secrets to each other. We mocked Nada's idiotic voice and her cadaver-like smell. I dreamed of recovering Ghada's soul and saving her from that executioner. I imagined him murdered; the families of his victims would thank Hossam and Bakr for avenging the people he had hung by their feet and forced to swallow their own faeces while he stood and watched, smoking greedily. Ghada would cry on my chest, and I would pass my fingers through her soft hair and I would make her relax in the arms of her only saviour.

Maryam and Marwa were surprised at my joy when I read Safaa's letter from Saudi Arabia out loud to them in which she informed us, sarcastically using the Bedouin dialect, that she spent her time sleeping and playing checkers with Zeina, Abdullah's other wife. In the picture she drew for us they seemed to be becoming close friends, conspiring together against the man they both loved. The few letters that followed were filled with tears and irritation at the enclosed houses, the Filipina maids, and Abdullah's long absences; he was accompanying Sheikh Nadim Al Salaty to gather donations in support of the men fighting the Soviet Communists in Afghanistan.

At the end of one letter, Safaa told us she was beginning to suspect she might be pregnant. Maryam wept like a happy child and Marwa let out a trill. Radwan led them to the shrines of the saints, where they read *mawalid* and wrote spells to ward off Zeina's evil eye, unconvinced of what Safaa had written about her generosity and their odd relationship. When I saw Marwa trilling with such power I tried to match her, but my voice rushed out like a sheep bleating as it tried to catch up with the herd. I remembered that such trilling hadn't been raised in our house for a long time.

142

I was annoyed at Ghada's reticence, and that she didn't take me to her secret house so I could see it for myself and submit my final report to my group, just as I was irritated by a young man who followed us surreptitiously. His shirt was unbuttoned and a silver chain decorated his wrist – he looked like a playboy searching for prey. I was reassured one day when I saw him get into a taxi driven by Hossam, who ignored me completely; I realized then that Hossam hadn't gone to Jordan with Bakr.

That night, I was haunted by anxiety and I trembled in terror. A journey abroad would keep Hossam and Bakr out of harm's way, but it also marked the beginning of a new series of assassinations. The victims, although they numbered no more than ten, were only the beginning of the organization's dream, which Hossam had explained by drawing a diagram of four circles and three triangles in the borders of an algebra textbook. I understood the few words, written in *ruq'a* script and decorated with green flags: these words informed the Prophet that the martyrs were coming, and they were followed by 'Our souls will be sacrificed for Islam,' written in perfect English.

I asked Zahra if I could see Bakr. She shook her head and finished sprinkling the *freekeh* with spices, advised me to use *bilun* to soften my hair which had begun to resemble thistle heads. That night, I stood in front of the mirror to look at my hair. My looks used to resemble a Pharaonic painting: sharp eyes, long brown face, drooping eyelids. I cut off my hair, wanting to remove any symbol of my femininity. I concealed my nipples in the depths of my breasts. I kept my long braids in my sketchpad. Laughing, Omar compared me to Mireille Matthieu; ignoring my questions about Hossam and Bakr, he enthusiastically described the horse he had just bought from an Arab trader, its svelte muscles and the magnificence of its form, and then he suddenly left us, as he usually did. Maryam confirmed that he had won the horse in a bet. As usual, she started recounting what was said in respectable houses about his latest scandals, and added that he would kill his horse soon. I tried to convince Marwa that we should go and see him, and she replied sarcastically that my uncles had all vanished.

She was alluding to Selim and his Sufism. He had begun to carry tambourines in Sheikh Daghstani's group, neglecting his family and my grandfather's shops, content to ensure that the veil between himself and the face of God had been drawn aside, and that columns of light had opened up before him. He no longer heard us; he would shake his head pityingly, and hope that the Merciful would live in our hearts. He emptied his wardrobe of all his English suits whose pinstripes he used to be very fond of. He now made do with coarse brown cloth, a woollen turban and rubbery shoes, like the ones worn in the villages. His careful money-management left him and he became bored. He didn't want to regulate the account books that formed the family's inheritance, in the midst of the storm which would leave nothing behind. Omar intervened quickly and skilfully, and managed the shops and work without wounding Selim's feelings. He told us that he couldn't trust a man who took three days to return from Bianun, which was only 20 km away. He sought out a craftsman and paid him double wages, asking Khalil to leave the arcade and supervise him. Everything seemed to be going well, but Khalil didn't like his task. He only sat in a cane chair, longing for Wasal; his new Aleppan wife couldn't make him forget the charm of the many dissipated nights he had spent in Wasal's arms.

That autumn, all of us in the house were like strangers exchanging courtesies. We hid our anxiety and didn't want to admit that we were afraid of revealing the truth we sensed; that Bakr, after his fight with the organization leadership, had made his choice. With three of his associates, he had become the most relentless of those responsible for the murders of sons from other sects. His allies in neighbouring countries rose up from their councils and welcomed him into their palaces, understanding his desire to return Syria to its natural course, and to threaten the other sect and 'the party that threw us into the arms of infidel Soviets', as he said after receiving a coded invitation to Beirut one Sunday afternoon in early October; it was to a private meeting Abdullah had arranged during his recent visit to Washington.

Safaa told us how surprised she had been at discovering that Bakr was in the room next to theirs in the large hotel in the Jounieh district of Beirut. She was a little confused but then kissed him warmly. Abdullah immediately took him away, and they left an irritated Safaa to her own devices for the afternoon. She waited for them for a long time, and then went out and wandered the streets of Beirut, struck with a sudden desire to go shopping. She thought of us, and bought woollen sweaters for us and neckties for my uncles which, still wrapped, were thrown into Maryam's clothes box. Safaa was worried when she worked out that Bakr had come to Beirut under a false identity: his name was listed as Jaber Antaby, and he recorded his profession in the hotel register as 'architect'. She was never alone with Bakr, despite her continual attempts to draw him aside. He would avoid private meetings, and she couldn't understand his reticence. At night, Abdullah took Safaa and Bakr to dinner at the invitation of an American friend whom he had bumped into. The men spoke in English about Lebanese food and Bakr calmly described types of kebab, showing great expertise in classifying food as he compared the cuisines of Istanbul and Aleppo by way of Lebanon. The men withdrew for less than half an hour and walked on the beach despite the strong breeze. Safaa couldn't believe that buying carpets required this level of caution. Bakr didn't sleep on his last night in Beirut. He reached Aleppo in the dark and came into our house a broken man; there was a strange, pale colour to his eyes. We were surprised to be gathered around him as he slept on his bed, snoring from exhaustion. Maryam put a hand on his face and saw how he had aged, even though he wasn't yet forty-five. Standing around her, we looked for some reassurance.

The entire family came together the following day, except for Hossam. It reminded us of a sweet time we had lost, as if recalling a dead man who had slipped through our fingers for a few moments, and after we had mourned him, he opened his eyes quietly and asked if there was anything left of the apricots from the previous summer. The family gathering, despite heralding the danger of a long separation, made Maryam optimistic about the possibility of recovering the moments of past intimacy – these would remind us of the position of our family and its inheritance – even though in recent years she had stopped enumerating the characteristics of our ancestors and had made do with wiping the dust off the pictures that hung in her room.

Omar didn't like family banalities (they reminded him of his ex-wife Rima's pickles) but on that day he recalled his memories with affecting nostalgia; we needed them to protect us. We brought out the silver table service, and our Chinese tablecloth.

My aunts and my mother sat down to eat dinner with Abdullah as an overt acknowledgement that he had been accepted as a full member of the family, and deserved to join us in the laughter which encouraged Bakr to make cheerful observations on Selim's Sufism. He sat on his own on the floor to eat from an aluminium bowl, and limited himself to vegetables, milk and dates, shunning the oily delicacies and cooked meats which covered the *freekeh* crowned with crushed almonds. He avoided drinking the berry and orange juices, and made do with a cup of water. I hadn't known before that Selim had such a tolerant and joyful spirit, especially when Bakr hinted at Selim's refusal to engage in sexual relations with his wife, and his abstinence from delicacies, even the fresh shrimps which my father used to bring him. Our happy day as a family passed in the blink of an eye. Maryam apologized for the circumstances that made us eat off one table. I said to myself, 'We need these banal moments so we can relinquish our dignity.'

Zahra came to stay in our house. She unpacked her large bag and hung her clothes in Safaa's wardrobe. We didn't believe her visit would last that long, but a month would become a year, and a year became years, and no one knew any longer when it would end. Bakr was totally absent. He became like a bat in the night which we couldn't get hold of; we could only hear the rush of his wings beating around us. Safaa and Abdullah left Aleppo like they were being hunted after Abdullah made a few swift calls to various countries, using my uncles' telephones.

We took up again our visits to the hammam in a reversion to our unchanging image; Blind Radwan led us there without enthusiasm. We were afraid to admit that the hot water and the smell of the cavernous baths couldn't save us from our depression. We resumed our chatter about details no more important than peeling garlic heads, or whether to store the hot pepper paste in glass jars or plastic containers. Zahra's perpetual preoccupation confused me, along with the way she avoided sitting around the pool on afternoons when the sky was clear and the winter sun brilliant.

Like a fugitive from everything, I went to school in the mornings as if it were my only sanctuary. I would look for Ghada as if she were my mirror, so I could see my image scattered in her sad eyes. She was losing her liveliness and had begun to wither. She didn't answer my questions, told me she would suffocate, and asked me to walk with her in the streets. I walked close, grasping her arm as we crossed Qouwatly Street and reached Jamiliyya. I was interested in one of the buildings; I knew that it was the secret house where she met her lover, and my desire to see him murdered returned to me. She opened the door and we went inside, where she broke down sobbing. She told me that he had abandoned her and she hadn't seen him for three weeks. He had told her that she was no longer suitable and had walked out on her, leaving behind only the smell of his shirt and her memories of him on the soft leather sofas covered with the heads of pharaohs and bulls.

As we wandered through the small house, Ghada wept. There were photographs of him everywhere. I imagined how many times he had taken her in his arms like a butterfly and lain her down on the wide bed to penetrate her, so feminine and delicate, like a beast. Jealousy filled my heart, and I was struck by a desire to weep, to smash everything, to burn the house down and reduce it to ashes. I dredged up all the hatred that had become part of my sense of the world, and changed myself into an interrogator – I sat Ghada down like she was the accused. He had left her some money, apparently, enough to help an abandoned woman forget, paid the rent of the house for three months, and offered her one of his colleagues should she miss him. She described him as vulgar and depraved but an unforgettable lover. She had offered to wait for him every day, like a maidservant waiting for her master, even if he came in only to look at her, and then leave. When I saw her wandering around the living room reliving his embraces, I realized that she was calmed by it. It was difficult for her to take in a word I said. I slipped away like a fugitive without saying goodbye. I wept in the street; I covered my face and soaked the black veil. As if seeing Aleppo for the first time, I wandered through it, lost. No one noticed me when I returned; they had got used to my absences over recent days as I spent most of my time with Alya.

I felt like I needed to see Alya, even though our next group meeting wasn't due yet. As I walked towards her house, a strange power welled up inside me. I wanted to be just like her. Her companions were surprised when I arrived, but Alya allowed me to stay for the trial of her friend Anoud. They had been tipped off that she kept an album of pornographic pictures within her *milaya* at all times; also, a young man she knew waited for her behind the Faculty of Literature after lectures every Tuesday and Thursday evenings. The trial was convened with all majesty, and Anoud swore on the Quran that she would tell the truth. She added that the young man had taken her hands and kissed them, and then she pointed to the place where the album was kept inside her black clothes – I rushed towards her without permission and searched her roughly. The album was produced and I asked God's forgiveness for the obscenity of the pictures, which showed the private parts of smiling men. Alya took hold of me and drew me away. She promised me there would be a horrible punishment which would quench our thirst and restore our reputations as decent mujahid girls. I couldn't wait; we left Alya's house and I felt my body was filthy, in need of a wash.

I related this to Zahra, and was frustrated by her indifference to my eagerness. I was surprised by her lethargy and her ardour for her mother's letters, which she still carried with her. She spent whole nights reading them, full of longing, wishing they would never end. I used to adore our house, but now I began to hate it. It was ruled by indolence, by silence, by a wait for men who never returned and about whom we never heard anything. The few hours Bakr had spent with us on his last visit were like a warning, or a dream we all craved. We knew that he had fled from us to the unknown; we had to accept it resolutely. During those hours, Bakr withdrew with Zahra and Maryam herded us into her room so we wouldn't hear their moans. We kept away, like silly children who didn't know what would take place between a husband and wife who knew this was their last meeting. Bakr later kissed my head and asked me to abandon Ghada and stay away from her. I informed him about the trial, and conveyed its details in their entirety, including the judgement to shave Anoud's head and banish her from our circle. Anoud had cried and sworn that she would never again swap nude pictures with her fallen friends. She was put under observation; Alya watched her at university, her sister Samia watched her at home, and God watched her everywhere else. In the same way, He watched us all and I sensed He was very close to me; I could feel His breath, and it calmed me.

Zahra reminded me of Hajja Radia and how I

hadn't visited her for a long time. I said to myself that I didn't love her any more, but I remembered how kind she had been when she used to sit me beside her so I could dream of Rabia Adawiya, crossing the *barzakh* like a white lark flying in a black sky. I thought of how stupid I had been when I believed that we needed hatred to enter Paradise. I saw her from afar: a calm woman with a heart full of fear, as opposed to Hajja Souad who illuminated a path of hatred before me, given meaning by cruelty. Her steady eyes dazzled me as they looked coldly into every person she spoke to.

I didn't know why Ghada had begun to avoid me once more. She suddenly withdrew from me and wandered through the school courtyard with Nada, and at leaving time she would climb into the death squad officer's car with her. My studies suffered. I wanted to escape from Ghada's remorseful glances whenever she approached me. I knew she wanted to cry and talk about how her lover persevered in humiliating her, how she hoped to be saved from the desires which made her crazy during those long winter nights. She would get up to smash everything within arm's reach – vases, ornaments, frames containing photos of the family – and afterwards, she would gather up the scattered glass silently. Her father, a well-regarded employee at the Ministry of Finance, wept in front of her lover, who laughed at him and asked him to leave, threatening to ruin his reputation and prosecute his daughter for debauchery.

I had my revenge on her when I saw her pale face; she could speak only a few fragmented, disconnected words. Finally she returned to me, but emptiness filled her existence. She was grateful to me because I greeted her during the morning roll call as we went into class. The other girls at school shunned her after news spread that her father had gone to that man; the officer's men circulated stories about the police's secret files on her, which confirmed that she visited cattle traders and slept with them in exchange for money. Alya definitively and firmly told me to stay away from her. I had no compassion for Ghada when I saw her expelled from school; she was vacant-eyed, and had lost all her sparkle. I was indifferent when she kissed me, or when I caught the scent of her perfume when she came close to me. I thought that ridding ourselves of those we loved had a similar function to our transformation into barren beings; it would give us strength, which we expected would turn into resplendent hatred.

I saw my future clearly in front of me. My feeling of strength made my presence at the rites marking births in friends' families, or at any other little celebration, into a gift I would give to them. I would intervene harshly when Maryam accepted such invitations, and I would limit the type of presents we took with us. Most of the gifts were copies of the Quran edged in gold leaf. When our acquaintances accepted the gift, I would ask them to kiss it and hold it to their foreheads and hearts in a show of humility. Back at home, I walked in the courtyard like an officer who has mislaid his troops. I ordered Radwan peremptorily not to leave his room at night, and he obeyed me silently and muttered something incomprehensible. I guessed that he was sighing after my old self when I was his companion who would join him to sing *nashid* in praise of the Prophet. I wished he had sight, so he could see my new image and know that everything I had left behind me was pale, unnecessary for a woman who wanted to become the *emira* of her group, who wanted to throw her weight behind things, and weave her own myth so that others would narrate it like a tale worthy of consecration.

I didn't like Zahra's silence, nor her wry glances at my ponderous footsteps that suited the dignity that possessed me after I received the decision that I should take on the role of an *emira*, princess and leader among these other students. Hajja Souad's voice trembled when she read out the decision and blessed it, enumerating my qualities and the force of my allegiance to my group; I swore to give my life to further our battle and to obliterate blasphemy from the face of the earth. The girls blessed me coolly, amid covert accusations that Bakr was the reason for my appointment as *emira*.

Before I became a princess I avoided going to

meetings of the group for two months. I was immersed in my studies, determined to realize my aunts' dream. My mother was depressed, and didn't believe that Hossam was all right despite the letter from him I took to her. He asked her to pray for him and described my father as a great man, me as everyone's greatest hope, and my little brother Humam as a pure-spirited bird. I loved his neat, regular handwriting. 'I miss him,' I said to Maryam, who nodded and continued reading the Sura Yusuf as if carrying on what she had started forty years earlier without interruption and in the same tone. She enunciated the ending of each word with the solemnity appropriate for the holy text.

I saw Hossam twice more. Bakr had agreed to a meeting after being assured of my perseverance and hearing about my cruelty, my zeal, and my requests to kill infidels. The first time, before he left us, Bakr asked me to go down to the cellar with him, gave me a wrapped-up bundle of papers, and told me to take it to Hajja Souad. Then he informed me of the predetermined time and location for my meeting with Hossam – in front of the Cinema Opera at three o'clock – and asked me to buy two tickets and pretend that we were a boy and girl fleeing school to spend a few furtive hours exchanging loving glances and brushing our hands against each other. I overdid the camouflage and wore vivid red lipstick like a doll who knew nothing of feminine secrets. My heart was beating hard as I stood and waited by the door. At that time, I knew that my brother hadn't yet been discovered by the Mukhabarat; overwhelming caution was required to keep him hidden. I looked at my watch; I lost hope. I was about to tear up the tickets and walk away when a young man approached me and looked into my eyes, almost penetrating them through the veil. He smiled at me. I knew him from his voice when he apologized for being late, like any young man wanting to get rid of the sweetheart chasing after him, hell-bent on marrying him. He took hold of my arm and we went into the half-empty cinema, where we sat at a distance from the few audience members idly watching Spartacus liberating Roman slaves and leading them to burn down their masters' palaces.

I wanted to kiss Hossam and embrace him, although it was enough to hold his hands in mine and feel their heat. I thought how he had grown suddenly over the last few months; his face had gained a hardness which would remain clinging to it. He didn't tell me anything, but listened attentively as I told him about our mother, father, brother and aunts. I wondered why I was so distant from them that I couldn't tell him more details than he already knew, just as I couldn't answer his questions about whether or not our younger brother Humam still believed that the fish my father sold were plucked from trees like lemons; he used to open his small hands and wait for them to pour down like rain. We laughed guardedly, and I told him about my meetings and elaborated on the girls in the cell, not forgetting my own heroism and the suggestion of hatred I planted in their minds when I stood up and spoke to them about our enemies, the other sects. I knew Hossam's face when it was flooded with contentment; his eyes shone so that he seemed like a sentimental boy, almost crying with grief for the bird that callous hunters had slaughtered in front of him; I could see he was pleased. He left me without answering any of my questions, and restricted himself to informing me that he was travelling a lot, without leaving me any room for further inquiry. He gave me money for my mother and left, turning into Bustan Kul Ab Street without bidding me goodbye.

A hideous loneliness afflicted me. I stopped wanting to speak. I immersed myself in silence which didn't stop me from thinking about Zahra who sometimes ignored me. She didn't care when I told her I was embarking on an important career. Her entire curiosity amounted to the five words she spoke coldly: 'God is gracious to you.' Then she sat by Marwa so they could finish spreading out the aubergine to dry. I asked Marwa about Zahra's about-turn and she replied curtly and with a tone of veiled rebuke that it was me who had changed, and that they were making allowances for me as my exam dates were approaching. I fiercely defended my changes, adding how sorry I was that they hadn't joined me in appreciating how wonderful it felt to kill the sons of the other sects and glorify the mujahideen, and then I rushed to my room. I took out the last letter Abdullah had sent to me alone, in which he described me as a little mujahida. I finished reading the lines in which he informed me that he was going to Afghanistan to support our brothers who were resisting the humiliation imposed by the Soviet Communists, a confidence given as if in confirmation of my position. Marwa, as usual, didn't care and went on discussing the *mahshy* and how too many spices ruined its flavour. 'I need some quiet,' I told myself. I arranged my room so I could study for the exams, and cut myself off from everything. Maryam stayed awake beside me for many nights, and took out a pure-silk bedsheet decorated with red and yellow flowers; she said it was the remains of Safaa's trousseau. I put it on my table, and the sheet imparted intense colours to it, which I didn't like. I added new notes in the margins of Hossam's textbooks, debating with him as if we were drinking coffee together, while cursing our uncles and laughing.

Twice, Omar came over to help me in Religion and Arabic. Sometimes he felt affection for the principles of *tajwid* recitation and demonstrated his skill for me; we were like two cockerels in a fighting arena, ruffling our feathers. Maryam was proud of our learning. Sometimes I would exaggerate in reciting information from a book to turn Zahra's head, who was as silent as a stone, ignoring our enthusiasm.

Radwan intervened to settle our dispute over the correct grammatical suffixes of the word *Fahawmal* in Imru Al Qays' *mu'allaqa*. We repeated its lines and added different grammatical inflections like scholars in the ancient souk of Akaz. Omar's company made the days pass pleasantly and easily, unpretentiously, but after he went abroad I returned to my hatred, confirming to them all that I had grown up and was not ashamed of disagreeing with my tolerant aunts, and of being close to Bakr, who I hoped would be the long-awaited Mahdi. I was proud he was my uncle.

On the day before the exams, I saw Ghada walking by herself. She had braided her hair carelessly, and she was trembling. I put her appearance down to worry about the exams and lack of sleep, so it came as a shock when she took a Makarov pistol from her handbag and said indifferently that her lover, the important officer in the Mukhabarat, had brought her back to him as an informer. She would wait outside his assistant's door to give him some reports, in which she vented all her lust and desire, but she never saw him. At the end of one report, stamped 'Top Secret', she reminded him of the tenderness of their trysts. He tore it up and pronounced her to be mad; she said, 'I can't live without him.' She went off without waving goodbye to me, and that same night she committed suicide with a bullet to the head, leaving a short note for her family in which she informed them that she loved them; she felt redundant; she didn't want to become an informer; and she concluded by saying she was no longer a virgin and was polluted, and that in a dark room she had aborted a foetus which should have had the right to live.

I buried Ghada swiftly, like a plague I needed to escape. I sat in her room, and looked at the pink walls and the pictures of Mickey Mouse, which she had been mad about when she was a child who didn't want to grow up or stop laughing. Friends of hers I knew wept and embraced her mother. Only I was stiff. I looked at the mourning ceremony for the dishonoured girl, rebuking myself but sure that she would go to Hell, and there would be no merciful intercession from the Prophet . . . On the third day, I went to her grave. I sat on the edge and wept for hours. I spoke to her and wept, recalling her smile and the smell of her neck. I sat in my room and didn't go out; I locked the door and lay on my bed alone. My mother came every day, expecting Bakr. She read out what Hossam had written in the letter I had given her, and avoided mentioning the money he had sent her through me. She hid it in her closet after crying and kissing it, searching for the smell of his fingers. I chastised her for her weakness. I seemed like her mother, and she seemed like my daughter, asking for guidance so I wouldn't leave her alone. All of us women were waiting for news of Hossam and Bakr, who were no longer seen in any place we knew of.

One morning, the army officer who had been a guest at Bakr's banquet some months earlier performed his prayers carefully at the mosque and recited a sura from the Quran. That night, he asked his servant for a strong cup of coffee, drank it quietly, and left the room of the duty officer to select seventeen young men from the military college – students who were due to graduate shortly. Coolly, he lined them up against the wall and executed them using a machine gun, like someone in a film. Ghosts left their dens to fly over the city; no one knew where they would finally alight. He left the corpses to fall in their own blood, their ribs and heads spattered all over the wall. He threw away his uniform jacket, kept the copper eagle on the pocket of his khaki trousers, and then left with the associates he had selected to guard the doors of the military college during the shooting. They all reached a house on the outskirts of Aleppo, where men welcomed them with cries of 'Allahu Akbar!' and showered blessings on them for having brought about funerals in the other sect's houses. No one knew why those students had died after having descended from the mountains with limitless ambition and vitality; no one but me, who celebrated hatred.

Maryam almost lost the ability to speak when she saw officers and Mukhabarat climbing down from our roof into the courtyard and drawing their weapons, bursting into rooms and cellars in their search for Hossam and Bakr. They crammed us into Radwan's room, who tried to push them as he cursed them, reminding them of my grandfather's rank and that only women lived in this house. One of them knocked him over, and I saw him put his boot on Radwan's neck, cursing my grandfather and his offspring and describing us as whores. More than sixty armed men were hysterically ransacking the rooms, overturning beds, opening wardrobes, smashing padlocks, scattering pictures and papers. They unrolled expensive carpets that smelled of mothballs; they didn't have time to contemplate their designs with wonder.

I almost exploded with laughter as we were barricaded into Radwan's room. The soldiers had turned out his boxes and poured all his perfumes on to the floor so that we almost choked. It would have been ironic for us to suffocate on perfume. Radwan cursed God and instantly implored His forgiveness, trying to convince the soldier that he was committing a mortal sin and charging him with immorality. Maryam shook him and asked him to be quiet, afraid that he would lead them to the secret cupboard where she had hidden Hossam's gun the day he killed the pilot; later, I had begun to hide my papers and pamphlets in there, paying no attention to Zahra's warnings.

The officer in charge called us into Maryam's room one after another. I thought, as I looked into his eyes, that hatred would make me calm and composed, heedless of the spittle flying from his mouth as he swore to cut off my hand and gouge out my eye if I didn't lead him to Bakr and Hossam. Zahra leaned on my chest, forgetting the coolness of our relationship in recent months. I sensed her fear, and thought, 'They don't know the secrets of our houses, or of the city's entrances.' I was the most composed of them all, as if my hatred were being put to the test. Maryam prayed for mercy on the souls of the victims; she didn't believe that Bakr was responsible for organizing any of the increasingly frequent assassinations, and clung to the hope that it was a nightmare which would soon be driven away and we would return to the security we had lost.

The military also occupied Bakr's half-abandoned house. Four soldiers lived there permanently, playing cards in an attempt to drive out their fear as they waited for him to enter their trap. My mother told me that they had grabbed my father by his moustache and soiled his face with their heavy boots, and that he had still not recovered his speech. His skill with fish had deserted him, and he hadn't slept for three days. I saw him sitting on the ground in filthy clothes, and my brother Humam, afraid, was squeezed into a corner. I talked to my father, but he didn't hear me. He was deaf, lost; he was looking for meaning in what had happened. They had taken him to their local head-quarters three times; there they cursed him, and insulted his manhood; he slept on the bare ground of a damp cell and the aluminium bowl in the middle of the floor gave off a stench of excrement and urine – but he was less upset by this than by the spitting of the guard who, all night, never stopped kicking him and cursing his women. He bore the blows from the four-lashed whips, and the pulling out of his fingernails with pliers. He remembered the men he had tortured in the same way in the days of Abdel Hamid Sarraj, as if he were being liberated from his painful memories and had expiated the sins that had weighed heavily on him for years. I sat beside him like a cat wanting to lick the wounds which he hid even from my mother.

Everyone lost their equilibrium, now that it was so abundantly clear what terrible danger Bakr and Hossam were in. My aunts and my mother were immersed in prayer and recitation of the Quran. They needed Omar, who came to our house. We understood each other by looks alone. Everything entered a dark tunnel and I waited impatiently, afraid that my mother would die of heart failure. My father's silence tortured me and I pitied him; for a moment, I almost sympathized with the murder victims. I wished that Bakr had remained a carpet trader who boasted to other families about his properties, praising his family like any man who took passing enjoyment from the absurdities of daily life.

Zahra recovered her strength all at once. She helped everyone keep faith that Hossam and

Bakr and their group had been chosen by God to bring back Islam, His word and His brilliance; to bring back the story of Bilal Al Habashy, who was tortured by the Quraysh in the desert heat and never yielded to their hell. We acted out a play: Radwan considered himself Bilal Al Habashy and Maryam the Mother of Believers, Khadija Bint Khuwaylid. I loved the role of Fatima Al Zahra and reviewed her *sira*. I rushed into Hajja Souad's council and asked to rearrange the prayer circles and redistribute tasks. I reproached a girl who questioned the validity of killing the sons of other sects and parties; she considered them innocent and quoted the Quran, which banned us from killing a soul whose murder God declared unlawful. The girls were astonished at the force of my expressions when I described the murdered as heretics; my voice trembled when I described our brothers as mujahideen and heroes, as if I were making a passionate speech at a ceremony. I volunteered to carry weapons and kill unbelievers, recalling the words Hossam had written in the margins of his chemistry books, and wishing him the martyrdom he wanted with everything he possessed and with all the vigour of youth. I took the largest section of the pamphlets which had to be distributed all over the city, and in which our group announced that we were at the beginning of our battle with the atheist party. People conversed with the pride appropriate for men who were committed to and believed in God. I

166

concealed the pamphlets under my clothes and one of the sisters walked in front of me, watching the winding street as I stuffed pamphlets under the doors of strange houses. I made their inhabitants tremble, and then think that the fear they lived in was nothing but an illusion which could be removed. I wished that I could knock on doors to tell them that I was bearing the good news of the green banners sweeping the country.

It was difficult to see the city from behind the twilight of my black face-covering, and I loved it; Aleppo seemed mysterious, cruel. In my heart I threatened unveiled girls. I imagined myself passing judgement on them; I would spray acid in their faces and disfigure them without mercy, hitting their delicate fingers so they wouldn't take hold of men's hands and laugh while dawdling and eating ice-cream. I thought there was no doubt they went to houses with men in order to have sex and desecrate marriage and their own virtue. Officers from the death squad now filled the city. They aroused terror with their powerful bodies and their machine guns, their scorn of death, and their unexpected siege of the old, narrow quarters of the city. Orders came to us daily as we passed through alleys like the breeze. Sometimes we felt like we were flying. We entered every house, and women were praying for our men. They wept when they imagined the danger surrounding us. We gathered donations, we sent letters, we distributed pamphlets, we didn't see the faces of those outsiders who in the quiet night came to the city in order to attack the Mukhabarat branches and the regime's headquarters; most of them fled back to their faraway villages. Every day, we felt that we were approaching our final pilgrimage when the soul of the Prophet would come out to welcome us, blessing our strength, and with his immaculate arms he would surrender to us the keys of Paradise.

Whenever the city's terror increased over the next few months, so did my certainty that hatred would make me into a hard woman, not the shy girl who used to stand on the doorsill afraid of loneliness and orphanhood. It was now summer, and for two unforgettable months, my vigour reached its pinnacle after a group of 'our best young men' were executed, as my uncle Selim described them in a prayer for the absent dead which was held for their souls. We passed on their brave words from the television coverage of their trial, when they explained their cruelty and their hardness. We envied them; they would reach Paradise before us, and their daring aroused the sympathy of the city's inhabitants as they denounced the government's corruption. Prayers were held in many different houses for their souls, and cries of 'Allahu Akbar' were raised at the moment of their execution. Their corpses were buried without mourners. My mother drowned in a whirl of wails and grief when she saw Hossam's friends, with whom she had broken

Ramadan fasts and exchanged jokes, going to the gallows. She was terrified of the same fate for her baby. Nightmares stopped her from sleeping. I saw her age – she was filled with tears and incomprehensible mutterings. She didn't have time to be happy that I was one of the ten best female students in Aleppo. I would become a doctor, she boasted to her neighbours and cousins, who didn't dare read our pamphlets as they were already banned from praying at the mosques. One of our oldest cousins cut his hair like the singer from the Beatles and put rings in his ears to avoid the accusation of being Hossam's relative whenever one of the patrols stopped him. I chose a strange way to celebrate my success: I founded a new prayer circle in the house of a divorced woman who taught girls sewing and embroidery. Its open windows banished suspicion about my frequent comings and goings with 'my girls', as I began to call them. We went to work in the morning and returned in the evening like any girls who worked and couldn't wait to leave so they could wink at shop-owners and laundrymen, while taxi drivers and patrolling soldiers tried to harass them; they would laugh and then run away.

In our house, I wore some white clothes which Safaa had left behind and I asked Radwan to bring some sweets. I arranged the bowls on the table as they all watched me, and Radwan sang an ode in praise of my excellent marks, suitable for a doctor. We ate the sweets and they kissed me and blessed me, and I hid my surprise. I signalled to Maryam to dismiss Radwan after he enthusiastically tried to recall that image when we were women led by a blind man, as if he missed that status now fallen to dust. Zahra served coffee after Radwan had gone to his room and I stood in the basin of the stone pool, arms open, and announced my desire to die a martyr. 'I want martyrdom. I am an *emira*.' I repeated it a few times: 'I am an *emira* now.' I stepped down and removed my underclothes as they looked at me. I walked to my room then turned towards them; there was bewilderment in their eyes. Before I left, I seemed to see them bowing as if in greeting to a princess.

# PART II

# EMBALMED BUTTERFLIES

It was butterflies that saved Marwa as she waited for Safaa, who never came. She missed Safaa especially on the nights when the death squad fell from the sky on to our plants (which occurred on an almost daily basis), showing off the skull emblems on their chests. They were disturbed by our contempt for them, for attacking a house full of women watched over by a blind man and lying in wait for the wanted men who had evaporated into the sky over the city. They tore up the rose bushes, which were Marwa's favourite flowers; like a madwoman, she ran from room to room, choked with tears and looking for somewhere slimy to shelter in, like a large snail.

The first butterfly she caught had wings of mottled brown and honey. It reminded her of the visit to the hammam she had made before her wedding when women smothered her in *bilun*, henna and perfumed soap, threaded her body hair, and ran their hands over her skin to ensure its softness. She adored the lightness with which the butterfly flew, and she embalmed it with Radwan's help; he loved the idea and laughed when she described its faded eyes and its mouth, which she likened to Safaa's small mouth. She kissed it like a lover who could never forget that powerful pressure of the other's lips which inflamed the pores. The insect's body became like that of a horse which, having received a fatal blow, cranes its neck to prevent its soul from escaping only to subside, cold, in submission to death.

Maryam disapproved of pinning butterflies to wooden boards. The sight of their wings affixed and outstretched in surrender impelled us to think about death, which had become as commonplace as a crate of rotten peaches flung out on to the pavement. It had lost its dignity and been turned into a banal tale told by the storytellers, whose zeal revived in order to narrate new stories about death squads and military divisions moving their tanks from other battlefronts to surround Aleppo. The soldiers' eyes were fearful and wandering; they felt that they were facing a pointless death because of the Party members who had fled to their homes, and certain college students who boasted of their pistols and their camouflage uniforms, after returning from camps hastily convened to train them up as paratroopers. The most indolent of them appropriated the best places in the universities, which had turned into barracks and areas for the military parades carried out by adolescent Party members; they didn't much care about the resignations of their respected professors, whose presence had become undesirable.

Most of the professors had fled and the rest of them closed their doors in the face of the oncoming plague, content to stare at their living-room floors and remember their glorious past which, it became clear, would never return. They dispersed in the streets between the tanks and the soldiers which had inherited the city they loved, trying to convince the fighters to listen to them and searching for one of their friends, a professor of English poetry who was about seventy years old. He couldn't bear to see one of his grandsons strutting around in his uniform like a turkey and kicking at his volumes of Shakespeare. He took down his grandfather's picture of T. S. Eliot and in its place he hung a photo of the commander of the death squad raising his fist in the air like a highwayman. In the meantime, his other grandson, who loved chemistry and had been predicted a dazzling future, wrapped belts of explosives around his hips and went out to hunt for prey. The poetry professor searched for his grandsons in various insalubrious places. He would leave his house at six in the morning, declaiming the poetry of Ezra Pound and snippets of Oedipus' story, a refugee from the smarter parts of the city. He aroused the pity of the policemen at the bus station where he spent the night among cardboard boxes. Whenever his students passed by, they sighed over the lost days of his brilliance when he had been the reason for their love of Shakespeare's language, whose vowels, he taught them, had been engineered for maximum musicality. He used to quote fondly from Latin texts which had been overlooked in Cambridge libraries, and he never forgot the smell which rose from their antique yellow pages – the same shade of yellow as the butterfly Marwa caught in the pistachio fields. She loved its lassitude and assigned it a central place among the specially prepared wooden boxes resembling coffins. She embalmed it in welcome and named it the Queen, and warned Radwan not to touch it or the place she had awarded it.

Marwa became like a stranger to us, someone we hardly knew. Her oppressive placidity and cold dignity suddenly turned into a feverish playfulness and a desire for adventure. She went with Radwan to nearby streets, gardens and fields, looking for butterflies. She neglected her appearance and abandoned our family tradition of women who spoke slowly and calmly. Like a peasant, she started using profane words and cursed without guilt or shame. We watched her every day as she astonished us further. Maryam hid her dread of a scandal which no one could save us from other than Safaa, who she knew had turned into an obedient woman without crazy dreams.

I didn't care about Marwa. I was convinced that we would have time enough in the future to rejoice over the mundane details of everyday life, when our voices and laughter would resound throughout the high-ceilinged rooms. I grumbled over Maryam's repeated requests to me to tell Bakr that Marwa had gone mad and that he had to intervene to save her. She believed that I could get word to the many hideouts that had made his disappearance into a legend woven throughout Aleppo. He became a terrifying ghost embedded in the wind, capable at any time of reappearing to walk the streets and greet his multitude of supporters. I nearly had a nervous breakdown because of the ceaseless demands from the district to me as its *emira*; they wanted me to organize yet more girls to make clothes, distribute pamphlets and gather donations. Other girls offered to blow themselves up in front of death squad officers, in revenge for the treatment of seven corpses of our brothers killed after a four-hour battle – Aleppo's inhabitants couldn't sleep, terrified by the scenes of soldiers' cars dragging bodies bound up with iron chains. They turned their eyes away from the cruelty that made Alya weep. She swore on the Quran that she couldn't bear it any longer; she wanted martyrdom and vengeance on behalf of those eyes which would sleep again one day.

Bakr blessed our fighting spirit and refused Alya's request. She had just decided to instruct me to organize students at the medical college that I had started at – without any accompanying trills from my mother, who had become an old woman who only ever spoke about death. She was very disturbed by nightmares in which Hossam appeared hanging from a rope, or as a body dragged over the asphalt. Sometimes he was a bridegroom wrapped in a shroud. My father's silences lengthened, and he was increasingly weary of the repeated summons to the Mukhabarat offices so they could ask him about Hossam, the son he hadn't seen for five months. He no longer paid attention to anything, and was no longer an ardent follower of the hatred which I displayed proudly, like a fabulous bracelet encircling my wrist. He would kiss me distractedly and mutter a few words cursing Bakr, and denouncing my sectarian fever which would lead us to disaster, he said. He would praise his friends from other sects whose elimination had become integral to our dreams; killing any individual from any other sect had become part of the plan. I no longer heard my father's voice, and considered his speeches on the poverty and generosity of his friends from the mountains to be unbefitting in a man to whom I was related and whose name I bore. I regarded him as an unbeliever and an apostate, and I was saddened to the core when I imagined him going to Hell; he wouldn't taste the nectar of Heaven or sleep, gratified, in its meadows. I asked for him to be forgiven, and prayed that he would be guided back to the right path. I wasn't sad when he took out his old metal suitcase, packed a few clothes, and went to Beirut to rid himself of our madness and our *fitna*, as he stated outright. The image of his sweet-featured face was lost from my memory; he became a coward who was unfit to belong to me.

★　★　★

Who ever really belongs to another? I thought while on my way to meet Hossam. I craved his presence; I missed him; I wanted to see the other face of my family. He took me to an Armenian restaurant and we sat together like lovers. I loved this role and my crazy infatuation with my brother, my lover, my companion, my leader. I looked deeply and passionately into his honey-coloured eyes, pressed my hand to his face, felt his skin, sensed his fear which seared me. He was distracted and didn't listen as I told him of my regret for my father and my fear for my mother, who had been forced to close up her house and move in with us in her father's house; it was as if we were all coming together and turning out panic and fear. Hossam was looking around cautiously and wouldn't listen to my descriptions of our victories. He took my hand suddenly and asked me to withdraw from the group and concentrate on my studies. In a few words, he confessed his remorse at his involvement in murder. I sensed how much he longed to lean back under the lemon tree and watch my mother cutting up beans and gossiping about the neighbours. He knew so many secrets about the disputes that were taking place among the leadership over the list of planned assassinations. His hand trembled as he drank his coffee and his gaze wandered; he asked me about Humam, didn't wait for my reply, muttered something, and left without saying goodbye – only with a few nervous words about wanting to flee to Mecca and seek forgiveness for his sins: *killing innocent civilians from the other sect.* This expression, which he kept repeating, frightened me. I stayed in the restaurant by myself and cried like a girl abandoned and deserving of the sympathy of the few patrons and waiters. I wasn't embarrassed.

It is difficult suddenly to discover that you are empty; that your shadow weighs heavily on the earth; that all around you, acid submerges your dreams and you appear corroded in the eyes of others. My father's features came back to me so clearly it made me rave at night that our family would only be saved, and Marwa's peace of mind would only return, with a swift victory. We would be reunited once more and all sit round the table, and Maryam would set out the neglected silverware like any lady secure in the knowledge that everything was as it should be. We all needed that image of the family, finally relaxed. I felt trivial; I hated studying biochemistry, and the students' insistence on exhibiting a precocious gravity. I asked our leaders if I could go back to my own prayer circle and be exempted from the college circle which I attended every morning. I was afraid that I would be arrested or hear that Hossam or Bakr had been killed. I thought of our destiny and, for the first time, thought that the murder victims would reach out their fingers to gouge out our eyes. Hajja Souad encouraged me to forget my fears. I couldn't admit to anyone that Hossam's remorse had shaken me and stranded me on an island of hatred, and I had thereby regained the dreams of a woman. I looked with clear eyes at my mother, who was in total surrender to a fate that hadn't arrived yet – whenever she heard the sound of bullets she burst out crying and beat her breast. Maryam would calm her and recite some incantations in a soft voice which seemed weak to me. She wove ropes of hope in the air and clung to them, like a child finding a swing in a pile of rubble that used to be a house.

I became less boastful of my kinship with Hossam. I paid no attention to the shattered family photograph. My parents' home was now occupied by soldiers; they scattered my memories, they slept on my childhood pillows, they flung sardine tins on to the floor and left them to let off a repugnant smell which mixed with that of their urine. Their shameless laughter was a necessity to them, so they could master their fear of the bullets which would come from unforeseen directions and pile them into coffins.

Bodies on both sides fell like ripened berries; the atmosphere was oppressive, saturated with the fear of nameless chaos. The state, which had expected a resolution to this battle in the most important of its cities, sought out its supporters as the situation grew ever blacker and more complex; our previous coexistence became a memory, and the subject of a cautiously exercised nostalgia – we were wildly optimistic of killing the people who were prone to such a longing. Retreat was no longer an option and hostility became like ripened grapes, dangling from a vine left to the passers-by. I would see Aleppo from beneath my black veil and it seemed like a fitting place to seek out the hatred I praised. I was hit by a delicious shiver, as if delicate hands were tickling my body and drawing me out of that state of indifference and depression endemic to the women of our household, along with their fear of the world I saw in my dreams. This world glowed as pure and bright as angels' robes, like those of the angels I drew as warriors carrying rifles and killing the death squad troops, who were growing increasingly violent and frenzied. They seemed to be firing recklessly and indiscriminately when, most of the time, they were only shooting to make jelly out of bats.

Omar came to our house soon after returning from his travels abroad. There were half-healed bruises on his face, and there remained beneath his eyes the gloomy traces of a frustrated man. He didn't tell us that he had been arrested and tortured for two continuous months to make him reveal Bakr's whereabouts, which he didn't know. He wasn't saved by his strong relationships with certain important officers and influential traders, nor by his hard-won reputation, which he had taken pains to develop in order to appear more dissipated than necessary. 'We all need Omar,' I said to myself as I scrutinized his stammering lips.

He assured Maryam that his bruises were the result of falling off his horse, and ordered my mother to make arrangements to travel to Beirut with my brother Humam. He wouldn't listen to her justifications for staying – she was waiting for Hossam, my younger brother was at school – and he wouldn't allow Maryam to back her up. He didn't care that Marwa went outside on to the city's streets with Radwan and tried to catch butterflies among the tanks and tents of the soldiers, who thought the pair were crazy and should be avoided. As time passed, however, the soldiers began to have conversations with Radwan. Initially they thought him strange, and then an amusing and necessary novelty; he made them forget about death, even if only for a moment. One of the officers was induced to buy a special perfume which allegedly acted as an aphrodisiac. Radwan unveiled it at a distance from Marwa who was standing and watching as if she were at the cinema. She was bewildered by the force of the fear of death, close to a desire to laugh; they overlapped to such a degree that it was difficult to establish where the separation lay between them. Radwan enumerated the merits of his perfume to the officer who appreciated his eccentricity. He paid in advance for the scent which Radwan spent all night preparing in an empty castor-oil bottle; he convinced the officer that the lingering smell was an intentional part of the perfume's composition, before leaving quickly and dragging his 'lady' with him – as he described Marwa to the officer while listing the imaginary qualities of another family who worked in weaving. He was afraid they would discover that the butterfly hunter was Bakr's sister.

Omar wouldn't listen to the story of Radwan's perfume. He asked us to help my mother pack her bags, and the following morning, a Lebanese taxi came to take her and Humam; it left hastily, as if protecting them from a coming disaster. Omar followed them to Beirut after a few more days, during which time we never saw him.

My mother's departure gave me a sense of ease. I was no longer afraid of her cowardly heart which had almost caused her to faint when she heard about the raid on the house where Hossam was staying; he had managed to escape over the roofs of the neighbouring houses, no more than two narrow streets away from us. My mother went outside to look for him and blamed herself for not sensing him when he had been so near that she could have hugged him and been cured of missing him. When she returned she was exhausted and disoriented. Fear gripped us so tightly that we lost our desire to gossip and we became strangers in one house, leading a life without structure but with one single goal: to be reassured every morning that Bakr and Hossam hadn't been killed; and that we hadn't had a heart attack, or succumbed to the madness which seemed even closer to us than Marwa's butterflies. They now occupied a quarter of the cellar and made the officer in charge of the latest search think he was entering a haunted house. He couldn't believe that this depressed woman was the same one who had gathered all these colours, mounted them in wooden boxes and covered them with expensive glass. The locks on the cases were golden, and their gleam resembled the stars and eagle on the officer's epaulettes which brushed the skull on his uniform.

His silence and Marwa's steadfastness in front of her butterflies agitated me. I was overcome with terror that I would discover just how much Marwa needed a man to look deeply into her eyes and set her body quaking, even if he was an enemy like this officer who was so pleasant, and who hoped that Hossam and his companions would fall from the sky so he could scatter their brains with his bullets. An idea occurred to me – that I might rip out his heart and throw it into the jar of pickled aubergines standing in a dark corner. I tried to visualize gathering the hearts of all the soldiers and pickling them. I imagined Rima exercising her passion and inventing new types of pickle and I laughed, reassured of the strength of the hatred in my heart. The officer praised Marwa and stopped his subordinates from smashing her boxes. She wouldn't listen to my reprimands and thanked him delicately, prayed for him to have a long life and eternal youth, and shook hands with him when he left. I swore to Maryam and Zahra that he hung on to her hand and pressed her fingers longer than necessary. Zahra was greatly worried by my insistence on smashing the display cases and on preventing Marwa from going outside, and Maryam calmed me down and asked me to help her tidy the rooms the soldiers had ransacked. Due to the frequency of these visits to our and Uncle Selim's houses, as well as to my grandfather's shops and the homes of all his relatives, we had perfected the art of swiftly returning objects to their proper places. The officers didn't believe that Bakr and Hossam weren't hiding in one of the secret tunnels which, it was said, could only be reached through passages in the spacious houses owned by families who clung tenaciously to their pedigrees. Marwa closed her bedroom door in my face and I heard Zahra mutter that I had become unbearable.

Safaa and Abdullah's letters were less frequent. We knew Abdullah had now gone to Afghanistan and was distributing donations and supporting the mujahideen on the ground. In my mind, he was almost on the same level as the Prophet's Companions, who I drew as mighty eagles swooping down from their mountain nests to tear out and devour the livers of their enemies. Safaa and Zeina had become sisters, shadows of each other. They agreed on how to divide Abdullah up between them and abandoned their jealousy in order to go out to the markets together. Their shared laughter provoked astonishment among the women of Zeina's social group, who listened ardently to the *sira* of Seif ibn dhi-Yazan as Safaa poured bitter coffee and circulated among the guests. In Safaa's most recent letter, before the Christmas festivals, she told us her pregnancy was going well. Maryam's eyes welled up; Zahra smiled and declared it a good omen, and then told us dispassionately that her mother was coming to Aleppo the following week, and she would have her to stay in our house. Maryam welcomed Zahra's guest; she needed guests to return warmth to our walls and to distract us from talking about and waiting for death, but I was angry at the preparations for welcoming a woman who would sully our house.

Maryam and Zahra ignored the officer when he came back on yet another search. He came especially to watch Marwa, whose eyes shone with happiness and desire as she greeted him without any concern for my anger. He exchanged a few words with her that I didn't hear; she nodded and he went and stood in front of her butterflies and looked particularly at the yellow one, which he asked to touch. She opened up the glass case for him and asked him to take his time. Unusually, his soldiers didn't overturn our cupboards, or scatter the photos from our ancient albums, or mock my grandfather's haughty looks while imitating Hitler, who was one of their greatest objects of admiration, despite his contempt for the Arabs.

I wrote a letter to Bakr, exaggerating Marwa's relationship with the death squad officer, and asking him to intervene to save our reputation and to prevent Wasal from entering our house. I had to leave the letter near a remote water tap at Bab Al Nasr, the same place he left his instructions. The following day a young man knocked at our door and asked to see Maryam on an urgent matter. He informed her of Bakr's decision to ban Marwa from going out of the house unaccompanied, and left quickly without answering our questions about Bakr's health or his situation. Marwa wept and spat in my face, cursing my father; we were dumbstruck when she still insisted on going outside alone to look for butterflies. I wondered secretly if I was repugnant because I had prevented my aunt from falling in love with our enemy. Her old image returned to me: a woman dreaming, crying on Hajja Radia's shoulder when she went to sing *nashid* for Rabia Adawiya who had spent the night by her lover's side. I completely ignored Marwa when we gathered in the morning to drink coffee before I went to college – despite Maryam's winking at Zahra, which was intended to remind me that Marwa had once been like a mother to me. I left, saddened.

The streets narrowed in front of my footsteps as I distractedly observed the tanks which I felt were pressing down on my chest, and the dense patrols on every corner. I imagined that they really were encircling the city and would no doubt seize all of our mujahideen; they would end the dream which had taken on a vivid colour and an unforgettable taste. That winter, Aleppo was weighing heavily on me, prompting me to reconsider my feelings towards our martyrs. I thought how hard it was for a woman to fall in love with men she didn't know; men who were dead.

Not long after this, Dr Abdel Karim Daly, a physics professor at the university, was killed. I saw him laid out with his chest blasted open. It wasn't known who had killed him; his blood could have been spilled by anyone, from us to the commander of the death squad. Our group disapproved of his murder and declared him to be innocent. That day, the paratroopers came in huge numbers and conducted rigorous searches of all the students before allowing them into their colleges. Hundreds of soldiers were crammed into the streets close by; they broke off tree branches to use as canes, stopped people, and made them stand rigid against the wall. When shooting broke out in nearby areas, it seemed as if Aleppo were burning. People were allowed to go out and I walked heedlessly, as if the sound of the bullets were music to which I was addicted. Soldiers fired into the air hysterically; they resembled frogs ensnared in a tunnel which had darkened suddenly and caused them to become disoriented.

That same day, when I reached the house where my prayer circle was usually held, I couldn't find anyone. I went on my way, afraid of hearing that our prayer circle had been disbanded and its members reassigned among the other circles directly subordinate to the group's leadership. Exhausted, I went to my room, flung myself on the bed and dozed off. When I woke up at dawn, Maryam was placing compresses on my head to lighten my fever. She told me that I had been raving about people she didn't know, as well as my father and Hossam. I got up but couldn't find a more soothing place to sit than in front of Marwa's butterflies. I drank a hot tisane and Maryam left me alone after covering me with a thick woollen shawl. I was curled up in the same leather chair in which Marwa sat for hours to contemplate the butterflies ranged on the wall. I gazed at them for a long time; the white butterfly speckled with black and brown made me pause. I looked for the secret of the officer's silence to answer the questions that kept me awake: did temptation lie in the butterflies, or in Marwa's calm smile and full lips? They were like her large bust which she no longer cared about fully covering as we did when we sewed our clothes, so we seemed like black seals which wouldn't reveal their shame. All of our bodies were shameful – every part of us, from our toenails to our hair. The butterflies almost stripped me of my strength with their delicacy and immutability.

My monthly cycle saved me from my concerns. It came on suddenly and heavily, two days before it was due. Maryam was understanding and tolerated my nerves when I insisted on going out early that morning. I missed Hajja Souad, and I needed her strength. On my way to her house I tried to appease my fear, and I bought *mamounia* and warm bread like a widow buying breakfast for her children. I was astonished by Hajja Souad's pale face and anxiety; she told me that we had lost more than ten mujahideen the previous day. The soldiers had raided a house in Hamidiyya and killed four men from the Abi Nour cell as they were preparing to leave it, having already accidentally revealed their hiding place in the Sukry quarter. They killed three of our brothers as well as destroying the entire arms cache behind the copper market. I felt terrified; she told me the names of the victims and I heard only some of them, sensing that she hadn't told me everything. I asked her directly about Hossam and Bakr, so she told me, 'Hossam was wounded and arrested.' I was dizzy and collapsed on the sofa. I felt like my heart had stopped beating. Just imagining the brutal tortures that would be visited upon his skinny body drove me mad. I was so weak that a breath of wind might topple me, and I barely heard Hajja Souad's voice demanding that I pull myself together and pray for him, and for the thousands of others squeezed into the desert jail and the putrid cellars of the Mukhabarat, oppressed by the smells of blood and excrement and anticipating a death already half-realized. She warned me about my thoughtlessness and weakness. I no longer needed to listen to anything; I said to myself I needed silence, and I was silent.

Marwa went out to meet Nadhir Mansoury, the death squad officer, and I didn't care. Maryam was bewildered; she slapped her palms against her knees as if she expected a catastrophe. She brought Selim over and sprayed spittle and harsh words into Marwa's face, saying she would destroy the family's reputation. Selim prayed with his *misbaha* of 999 beads and asked God's forgiveness without raising his eyes to our faces, contenting himself with repeating, 'Do not throw away your virtue.' Marwa's face was rigid. Coldly she said, 'I love him.' Everything collapsed; our dreams fluttered apart like wisps of straw. We were as silent as if we were dead. We felt the need for a man to lead us by the hand to safety; we no longer knew who might throw us a lifeline to save us from disappearing.

Omar had by now settled in Beirut. He could no longer bear the lot of being related to Bakr, whose family name had thrown suspicion on his relatives and exacted a cruel price. Selim's son Jalal, who was performing his compulsory military service, had his nails pulled out under interrogation and was transferred to a division close to the airport out in the desert, where scorpions climbed the tent pegs and colonized empty gun barrels. The officer in charge was half-mad and thought he was Stalin.

He brought the soldiers out of their tents and asked them to lay a railway through the desert all the way to Berlin, and then laughed hysterically when he saw them looking at each other and beginning to pile up the few stones they had found on the edge of the camp when he had ordered them to look for truffles. On that occasion, they had spent three days scrutinizing the desert, rummaging for plants and looking for that delicious fruit which was ripened by thunder and grew freely in the earth – anyone who didn't find a truffle had his backpack filled with stones. The commander gathered up these truffles and sold them in the souk Al Hal, along with the soldiers' leave papers. Patience was the only thing that prevented them from killing him and fleeing across the border into Iraq.

After six months, Jalal returned on a short leave, utterly withered and speaking in fragments rather than fully formed sentences. He wept in his mother's arms as he described to her how the commander had made them walk over thorns because their voices were too weak in singing the praises of the Party. In the scorching summer heat, he smeared their bodies with jam and left them stretched out beneath the sun, enjoying how they were burning and fainting; he was taking revenge in his own special way on the treachery of those who had banished him to this barren camp after an honourable military career.

Selim advised Jalal to be patient. He didn't join

him in cursing Bakr, but went to the corner of his room which he prepared for a meeting with the other dervishes, even though they no longer came to recite *dhikr*, afraid of being accused of terrorism. They had dispersed and now chanted *dhikr* on their own, after one of the most important officers from the death squad had plucked out their imam's beard hair by hair, all the while reminding him that they wouldn't kill him so that he would know their mercy. Most of the dervishes shaved off their beards and their faces were no longer blessed with rays of divine light.

Jalal made a decision and returned to the camp's commander laden with alcohol. His new behaviour seemed odd at first, but before long all was settled in the colonel's mind; Jalal told him about the fugitive Omar, the originator of many famous scandals in Aleppo, while cursing Bakr and his organization; he now abstained from the prayer he had earlier been practising in secret. Jalal admitted to himself that the taste of alcohol made the camp's nights of hard labour seem almost delightful. He remembered Omar's face and swore that he would relive his uncle's life, and outdo him in shamelessness. He reassessed his life, family and religion. He withdrew from his tent mates and grew closer to the colonel, who appointed him as his orderly. Jalal prepared the colonel's food himself, drawing on his recollections of dishes his mother excelled at, and discovered a new outdoor hobby. He turned a deaf ear the first time his friends told him about the rumours of a sexual relationship between himself and the colonel, describing his soft moans and his position in the colonel's embrace. No one would listen to his complaints after he had been granted several spells of leave so he could bring back from Aleppo bags of pistachios, crates of excellent whisky, carpets and cured meats. He dredged up memories of his studies of the city's markets, where he had been raised after leaving school at the age of thirteen in order to learn pragmatism and how to bow before the wind. Jalal thought that his fate was dependent on his leaving military service neither deranged nor resentful towards his future partners, of whom the colonel would be the most important. He began to tell him his story as if they were friends, on the rainy winter nights when silence settled over the camp so it seemed like the grave.

All night, I tried to rid myself of the image of Hossam at their hands, like a duckling caught in the fangs of a hungry leopard. I thought that his confession might lead to disasters for the organization that no one had yet imagined. Marwa stayed alone in the courtyard despite the biting cold, sitting on the cane chair as if waiting for her lover or considering her fate. Maryam sternly asked Radwan to watch the door, which she locked. She placed the key in her breast pocket, so she could sleep and be assured that the high walls and locked door would prevent Marwa from fleeing to him, despite Zahra's requests to leave Marwa to her, her night-time companion and confidante. Zahra nodded off and Marwa didn't come to bed. In the morning, we found her asleep on the abandoned cotton ottoman beside her butterflies, with her arms wrapped around herself. Her fingers were blue from cold. Radwan refused to leave his room, avoiding our anger and sudden agitation. To his blind companions, he described us as crazy women who had lost all desire to laugh. He recalled the insulting severity of my grandmother and mocked Maryam, imitating her until she seemed like a broken-jointed puppet at the hands of spoiled children. Maryam muttered angrily; she had no sympathy for Marwa, frozen with cold.

Quietly, over the morning coffee, I told them that Hossam had been arrested. I allowed myself no opportunity to see the terror in their eyes; I left for college, where studies had been suspended for the funeral of Dr Abdel Karim Daly, considered a martyr. I walked in the funeral procession thirsting for revenge, even though his life did not really warrant it. I urgently needed to regain my hatred in the midst of these hordes who clamoured for our blood as they followed behind the coffin carried on the shoulders of students with flushed faces. They cursed the murder of the professor who had left a pleasant impression on everyone he met. I tried to find a justification for his death and convince myself of our group's statements, although I felt no compassion for him. The students insisted on his funeral cortege marching to the gates of Aleppo, and they climbed up on to both lanes of the motorway; I could see his colleagues weeping bitterly for him. Dr Daly was known for his biting speeches attacking the authorities and the death squad in particular, which he categorized as a Nazi sectarian faction. He described our group in the same terms, and didn't conceal his resentment at the cruelty with which the city was treated by all sides.

He had studied in Aleppo's university at the end of the sixties, when he had arrived from his nearby mountain village and rented a cheap room in the Siryaan district. With three fellow students, he gained a distinguished reputation that tempted some Parisian scientists to take up their never-ending projects and lure them to France. Nevertheless, he preferred to return to his city with his Aleppan friend, Adham. They left their companions at work in secret Parisian laboratories, where they could become French, lisp their 'r's and write to their friends who had returned to Aleppo, deriding their love for the city and their stupid patriotism.

In silence, Dr Daly stoically bore the obstructions to his scientific projects, and the pressure exerted on him to affiliate himself to the Party. His initial refusals turned to ridicule. When Aleppo began to drown in a fever of murder he announced his position publicly in front of his students, whom he spurred on to reject the tyranny of both sides, attacking the recklessness of students of the Youth Wing of the ruling Party. The university administration was forced to compromise and made exceptions for his lectures; when he refused to allow paratrooper students to enter the lecture hall dressed in military uniform and carrying weapons, they didn't dare oppose him. He failed to hand over a student of his who was wanted for being leftist and threw the Mukhabarat out of the hall, which allowed the student to escape through a window. This tale reached near-legendary status in the university, and spread throughout the city after he turned down the protection offered to him by a Mukhabarat officer. He refused to leave the house he rented in Bab Al Hadid, a district famous for its bigotry.

I said I needed to restrain my sympathy; hatred was our great weapon to make the majority defend their sect against the ruling minority, even though there were many officials belonging to this majority among those who had built the regime, and their hands were equally stained with blood and corruption. I didn't approach the car on which the bier was placed. The students wept for the dead man as a father, brother and friend, recalling the wonder of his lectures which never lacked joy or freedom. He supported the lifting of the veil and rejected the sectarianism that he said was the decay that would lead to the suffocation of our souls. He praised physics which he loved and which, in his opinion, would guide us to the scientific thinking of which we were in need. It was widely known that he could be found with his students in theatres and cinemas, and after their graduation he maintained friendships with many of them. He received letters from all over the world, quoting him in matters of love or scientific research, together with wedding invitations.

I looked at the photograph his students raised over the bier and contemplated his honey-coloured eyes. I rationed my glances so as not to fall into ardent love with yet another dead man whom I considered my enemy. I moved away from the crowd and walked on my own, weeping for Hossam and afraid of my fate. I went back to the house where my prayer circle met and found it still shut up; I was confused and quickly went on my way, afraid of revealing its purpose. I didn't dare use my key as someone had closed the blinds – a pre-arranged signal of danger and a warning not to approach. I later said to Hajja Souad that I wanted to know the fate of that house, but she didn't answer me. She ordered me to stay away from any activity or meeting for the time being, and relayed Bakr's desire that I keep away from the organization, and that I travel to Beirut to be near my mother who had collapsed after seeing Hossam in a dream, strung up from a gallows and left dangling. I then found out that Hajja Souad had misled me; when she told me that my brother had been arrested, she hadn't made it clear that this was only two days after my last meeting with him; so Hossam had been in custody much longer than I had realized. With horror, the inhabitants of the quarter of Bab Al Ahr related that four young men had prepared an ambush for the car of a senior officer in the death squad, who sometimes visited a friend in Aleppo. Their carelessness in an area they considered to be entirely loyal to them made rounding them up in the forest an easy affair. Hossam at first escaped across some roofs to the cemetery at Bab Al Hadid, but his meagre ammunition ran out after two hours and he was captured after being wounded in the chest and losing consciousness.

I immediately ran to the cemetery which was situated nearby, looking for spots of his blood which, to me, formed mountains out of the dust. I sat at the graves of strangers as the guard described Hossam's terror and his attempts to kill himself so he wouldn't fall into the soldiers' clutches, and he pointed out to me where a headstone had been chipped by a bullet close to where Hossam was captured. His blood was scattered all over one fragment; I carried it away with me as a closely guarded icon and put it on my table. I surrounded it with the reverence it deserved and everyone was wary of touching it, even without being informed that Hossam's blood was in our house.

Hossam lay handcuffed to a bed in the military hospital. He was guarded by four members of the Mukhabarat who kept their fingers on their triggers. He tried to kill himself again but was prevented by the doctors, who then kept him heavily sedated for seven days. His companions couldn't reach his isolated room and they grew desperate after he was transferred to a building of the military Mukhabarat where he would be exposed to the whips and the dread of brutal torture – they would try to make him confess and reveal secrets about Bakr, arms caches, and the rebel leadership, who appeared in fuzzy pictures to be like birds, or moles digging into the earth to hide away despite their blindness.

The festivals of Christmas 1981 came and went. Aleppo's Christians rang their church bells timidly and prayed silently. Aleppo became a funeral city; the smell of death had spread into every corner. There was a curfew at night and the city was under siege. No one was allowed to enter or leave for a fortnight, which was long enough to search all its houses. No drawer was left unopened, their secrets confiscated by the forty thousand troops of the death squad and the special forces, together with the military divisions that surrounded the city on all sides; the inhabitants of this fortress grew weary of the blockade imposed by the President's unwelcome envoys. Danger drew ever nearer to the President himself, and his face on television seemed tired. He made passionate speeches every day about his grief, and asked his military leaders to resolve the conflict which no one had thought would be this acrimonious. They were terrified when other cities were set alight; the small town of Hama became an unexpected battlefield. It dreamed of recovering the leadership of the country for our sect, with the Quran raised above the sword. Its caves and old houses, its gardens and river banks were all under siege. Hama received its allocation of the dead, who would no longer walk through the forests, steppes and mountains during summer holidays.

I told myself that the siege of our city was an opportunity to reassess our house, to contemplate my surroundings. I started to become lazy and slept until the afternoon. I thought of my mother from whom we had decided to conceal Hossam's arrest. The soldiers searched our house three times more. On one occasion, they even insisted on opening the jars of pickles and left behind them a strong smell of vinegar, which lingered as we returned to our isolation as sad, lonely women who had lost all sense of security and pleasure in life. Our movements through the courtyard were detached, and seemed to herald even greater disasters. The mere anticipation oppressed our spirits and made us caress our wrecked bodies, which had relinquished escape, in the bathroom among the foam of the perfumed soap now grown dry and leathery. One day I said to Zahra that we had become hideous but she didn't reply, still waiting for her mother who had postponed her trip. Maryam weighed and sifted lentils, and for the umpteenth time asked Radwan to bring up another sack from the cellar store. She would weigh them and watch Marwa sitting silently in front of her butterflies.

I went out on the tenth day of the siege and it was as if I didn't know Aleppo. The sound of guns and mortars was uninterrupted at night, and the shelling had devastated Bab Al Nasr, Bab Al Hadid and Jalloum. I saw Hajja Souad, who urged me to go abroad and asked me to stop visiting her; things were not as they should have been. The final battle, which we had all been waiting for eagerly, had panicked our leadership and our militia was once more riven by internal conflict. I continued on my way to the college (closed since the beginning of the siege) and wondered about the fate of the corpses there – and of the frogs and laboratory rats smothered in chloroform and awaiting dissection; I thought about that sad lizard and how my hands trembled as I sliced open its stomach to take out its intestines and extinguish its life for ever. I looked for the blood that covered my recent dreams, in which Hossam came to me carrying his shroud, laughing as he waved it. I woke up afraid, took out his books and kissed them over and over again. I became absorbed in his neat handwriting and his powerful expressions in praise of the martyrs who had not been washed before their funerals so that their blood could be witnessed by the mourners.

The dream kept returning, and my terror

increased in proportion to the impossibility of knowing Hossam's fate. The dream grew longer: now Hossam was included in a host of people, most of whom I recognized, despite their flat and featureless faces. They muttered an incomprehensible song resembling an old Syriac hymn. Any meaning in my dreams died, and they became riddles I couldn't master. The swallows and meadows fled, and the siege of Aleppo penetrated our very skin; we could smell the soldiers as we sat beside the silent fountains and exchanged glances. We all tried to recreate dim memories, but our fear scattered them and transformed us into lizard-like beings. Feigning bravery, I left Maryam's room to enjoy the moonlight which emerged from behind the gloomy clouds, indifferent to the silent city and nightly curfew, which a poet known for his homosexual tendencies compared to a paradise buried alive.

The poet had insisted on celebrating his sixtieth birthday on the steps of the Citadel with his friends and his lover, whom he had picked up one day at the warehouse where he was working as a porter, and publicly serenaded him with an ode full of powerful feeling. He was reviled by the city whose pain he had immortalized in a long *nashid* written in *kamil* metre, in imitation of the *mu'allaqat*. He prefaced it with a historical description, mourned the days of the Hamdanid dynasty, and dwelled on a description of his beloved's broad shoulders and virility. He likened the death squads to vampires and the city to the neck of a beautiful youth fleeing the court of Haroun Al Rashid in diaphanous Abbasid clothing. The poet was most prominent and generous in gratifying his lover, who was made to forget bowls of lentil soup and being groped by men who winked at him coarsely; he revelled in a spacious house with blue windows, relaxing like a husband on a holiday from work. Lines from the ode were spread among the people, who never again hurled stones at the poet, as they had done whenever he walked in an elegant and effeminate manner past the coffee houses in Bab Al Faraj. The coffee-house patrons would wait for hours for the waiters from nearby restaurants to bring them plates of rancid meat, and they would scold them in loud voices which were silenced as soon as the foot patrols went past, the soldiers scrutinizing everyone, their fingers on their triggers in fear.

I ignored Marwa who braided her hair with colourful butterflies, jeered at modest head coverings, smoked openly, and sat in her room beside the fountain watching the sky, expecting it to rain with butterflies like the ones covered with glass and hung on the cellar wall. They cast a shadow over her bed, which she had moved to the damp corner beside the sacks of okra, beans and dried tomatoes. Her tears dampened her woollen pillow, wrapped carefully in a case which she had embroidered in the Yazidi style.

Marwa only smiled around Zahra, who was

absorbed in her two children. They lay on the bed and ate seeds fried in spices. I wished that I could approach them and share in the chatting I missed so much. My separation from the girls in my group had increased my isolation and made me feel that my emotions were worthless. I was afraid of sleeping alone but I didn't want to shatter my image of being a strong mujahida who didn't care for the trivialities of life which were unbecoming to me. Hossam was present in every detail of our life: Maryam mourned him, and Marwa and Zahra wept. My tears remained concealed in my heart only to gush out once I was in my bed. I lost all desire to draw my dreams, along with many other things that used to give me happiness, such as reading and sympathizing with Radwan whenever I sensed he felt lonely and repented of acting as guardian to women who didn't value a man possessed of strange talents and filled with joy.

I looked for Hajja Souad and found her after three days, trembling with fear as she sat in her prayer clothes. In February, news came from Hama that the rebellion had begun to sow fear that the small town would be utterly destroyed and its inhabitants brutally murdered. The battle approached its end, but we believed that our young men would be plunged in it for years to come, and that few families would be able to escape to the plains. The bodies of the victims were lined up in the streets of Hama but no one could be found to bury them. The presence of our militia on whom the desperate muezzins called was a confirmation of the show-down everyone had been waiting for. Trained fighters mixed with civilians who brought weapons out from abandoned wells and other hiding places to defend their lives against the insane bullets whose source no one knew any more. Thousands of soldiers read the Sura Fatiha for their souls and rushed into the small city whose narrow streets were besieged by hundreds of tanks; not even a bird could escape. Future generations would narrate the madness which could have been avoided, thus granting the chance of a life to the children who had loved jumping into the Orontes River from the wooden waterwheels. The ceaseless grinding of the waterwheels was the only reality; a voice of constant yearning, of a grief whose cause no one inquired about any more. Bereaved mothers swore they would never take off their black clothes; they would remain in perpetual mourning for the dead. Many of them ripped their clothes in a state of delirium and went out into the streets half-naked, mourning for the city of Hama and their sons with elegiac *ritha* which would 'make rocks weep', as Khadija Al Mufti told us. A member of the Hama branch of our organization, she had been able to flee with the assistance of a senior paratrooper, who later wept and trampled on his military insignia before his companions killed him; they were afraid that he would kill them at night when they returned from restocking their ammunition. Hajja Souad and I were silent as we listened to Khadija. We waited for her crying to abate, as our words of consolation couldn't halt it. When she finally stopped, she announced she was withdrawing from the organization. In the morning, she gathered her few clothes in a bundle and disappeared like a pinch of salt thrown into a torrential river.

Marwa wasn't impressed by my zeal to burn down all the houses belonging to the other sect. She laughed derisively and left the house without turning around to hear Maryam's pleas. Maryam had lost control, even over the keys. She tried to convince Radwan to guard Marwa, but then gave up and sat on the step to her room. She was silent, like an unburied mummy displayed in a glass case and reeking of embalming fluid. Marwa returned in the evening, glowing and loudly repeating a section of the song 'You, Who Keep Me Awake' by Um Kulthoum. She closed the door to the cellar, turned off the light, and slept beside her butterflies. Zahra convinced Maryam to wait till the morning before tackling Marwa. But the next day, Marwa went out again, leaving her door open behind her and her bed in disarray. After the evening prayer, she sat on the sofa and said quietly that she had seen her lover and they were getting married. Then she rose, turned to us, and said, 'I am leaving the refuge of Heaven. I love Hell.'

We were left reeling. This calamity was even

greater than that borne by weak women when their men became corpses; it wasn't very important whether they were martyrs, or just cadavers with flies swarming around their faces. For the entire night, Zahra spoke quietly with Marwa, who insisted on describing the smell of her lover's hands and chest and, with even greater courage, lauding his virility. The affair had returned something to her body that she thought she had forgotten for ever, and now she was concerned with restoring grace to a body which had regained its vitality. Her movements in the court-yard became sensuous and coy. She walked coquettishly and looked several times at her watch as if a rendezvous were imminent. She kept going out unexpectedly, in total disregard for our fear or our reputation. The officer, Nadhir Mansoury, was waiting for her in front of the gate to the Bab Al Hadid district, and she boldly got into his car to set off for an unknown house in which a bed had been hastily prepared so they could pass a short time in fleeting pleasure.

Zahra had been expecting this calamity and surrendered to it silently. She distracted us all by talking about her mother's visit, which had been postponed yet again. Maryam sought help from our absent men, and her anger exploded the moment Marwa came back, shameless, half-drunk, and singing like a cheap bar-girl. She took off her shoes and walked barefoot on the floor. She removed her long coat and her head covering, and stood only in her flimsy dress which showed off all her features: breasts with nipples like cherry stones, rounded posterior, soft stomach, long legs hairless and gleaming – like a dancer showing off a licentiousness which bewildered us. I felt that everything was breaking down; I hated my backside; I wanted to leave this void, this vacuum within the storm, a feeling enhanced by a torrential downpour that night.

I thought of writing to Bakr but guessed that he might be dead or in custody, and that if he was alive he would care only about hanging on to his life. (Thousands of young men had been arrested: not only members of the organization and sympathizers, but also people with no discernible relationship to them. New prisons had opened and we were regarded with suspicion; a relationship with us might cost someone their life.) Zahra intervened harshly. She slapped Marwa, then led her to her room where she embraced her and let her cry on her chest dramatically as if both women were actresses in a movie. She listened to Marwa's fears as she repeated that she loved him, and even if she were to be slaughtered she couldn't be parted from him.

That night Maryam couldn't sleep and read the Sura Yusuf ten times. She performed the dawn prayer five times, immersed in a strange calm. She didn't get up to welcome the three young men she saw entering behind Radwan; they checked the time, then asked to speak to Maryam alone. After a short conversation she led them to Marwa, who hadn't woken up yet, and asked Zahra not to interfere. She knew they had been dispatched by Bakr to halt this farce which had almost destroyed our reputation. Two of the young men carried Marwa and the third stood beside the door and drew his weapon. With swift movements, they gagged her and attached her to the leg of the cast-iron bed on which my grandmother as a married woman had first enjoyed the delights of passion, before she exchanged it for a brass bed; Maryam had inherited it and marvelled at the skilful moulding of plants and the incantation 'Ma Sha' Allah' in Kufic script.

Marwa was chained to the leg of the bed by her ankles. She cursed her assailants and wept when one of them informed her that her lover, Nadhir Mansoury, had been assassinated that morning. They added that Bakr had sworn to kill anyone who attempted to free her with a thousand bullets. After one of them kissed the satisfied Maryam's hand, they made a swift exit and left Marwa to rattle her chains in fury. Bakr had designed them so she could reach the bathroom to wash and attend to her needs, and sit beside the window like a prisoner. It occurred to me that she couldn't see the moon from her small window, overshadowed as it was by the terrace roof which stretched along the top of the wall. The lemon tree, which we no longer expected to bear fruit for us, revealed the flightiness of happiness, which we had discovered was just a delusion. We couldn't believe that what had just happened could earlier have been imagined, even in our wildest dreams.

Deep down, we each envied Safaa for escaping the depression of our house, which had begun to resemble a vial of vinegar. Marwa had resisted and I believed she would go on to smash her iron chains, but then she suddenly subsided like a lioness whose wildness has been tamed and which has now grown used to being a child's plaything in the zoo. She refused to speak to Maryam or even respond to her morning greetings. We became non-existent for her, and I felt her contemptuous looks penetrate my body like burning arrows, confusing me as I tried to enter the circle of her dreams.

The bereaved opened the city gates three days later and, the siege being lifted, the tanks withdrew to the pistachio fields. There was grief and fear in the eyes of people who had grown used to bowing their heads, cringing like chickens who cared only about returning safely to their coop at night. The bullets' randomness had made Aleppo's men hollow, bereft of dreams. Our organization lost internal cohesion. The leadership's meetings were brief, rushed and inconclusive; accusations were exchanged and no one could look into his companions' eyes with satisfaction, as they had just a year before when they confidently approached the steps of the Republican Palace.

★　★　★

Thousands of corpses perfumed Hama's air, saturated with the smell of the river. The lists of countless detainees which were thrown on to the table in meetings were deeply frustrating for our leaders. We heard that at one meeting Bakr stood up and announced his resignation from the leadership – and he immediately left for Jordan on a false passport, and from there to London, where he arrived at night in the middle of fog. He wanted to walk to London Bridge and cry into the River Thames. Like any man, he didn't want to look back so he wouldn't have to remember the hundreds of young men who had sworn on the Quran and left to seek out paths to Paradise and certain death.

Marwa had missed her butterflies and calmly drew them in her room. Anyone seeing her might have thought that she loved her bonds as she gleefully pestered Maryam to ask Radwan to bring her some acrylic paints. She started to draw on her shackles and colour them in, and Zahra laughed at her commentary on her pictures. They made me miss my old self, when I didn't praise hatred and drew my dreams with only childlike malice. When Marwa came near me, I sat beside her and told her how beautiful her lips and butterflies were, and how much I missed my brothers, like any obedient girl sympathetic to her plight. I tried to break her chains, but I couldn't. Marwa was indifferent, as if she couldn't hear me. She finished painting a sunflower on one ankle fetter, which was resplendent in dark yellow with clumsy details like the unintentional smears of a child's drawing.

After Hajja Souad disappeared and the existence of our cell was discovered, I began to look around me in fear whenever I walked in the streets. I approached Hana one day when I saw her outside the chemistry lab, which had now reopened, and she ignored me completely, as if saying, 'Get away from me. I don't know you.' She found me later, and told me that Alya had been arrested and they were still looking for Hajja Souad. I felt the weight of handcuffs settling around my wrists; I couldn't contact anyone to take a letter to Bakr. I was alone. I would leave the house in the morning and walk in the streets, draped in black, rejected; like a fish striving for the shore and which, having reached it, can no longer return to the safety and care of the sea. I reproached myself for disdaining the smell of the white coat that had delighted my mother and aunts when I put it on for the first time and came out of my room, spreading my arms in the guise of a doctor. I took my mother's wrist in order to take her pulse in exaggeratedly coquettish movements which made them all laugh. We had needed my white coat, so we could believe that the future would not be as black as our clothes.

Everyone was preoccupied with Wasal, who had finally arrived in Aleppo. Zahra hugged her warmly, a daughter in need of her contrite mother. Wasal wore a long, modest dress and a hijab. She was elegant and earnest in her penitence and feverish efforts to get to Mecca. Maryam marked her arrival with gloom initially, and then with increasing enthusiasm. The soul returned to our house along with movement and laughter, and cooking aromas wafted from the kitchen. Marwa's chains incensed Wasal; she asked for her forgiveness, which no one else had, not even Omar who dropped in like a passer-by before quickly returning to Beirut, and from there to other countries. We lost track of him as he became afraid of death. He closed the family shops, and informed us that back in Beirut my father was immersed in alcohol, fishing and silence.

Wasal was proud of Zahra; of her strength, of her deep faith that it was God who had calmed her heart and expelled the fear and night terrors from her life. The two women were at ease as they sat together, scolding and laughing and going to the markets with Maryam and Radwan, ignoring my presence and my requests not to let a dissolute woman enter our home. Marwa shouted at me to fear God and turn my gaze inwards to see the ugliness inside me. That night I felt like I was full of decay; I needed to sit by myself and cry over my broken image as a girl who had once loved life and tolerance. Maryam heard my whimpers and embraced me like a mother, and I thought of how much I needed compassion. She took me the next day to the hammam, and we left Marwa fettered without any feeling of guilt or pity; she had inquired after

Nadhir from the death squad soldiers who were still periodically raiding our house, overturning our things and moving around like passengers at an abandoned train station. Marwa smiled when they told her that Nadhir hadn't died, nor were his wounds serious. She asked them to convey the message to him that she was chained up because of their love. The young officer was enthusiastic about this, astonished by the woman surrounded by embalmed butterflies and attached to a heavy cast-iron bed which even an ox couldn't move. Two days later, he returned with his soldiers and went directly to Marwa's room. He gave her a sealed letter and left without repeating his usual idiotic questions about the contents of the abandoned well, which had been sealed with a metal cover to prevent scorpions and snakes crawling out of it. He looked at her respectfully and greeted her with the consideration due to the wife of a superior officer. We couldn't take the letter off her; only Zahra knew everything and she kept her friend's secrets, ignoring Maryam's questioning and responding enthusiastically to the suggestion we take Wasal to the hammam.

For the first time I knew what it might be like to be considered a fallen woman – women crossed in front of our compartment to spy on Wasal's withered breasts, imagining what they had looked like forty years earlier when they were like fruits of Paradise. Wasal rubbed down Maryam's body with the experience of a woman who had encountered many men and who had moaned in pleasure at their hands. Maryam's dead body woke up, and she was dreamy, as if recalling the son of the Samarkandi and desiring him. She imagined his hands and his chest and regretted a wasted youth. The hot water and the smell of the cavernous hall made Wasal recall her story; she recited some English obscenities, which I understood. I smiled in an attempt to attract her attention and get closer to Zahra again, who didn't comment on the few spots, boils almost, scattered over my body. They stopped me from undressing in front of the other women in fear of their ridicule, despite my firm breasts whose full bloom I restricted in a bra made of a rough, coarse material which was more suitable for an old woman.

We were astonished by our liberality and avoided exchanging looks so we wouldn't discover that our relaxation was fleeting: it would ruin our deliberately excessive laughter. We tried to forget the nightmares and recall the glories, and engage with the trivialities of life – we hadn't realized at the time how necessary these were to help us carry on. Our career as the women led by the blind every Thursday evening was now impossible; undertaking this visit to the baths at all was a cause for celebration. Gathering in a circle around the dinner table every Friday became a miracle whose future recurrence we couldn't count on, any more than on a night's restful sleep in our own beds. I left our compartment in the hammam,

217

looking for the footsteps of the child I had been and the galleries in which she had got lost.

I didn't notice Hana until she approached me and whispered that we had to meet; she set a precise time and place and warned me not to miss it. She left, so we seemed like two women swapping razor blades to shave our legs. I almost choked and drowned in the steam. I didn't want anyone to see my terror of going to prison, whose rot I had already been able to feel under my tongue. I imagined the feel of handcuffs and remembered Marwa – I had spent the night beside her and she asked me resolutely to go away and leave her to her wait. I gazed at her and felt for a moment that she had become used to her chains, and that the feel of their rusty links no longer disturbed her; she walked slowly in her room and attentively watched the sky through her window. On moonlit nights, she would sit in the courtyard for hours following the path of the moon like a white ship gliding over the horizon. Her silence was an expression of her contempt for us, and we felt it even more when we heard her peal of laughter with Wasal, who loved her and shared her room. At night, Wasal would sing Frank Sinatra songs for her, and Marwa requested 'If You Go Away' after hearing a translation of the lyrics. Marwa paused for a long time over a section she had learned by heart, and made Wasal burst out laughing when she playfully dragged out the consonants as she sang.

Wasal was a good listener. She spoke with the politeness of a woman who wanted neither to ruin her daughter's life nor exact a high price from us, and before long she had absorbed our dreams and desires. She began to tell Maryam her life story in an attempt to depict herself as a wronged woman, lonely but desired by thousands of men – from the Khan Cordoba to London and New York, where she had arrived on a cargo boat with one of its Spanish crew. The Spaniard's languishing eyes made her believe that he had been waiting for her for a thousand years; the way he wept at her door and bent over her feet to kiss them awoke her wild dreams of wandering along the Atlantic shore, of living with a man who could recover the taste of her first days with Khalil. She acknowledged that she had loved Khalil and cried for him during the nights when she was deprived of Zahra.

Later, when she began to send letters to her daughter, she realized she had squandered her dream of a warm home to spend her old age in, surrounded by the two clamorous grandchildren who loved her, who didn't cry when she came near; she would pet them and wipe their noses and they would look at her in wonder. When she came to my grandfather's house, she opened her bags and distributed presents like any grandmother returning from a trip. She needed to take out a velvety photograph album and point to pictures of her grandsons' mother as a baby, so they would know that she was their grandmother and not some woman passing through their lives. They exchanged long glances with Zahra and after a short time rushed towards Wasal with a recklessness which delighted her. She became a horse they rode and a cat who miaowed and licked their feet. She sat them beside her at the table and taught them how to hold a knife and fork in a more elegant way and to eat sedately after the English fashion. Her insistence that they wear ties, and their swift acceptance of the 'horse collar' as they called it, provoked astonishment in Maryam, who was jealous of Wasal's ability to make her grandsons sing English songs along with her like her backing vocalists. She felt the gravity of her understanding with Zahra about rescuing the children from this hell, and ensuring a future for them away from the smell of death which rained down ceaselessly over the city, and which would only stop once the city had been drowned.

Zahra was desperate. She surrendered to dreams that seduced her with a different type of recklessness. They woke the desire to arrange her life anew, away from Bakr and his ambitions. She had also believed in them once, on the day she lay next to him on their bed after making feverish love which had taken her breath away. He whispered confidently about the Islamic state which was on its way, where everything would be washed clean, radiant like crystal. Dreams appeared to them both, so close that the smell of them lingered on their fingers, as they immersed themselves in a sublimity of touching and desiring which they hoped would never end.

Because of her memories and her dreams, Zahra endured being taken to the Mukhabarat in handcuffs by Bakr's side more than twenty times, and coped with the officials' insults when they described her as an unfaithful, whorish wife. Later, she bore the torture of being hit with a four-ply cable until her back split open, secure in not knowing of Bakr's new hideouts, nor the colour of his pillows and sheets; she no longer worried about these much after witnessing the cruelty and rage of the Mukhabarat at Bakr's escape from ambushes they had set for him, like a wounded bird who had the measure of their traps. Zahra realized that quietly drinking coffee with him in the mornings was a dream that had come to an end for the time being. She explained to Maryam how much she needed Wasal, who could ensure a future for her children. Hope returned to her when one of Bakr's associates handed her a hastily written letter: *I'm abroad. I miss you and the children . . .* She hugged the letter to herself and basked in the comfort it provided. Bakr's arguments with the leadership had reached an impasse, and he accused everyone of abandoning Hama to pursue a holy jihad on their own. In his words she felt the unexpressed regret that oppressed him – until he remembered his position in London as a skilful political speaker, worldly-wise, endowed with the sworn allegiance of thousands of young men.

Zahra laughed as if receiving a gift from God on her final visit to the Mukhabarat. She didn't curse them and they didn't torture her; they made do with looking at her with contempt, and she sat calmly at the investigator's desk as he informed her that she was subject to a travel ban. She nodded and knew from his ease that he was triumphant, no doubt aware that the battle was nearing its end. She had to reassess her daily life as a married woman whose husband had fled from certain death. Maryam marked the occasion of Bakr's letter by bursting into noisy tears in front of a photograph of Hossam, who was drowning in the labyrinth of a desert prison. He had been led there with thousands of his comrades to be crammed into old, damp prison cells in which no one could make out the partitions, nor even the succession of night and day.

The spacious house grew cramped. I said to myself that Bakr had abandoned me, despite his urging me to go to Beirut and join my parents. My father no longer listened to the news of me which my mother would relate to him after he returned in the morning from hunting. He would ignore her as if she were a stranger, lie down in bed, and fall into a deep sleep devoid of hope. When he woke up, he dressed hastily and went out to sit in the bar which he almost never left, recalling his misspent youth when he used to laugh like a bull and compete with his companions in gulping down arrack after accompanying Abdel Hamid Sarraj on his nightly errands.

I was scared when I was in the streets and let my feet drag over the asphalt with the diffidence of the defeated. I never used to think that misfortune had this kind of taste. I no longer recognized places; I was like somebody lost who needed hatred in order to regain a little of her balance, to feel that her life was not just water, spilled on to a pavement and disappearing into steam. Marwa made me feel that I was a stranger, that I was surrendering to a fate I couldn't grasp, blowing away like a feather which hadn't found a wing to be part of. Her glances turned me into a plank of wood drowning in a tumultuous sea. I didn't dare look at her chains. She didn't encourage us to think of smashing them as she tortured us with her silence; she ate from Wasal's hand and wiped the dust from her butterflies. She ignored Radwan's pleas to sing along with him as before; he believed singing would save her and our house from the rot we had begun to feel in our mouths. Radwan prayed for the days of Safaa and my grandfather, who never used to leave the house without first reassuring himself of Radwan's welfare. Now no one cared for him; Maryam no longer paid attention to his clothes and they became soiled, and he appeared more like a tramp than the servant who had once kept clean and perfumed in order to defend his masters all the more fiercely. I saw him sitting by the pool, and his blind eyes moved restlessly as he followed the twittering of the sparrows flying across the sky. He didn't stand up, as he usually did every year, to announce the early arrival of spring – instead he restricted himself to listening to the silence which had settled before long over our gates, which no longer opened and caused a din with their eternal creak. We missed the noise – it had made us feel we weren't living in a tomb.

Maryam asked for Wasal's help in convincing Marwa to allow the removal of the chains which tormented her. Marwa had begun to compose a song, glorifying herself and depicting her tortures; as she wanted it to be heard, she had to relent and once more sing with Radwan, as part of an imaginary troupe, performing for an audience deaf to the tale of her epic battle. Radwan tried to regain a flavour of joy but his first notes seemed cold and sad; they left the impression that his voice was growing old, and what remained of it was insufficient for leading the women of the family. His voice was harsh and he made mistakes when reciting, but Marwa flattered him, praising him and encouraging him to continue with his composition of an epic love poem whose heroine has been chained up by her tribe; they keep her and her dreams under guard so she can't slip through a gap in the tent and corrupt all the other daughters of the tribe.

One day Radwan left the house to look for his friends and found that most of them had shaved off their beards, like roosters whose feathers have been plucked. Most of them now wore suits and ties. The fear in their eyes and their slow movements betrayed that the mosques were no longer safe for their work, their *dhikr* and their improvised *mawalid*. A wrong turn that had resulted in three of them being killed by stray bullets had robbed them of their enjoyment of being blind. Radwan tried to convince them to return to their singing, and he listened patiently to their odes of lamentation for their friends, which opened with a verse in praise of the President and concluded in agonizing grief for the three believers, killed by infidels who had turned Islam into a religion of murder. 'It's all finished,' Radwan said to himself as he left the Umayyad Mosque and passed through the main souk, stopping in front of my grandfather's shops whose locks had lost their shine and rusted. He sat beside the shops, and perhaps he heard Khalil's groans, Omar's laughter, my grandfather's footsteps. He tried to hold back his tears, but the sounds around him were a sign that everything had come to an end.

Radwan returned home along the road which swung around the Citadel, the same route he had taken with my grandfather on their last walk together. He went into his room, carried his boxes out into the courtyard, and began to take out and smash the perfume bottles. Their scent was released throughout the courtyard and mingled with Maryam's wails; she grabbed hold of him and thought that it was the first time she had held a man with such strength. She realized that her desires really had died. Her determination did not have to last long. Radwan left the remaining vials alone. He returned to his room and would not come out even to bid Wasal goodbye. She kept one of the bottles from which emanated a strange smell, similar to that of rare wild roses. Khalil had covered her neck with garlands of them when Mosul first appeared to them on that day now so long ago. Neither of them had been able to forget the aroma of that dawn, of damask roses whose scent remained long after they had withered.

Maryam suddenly displayed a generosity Wasal greatly appreciated; she had been trying to find a small carpet to take back as a souvenir to London, and Maryam gave her Bakr's carpet. Contentment radiated from Zahra's face as, on that last day, she reached an agreement with her mother on many things they hadn't discussed outright. 'Those two have secrets now,' I told Maryam. She would wake up alone, drink her coffee, pray and cook food for men who never came; Radwan would carry it away silently the following day to distribute among poor families. He knew the road to their houses very well and didn't linger to hear their profuse thanks; he would just throw a piece of cooked meat at the door, knock on it, and continue indifferently on his way. He grumbled at this task, but only under his breath.

Maryam missed quarrelling with him. His silence

filled her with a premonition of evil. She saw a fear of death in his shaking hands as they sought out his cup of tea when, at her order, he sat beside the pool. It was part of her attempts to reclaim the traditions and rituals she had boasted of in front of Wasal, when she saw her teaching her grandsons some English phrases. Maryam realized that the children had a cold haughtiness that would cling to them throughout their lives. They belonged more to Wasal than to her, but Maryam was no longer concerned by loss. She sought news of Hossam, which we all needed. Women were now meeting more often in the old city so they could exchange the latest on the arrests spreading among their sons and husbands. The men were sure that they would end their lives within their prison walls. They got used to the smells of the prison and became almost addicted to the bouts of sadistic torture to which they went without protest or discussion, as if they were going to play football.

My dreams were absent once again, so I lured them to me like a flock of doves. I tried to get to sleep early. I sat on my bed like a Buddhist, meditating on the carpet hanging on the wall. I slept like a corpse – as if my body were trying to expel its worries, but on waking I couldn't move. I felt paralysed. Emptiness couldn't save me from my hatred which only grew. My cries held no meaning any more. I watched Marwa – she had received another letter and hidden it from everyone, even Zahra.

Zahra had begun to go out every day to care for her father; a stroke had left Khalil bedridden. He asked for my grandfather whenever he was awake, and in moments of delirium he cursed God and dwelled on descriptions of Wasal, comparing her vulva to a coconut. When he was lucid, he would weep and spit in his Aleppan wife's face, who had left him without food as a punishment for remembering Wasal. She quarrelled increasingly with Zahra, who sought Maryam's permission to move him to our house to die there. She suggested installing him in Radwan's room, who was solicitous of his friend. He liked listening to Khalil's life story, especially the part when Wasal stole him away from my grandfather. The memory of Wasal remained like a lump in his throat. He couldn't forget her, or talk about her. Radwan rekindled joy in Khalil, so he related his story more than ten times, every time using the same vocabulary and exactly the same sentences. Maryam didn't care and was silent. She remembered that Khalil was not that old that he might be expecting to die.

Marwa's determination and Zahra's support ensured Maryam's willingness to attempt a reconciliation with Marwa. She began to emerge from her silence, while still in chains, in accordance with Bakr's instructions and our respect for his authority – as we rotted away. We didn't know the secret of the almost daily visits of the death squad soldiers who would cast a cursory glance over our

228

things, stay in Marwa's room for a few moments, and then leave. After their visits she seemed glad, as if she had just said goodbye to some dear friends. She began to drink coffee with Maryam, and was happy to peel an onion or chop garlic when helping her make stuffed aubergines in honour of Khalil's presence (he loved them so much that he once prepared sixteen different types for his wife, who didn't share this love, especially when he didn't apologize for the rancid smells filling the house).

Radwan cried when Khalil was carried in on a stretcher. He perfumed his friend's body with a strong-smelling scent and shared his room gladly, eager to break his loneliness. Zahra's solicitude reminded him of Safaa who, in her letters, still seemed to be fond of him to the point of infatuation. His replies were more detached and contained numerous complaints that we were neglecting him. He promised to compose a book for her whose lines of verse would be arranged as if they were pearls, and praised her husband, Abdullah, who was travelling increasingly often to Afghanistan and America on missions described by Safaa as *top secret*. She was proud of him, his appearances with Prince Shehab El Din at his councils, their confidential conversations, the approving glances – they described him as a mujahid who upheld Islam by expelling the unbelieving Soviets and smashing their tyranny of iron and fire over Muslims. Safaa wrote that the homes of other princes were thrown open to Abdullah and his presence became a cause of much boasting; he would drop hints about the generous contributions bestowed by their peers exploiting their feverish rivalry to buy Paradise; he was an exceptional ambassador who decided all kinds of matters.

Abdullah did not neglect his friendship with Bakr, who had come limping to him in London. Abdullah spent three nights with him during which they never left the hotel room, quietly reviewing everything that had happened. Abdullah tried to convince Bakr to come to Afghanistan with him, but Bakr was still incapable of forgetting the image of his brothers blown to pieces. They had vanished into the air as their blood rained down like coal dust over his beloved city. Bakr couldn't look into Abdullah's calm eyes as his friend tried to suck out Bakr's rancour at his fellow leaders for deferring the announcement of the civil militia, which Bakr believed would have been sufficient to destroy the death squad's authority and control, and thereby decide the conflict.

On the second night, Abdullah let Bakr rave about his belief that they could no longer organize the thousands of young male volunteers who believed with absolute certainty in the Islamic state, adding sorrowfully that they were now mere playthings in the hands of neighbouring heads of state, to be haggled over, bought and sold. Abdullah said nothing and Bakr was surprised at his politician's cheerfulness. On the third day, Bakr came down with a fever and a doctor was hastily summoned; he ordered complete rest.

Abdullah was reassured as he sat in an aeroplane heading to Washington. He looked out of the window over the ocean and saw shadows descending; he leaned back and thought about the old dream that had seduced him when he and Bakr used to wander through countries looking for the carpet of the prince's dreams. He had to convince the Americans of the necessity of establishing a unified Islamic army in order to liberate all the Arabic states currently under Communist rule, and expel the Soviets from Afghanistan.

He didn't sleep, but closed his eyes and brought to mind an image of Safaa – who had become a powerful female presence in his life, after his first wife, Zeina, had become absorbed in her children, Nabataean-poetry competitions and hunting, now with her uncles, now with the princesses. She left her children with Safaa who looked after them and watched over them, so that they began to call her 'Mama'. She found the word pleasant, then placed her hand on her swollen stomach and remembered her craving for dates. She took the children to the market and joked with them, without a care.

But the happiness in Safaa's grasp was incomplete. She would sit for hours as she thought about our fate, which had entered an endless, shadowy tunnel. She missed Radwan and gossiping with

Marwa, she told Abdullah over the phone when he reached Washington. He reassured her about Bakr and serenaded her with a graphic description of his desire for her.

Abdullah felt a strange energy even though he hadn't slept even for a moment on the flight. Hot water and strong coffee restored his clarity of mind, and he sat down to wait for the meetings. Six hours later, there was a knock at the door of the modest hotel room in which he had been ordered to stay and a man in his fifties entered. He spoke Arabic fluently, and introduced himself as a representative of the Agency; he enquired briefly after Abdullah's health, and asked him to relax until the evening. He left and Abdullah fell into a deep sleep. He thought all these precautions very strange. He realized that his past interested them, judging from the CIA officer's questions about the extent of his former relationships with Russian officials and his comrades in Aden. That evening, he quietly left the hotel and gave an address to the taxi driver. In the back of the cab, he was struck with sudden boredom. He loosened his tie and felt the necessity of returning to Riyadh. He was confirmed in his suspicions when he sat down at the meeting table and saw in front of him Philip Anderson; he had the face of a professional killer, cold-eyed, revealing little emotion.

Anderson proposed to include Abdullah in a spy ring, and granted him the prerogative of choosing the places where he wanted to work – anywhere from Moscow to Riyadh. He brought out a dossier of 180 pages and allowed Abdullah to examine it, whereupon he found his entire life story before him. Anderson was not pleased by Abdullah's sardonic tone when he laughed and suggested that Anderson sell him the dossier to help him in writing his memoirs. Threatening to return to Riyadh immediately and seek out other partners, Abdullah got up angrily and curtly informed Anderson that he was a politician not a mercenary, and one convinced of the necessity of killing unbelievers and driving them out of Afghanistan. He mocked the American's depth of analysis; from the way Anderson spoke about those matters, they might as well have been ordering a quick breakfast in a diner. Abdullah took his leave abruptly, without asking permission. Anderson watched him from the window of the apartment as Abdullah put his hands in his pockets, whistling like any carefree man, and looking in shop windows.

Abdullah waited in a deserted restaurant for his former student Saleh, whom he had mentored in the Communist Party. He had nominated him for several successive posts, until Saleh had become an important man in his own right and tried to convince the Americans to increase the level of their diplomatic representation in Aden. Once the two were sitting together, Abdullah quietly asked, 'Why have you betrayed me?' He pushed away Saleh's glass of whisky and soda, and asked for a portion of chicken and a plate of Russian salad.

Saleh cleared his throat awkwardly and then launched into a confused tale of dispute within the Party. Abdullah ate calmly and thought about what a good student Saleh had been, as he was drowned in a torrent of the other's words. Abdullah's silence was unbroken until Saleh surprised him with an invitation from his old comrades to return to Yemen. He took out a letter signed by the head of the Yemeni Mukhabarat, who had shared his room in Moscow for four years. He took hold of the letter and calmly tore it up; then he rose to his feet and spat in Saleh's face. Abdullah left swiftly, leaving his old pupil in utter disbelief at the transformation of the teacher who had taught him the art of diplomacy, and how to smile to the enemy's face while searching his eyes for his weakness.

Saleh wiped the spittle away and finished drinking his whisky, as if what had just happened was an old folk tradition of farewell in some distant country. He regretted telling Aden of their meeting, blamed himself, and remembered the sweetest moments of his life, when Abdullah spoke to him for the first time at one of the Communist Party meetings. Immediately, he could see his talents as a statesman who had perfected demagoguery and a certain economy with the truth. Saleh came out of the restaurant feeling depressed. He left his car behind and walked absently along the crowded streets, recalling discussions which used to carry on till morning. His teacher's contempt pained him. He remembered when Abdullah sent him to study law at the University of Damascus, bearing enthusiastic letters of recommendation to Syrian officials. Saleh played backgammon with them and taught them the basics of chewing *gat*. He joined the staff of the Ministry of Foreign Affairs, demonstrating to all his talents. When he and Abdullah were later walking alone in the streets of Aden, they would recall their nights in Damascus, when Abdullah would arrive as a surprise guest for a day or two, and they would escape like two impish young men into the alleys of Bab Al Tuma, taking note of the Levantines' *politesse* in evading difficult questions. Saleh felt choked up. He resolved the matter by delivering a long report in which he advised Abdullah's assassination, because he had sold Communist Party secrets to the Americans in exchange for a steady supply of arms to the Arab fighters in Afghanistan so they could overthrow the Soviet-backed government.

When Abdullah returned to his hotel late that evening, he found Philip Anderson waiting for him. They embarked on a deep mutual understanding which turned to friendship; this would later cost Anderson all his ambitions for advancement through the upper echelons of the CIA. The pair stayed up till morning, outlining the necessities for supporting the mujahideen. Anderson understood the need for military intelligence and hardware. Abdullah spent four days in Washington to ensure that Philip recognized his dedication.

He respected Anderson for his precision, his ideas, his elegance, his wide-ranging knowledge, and his passion for antiquities.

Abdullah was not surprised when he found Safaa waiting for him at the airport with her driver and his children, who noisily asked him for presents. He took her hand in the car and desire coursed through their blood. From his pulse, she felt that everything was fine. That night, Safaa didn't take long to convince him to let her travel to Aleppo to give birth to her baby there.

We had needed Safaa so much. She was as welcome as a cool breeze in the long, scorching heat; she was laughing, warm, engaging as she swapped reminiscences with us. Radwan observed everything from the threshold of his room, waiting for a question from her which wasn't long in coming. She saw the sad smile of an embalmed man, barely recognizable. When she saw Khalil lying on the hastily prepared bed, it seemed to her surreal – our house had become a nursing home and the dead left it in coffins. She didn't need long to understand everything. She lost hope that the situation might be less grave than it first appeared when she saw Marwa celebrating her chains, waiting for her butterflies to rise up from their torpor and liberate her, as she said sarcastically when showing off her drawings full of glowing colours. We all shared Safaa after she felt our isolation from each other. She drank tea with Khalil and Radwan in their room; we heard laughter and the sound of Radwan singing, which we hadn't heard for some time. He regained his joy; the fool returned, who loved playing, making perfumes and composing odes in a heroic attempt to leave something behind which might immortalize him – after being emasculated by life in a house of women whom he led on their few, repetitive walks. They were ladies, and he was sometimes a servant, sometimes a family member. Safaa sensed his regret at having wasted his life with us, but despite repeatedly gathering his possessions in a bundle and leaving without even saying goodbye, he had always returned sheepishly after a day or two.

It is difficult to be alone – for solitude to be a never-ending fate marking you like a tattoo. With Zahra's care and Safaa's presence, Radwan was made very happy and he returned shyly to sharing our meals, filled with hope for a proper old age. Safaa didn't succeed in getting Marwa to sit with us, however, and Maryam's heartfelt tears as she implored Marwa to forgive our cruelty were of no use. Marwa and I had exchanged our roles in hatred, which added a piquancy to her glances at me and Maryam, who now seemed like my grandmother. She lost the gleam of a woman who hadn't celebrated her fiftieth birthday yet, and had never blown out a candle in her life. Her bottom grew fatter and her anxiety ended; she was relaxed after bouts of nerves which had almost led to madness, when she used to go out into the courtyard at night and doze on the large cane chair. She hated her bed; it distressed her with dreams that kept her awake. The Samarkandi's son returned as a distant memory, with his quiet smile and his scent. His image mixed with those of other men; I thought Radwan was among them – Radwan standing in front of the door to his room at night listening to the city's sounds and smiling; or, on one occasion, undressing to perform his ritual ablutions and exposing his sexual parts which Maryam saw as they dangled and proclaimed his inactive virility. She was furious – she couldn't move, or he would discover her presence. She was overcome with confusion as for the only time in her life she watched a man wash his body. He celebrated his body with his fingers and smiled.

It was a critical year, in which we saw Maryam pray for God's forgiveness as she begged for the death of her desires. She grew dizzy when she wondered, for a moment, why she hadn't married and immersed herself in pleasure – but at a glance from us she soon regained her senses and thanked God she had never tasted that murderous need for men which transformed girls from good families into shameless whores. Her conversations were tedious for Safaa, but Safaa bore them out of love and respect for an older sister who had begun to behave like a mother to all the family. Like a grandmother, Maryam destroyed her own dreams; she began to resemble a snail with its calm, submissive slide.

Safaa spent a night in my room, and her affection made me very happy. My equilibrium was restored; we spoke like friends and I didn't object when she opened my wardrobe, reproached me for neglecting my body and tossed aside my coarse clothes which looked like they belonged to Maryam. Out of her bag she took two glass bottles of perfume which I kept but didn't use for a long time. I asked her about Abdullah and she replied tersely. She had returned to me, and I gradually came to comprehend my anxiety, and the fear of being arrested which had clung to me for weeks but now no longer – as if I no longer cared after the news of how thousands of our young men had been tortured, suffering broken limbs and skulls, death, exile to unknown destinations. I had an equal chance of death or life. Safaa possessed a strange power; I wasn't aware how much it helped me to master myself and my anxiety, and my misgivings disappeared.

My hatred only increased for the death squad soldiers, vain as painted peacocks. One day I saw a large military lorry crossing Baron Street with six bodies of our mujahideen on display. A soldier smiled and pointed to the lifeless eyes. Behind them, a Soviet-made armoured vehicle dragged a corpse bound with steel cables; it was being torn up by the rough asphalt, while the driver joked with his friend, relaxed and unafraid of any sudden gunfire. They were assured of their victory and our defeat. Their movements through the city grew more confident, more light-hearted, as they felt that they had been saved from the death that had been looming over them, making them afraid that bullets and shrouds would pour down along with the rain.

Marwa grew quiet; she returned to her silence, then closed her door and her window after receiving the most recent letter. She didn't open the door and made do with a few dates and a pitcher of water. On the third day Nadhir came, leaning on a crutch and limping a little, and he brought with him a sheikh, two witnesses and three soldiers. Marwa opened the door to her room and hastily adorned herself like a bride. The two exchanged smiles as one of the soldiers sawed through her chains, and they all sat together in the courtyard where the sheikh began to prepare the marriage ceremony. Maryam hit her head with a shoe, wailed, and then threw herself at Nadhir's feet, pleading with him not to open up a river of blood which would drown us all. Safaa took Maryam by the hand and led her back to her room, trying to understand what had happened. Nadhir took out of his pocket thirteen love letters Marwa had sent him, and his replies in the same vein. He was kind as he tried to explain their mutual desire to marry despite coming from different sects. I couldn't bear it; I wished I had a pistol or a rifle to take my revenge on a smiling Marwa, who didn't object when Nadhir reached out a hand to her hijab and removed it. She shook out her long hair like a

240

gypsy and released the smell of sweet perfume. The marriage was quickly concluded and one of the soldiers carried away her small bag. Marwa waved to us as she went out of the door, dawdling like a bride and without properly bidding goodbye to any of us in the midst of our bewilderment. Zahra distanced herself from it; she didn't try to explain what had happened. She gathered up the chains still attached to the bed and put them in Marwa's emptied wardrobe, its doors hanging open. Marwa had taken a picture of my grandfather, her small carpet and a few clothes with her, and left everything else in a pile on the bed as witness to her permanent escape from our life.

Maryam rushed outside like a madwoman, and I followed her. Radwan couldn't keep up with us; Maryam's quick footsteps frightened me. We went to Selim's house and found him sitting in his inner room, completely bare of furniture except for a rug and a few pillows; incense burners were ranged around him and green fabric hung from the speckled walls. A dozen copies of the Quran in various sizes were stacked on the low table. The place seemed neglected. Maryam didn't reply to his wife's welcome; Um Jalal seemed demented to me, nodding and praying to God to keep everyone safe while her children sat around looking like vagrants, dividing up brown bread and bowls of soup and wearing robes made from some coarse material. It was as if I didn't know them; Uncle Selim's house had changed so much. Maryam took hold of his shirt and shook him, weeping and pleading with him to do something to protect his public standing. He shrugged his shoulders as if he was high on drugs and hadn't heard what she'd said; or as if, faced with a barrage of stones from children attacking him and blocking his way, he was content to pray and place his hands on his head, escaping even from self-defence.

Maryam wept and related Marwa's abduction, calling her a prostitute who should be slaughtered, and a traitor who had gone over to the other sect. I didn't recognize Maryam when she was angry. Selim listened to this leaden speech, so distant from his own vocabulary. He turned away and began to read again from the Quran but she snatched it away from him and flung it against the wall, screaming at him to get up and return to the world to see what had happened in it. The blood froze in my veins; Selim wept and gathered up the scattered pages, kissing them and calling Maryam an infidel and a madwoman. His gaze scared me when he looked at us like fallen women and then left us to rush to the nearby mosque. He sat beside the head of the *wali* who had been buried in the courtyard, bemoaning his fate and grieving that Maryam had been overwhelmed by the material world; he was bewildered by the idiocy of forsaking the Quran like any atheist who had abandoned Paradise for the absurdities of this world.

Maryam sought refuge in God and calmed down a little as she walked in the street. She leaned on me and we sat with Sheikh Daghstani who listened to her, nodded, and promised to visit us; we needed visits from strangers so we could complain to them of our weakness and reaffirm our hatred for the other sect to which Marwa now belonged, our virtue turned to delusion in the wake of her departure.

For days I thought that what had happened must have been a nightmare or a prank, were it not for the evidence of Marwa's empty room and her abandoned clothes, which Maryam distributed among the poor as if Marwa had died. There was no possibility that it wasn't as true as the evening which descended heavily. Maryam observed everyone's silence and indifference; she took the few photographs of Marwa out of the family albums and burned them. She looked at me unhappily out of the corner of her eye. Safaa salvaged what remained of the pictures before I could be fully satisfied at their transformation into ashes, which floated on top of the water in the pool for a few minutes before disappearing.

Everything began to look the same to Maryam. Night was like day, hunger like plenty, black like white. She surrendered to a fate she had prepared for herself in silence and without consulting anyone. She learned to play deaf skilfully when she heard a conversation she didn't like. Marwa's marriage turned her existence upside down, as it made her think of certain things again, especially after Omar arrived on a visit and we heard the laughter we hadn't heard for some time. She told him all the details; he patted her hand and said something which confused us: he mocked our doubts, and I learned from this that he had already visited Marwa in the home – an officer's house on the outskirts of Damascus – she shared with Nadhir. He got to know her husband, and they became friends. Maryam knew that she had now become totally isolated. Her dreams came to a virtual end and she had nothing left but to chase the wasps away from the jam which no one ate any more. She stacked the jars in the larder so we could give them to passers-by.

The first days of Marwa's absence were very hard. Zahra wiped pus away from her father's sores and helped Safaa with her preparations for the birth. I went to see Uncle Khalil and expressed my sympathy for his pain. My concern for him meant I regained Zahra, the friend I had lost long ago and whom I needed now. Radwan helped me feed Khalil, and I recited the Sura Al Baqara for him. I tried to recite it using *tajwid* and Radwan nodded approvingly, joining in where he had memorized it by heart. We became a duet, mourning a man we loved and refusing to listen to his ravings which interrupted our recitation, as if we were reciting to ourselves and not for his soul. We had decided to wait for it to ascend from his body and flutter away over the city – along with the countless number of souls that had crowded together over the preceding months, until

244

Aleppo turned into a city of wails, curtailed funerals, silent elegies and deep sadness in mothers' eyes as, a few metres away from them, murderers strutted about in their uniforms and boasted.

With my own eyes, I saw Samir Nirabi trying to escape from a night-time ambush by one of the Mukhabarat patrols. He shot at them from his hiding place and used up all his ammunition. There was nothing in front of him but the bakery at Bab Al Nasr, so he threw himself into its large red-hot oven; the few customers vomited in horror at the sight. Madness took possession of the soldiers and they emptied their magazines into his corpse, which was badly charred, amid cries of 'Allahu Akbar' and 'Bismillah' from passers-by. The soldiers circled the area to take futile revenge on the blackened corpse. The baker couldn't believe his eyes when Samir Nirabi rushed into the oven; he had a breakdown and was afflicted by nightmares. He didn't leave his house for a year, after which he returned to his village to look after livestock, and escape the malice of the children who bashed on tin cans, swarming after him like the insects which rush to the watermelon fields and leave scars on the fruit's smooth skin.

I saw Samir's mother walk barefoot through the city, cursing both sects and wailing with bitter tears as, behind her, her sons and daughters raised their fists like they were mourning the air. The soldiers prevented her from touching Samir's remains, so she spat in their faces. I didn't dare approach her; I felt that words were worthless. I remembered Samir Nirabi's lean face when he passed by me in the college corridors, avoiding either looking at me or hinting at our relationship. Hossam was only one year older than him, and had recruited him from one of the secondary schools. They went to the swimming pool together and Samir was transformed from a frivolous young man who followed young foreign girls home from school, serenading them openly and showing off his gold jewellery, to a harsh defender of the Islamic state and its martyrs. His mother would remain openly hostile to our family for the rest of her life. She swore that she would have revenge on us, and on the death squad who banned her from leaving her home. She would open her window every morning to curse everyone tirelessly until the day she died of a sudden heart attack.

We all took prodigious care of Safaa as her due date approached. She regretted having returned to give birth amongst us; she missed her Saudi home comforts, and was worried and afraid for her baby. We needed a joyful event in our house to taste fully of life. The midwife came several times and examined Safaa in her primitive way, and watched over her closely in the final days. She shared the task of bringing in anise and algae with Maryam; I prepared and perfumed the baby clothes for the new arrival, and was delighted by

Safaa's interest in them. Maryam stuck to Safaa like her shadow; she even slept on the floor next to her bed. Maryam needed to worry about someone to this impassioned extent in order to forget about everything that had happened.

No woman had given birth in our house for some time. The clan all gathered along with other women I didn't know, and Zahra ordered me to fetch towels and hot water. When the child's first cry was heard none of us trilled, as if we had forgotten how to do it, but there was joy on everyone's faces. Radwan laughed as he investigated the baby, carried him around and approved the name Amir. We became very attached to Amir and he offered us an escape from the truths drowning the city – the chaos of revenge murders, hatred and cruelty.

Around this time, there was widespread resentment at the murder of a famous doctor whose clinic had been crammed with the poor, and who had been well known for his ardent Marxism and frank hostility to our movement. Then Sheikh Jamil was killed; a sycophant well known for his loyalty to the authorities, which was exploited by his children in order to inherit his sheikhdom and influence, and so pillage the country in partnership with corrupt officials. Most people were afraid of having even a minor political accusation raised against them as it might lead to a spell hiding underground; Sheikh Jamil spent his entire life without anyone even daring to question him. His family made sure he was fully exonerated, so that no similar fate would befall any of its members.

Thanks to the face of the young child whom I began to call 'my prince', I regained both my dreams and my optimism. I wondered how such a being would blossom, how his little face would grow, and his fingers, his eyes, his feet. Safaa stopped trying to get in touch with Abdullah; he was lost on the paths of Afghanistan along with the volunteers he had gathered from various Arab countries. Their asceticism left a considerable impression in the hearts of the Afghans who welcomed them and shared their slices of stale bread. They respected the volunteers' neutrality towards the internal factions who argued over how to divide up the country. Abdullah didn't sleep for nights at a time as he established regiments of volunteers to help Sheikh Nadim Al Salaty, whose respected presence prevented murder between the factions. Abdullah disguised himself in women's clothing to reach a house in a remote suburb of Kabul so he could break bread with his new companions. In that outlying house, Abdullah announced to all the leaders present that the Arab mujahideen would stand on their neutrality; their role was to provide the support needed to expel their enemies, and they would not fire a single shot against any Afghan.

Afghanistan was forgotten until the Soviets entered it, and then the world was reminded of it once again. The Afghans, who wanted nothing from this world other than food for their children, became ensnared in difficulties. They became mercenaries for the warring factions that each wanted control over the marijuana fields they believed were full of money. Abdullah fell in love with the country when he saw its mountains, caves and plains. He considered its terrible silence appropriate for a reassessment of his sense of self and his ideas. After several trips to Washington when he used all his wiles to convince the Americans not to leave Afghanistan to its inevitable fate, Anderson followed him to Pakistan and they spoke like old friends about a new Islam, which wasn't content with five prayers a day but pored over hundreds of texts calling for an Islamic state. On the first day they ate dinner in a local restaurant in Islamabad like tourists looking for traditional curios and Kashmiri silk. They haggled with a market trader and bought things they didn't need. After being assured that Safaa had been delivered safely, Abdullah was as happy as a young child and insisted on celebrating with Anderson by going to the most luxurious restaurant and eating Saudi *kabsa*. They agreed to transport arms through a network of workers whom they didn't name.

Abdullah would be alone for years. He vented his desires for Safaa in love poetry which had a broken metre but also a strange charm in its composition, and which was limited to words which rhymed with 'Safaa'.

When we had to say goodbye to Safaa, we did everything for her and packed her bags with all the baby things; it became a necessity for us, so we could get used to her absence. After she had gone back to Saudi Arabia, the three of us, Zahra, Maryam and I, sat down together and we were silent. Maryam no longer felt a connection to anyone; Zahra was weary, moved automatically and didn't reply to my questions about the secret of her soft feet and youthful face. There was nothing for me to do but return to my room and my dreams so I could draw them as I liked. I drew Abdullah wearing a turban, rifle in hand as he led the large army which would enter Kabul behind him and destroy the Russian forces being swallowed up by the quicksands in the swamps. Their remains turned into skulls which women collected to make necklaces of coloured beads that Afghans hung in their mud houses. For an entire week after Safaa's departure, we ate our breakfast in silence and without enthusiasm. I was back at college; at the end of my walk there, I tried to recall the faces I had seen on the way. Everything had become decrepit: streets, faces, trees; now the obituaries no longer bothered to say 'martyrs' or even 'killed by stray bullets'.

I spent a long time with Khalil and listened to his ravings as he described the taste of Wasal's vagina as 'spicy' at one time and 'like a pineapple' at another. Afterwards he repented and wept to his friend Radwan, who smiled foolishly as he recalled memories of a young man about whom no one knew anything. One night, I heard Radwan speak to him about a mute girl the two of them had once met in the courtyard of the Umayyad Mosque. Radwan had convinced her of his ability to break the knot in her tongue, so she clung to him as he went on his errands; this eventually ended in a civil marriage performed by one of his blind friends, and which Radwan tore up after six months, during which time she had grown passionately devoted to him. She looked for him among the blind men of the city, who didn't understand what she meant by the hand gestures she used to describe him. He told Khalil she was a poor woman who made straw baskets which no one bought; she exchanged them for herbs which would help her have a child, even if it was with Blind Radwan, who escaped from her only to become entangled with a family whose depression he couldn't bear.

It is difficult to be constantly searching for the choices we want. Fate, to the same extent as it opened up secret caves in front of Abdullah, closed its doors in front of Maryam. Omar moved in with us after failing in his search for an elusive refuge – but she wasn't saved even by his long stay. He would circle around the room, then leave wearing a limp suit, sad and devoid of any desire for frivolity or dissipation. He tried to open the family shops again, having lost much of his money in

Beirut. He didn't know how to get involved in any other trade.

At first Beirut had been entirely the right place for Omar's new life, but the chokingly humid climate by the sea didn't suit him. His homesickness never left him, and his friends lost their gay laughter. He eventually decided to return after the Mukhabarat confirmed that they would not harm him. He presented many expensive presents to the wives of officers who proved influential in pardoning the family name. He brought all his possessions, and tried to be involved with us, convincing Maryam that Marwa had committed no crime, and that members of the other sect were not our enemies but people it was possible to live alongside. His repeated visits to Marwa no longer roused anyone's fury, and instead became a bridge with which he returned her to us. It is difficult to imagine yourself pardoning your enemy.

Omar never ceased to surprise us. He never doubted that life was short and did not deserve to be taken so seriously. The previous months had made him careworn, as if he was no longer in control. His beloved horse died and he couldn't find anyone to bury it; he looked sorrowfully at its great skeleton, which was all that remained after the stray dogs had torn at it. He took its skull, cleaned it with alcohol, and dried it out in aniseed. Omar would boast of this new cup in front of guests who were used to his eccentricities. When he opened up the family shops there was a strong smell of mothballs, as he had stuffed large quantities of them in the more expensive carpets, to keep the mice away. They hadn't found anything to gnaw on apart from one small carpet which Bakr had picked up from one of the markets of Izmir and considered a treasure. A rumour was circulated around the market that it had been presented to Sultan Abdel Hamid so he could pray during one of his visits to a famed *shatranj* player. Omar patched it up, but he was certain it would be too difficult to restore it properly. Bakr's deviousness, which had once almost succeeded in getting an inexperienced antiques collector to pay six thousand dollars for it, was gone. Omar burned the carpet without a second thought. Smoke rose from the shop as he sat silently and observed his surroundings. He was overcome with nostalgia for the long-gone mornings spent here, as he drank tea and exchanged news of the latest murders in the narrow-laned quarters whose inhabitants were afforded no protection from their high walls.

Omar went to check on his farm which had been occupied by the death squad. They had ruined everything: they went down to the cellar where expensive wines were stored and drank them down without any regard for their taste; the bedding became filthy, and the smell of fat stank out the kitchen. Omar entered the house, accompanied by a senior officer, and threw them all out. He felt frustrated when he saw what they left behind and walked out again. He lived in seclusion, and didn't respond to his friends' entreaties to bring a bit of the joy to their lives which had faded after so many of them had fled abroad. He couldn't find anywhere better to rest than our house. He sat and relaxed, a man returned to the family who needed him after a long absence. In the mornings he would have coffee and ask if we needed anything. I wouldn't have believed that Omar could concern himself with parsley and cheese and would go to the Souk Al Hal to buy them while they were fresh. Maryam didn't discuss how long he would be staying with us. She waited every day for him to gather his clothes and his things and leave us again to our lonely fate. We endured our relationships with all these males, whose lives began with dreams of the Republican Palace, and ended in homelessness, exile and prison.

Whenever Hossam came to me in dreams, I felt that all was not well with him. He would call for my help and ask me about the chemistry textbook; his face looked like that of a dead fish on a distant shore, stinking as its body disintegrated and vanished. I sat on my bed and drew a palm tree on a beach. My fingers and my coloured pens failed me. All colour faded to a monochrome where nothing held meaning or distinction; it was all featureless, without structure: a face without a past, present, or future. Our loss was manifested in our disconnected conversations, in the neglect of Marwa's butterflies whose cases became covered with dust. 'My only connection to her is her genes,' I told myself. I cleaned the boxes and rearranged the butterflies, carried them to my room and watched them for days in a search for the meaning inherent in them. I paired up the colours, trying to create an order with a meaning specific to me. Radwan wouldn't help me hunt for any more. He was engrossed in Khalil, whose last days were filled with delirium. Omar didn't care about Khalil's final moments and was just waiting for him to die – he hated this disruption to our routine which had turned the house into a staging post for the dead.

We were pleased with Omar and the severity with which he ordered Zahra not to coddle her father, and Maryam not to let things slide. Omar saw that Maryam was exhausted, her existence was tedious, and that she was certain that nothing would go back to how it should be. She was like a woman who has always taken great pride in her possessions, and who then returns from a trip to find that her apartment has been ransacked, that little thugs have crept in through the window and smashed the fragile ornaments she had been so careful of, so that they can hear her bemoan their ignorance that she should be surrounded by objects that reminded others of her status. Omar felt that Maryam's disconnected sentences made her crumbling world into a mirror of events to come. 'She doesn't believe in anything any more,' he thought as he watched her get up suddenly, leaving him to drink his coffee alone as she carried food to Khalil.

By now Khalil was only rarely conscious, and he seemed like a different man, as if he had been sleeping after a long night spent awake. He would look around him in astonishment as if it were the first time he was seeing Radwan's room and the damp bed smelling of sweat. Zahra made a great effort to keep this stench from spreading through the house. She was worried by Omar. She saw disapproval in his eyes; his courteous visits to Khalil when he was conscious were no consolation; nor was the fact that he paid the doctor's bills. Zahra considered the payments as alms to the long-time companion of my grandfather, as charity from a man who wanted the city to talk about his affectionate heart. She asked Maryam for permission to move to a rented house and there look after Khalil like a dutiful daughter until his death. Then, she added, she would reassess her life as the wife of a wanted man, who had no hope of ever again sitting down to eat breakfast with her and their children. Radwan also threatened to leave with his friend.

In order to explain fully, Zahra handed Omar a letter reminding him of their long history of silent, mutual misunderstanding; she had always looked dimly on his lifestyle. She mentioned his quarrels with Bakr, which had eventually caused a near estrangement, and which were only resolved by the stern intervention of their mother. Bakr then was silent to an irritating degree. The way he jealously guarded his secrets, his harshness and his logical thinking made him my grandfather's true heir, in direct contrast to Omar who filled places with noise, idly criticized our banal existence, and went out of his way to appear excessively frivolous. Our daily life had been ordered in a way that amply demonstrated our chastity, so that my uncles heard compliments about us when they exchanged civilities with their acquaintances; our men had only to kiss a sheikh's hands to be granted blessings as he patted their hands like he would a pet cat. There was a hidden conflict between the brothers, in which Omar didn't respect their age difference of ten years.

Now I saw Omar wandering alone in the courtyard, brushed by the breezes of spring, which this year we didn't celebrate with barbecues as we usually had. Maryam used to insist on making it an occasion for a family gathering, tolerant of the younger children as they played with the flowers and roses. She would be set apart from her brothers' wives and her sisters by virtue of being the lady of the house, striving to be a virgin grandmother. They would laugh and wink at each other with each of her ponderous movements and her increasingly grandiose speech. They all loved her in this role which she performed like an actress who had perfected it throughout her life; the audience would applaud every night with the same warmth, but then whisper in the corridors about her advancing age, and about the decline in the numbers of fans flocking backstage to have their picture taken with her.

Omar was recalling Bakr's repeated rebukes and warnings not to interfere with the craftsmen repairing a particular Persian carpet to conceal its flaws from admiring customers; the death squads examined it more than twenty times while looking for Bakr. My grandfather used to call this carpet a rare pearl, and it spent fifty years being carried backwards and forwards between its own special place in the warehouse and the main wall in the shop, on which pictures of our ancestors were also hung. The carpet was there for no purpose other than display: my grandfather refused to sell it. He prominently exhibited a photograph of it where it was laid out in the bedroom of the Iranian Shah Mohammed Reza Pahlavi. That carpet had 'crept' from the Imperial Palace clearly as a result of some conspiracy or subterfuge. My grandfather, and Bakr after him, waited for the Shah or his loving wife to send intermediaries to reclaim it, at a suitably high price. He dreamed of the arduous negotiations that would be miserable for the envoy of the emperor and empress, who would try to recall how their feet had been positioned on it when they were newly married and proud of their glory.

In one of their raids on the warehouse – in search of the weapons an informer had written were buried amongst the best of the rolled-up stock – the soldiers grabbed the carpets roughly and unrolled them on the floor. They trampled their boots all over them and threw down on to them the cigarettes Khalil had rushed to light, like a waiter in their service rather than a man who knew the true value of these gems. Khalil breathed a sigh of relief after they had left, because in the darkness of the cellar they hadn't seen the designs of strutting peacocks, and swans swimming in small pools, surrounded by a delicate, symmetrical decoration of jasmine stems overlapping with strange flowers. My grandfather was convinced that they were wild lavender, and had once tried to persuade an American journalist to publish an article in his magazine. The man had stopped accidentally in front of the shop, as if he were lost, or a tourist who had let his feet carry him wherever they wanted. The journalist understood from my grandfather's words that he was looking at a rare treasure, nodded, and left without caring. A rumour subsequently spread through the souk that an American magazine had attempted to run an article on the carpet, but my grandfather refused to agree to it unless they put a picture of it on the front cover.

Hundreds of images of Bakr passed in front of Omar as he sat in our courtyard daydreaming. He was avoiding Bakr, who was trying to talk to him from London and convince him to join him there. He hadn't forgotten Bakr's rebukes when Omar had signed a document of disassociation from his brother, along with offering up information which helped investigators draw up a more complete portrait of Bakr. This had made disguising him very difficult: for example, Bakr's left hand flexed involuntarily when he was at rest, and he had a very slight limp when he walked quickly. Omar thought, 'Why does he ask us all to be like him?' and did not regret his actions.

As we ate breakfast together the following day, he asked Zahra to consider him a guest and to act as if she were the lady of the house; he swore that if Khalil left, then he would as well. He generously suggested moving him to the room into which my grandfather used to withdraw by himself during Ramadan. He would devote himself to worship as if he were an ascetic sitting in a distant cave with his Lord and forsaking the material world. Back then, Omar would wink and say sarcastically to Maryam that their father was 'waiting for a revelation'.

Maryam understood Zahra's moving words of gratitude. She was keen for Khalil to stay with us but ignored Omar's offer to move Khalil to my grandfather's room, aware that Omar hated it. It was also the room where Bakr used to withdraw with my grandfather when they wanted to review their accounts, or to discuss family affairs without being overheard. I saw that old, jealous gleam in Omar's eyes after he had spent the night alone in the courtyard, his sleep disturbed by pictures of Bakr hunting him and gaining ground. He felt a particular affection for his past, as if understanding for the first time why people needed their memories so much.

That night, my dreams turned into disturbing nightmares. I saw corpses hanging from nails hammered into the sky and laughing as their teeth fell like hailstones on to the heads of naked passers-by, who disappeared inside coffin-like buildings. I woke up terrified and trembling, and I heard noises and mutterings in the courtyard. Radwan was whimpering and I saw Zahra prostrate in Maryam's arms, who was muttering verses from the Quran. Uncle Khalil had died just after the dawn prayer. He had spent his final night raving deliriously, and Radwan knew that the end had come. He turned the pages of the Quran to the Sura Anfal and lost himself in whimpers that woke Zahra, Omar and Maryam, who pronounced the *takbir* and the *bismillah*.

Omar remained calm and insisted on holding Khalil's mourning ceremony in our house, as if apologizing for the humble funeral which was only attended by a few of Khalil's distant relatives. He had been buried soon after the afternoon prayer in a tomb which Zahra heard of in the overcrowded Cemetery of the Righteous, now jammed with the new graves of the dead whose mourners didn't have the time to care for their tombstones.

The days of the mourning ceremony were laden with duty and expense. Omar didn't discuss the details. He allowed Radwan the freedom to go out and roam the city for three days, as he wished to

261

look for his friend's soul and escape the smell which still filled his room. He returned in the evening, exhausted, and his clothes were filthy as if he had been sleeping on the pavement. He sat by the pool and told Maryam that she needed parsley and aubergine, which he would bring from the souk. I thought that he didn't want to be alone; he wouldn't enter his room until all our doors had closed, mine last. The terrifying dream returned to me in new colours; blue and black faces, and eyes which were sometimes red. The dead were walking along Telal Street, eating cake, smiling, and carrying shrouds streaked with bright colours. There were faces of people I knew, both living and dead, and faces of strangers I had seen once, but couldn't remember where or when. I wept bitterly when I saw Amir, Safaa's son; he took me by the hand and led me to his wide tomb, saying mockingly, 'Look how we play when we're dead.'

Depression settled on everyone's faces after the hastily prepared mourning ceremony came to an end. Only the empty chairs remained, along with the yawns of the three servants in formal uniforms whom Omar had brought in from a specialist funeral service, recommended for its propriety.

On the fourth day, Zahra wrote a long letter to her mother to inform her of her father's death. She described his final days movingly, and Wasal cried bitterly for her past and her memories. She considered herself responsible for the misery of his final days but, at the same time, felt that she had regained Zahra for ever. She replied with long letters in which she remembered Khalil charitably, and prayed for mercy on him with carefully chosen phrases from which she tried to hide the coolness of her feelings towards him. She quoted verses from the Quran and snippets of the sira of the Prophet's Companions. She preached to Zahra, who needed someone to wipe her eyes which gleamed with sadness, and to give back to her body the vitality of a woman who had inherited all the talents of giving and receiving pleasure.

Zahra never disclosed her secrets so she seemed, to anyone who didn't know her, like a cold woman who was proficient only in drying figs and looking after embroidered bed sheets. Bakr alone knew the taste of the flames which his beloved Zahra appeared to keep permanently lit. His memory of her remained unextinguished despite the long nights in London, and the days spent hiding in secret houses where he never stayed long. He missed her perfume and the way she lingered over removing her clothes to unveil her firm breasts. Then she would lie down beside him: quiet, deliberate, confident, desiring, passionate. She was like a sinner whose footsteps gradually slipped until, at the same moment as she was entirely immersed in sin, Paradise took shape in front of her in all its tranquillity. Souls hovered in the skies like white, pure birds whose wings had never known the hunter's snares. Bakr had nothing more than memories now as he sat with Wasal, looking at her for hours and waiting for her to blink her white eyelids that resembled the marble of Zahra's face. His wife's future appearance was already present in Wasal's features and gestures.

Both Bakr and Wasal were apprehensive at first of the forced relationship between mother and son-in-law; he still had a lot of unanswered questions about her past – thrilling, vague and morally unacceptable in his view. He was tense during his first visit to her, but surprised by the care she took of him, and even considered her overt generosity to be excessive. Bakr, according to Wasal, was a fundamental part of her picture of the family that would ensure she spent her final days enjoying a feeling of deep contentment. She listened to him and was astonished by his desire to talk, as he abandoned himself to describing his situation, his homesickness, his worries about the coldness of the English and how much he missed Zahra. Wasal concealed nothing, and repentance lent her the ferocity of conviction. She knew that the misgivings roaming through Bakr's head had to be eliminated if she was to enter his house and wander freely with him through the streets and suburbs of London on Sundays, like an old woman spoiling a younger lover. She spoke dispassionately about her husbands, from Esmat Ajqabash to Khalil and John, disregarding the scores of lovers whom she had left longing for another taste of her kiss; she did this whenever she wanted to leave an ineradicable impression on a man, whether she hated or loved him. The worst men, for her, were those who aroused neither rage nor longing; she would turn her back on them with no regret for their vague, insipid image.

They announced a truce with Zahra's blessing, who had begun to behave like an orphan. She was lonely, and weary of the probability that she would remain alone without a man for a long time. Forbidden to travel, she withdrew into her own house and paid the price of Bakr's dreams, which had once been her dreams too. She freed herself from the oppression of her hatred for the other sect, blessed Marwa's marriage and tried to convince Maryam to come and visit her, which was no longer so difficult.

The streets were still unsafe, and murder became the only outlet for the soldiers and the men of our organization, who were stumbling blindly through their latest operations. The leadership had failed to re-establish communications with the warriors equipped to blow themselves up in revenge for companions who had had their faith mocked openly. Mukhabarat officers treated those they arrested like redundant humanity. If one of their prisoners died under torture, because of the beatings or electric shocks, it meant nothing and it would never cause any disciplinary action; but it did invite some irritation over the dilemma posed by the corpse. Delivery of the body to its family seemed pointless to them, so it would instead be thrown hastily into any available hole and dirt piled up on top of it; the decay of a cadaver aroused boredom and disgust. It restored to death its true nature. Sudden absence and the earth's gravity returned the bodies to their point of origin, which was a complete fusion with natural elements. The living became more engrossed in retaining their lives than venerating the dead, in a city which death surrounded with exaggerated respect.

Safaa had been staying with us on another extended visit. But occasional letters from their husbands were no longer enough to enable Safaa and Zahra to relax like two women who were simply taking a short holiday from the monotony of their domestic lives in their old family home. The most recent letter from Abdullah had been short, strange and enigmatic. He asked her to return to their house in Riyadh immediately, but without informing her where he was. Despite the Saudi postage stamp and his seal, she was worried by his addressing her in this manner. She consulted Omar, who wouldn't discuss the matter; he usually avoided mentioning Abdullah altogether.

Nothing remained to Maryam other than the small details of the family's past that she tried to restore with great enthusiasm every now and again, before finally losing her spark and returning once more to her choking isolation and a fate which she felt was close to a tragedy. It was reminiscent of the stories woven around an imprisoned hero and the torture he had to endure before the

266

princess came, fell in love with him and sacrificed herself in order to save him and bring an end to his captivity; for a window to be opened again, so a breeze could blow in and sweep away the heavy shadows, and return lightness and sincere joy to wandering souls. Maryam went back to being the only one to wake up at the dawn call to prayer. She would perform her ritual ablutions and pray, and then return to make breakfast and wake us up. We would rise sluggishly and exchange morning greetings coldly, and we sat at the table like guests at a hotel.

Omar was supposed to take Safaa to Damascus Airport; the two of them hatched a plan to visit Marwa on the way, and took Maryam, Zahra and Zahra's sons with them. Maryam read Sura Yusuf by heart and repeated prayers for travelling, so that God would keep them safe from the patrols which thronged the road to the airport and which were alerted by the family name to delay and search them, and repeat the same questions about their relationship to Bakr, which Omar resolutely denied. He then travelled along the country roads between the villages so he could avoid the obstructions on the main road to Hama, and it provided an opportunity for everyone to contemplate the mountains of Masyaf. They sniffed the clean air and chattered as if they were on holiday. The guide showed off his knowledge, which proved tedious before long, and they arrived late at Marwa's house, and she sobbed and hugged them one after another. As she kept on embracing them, they all sensed her longing for the house which she had left without the customary trills from my aunts – who had once been famous for not even having to use their fingers to create such a long and musical sound.

Like a child, Marwa listened to Maryam's comments as she looked over the small house consisting of two rooms and a living room. It was located in the area designated for death squad soldiers, shaken by the barks of wild dogs in the waste ground nearby. Maryam felt Marwa's homesickness keenly, and decided to ignore the fact that her face wasn't veiled. It caused a lump in Maryam's throat which she could tell only Omar about; he just laughed and didn't pass comment. He drank his coffee and waited for Nadhir, who arrived a little late for this last-minute dinner party. He welcomed his guests but the gathering seemed rather formal, unsuited to his revealing his low spirits or talking about how the siege of Aleppo had killed off in him any further ambitions. How to extricate himself from his position as an officer occupied most of Nadhir's mind. He remembered his enthusiastic beginnings at the army college, followed by the parachute training at which he had excelled. Whenever he looked at the medals on show in the small cupboard, he felt a disillusionment that his companions couldn't understand as they rushed to defend the regime; the holy task of protecting their threatened sect was a frequent topic in their private conversations.

Nadhir's commander reproached him, and reminded him that marrying the sister of one of their chief opponents couldn't be viewed as a minor indiscretion nor a passing whim, but as showing prejudice in the enemy's favour. No one would listen to his description of her innocent face beside her butterflies that afternoon, when her gaze turned towards him and dragged him from the terror that blended with everything, and his worry at the role assigned to him. He hadn't learned to jump from a plane with a parachute in order to besiege cities and murder civilians. Marwa saved him and gave him a feeling of absolution. Her deep desire wiped clean his soul, which was besmirched with hatred. She revived his old dream of living outside the holy sect.

After a while, Nadhir found the voices of the four women and Safaa's laughter disconcerting; he suggested to Omar that they wander around Damascus during the few hours that remained until Safaa had to leave, and they lurked in the coffee houses of the city, leaving the women to their own affairs of indulging freely in nostalgia.

I didn't realize I had been left alone with Radwan until the shadows fell and I remembered that I hadn't eaten any dinner. I got up quickly and went into the kitchen to examine the various dishes Maryam had left us. I tried to summon up some enthusiasm but the feebleness of my body made my movements heavy and unstable. I collapsed on to a chair by the fountain and weariness began to assail my heart until I could feel it like a pall over the whole house. I reflected that it was the first time I had ever been alone amongst all those empty rooms and cold beds. I convinced myself that I would never forgive Marwa, and that Maryam would return to her previous stance. Like a scared mouse, I sat without moving, contemplating the night which descended with a cold, light, refreshing sting. It made me go into my room and watch Marwa's butterflies quietly, as if searching for the truth of my feelings towards her, or trying to describe the constriction which gripped my heart and turned me into a shuffling, heavy lump. I thought for the first time of the weight of things; of our bodies, of our souls which were so dense they lacked any sense of lightness.

I seemed to discover what I was looking for when I saw the butterfly with azure wings dotted with yellow crosses, fixed to the board with a lotus blossom at its head, pleading with me to save it from the gum that had solidified it and prevented it from flying away. I brought my face right up to the butterfly; I almost saw the ghost of a smile on a patient woman's lips. I continued thinking about weight and density: our weight upon the earth when we tread on it with indifferent footsteps; the weight of trees in a forest surrounding us; the weight of the dead when they are liberated from their lightening souls and become precisely determined loads, no more and no less, fixed in the cavities of the earth which swallows them back up while their souls, like butterflies, roam freely. It occurred to me to take out the butterfly and pray so that its soul would return to it. I missed Marwa. But my next thought was, 'I won't forgive her,' muddying my palette once again. I felt nauseous and choked; the hatred was like pus coagulating thick and yellow within us, without any possible release.

I left my room and went towards Radwan's. I walked slowly so I could catch the movements of his hands as they mixed a perfume or groped about for things, but I heard only snoring. I opened the door and saw him in the shadows stretched out on his bed fast asleep. I quietly turned on the light and looked at his skinny body; his head seemed small without its cap, which he insisted on keeping rather than the turban the other blind men wore. His eyes were cavernous and his shadow light, as if he were flying rather than disturbing the earth with his weight. I felt sympathy for him and rebuked myself for the hatred that he found an obstacle to talking to me on my own in the evenings. It occurred to me to wake him up and cry on his shoulder, but the idea of behaving like that with a servant terrified me. I closed the door and went back to my bed, burdened with hatred. I was convinced that it would save me from the absurd compassion that threatened my inner strength, that would turn me into a feather searching for somewhere to settle on a fluid, unbounded earth.

The house became immersed in darkness and quiet; however, this was soon pierced by the sound of shooting very close by. It was at first intermittent, but then turned into a torrent of machine-gun fire, grenade explosions and calls of 'Allahu Akbar': the battle was so close it could have been in the next room. At first I was horrified, but I pulled myself together and went out into the courtyard, unafraid. Radwan was worried, blundering about. I stood still so he wouldn't realize I was also there; I wanted to watch him, not help him. He shouted my name a few times and I didn't reply, but followed him back to my room where, afraid, he patted my bed. I stood in the door and reassured him, 'I'm here.' He relaxed a little and, like an actor in a play, announced what everyone already knew, 'They are fighting.' My silence was a hint, picked up on by Radwan, that I didn't want to talk. He sat on the kitchen step as if he were hiding in a safe place. The screams of 'Allahu Akbar' were pleasing, and I involuntarily muttered a long prayer I remembered from the time when I used to sit next to Hajja Radia in her prayer circle and tremble with deep emotion. At that time, all I wanted was to be close to God, and for Rabia Adawiya to appear in my dreams, a woman made of light slipping into our hearts to grant us reassurance. I muttered another prayer and the fighting intensified.

I was trying to draw as ambulance sirens grew ever closer. I calculated that the fighters were stationed at the corner of our street, and imagined that I would see one of them climbing down to me from the roof. For the first time, the dawn call to prayer was not raised. We were prevented from opening our doors. The firing finally stopped at dawn, and then the soldiers came into our house. They overturned everything furiously and kicked at the doors. Radwan tried to find out what they were looking for, but they cruelly flung him to the ground. I saw him trembling with fear as he replied to their questions and told them that the house's owners were away. For the first time ever, I heard him describe himself as a family servant. He also reminded them that this house was under the jurisdiction of Lieutenant Colonel Nadhir Mansoury. The soldiers exchanged glances, trying to work out what their colleagues might be thinking, and then they left, angry and tense, inflamed, fingers on triggers. I made do with just hating them, without voicing my objections to their accusations as they savagely hurled all our things out into the courtyard. They searched all the houses in the alley, spat in men's faces and made them stand awkwardly for hours at a time – no one dared to move or object. The soldiers' faces expressed a powerful fear they thought they were keeping concealed. It was clear from the search that the reason for targeting these particular men was merely their proximity to that morning's battlefield. Most of the city's residents declared that they had had nothing to do with it, and the death squad withdrew from the area after the afternoon prayer. We breathed out.

I went out of the house and left Radwan trembling with fear. There were smears of blood on the wall of the house next to the water tap. Few people had dared to stop and examine the destruction and traces of the battle. No one noticed the tears which soaked my veil when I saw the local newspaper a soldier from the death squad was distributing free of charge. It had published photographs of twelve swollen faces and of a blackened corpse, beneath a broad headline which described them as murderous criminals, along with a picture of soldiers raising a victory sign. They were dancing around the corpses and the captured weapons, which had been carefully lined up so they could be photographed with their owners. I regretted that I hadn't noticed this particular house before, and that I hadn't helped the young man in the third picture from the right; the marks on his neck looked as if he had been slaughtered hastily with a blunt knife. I used to see him in the alley, and he would quickly lift his gaze towards me as if he wanted to see all the details of my figure, to see my eyes beneath my face covering. I didn't appreciate his audacity. It was only later that I found out that he was afraid and had wanted my help in securing protection. His soft, smooth face and elegant clothing had made me think he was a womanizer.

I didn't sleep that night; I was worried, and tossed and turned on my bed. I had prepared a rich dinner of boiled eggs, meat, pickled cucumbers and lots of white cheese. Radwan wanted only a small portion. I tried to draw out the time he would spend sitting with me at the dinner table in order to banish my desolation. Tedium slunk in, however, and formed a heavy barrier between us. We almost rushed to our separate rooms, where I was content to gaze at the dead flies on the light shade. That game didn't last long, nor did summoning up old pictures from secondary school. It was impossible to escape from the faces of the victims in the newspaper; that young man's face lay siege to me. I gave myself up to a long daydream and constructed it like a feature film. I dared to desire him and tried to drive out the image of him as a murder victim. I brought him to my bed but couldn't complete the scene, as if he wanted only to be dead, abstaining from all the pleasures he had anticipated in life. His image leapt up from my bed, and he was dead, and everything was ruined. It nauseated me to imagine myself lying with a man who had died that morning – no one knew whether his corpse had been buried or was still in one of the hospital mortuaries.

The death of these fighters reproached my conscience as if I was the one who had fought them, because in my mind I had abandoned them, despite my faith that they were clearing the way for the Islamic state we dreamed of. We could almost touch it, just as I touched the cool wall now and pleaded with it to shift just a little so I wouldn't be choked like a mosquito in a hole. I was horrified by the idea that my body needed sex. I blamed Maryam for leaving me alone, despite my keenness for solitude.

I had thought it would be an opportunity for me to gather my thoughts, especially about why the organization had so completely cut me adrift for two whole months. I guessed that this was because of Bakr's orders from London, or fear on the part of the leadership; Bakr disagreed with them over fixing a date for a ceasefire and returning to negotiations with Sheikh Mahmoud Haritany. With his modest clothing and prominent prayer beads he gave all the signs of being a pious man, but he was ultimately a puppet of the authorities who dispatched him to the meetings. He called for a laying-down of arms, and described our organization as perverse, a departure from the teachings of Islam, as it killed the innocent. No one found any way of silencing him other than killing him, leaving his spilled blood to meander between both sides. This cleared the path for Sheikh Jamil Al Nirabi, known for fatwas that exonerated the authorities; he declared their deeds acts of self-defence, which gained him our bitter enmity. His much-vaunted popularity was in fact limited to his disciples, who benefited from his influence.

However, over the years, officers from the Mukhabarat had made numerous additions to Sheikh Jamil's file, particularly after the infiltrators in his retinue increased: documents and photographs relating to his profligate children who had entered into smuggling partnerships with important officers and traders; a full inventory of the gifts offered to the sheikh by the authorities; a tally of the cost of his great services; a list of the titles conferred on him which described him as a magnificent man, a true believer, which almost elevated him to the level of sanctity. His students spread rumours of his miracles until they were considered facts. Whenever he was asked about them, he would shake his head and his tears would flow – they were divine messages which proscribed his footsteps and sanctified the foam sputtering from his mouth as he stood up and spoke in all the mosques which claimed him. He considered himself the next *wali*. He hid the details of his relationships with Mukhabarat officers, who made him understand, in their own special way, that his file had reached six hundred pages and could be published at any moment; he had no alternative but to bow ever lower and kiss the ground beneath their feet.

From the first statements distributed by our group declaring the beginning of jihad, Sheikh Jamil realized that the situation had become complicated. This crisis might ruin everything he had built up; there was no opportunity for silence or retreat. He publicly attacked our group's operations, and surrounded himself with bodyguards for fear of being killed. He became a familiar face on state television as he enumerated the President's qualities; he praised the President's faith and made an effort to maintain respect for him among the populace. When the President chose him to negotiate with the group to end the dispute, Sheikh Jamil tried to ingratiate himself with the opposition early on in the session by speaking elaborately about the Treaty of Hudaybiyya. He hadn't expected the file that was placed in front of him: all his words and speeches were recorded there, together with the fatwas he had made which were incompatible with Islam, and a comment describing him as a traitor to the religion.

Not one of those gathered in that house where Sheikh Jamil had been led, blindfolded and unprotesting, ever forgot that candid conversation which had a whiff of conspiracy and politics rather more than a respect for dogma. Sheikh Jamil placed the authorities' demands on the table in front of Bakr's comrades who read them carefully. It didn't take them long to list their reasons for the need for negotiation, hinting at a lack of trust in the authorities. Sheikh Jamil tried to prolong the discussion, which was like any other between rival gangs, and got lost in interpretations of Quranic verses and hadith and esoteric explanations of historical events, quoting extensively from the days of the Rashidun Caliphs to Mu'awiya. Sheikh Jamil spent three days among papers and discussions. He tried to be silent as far as possible, in order not to make a mistake in an atmosphere made heady from the smell of blood on both sides' hands. He demonstrated considerable resilience in withstanding insults from both parties.

On the fourth day, the communications officer informed him that the negotiations had come to an end. After darkness fell that night, during a curfew which would continue for months, military vehicles and personnel carriers left the barracks in unusually heavy numbers in order to besiege every single quarter of the city. They raided seventy-six houses, six of which were meeting places for our group's leadership or weapons caches. Battles continued for more than twelve hours, the details remaining uncertain while rumours were spread throughout the morning, and statements were issued in which each side claimed victory in the previous day's battle. The painful losses incurred necessitated an emergency meeting among our group's leadership after three days, and it was focused primarily on revenge.

A few days later, four young men with covered faces went into Sheikh Jamil's house while he was performing his ritual ablutions. One of them took hold of his neck and another sliced it open; they left his body beside the alcove where he would drink his evening coffee before going out to hold council. His children came across it, drenched in its own blood. They were upset by the manner of his death, and remained unsatisfied by the huge funeral held under military protection; they used the funeral's extravagance to demonstrate their strength of influence. They displayed the telegram from the President which promised revenge on the sheikh's killers. At the same time, the leaders of our organization hurled accusations at each other for this murder. They all swore on the Quran that the group had not killed him, and the sheikh's children and followers received a letter from the organization denying responsibility for his murder, although the wording was dry and harsh and contained no decorous formulas of respect.

Sheikh Jamil's oldest son concealed the letter and began to prepare for his inheritance after a long night spent alone in his grandfather's shrine. In the morning, he placed his father's turban beside his bed and recalled the knowledge he had inherited about the new professors in the Sharia College, the sons of the market traders, and his father's partners and friends. He was well aware that asceticism created prominent men, and power created statesmen. He fine-tuned his preparations for extracting the price of his father's blood without delay.

All night, I tried to expel from my mind Sheikh Jamil's image and story. He had transformed himself – from his origins as the son of an ascetic sheikh – into the turbaned man of power who justified the supremacy of the other sect and the injustices heaped on ours. Desolation settled over the courtyard. I sat on the step, watching the plants and the branches of the giant cypress which leaned over the corner of the courtyard next to Radwan's room. I decided to take a cold shower and made myself imagine it was still May. I stood under the shower and closed my eyes, trying to resist the cold which penetrated my pores. I crossed the courtyard wrapped in an old bathrobe I had found lying on a sofa in Maryam's room; I liked its colour, red with bright blue stripes, so I kept it. Like any shameless girl who didn't hide herself from prying eyes, I left the bathroom wearing only that; I slowed for a few moments, a dove with cloth wings, tickled by the breeze and the cold sting of morning.

I lay on my bed and felt my body, starting with my breasts. I let out a soft gasp of surprise at the lightness of my fingers as they moved over my stomach and returned to my nipples, fearing to complete my rebellion. My body relaxed as I felt myself with a soft touch; I closed my eyes and let my fingers wander somewhere which moistened as soon as I reached it. I felt a surge of defiance which I tried to suppress for a short time, but I returned, blissful and squirming, on to the soft cushions. I wasn't aware of the open window, nor of my voice, afraid and faltering at first, then rich and harmonious while images of the dead men

281

whom I had dreamed of passed over me to the sound of limpid, girlish laughter.

I don't know how much time passed until I weakened and wanted to sleep. Nothing else could save me from the reproaches of my conscience which continued to haunt me; even so, I kept touching my body and summoned up lust, a tremor which came gushing, warm and delicious, as if I had discovered some sort of magic which relieved me of my tension, but left me burdened with coldness afterwards. I woke up to the sound of Radwan's footsteps and the afternoon call to prayer. I rushed to make the prayer, with weakness in my knees and pain in my joints. I was exhausted, and guessed that that strange night had enfeebled my body. I hadn't been in the courtyard of the mosque for long before an old woman approached me and asked me to help her get back home. She calmly gave me a code word, then reached out a hand as if she wanted to lean on me. We got into a taxi silently, and arrived on a quiet street in a new quarter of Aleppo where we went into a ground-floor apartment in a building still being decorated. Hajja Souad was sitting, visibly worried, in the middle of the spacious living room. I was the last to arrive. She kissed me quickly and asked me not to remove my hijab. After a few moments, the door opened and Prince Shukry came in. I almost gasped in surprise at finding myself face to face with such an eminent member of our organization, a man known for his tenacity and self-confidence; amongst ourselves, we called him 'the prince of believers'. His sad smile radiated and he watched us quietly, his eyes on me for a long time. He enquired hastily about Marwa and her marriage, and about my uncle Bakr's situation. I murmured something incomprehensible and confused, and then I gathered my strength to speak my opinion: that I considered Marwa to be an apostate, that she was acting against Bakr's interests, and that she was damaging the whole family. He nodded, understanding of my zeal.

The time he spent with us was to be short, and he repeatedly looked at his watch. He began speaking when the girls fell silent after having tried to create an atmosphere of joy; they reported the opinions of the people on the street which emphasized their stand alongside us, and the thousands of prayers for our victory. I was astonished at this optimism so confidently displayed; the girls avoided mentioning that the people blamed us at least partly for the destruction that had settled on the city. I decided to express what was inside me by drawing a true picture of what I had seen. I asked for permission to speak, and waited until after the prince had finished. He opened with the verse we repeated every day: *Make ready against them all you can* . . . He spoke authoritatively and calmly. He told us that negotiations with the authorities would not resume, that victory was near, and that the painful strikes directed at us hadn't deterred the organization. He prayed for our martyrs, praised our members who had been imprisoned and had resisted brutal torture, and asked us to pray for them. He entered a labyrinth of language which clarified nothing other than the establishment of some sort of an educational institute, which I doubted would be of much benefit to us, and he avoided answering our questions; we no longer knew who would answer them or calm our worries. He threatened the government with surprise attacks of vengeance, and with putting on trial every symbol of the regime after the 'great victory', as he called it.

My desire to talk paled when the prince indicated I could now stand up to speak. I got to my feet and looked around at the six girls, and Hajja Souad encouraged me with a slight smile. I asked directly if my enforced leave from the organization during the previous two months was as a result of Bakr's wishes, or, rather, of his being abroad. My uncle's absence had opened the door for his detractors to start rumours that he had opposed the recent murder of a renowned doctor. (This doctor had been accused of surrendering up one of our wounded who had taken refuge in his clinic when there was nowhere else for him to hide; he was being pursued by a patrol of the death squad for shooting at them.) I spoke at length to explain how people were tyrannized by fear, exhausted by waiting for the victory we had promised them. I said that people had begun to hate us, and the city was no longer safe for us.

Furthermore, I enquired about the leadership withholding essential information about a suspected Mukhabarat infiltrator, whose activities allowed successful strikes by government forces on a number of houses in April: an omission which stank of betrayal.

The prince's eyes were fixed on me, revolving angrily in their sockets as if looking for the reason for me to utter such an accusation, unsuited as it was for a small prayer meeting of girls who should think only of implementing accepted teachings, of their faith in the magic of their leaders, and of their absolute trust in them. The prince interrupted me harshly to say that it wasn't any business of mine to disclose the group's secrets. He praised Bakr, described him as a great mujahid, and hinted that his departure had been at the behest of the leadership, which had charged him with tasks abroad. He rather curtly answered my last questions, about my brother Hossam. Then he rose, signalling to us to remain seated. Hajja Souad led him to the door where he once again donned his disguise, which made him look like a porter from one of the souks, with a neat moustache, long black trousers, gold-embroidered shirt, and the *misbaha* of large yellow beads whose clacking could be heard clearly from a distance. He spoke a few words to Hajja Souad and left without turning round as our gazes clung to him. Sighs of pleasure wafted from the girls as they prayed for his safety, and that his enemies might look away from him and from all the companions of the mujahideen.

Hajja Souad ordered us not to leave before an hour had gone by, and suggested that we first make tabbouleh and chips before she allocated our new tasks to us. The laughter of the girls in the kitchen and Hajja Souad's voice oppressed me and reminded me that I hadn't acted like an *emira* at all. I felt that they knew the rebellion I had committed the previous night. I was dizzy, and the only person nearby was Um Ramez, the woman in her sixties who had brought me to the meeting. I saw her engrossed in telling her long beads with closed eyes; she moved with the gestures of a woman assailed by lethargy, trying to blot out her surroundings. I watched her and tried to catch her eye but she continued to mutter her incomprehensible prayers. The sound of girls' voices didn't suggest a covert meeting, but rather the preparations of a group of friends gathering to go to a wedding.

I was alarmed at Layla's snobbery when she was named *emira* in my place. When I told Hajja Souad that withdrawing the title from me in this way without any justification was very frustrating, she took me by the hand and we went into an opulent bedroom. She sat me down on the bed and recounted the organization's history. She also accused me of recklessness, reminding me that I had come to her house without a proper appointment, as if I was out for a stroll. She patted my shoulder, told me that titles had no importance, and reassured me that I would soon get some pamphlets to distribute around the university during exam time. I understood that I should now leave, as she was intransigent in the face of my protests about Prince Shukry's refusal to reassure me about Hossam. All he had said was that Hossam had been transferred to the desert prison, and that the leadership was satisfied and proud of his resilience. Hossam wouldn't divulge the important information he had gleaned from accompanying Bakr in recent months, as he moved from one safe house to another in order to stay alive and run operations. Prince Shukry had enthusiastically asked me to be proud of what we as a family offered to the organization.

I was the last to leave, determined as I was to see the eyes of Um Ramez – I knew that she had asked permission to kill a death squad soldier in revenge for her son whose fingers had been cut off in prison, and whose back had been broken, leaving him paralysed down one side. I couldn't wait any longer; I was already late in leaving that flat, and it was an infringement for which I might be held to account by the organization. I wandered the streets of that neighbourhood while evening gradually fell, and it coloured the sky in a way I had never seen before: over the open ground to the west there was a translucent twilight coloured red and pink with clouds whose persistence revealed an early summer. I said to myself that being able to see such a sight might be a rare opportunity for me. I lifted my veil, and for some minutes I looked at the sky. I thought of Hossam, and how he used to lead me by the hand to our roof and point to the full moon, showing off his skill at calculating the *hijri* calendar which he had been occupied in chronicling since he was a young child. I missed him, and that distant childhood. I reflected that absence gave birth to illusions. An image of my mother appeared to me, with her kind face and her peaceful nature. I wished that my room had this wonderful view of open horizons, with olive and pistachio trees in the distance; the wind carried to me the unmistakable scents they released at the full moon.

There was hardly anyone around. The area was deserted apart from some animal droppings and some late, exhausted builders trying to reach the bus stop. A layer of white dust covered their clothes, bestowing on them the fairytale colours I had seen in my dreams of crowds of people draped in white. I walked behind an old man and felt protective of him, abandoning my wish to walk in these wilds until I reached the horizon, in expectation of the rising moon. Then I was terrified by the scene of a Mukhabarat patrol scanning the faces of the people waiting for the bus. It was very late for me to be so far from home.

It must have been about half past eight when I opened the door to the house and went inside. Radwan rushed towards me and protested at my being so late and leaving him to worry. I reassured him coolly, and heard from him that Omar and Maryam, after their visit to Marwa, had gone on to Beirut; Zahra was staying on in Damascus, and they would all return in two days' time. I sighed angrily and wished I was with them. I flung myself on my bed and fell into the deep sleep I had been begging for for months – a sleep so deep that I didn't hear the rain which fell later that night and soaked the woollen jumpers left on a chair by the fountain, along with the copy of Sayyid Qutb's *Social Justice in Islam* I had been trying to read. Its pages were wet through and it was impossible to salvage. I threw it in the bin, along with all the food Maryam had left for us, which had now spoiled.

Radwan was delighted the following day when I acted like a proper housewife making food for her family. I wanted to cook, and I welcomed his comments; he would ask me to add a little salt or some spices after tasting the *freekeh*, like a connoisseur whose opinion was much sought after. In the two days we had been on our own we had reverted to being friends who had recovered the warmth of their relationship without any reproaches. I thanked him in my heart whenever he called out my name, as it was the only means of feeling a presence within this vacuum I had begun to escape from. In turn, I suggested he use organic compounds when composing a new perfume so it would resemble the smell of old stone after rain. He smiled at the idea but kept silent.

While we were drinking coffee in the evening beside the tub of red damask roses, I asked him to think about joining me in a play I would try to write to welcome the others home. He laughed sarcastically and, in a deep voice and with ponderous sentences, informed me that he no longer expected anything but death. I saw his face colour and he concluded his speech like an actor who is carried away by the power of his own voice and cares neither for the pleasure of the crowd nor for their applause. He gave himself up to cursing the idiots and the unjust city that had turned his dreams into piles of filth that could be purified only by fire; the ash in the rising smoke would swirl around in the atmosphere looking to join up and form the cloud that would one day rain down black on Aleppo, on its pedestrians and buildings, in revenge for the years of his alienation and their deafness.

Radwan spoke about death like an ancient Greek warrior in mourning for his own life, now cruelly reduced and far removed from the adventures and glory of war. I was seized by dread as his voice flowed tunefully, pure and deep. It was as if I didn't know him. None of us knew him; we didn't perceive his pain, or pester him with questions so he would talk about himself. To us, he was a servant. He heard all our whispers, and kept all our secrets. He worried about us, our illnesses, our concerns. He had witnessed my birth and read the sacred verse to me after putting a charm round my baby neck. I wore it until my neck grew too large for it, when my mother stored it away carefully.

Radwan started to tell me about the child he had been sixty years before. He was five when he realized that he was blind and different from the sighted. His family were offended by his blindness, so they ignored him and left him to wander as a vagrant in the streets of Ain Arab, a miserable child. He would sit on the ground by the mosque and listen to the *tajwid* recitation of the Quran which emanated from Sheikh Bihzad's prayer circle, although he didn't dare intrude. When he sat under the large tree in the courtyard of the Amri mosque others tripped over him, not having noticed him there. Silence and estrangement caused him pain; he tried to demonstrate his skill and the flexibility of his young body in front of the other children, and he would leap into the air and somersault, and then land on his feet with a smile. The children clapped and cheered him, but then left him to wander further on his own. He was protected by the night guards, who took pity on him and allowed him to sleep in the door to the souk, and threw him odd bits of watermelon.

On long winter nights Radwan would take refuge in the lonely Khan Al Duwab, where the wife of the owner took pity on him and allowed him to sleep in straw warmed by the breath of the oxen and donkeys chained to the manger. Ain Arab was familiar to him, and he was familiar to it. He would occasionally walk in front of his mother's house and slacken his pace so she would notice him, change his coarse woollen clothes for the only other set he possessed, and then once more leave him to his fate. She was afraid of her husband's anger; he had married her after her divorce from Radwan's father – he had gone off to preach the Day of Resurrection in the villages and Bedouin camps, leaving her only some tattered rags, a mud hut and a decrepit donkey: a dowry for a woman doomed to be torn to pieces by men. They circled her house on cold nights and she didn't know how to protect herself from those who had designs on her and her blind child. She didn't prevent Radwan from leaving to live with his grandfather, which was in fact the condition laid down by the only man who had asked for her hand – as his third wife, so he would have some help with the harvest.

Radwan was choked by the hatred for his blindness he encountered at his grandfather's house. He ran away, and had nowhere to go other than the alleys and the open countryside. On moonlit nights, he dreamed that he was flying over the earth like a sparrowhawk. He hated the nickname of 'Mole', chanted by the children when they tried to hurt him. He knew the smell of each and every stone of Ain Arab, and imagined the faces of its inhabitants: using their voices and smells, he was

292

able to draw conclusions about them and mock them. He didn't surrender to his misery and grew addicted to solitude, despising the idiocy of the peasants. He sang in Kurdish and memorized the lengthy tales and elegies of the Bedouin. He tried to become a professional mourner but was driven out more than once for the sardonic smile which revealed his mockery of the tribesmen.

At one stage, Radwan was struck by the idea that he might be blessed, so he prayed in front of a large gathering for the power to heal the lame. When the woman beside whom he was sitting did not get up after he had muttered his prayers over her and drawn his hand across her forehead, her seven children kicked him out into the street. He abandoned this idea, now convincing himself that abstinence from worldly enjoyment was foolish, and did not tally with his dreams of unending pleasures. In the summer, he slept in an abandoned camp and foraged for food, gathering up the ears of corn that fell from the harvest carts. He struck bargains with the women who betrayed their husbands, after he caught their lovers' voices and the women's entreaties through the walls of their mud huts. In the morning the women would give him eggs, milk, and wheat which he could sell, and he kept the little money he saved in a bag hanging from his neck in readiness for he knew not what.

When a circus came to Ain Arab for a few days, Radwan was fascinated and he pleaded with its owner to try him out, to teach him to juggle and make tigers jump through a ring of fire. The Moroccan circus master liked the idea, tickled by the idea of a blind gymnast. He tried Radwan out more than once, but the elephant almost trampled him. There was also a fire-eater who cursed in German and brought forth flames from his mouth, to the astonishment of the Ain Arab folk, who sat for hours watching him. He tried to teach Radwan how to draw scarves out of his mouth, but when he jammed them in his cheeks he almost choked. After three days, he abandoned the idea.

Radwan went back to the countryside like a hawk unsuited to a cage. He learned to sleep on tree branches, thus avoiding the perverts on the prowl for children to rape. Dreams unfolded which he couldn't explain, and the call to travel pulled at him after he felt that the smells of Ain Arab were choking him. He cried in front of the khan owner's wife so she would order one of the drivers, who he guessed from his calm voice wouldn't simply abandon him in Aleppo, to allow him to bed down on the bags of barley he was transporting. She spoke with all the skill of a lady to the carriage owner and paid him a fee to take Radwan to the city's Umayyad Mosque.

On the way, the owner of the carriage watched Radwan as he smiled and inhaled the scents of the villages and of the river. The driver found Radwan entertaining and didn't weary of his incessant chatter. He thought he might do him a good turn: after hearing him sing for two consecutive hours, the driver took him to the house of Hamid, a record-seller who was looking for new talent so he could form a band. Radwan leaned back in a chair and asked for a cup of water sweetened with sugar. He then sang a Kurdish song he had learned by heart and offered a confusing translation of it for Hamid. The record-seller imagined him in a band that he never managed to create, however. After six months, he was forced to turn Radwan out.

With a smile and without regret, Radwan left – he didn't plead to stay. He didn't like the way Hamid's house smelled, nor the tedium of having to listen to Hamid's daily fights with his shrill wife, who often left Radwan without food. Radwan said to me that he could still remember sitting in that small record shop listening to Zakariya Ahmed, with whom he was infatuated. He had thought that fate had led him to this cramped place so that he could relive the tale of this great musician, who was 'just like him', as he would proudly repeat. Radwan knew many of his lyrics, and was determined that his own voice, husky as it was, would acquire the sweetness of Zakariya's when the song 'Ahl al Hawa' inspired a painful sorrow. Radwan was carrying some of those records inside his bag when Hamid left him in the courtyard of the Umayyad Mosque. He breathed in deeply, yielding to the smells he loved. He felt that he had found his niche at last, and he relaxed for a few days with the blind men who welcomed him in their own sarcastic manner, trying to keep him from participating in their livelihood of reciting *mawalid* to the women who fulfilled their vows every Friday. Radwan liked their plotting and joined up with them. He never felt homesick when he lay down on the rich carpet in the mosque at the end of the evening and fell into a deep sleep beside his few companions who, like him, were all homeless.

After seven years, Radwan was proud of his Aleppan credentials. He now looked for a new place to belong to, and started to make up strange stories about non-existent relatives, claiming kinship with certain ancient families whose names, works and status were well known. The city still boasted of its affiliation to these families; sanctifying them was part of the essential social mores, along with the retention of certain other conventions whose affectations seemed peculiar to Radwan. He kept silent, trying to pierce the web of secrets which the blind men had spent years quietly weaving around their world.

One day he went out of the mosque on his own after his blind companions had left him behind, arguing that he was too young to accompany them. He went to the souk, excited by the new smells and the loud sounds there. He stopped in front of my grandfather's shop; my grandfather sat and observed Radwan, watching as he kissed Hajj Abdel Ghany's hand and asked him to teach him to make the perfumes he found so stimulating. Radwan was haunted by a strange feeling which almost amounted to rapture. He exhibited the originality Hajj Abdel Ghany loved. My grandfather allowed Radwan to sit in front of his shop and sing Zakariya Ahmed songs, and sometimes helped him to distinguish the smells that he then archived in his memory. One day, about two months later, Radwan stumbled while carrying some bottles and this made the Hajj so angry he slapped him. Crying bitterly, Radwan went back to the mosque and didn't leave it for an entire year, only keeping alert for my grandfather whenever he came to pray so he could greet him. He spoke to him openly about his troubles and his life story. He spent a long time describing his dreams, and accepted my grandfather's charity during the festivals: the new suit my grandfather bought him then would become one of their traditions. He liked Radwan's joy and voluble conversation; Radwan eventually convinced my grandfather to add him to his family as a kind of servant, and not to worry about his blindness.

Carrying his small bag, Radwan walked into my grandfather's house, and there became such a necessity it was impossible to dispense with him. He instituted reforms which my grandmother didn't like but agreed to so as not to anger my grandfather. Radwan reassured him and acted as his confidant during rainy nights when he felt lonely and disinclined to knock on anyone's door.

My grandfather found a haven with his servant, who became his friend.

'Maryam was five years old at the time,' Radwan said to me and laughed, then continued to drain the mint tea which I had prepared for him as a bribe so he would finish the story I found so fabulous.

I was afflicted by desolate ideas for a moment; I looked at him as if he were about to get up from his chair, lay down on his bed and die. I was afraid for him and tried to encourage him a few times with a question, or to cajole him into sharing further details, but he now turned a deaf ear. He was drinking his tea in silence, and then he got up and walked to his room without wishing me goodnight. He walked sluggishly and dragged his feet, contrary to my expectation that he would have grown lighter after throwing off the weight of the childhood memories with which he wrestled in order to stay alive. I remembered the reply which he kept repeating when I asked if he missed my grandfather; he told me gravely, 'His smell is still here. I loved this house, and its smell.'

Dawn crept in and I was still there, focused on the empty chair in front of me. I thought that Radwan must be in love with one of my aunts, and I guessed it must be Safaa. He had described her birth and how he looked after her when she was a child. Maryam I regarded as unlikely; I felt that he pitied her, and considered her to be wretched and to have wasted her life on delusions. She was like a silkworm which has patiently woven its cocoon when, choked by the smell of its own body, it tries to carve out a little window for some fresh air and the whole structure caves in. She could only weep among the ruins of eternal prosperity.

The rest of the night passed quietly, and I didn't hear any shooting. I slept like the dead, devoid of the anxiety of the past days, and woke up to the clamour of the returning travellers, whose depression seemed to have been lifted by their holiday. Maryam had missed her things and, on finding them scattered about, set about rearranging them with great care: her few pictures; the clothes which aged her terribly; an antique tambourine left behind by Hajja Radia when she came to our house; her carpet. There were also two small boxes filled with obsolete accessories, as if they belonged to a woman who had fled decades earlier: copper kohl pipes engraved in Persian with the name of a princess famous for the beauty of her dark eyes; a piece of laurel soap particular to Aleppo which Maryam used very sparingly, believing it to be rare; and a circle of beads that had been briefly fashionable in the fifties among the more sophisticated class of women. Maryam still used these beads, as if she didn't want to believe that the joy, warmth and chatter of those gatherings had disappeared.

My aunt told me at great length about my father,

mother and brother Humam in Beirut, and smothered me in reassurance. At first she sounded indulgent even towards Marwa, but in subsequent days all her anger came out: she spoke disparagingly of Marwa's removal of her veil; and of my father's alcoholism, and the fact that he cursed my mother and Bakr and our group, and praised the other sect. He still had many friends who belonged to it; back in the late fifties and the days of the United Arab Republic, they had accompanied him to Alexandria and taught him to fish. 'Like he was angry and didn't want to see us,' Maryam said as she waved her hand, trying to drive away the image of her journey, and burdened with the disgrace of the picture she drew of her sisters and her brothers-in-law.

Tedium soon returned to our house. We seemed to be waiting for a miracle to save us from our monotony and fear, which only escalated again after the violent clashes that took place in Jalloum and reached all the way to Jamiliyya. We all hunched up in the cellar, silent amidst the smell of the lentil soup which Maryam had begun cooking, trying to affect indifference to the events taking place less than two hundred metres away from our house. Then she burst out crying, expressing her annoyance at the curfew, at all the killing, and at the searches that revealed her secrets to strangers.

Her weeping frightened me. And all my anxiety

came back, some time later, when Omar told me about another letter from Bakr asking me to withdraw from the organization, as I was under surveillance. Omar couldn't bear taking on this role of 'man of the house', when it was a house inhabited by cranks who opposed him in everything and didn't respond to life's opportunities. He had reverted to his former scandalous behaviour, but Aleppo no longer cared about this in the midst of the ruins and the mothers wearing mourning for the sons lost to them in prisons and tombs. It is difficult to remain objective when your life is threatened, and I thought for a moment that I had no choice but to walk to the end of the road I had chosen. I had been avoiding college, as it had become a place where I was informed of my tasks for the coming days. They would leave me pamphlets in one of the bins, or a woman would stuff them under my coat when I sat on the bus. She didn't even have time to press my hand in solidarity.

Fear drew me to pleasure and irreverence. All I could think of was how hard it was to be under constant surveillance, when someone counts your breaths and your steps, trying to get inside your mind to review your memories and the pictures you love. I was terrified by the idea that they might be able to spy on my dreams. I went cold when I felt that I was really being watched, and by several men at that. I wandered in their chains, under siege from their gaze. I tried to look into their eyes in defiance, so I wouldn't fall down in a faint in the middle of the street. I focused on the middle-aged milk vendor who had settled at the corner of our road two months earlier. I wasn't duped by his candour or his quiet voice when I approached him to examine his cart, and ended up buying milk which we didn't drink. I began to hate him and looked at him spitefully, hoping he would die. I wrote a report and dispatched it to the leadership of the group in which I cursed him and asked for him to be liquidated. I waited for his death (which seemed to be running behind schedule) and I began to think of him as a man who was running out of time to put his affairs in order for his family. I dumped some of the pamphlets in a narrow, empty alley, ashamed of carrying them. I tore up the rest, threw them in a dustbin and fled after I saw a young man who I felt was tailing me, but I regretted it when I saw him go into his house.

Omar's words about Bakr's letter had robbed me of courage and left me as brittle as blotting paper. I swallowed hard whenever a passer-by looked at me; my dreams died in silence and the city started to resemble a large tomb. I thought of fleeing and living with my mother again, and that trying to reconnect with my father might save me from this maelstrom. I looked for Omar so I could tell him my decision and sat on the steps to his house for hours, in defiance of the neighbours' looks which condemned his immorality. I went to my grandfather's shops and asked the new craftsmen about Omar. I couldn't find him, even though I left word for him at every place he might be. I felt lost without him. He was the only one who could save me. I needed someone who could end my turmoil and return tranquillity to me, so I could stand still and watch the flowers wither at the end of spring, and praise the laziness of a late-blooming rose.

Omar's shamelessness grew increasingly worse with his new friends. They were traders who had suddenly acquired influence in the souk after carefully ensuring a monopoly in smuggling goods from state warehouses; they dealt in household utensils, cigarettes, and so-called 'intermediaries' – aimed at mothers who were pining for their sons in prison and craved to hear any reassuring news. They sold their jewellery and bedroom suites in exchange for a snippet of paper which assured them that their sons were alive. Trade was brisk, and partnerships with death squad and Mukhabarat officers much in demand.

What little hope remained dwindled still further, and the city was left to instinct and hatred. But at the beginning of that summer of 1982, the sounds of tambourines were once more heard, along with voices raised in supplication to God. Everyone climbed on to their roofs to see the lunar eclipse, which granted the people a rare opportunity to shout and drive out the decay which now penetrated each moment. The city re-enacted the rituals which had fallen into disuse because of all the suffering which had stifled them, and because of Aleppo's massive expansion to accommodate hundreds of thousands of migrants from the countryside who came in search of work. Native Aleppans remembered the last time they had gone out of the city, to climb Mount Ansari to pray for the rains, which had been late that year. Since that distant occasion, no one had heard the sound of tambourines or voices pleading for rain and mercy; but now they begged fervently for the withdrawal of the death squad. Most of its soldiers had never witnessed such a display in praise of God and Heaven; nor the tears of the mothers whose deep emotion swelled until they tore at their clothes. The women's wails rose above the sound of the tambourines and the chanting of the singers whose throats were regaining warmth from reciting religious poetry.

Maryam had spent all day enthusiastically adorning herself, and now she went up on to the roof with her tambourine so she could sing, despite her tears which rained down at the cries of 'Allahu Akbar'. The tambourines all around fell into one quick rhythm. The eclipse began; the colours of the moon changed and merged, and the city was covered by a ruddy glow almost orange; it was a magical scene that pulled me for a few moments out of my anxiety and made me believe in the awesome power of nature. These rituals continued until a little after midnight, and a truce was adhered to by both sides out of respect for the crowd, which was so burdened by its loss of the tolerance Aleppo had once been famed for, when its population had been distinguished by the intermingling of all its languages and customs.

Maryam came down from the roof a different woman, still carrying her tambourine, which she kept on banging. Even in the darkness I could see that her face was agitated. She concluded her singing with a lament for my grandfather, the city, her body, our family; she summoned them all up with moving expressions, calling on them to see the devastation which had settled on our house. Zahra was trying to calm Maryam and stop her from going inside in this hysterical state, but she began to dance in the courtyard and, in a loud voice, to curse the era which had made her into a woman to be overlooked. She called on Bakr to come, describing him as her beloved; she called on Selim to wake up from his sleep; she called on Omar to join her in the courtyard, which had missed all of their footsteps. I didn't approach her; I was powerless to help her as she fainted. We put her to bed. I couldn't hold back my tears – I kept thinking about dying. I imagined that my body was extricated from its density, and that the blood in my veins was solidifying and losing its heat. I held Maryam's trembling hand as she seemed to surrender to an uncertain fate. She slowly relaxed; weariness appeared on her face and her body twitched as she fell into a sound sleep.

In the morning, Maryam couldn't get up. Her voice was weak, her eyes sad. She needed all of us; she wanted to forget how she had been possessed the night before, and how she had disgraced herself. She was like a woman bitterly bidding goodbye to her girlhood and who now regretted having kept her body and soul pure. We sat around her for three days, telling her stories; she wasn't cheered by Zahra's and my praise of her voice and lithe body; she turned her face away from us and looked at the wall for hours at a time. She focused her gaze unflinchingly on a single point, as if trying to bore through the wall and see beyond it; it was an indication of her dismissal of us, despite the gratitude we heard in her quiet, affectionate voice.

Some days later, Omar arrived early in the morning, exhausted after a long night out and smelling strongly of alcohol. He didn't seem to care that there were lipstick marks on his shirt. He drank his coffee in a rush, listening to us distractedly, and missing half of what we said. Maryam didn't care that he was there; we had expected his visit would lift her depression. He briefly encouraged me to go to Beirut if I could, but added that I was forbidden to travel abroad. He gave us a considerable sum of money, shared a joke with Radwan, and then left; everything was done at top speed, as if we were a plague he had to stay away from.

★   ★   ★

How cruel we are, when we act carelessly with others' dearest possessions. We leave them to their fate, unheeding of what they mean to someone else. Marwa's butterflies no longer provoked anyone's interest, and I had thrown her boxes in a corner of my room (which had begun to look like a junk warehouse offering shelter to a vagrant each night). Marwa cried bitterly when she saw our neglect of them. She kneeled down to wipe the dust away with the hem of her clothes, calling each butterfly by its pet name, which she still remembered.

I had believed that Marwa had been definitively expelled from our house; in time, we would forget her and turn her out of our memories, trying to ignore the pain she had caused by departing from our sect's traditions, and in the company of an officer, who had once threatened to kill us and shatter our unity. I hadn't taken Maryam, Omar, Safaa and Zahra's visit to her in Damascus very seriously; I didn't believe that she would ever return to her old home, or feel comfortable there with her husband.

She came back without asking permission. One day, she just opened the door with her key, and Nadhir followed her in, carrying her bag. He was shy, but Maryam's warm welcome of them both broke the ice. They stretched out on her bed at night as if they were returning from a short holiday. Marwa said she forgave me, but I couldn't ignore her blue clothes which showed her knees, nor her uncovered and subtly made-up face; this all made her a stranger to me. I didn't understand where she had hidden all that confidence before – her new freedom revealed her as a tolerant and intelligent woman. She pitied our life beneath the veil. Our souls were weighed down and we walked in fear, ponderously. Her graceful footsteps in the courtyard and her laughter reminded us of Safaa. She began to resemble her so much that I thought they might have exchanged dreams, as if they were playing merrily with their destinies.

When Nadhir received news of an assassination attempt on the President, he kissed Marwa on the cheek, and went off quickly, in a state of great tension. Anxiety tore at him as he made his way to Damascus; the old itch on his neck returned, which always heralded danger. It had saved him from a certain death during the October War, when his battalion's position was bombed only a few minutes after he and his troops had withdrawn. He summoned up other memories which he feared had long faded, and which led him to look back on his early life. He thought about his father, Sheikh Abbas, who had taught him the tolerance that had cost him dearly. Sheikh Abbas had relinquished his position to other imams, who expounded on hatred, the necessity of maintaining solidarity within their own sect against all others, and the strict retention of political posts in order to guarantee that authority remained in their hands.

There were lots of whispered rumours about secret debates where Sheikh Abbas argued in defence of tolerance as the only solution to protect the sect and keep it unsullied. He would quote the words and deeds of the great historical imams, displaying his wide knowledge of the Quran and the Hadith, as well as making use of his dignity and popularity; his family's power prevented the other sheikhs from attacking him publicly, despite what they said quietly amongst themselves about his determined inattention to the cruel injustices propounded by the other sects.

Fear didn't push Sheikh Abbas into a bickering match with the others; that had been the aim of one of the sheikhs, in order to diminish his prestige. Instead, Sheikh Abbas sought seclusion in his home which overlooked pine forests and orange groves, and remained there to this day. He was aware that what was coming would be even greater, and he couldn't prevent it if the people were tempted by the fatwas of Sheikh Mudar to kill others merely because of their membership of another sect.

Nadhir tried to recall an image of his father, but it was blurred. The smile which never left him gave his son the strength to quash his worries. Nadhir said to himself, 'The President wasn't harmed at all. As for the President's associate who threw himself on to the bomb and was blown up, his family will receive an appropriate sum and influence as a reward for his devotion.' He arrived at

the government building in the evening and realized from the faces of the guards who greeted him
that something was seriously amiss. He climbed
the steps calmly and sat in the room of the
commander's secretary, turning over the pages of
a calendar in a bored manner for over an hour,
waiting for the summons whose origins he had
tried to trace in his mind several times. The gestures
of the guards, secretaries and officers in the building
communicated a general nervousness.

At exactly eight o'clock, Nadhir entered the
room where four officers he knew well were already
waiting. As he greeted them he noticed they were
acting coolly towards him; they didn't kiss him,
as they usually would have done after a long
absence. The secretary opened the door and
gestured to them to go into an inner office. The
commander of the death squad was waiting for
them quietly, and the traces of exhaustion around
his eyes showed that he hadn't slept well for some
time. It was well known that he was a pleasure-
seeker, so his state wasn't in itself indicative of
anything exceptional, given his frivolous disposition and his utter disregard for the consequences
of his actions. The commander motioned for them
to sit and directed his curt words to the highest-
ranking officer. He explained the details of the
assassination attempt and, without a pause, added
coldly, 'We're carrying out a strike on the desert
prison tonight.' Then he banged the table with his
fist. 'Don't leave a single one of them alive to see

the sun rise.' He handed round the files, labelled *Operation Sleeping Butterfly* in an inappropriately ornate script, to each of the five officers. He bid them an authoritative goodbye, and left his office through a concealed door.

Nadhir felt dizzy at this knee-jerk reaction; this meant the murder of vast numbers of political prisoners, attacking them when they were trapped like dogs in a cage. All as casually as if one were swatting flies. The scene he imagined made him nauseous; his stomach heaved and his knees buckled. He didn't think he could walk. He inhaled the air of the Al Mazza quarter and tightened his grip around the folder with his orders, aware that time was racing away. In less than an hour, the aeroplanes would be on their way to the desert, carrying heavily armed soldiers that might have been simply on a hunting expedition to the plains for wild ducks or gazelles. Nadhir drove to the airport where the head of the operation had preceded him. The commander was a very distant relative of his, and Nadhir greeted him and asked to speak to him alone for a few moments. He informed him that he would not be able to carry out his orders, then he reached for his military insignia and removed them from his uniform. He spread his arms wide, as if accepting the court martial that would sentence him to death for his refusal. He announced his readiness to go to any Israeli position they named to destroy it in a suicide operation.

311

The commander was worried; he knew the implications of this refusal, especially coming as it did after Nadhir's controversial marriage to Marwa. This had been the subject of discussion amongst the top brass, who said that Nadhir had crossed all boundaries and was lacking in loyalty. The commander didn't let him finish his sentence. Nadhir handed over the key to his staff car and walked out, avoiding the troops who were shouting their allegiance to the death squad commander. They raised their fists in the air and climbed into the ten aeroplanes squatting on the runway in the growing twilight. Nadhir turned around and saw them take off in an orderly fashion. He didn't realize that it was his tears that were blurring the narrow road through the cactus fields. He thought for a moment that maybe he had heard the orders wrong, or that the previous night had left him exhausted. He couldn't grasp that this mad fantasy would actually murder prisoners held in an isolated jail. He thought it would be a miracle if anyone left that prison alive.

Nadhir found himself sitting in a taxi with three other passengers, who eyed his uniform warily, and couldn't understand the presence of this officer – alone, silent and distracted – among them; he imposed a silence on them, which was a measure of their fear. The old Mercedes swayed patiently on its way to Aleppo like a sealed coffin borne aloft. Nadhir tried to sleep, but nightmares attacked him; awake, dark thoughts agitated him.

He almost started to mutter to himself like a madman as he tried to imagine what was happening when, checking his watch, he calculated that the aeroplanes had landed next to the prison gate half an hour earlier. An expert in this sort of operation, he guessed that his colleagues had had more than enough time to ensure that their rifles were in order. As in some sort of perverse fairytale, their enemies, at the moment still bound in iron chains to the walls of the prison, would be transformed into live targets on an imaginary shooting range.

The following morning, a hot summer's day, the country woke up to stories which had spread like lightning, already retold thousands of times. I understood why Nadhir stood at the door looking exhausted and broken, asking for Marwa to call him another taxi. He apologized for drinking Maryam's coffee with a shamefaced smile, and he spoke almost incomprehensibly and with great difficulty. He said that he had resigned from the army, and that what had happened that night would never be forgotten for a thousand years. Then he left like a fugitive along with Marwa. In the taxi, she put her hand tenderly on his hair and face and whispered, 'It's all right, darling.' He kissed her palm and took refuge in burning tears, not caring about the astonishment of the driver, who shook their hands. He stopped the car and got out to leave him alone with Marwa, who was almost speechless at seeing him like a small child.

She pulled herself together, wiped away his tears and kissed him on the lips; then she ordered the driver to hurry: they were rushing to someone's bedside to witness the last, warm breath of the dying man before his body turned cold and he left them for ever. Marwa thus freed Nadhir from the need for any further explanation or a response to the sympathetic glances of the driver, who now ascribed this man's tears to the imminent loss of a loved one. He concluded this passenger was like any other person, despite the uniform he wore, which should have indicated that he was just one of those terrorizing the country and revelling in the bloodlust and the fear in people's eyes.

Reports had spread of how the troops had calmly left their planes, gone into the cells of the desert prison, and cold-bloodedly opened fire on the prisoners, whose brains they splattered all over the walls and ceilings. The corpses were piled up in the corridors like rotten oranges thrown carelessly on to a rubbish dump. More than eight hundred prisoners had been killed in less than an hour. Later the bulldozers carried the bodies to a secret location where they were thrown into a pit whose size, shape and smell no one could possibly imagine. The accounts of the few survivors would offer yet another opportunity to examine the extraordinary resilience that humanity can show in the face of the most extreme circumstances.

All over the country, black flags were hung from balconies. Anyone entering Aleppo or Hama in the early evening of the following day might have thought a festival of weeping had begun, and that it must be the preamble to the festival that recalled the martyr Hussein, which had so often inspired artists, scholars and strangers passing through Karbala. Hajja Souad rushed towards me weeping. She hugged me before I could enter the house, and I heard her prayer for Hossam to enter Heaven. Everything I had tried so hard not to believe was embodied in front of me, like a truth which now had to be heard clearly. I couldn't move my tongue; I felt paralysis creeping through my limbs. I shook my head unthinkingly and fled. When I eventually got back to the house I found my mother sitting in the courtyard and crying. She was kissing a picture of Hossam she held in her hands, and she stood up to trill and dance like she had gone mad. Maryam, Zahra, Omar and Radwan all formed a ring around her to prevent her from running out into the street until she fainted, and then they carried her to bed.

Before dawn the next day, we set off in Omar's car for the desert prison. We had been preceded by groups of mothers who came from all over the country to seek out their sons. They didn't want to believe a story they thought must have been invented. Road blocks and armed soldiers prevented the thousands of people who slept outdoors that night from reaching the prison, which was entirely quiet after the corpses had been moved and the building washed down with power hoses. It was as if the soldiers had carried out with precision a job they considered to be no more than routine, and now they were keeping aloof and distant from the inanity of the crowd milling around.

My mother was silent in the car. We remembered, halfway along the desert road, that we hadn't exchanged greetings. We didn't clasp hands like other mothers and daughters when they meet after a long absence; I quietly placed my hand in her open palm and she leaned slightly towards me with a strange coolness. Were it not for her eyes, which had an irresistible strength, I would have thought she was dead. I couldn't say a word. When we got near the prison, the scene was like something from an extraordinarily vivid and life-like film. But the hell of this mass execution was beyond imagining. Women veiled in black were holding up pictures of their missing husbands, brothers and sons, kneeling in rows as if praying to a god they had believed in for a long time; the fear on their faces seemed to have been caused by the loss of His compassionate image. They persisted in their prayers and pleas to see their men, hoping against hope that the story was just a lie told in various forms; as if it were an exercise dumped on the public to train them up in creative writing, or a revival of the traditional Arabic tales which the Caliphs had once enjoyed.

'We need Scheherazade,' I said to myself when my mother bolted from Omar's car as soon as it stopped. She broke through a group of women who looked just like her and rushed towards an armoured car, which belonged to the death squad soldiers who had closed the road, and started hitting it. She cursed the troops, who looked at her dumbfounded from their hiding place inside the car. They were afraid that the crowds would attack them.

Hysteria reigned among the assembled carts, cars and broken-looking people. No one noticed that the children had sand stuck to their snot-covered faces – they had been gathering rocks to build small tombstones and then they threw pebbles at them to knock them down, trying to break their intense boredom. Sandwich and snack-vendors saw an opportunity and came rushing from the neighbouring village. They hastily set up stalls and soon there rose up the smells of cooking meat and salad which no one ate. The burning sun did not deter the women from wailing, even though their saliva dried up and their lips cracked from thirst. They punished themselves, and abstained from material comforts; they called on death to reunite them with their loved ones.

I tried to order in my mind the stories that men and women were circulating – they spoke cautiously at first, but by midday the narrators' voices rose up and no longer bothered mentioning the sources of their information. I imagined Hossam as a cold corpse, carried away like a piece of garbage by a bulldozer and thrown into some place where it might be uncovered and torn at by dogs. I felt sick when stories were told about those who had been left alive, those carrying their own guts in an attempt to cling on to life and trampling on the corpses of their brothers piled up in the narrow cells. Ten metres square had teemed with more than eighty prisoners who had for months or years outsmarted the whip, tuberculosis and scabies. But no one could save the injured after the death squads left in their aeroplanes.

A long time would pass before the full details were revealed of how the soldiers had entered the prison, and of the names of the officers who had issued the orders in cold blood. They would be pursued by the curses of the dead which did subsequently drive six of those soldiers completely mad, fleeing in perpetuity the imaginary enemies hunting them. Earlier they had returned to their homes laden with medals, conferred on them by the commander of the death squad, who had personally welcomed all the soldiers back to head-quarters. He gave a speech in praise of their courage, and presented them with a small amount of money, which they then spent on falafel sandwiches before returning to their miserable rooms in the suburbs of Damascus.

As we drove back along the desert road, in the dark, we were despondent and silent. My mother was sitting on the backseat beside me, and Omar avoided looking at her in the mirror. Next to him, Maryam sat with her eyes closed, her hands on her *misbaha*. There was no sound other than the regular clack of the beads and the muttered prayers I couldn't quite make out. The desert road was boring at night, and the futility of speech rendered us silent. I recalled images of the bereaved women, who were determined to remain outside the prison gates until they received their men's bodies. It was a surreal scene, and surely one impossible ever to recreate. I suddenly felt that the confined space of the car, in the surrounding darkness, created some sort of unity between us. In the scant light, I could see my mother staring at a fixed point ahead of her. I closed my eyes. Before we reached Aleppo I realized again that I hadn't offered her a single word of condolence. We couldn't believe that Hossam had become just a photograph on the wall that we would look at, heartbroken and sobbing, remembering his elegance and his beautiful eyes. I thought about the fear he had shown the last time I'd seen him. I was certain now that he had known that death was his only way out, and that he wouldn't survive if there was a delay in the victory which he had begun to understand was impossible.

I wanted to hug my mother and cry in her arms like a little child, but hatred dominated me to my very core. My extremities went cold. I felt paralysed and indifferent. I didn't care if I ever emerged from the dark tunnel I had entered. 'I have to control myself,' I thought as I saw the lights of Aleppo and the statue of the goddess of fertility and beauty, which we considered heathen. I tried

319

to look at it. It seemed beautiful, and so did the symbols of fertility and femininity she carried. For a moment I was overwhelmed by the idea of immersing myself in heathen ideas, but then I imagined Hossam in Paradise and my thoughts cooled. I reached out my hand towards my mother's open palm and pressed her fingers gently; I felt how cold they were as she failed to respond. I used to need her support, but her coldness delighted me now. Judging by the empty streets, it was now very late. I looked at my mother and took hold of her hand again and pressed it firmly, but it remained limp. I tried yet again. I started to cry silently, and no one noticed or cared. Omar drove into our street where tanks occupied all four corners. My crying grew louder and the car stopped. Omar and Maryam were stunned when they turned towards me and saw my mother was dead.

Everything was over quickly, except for the rest of that horrific night. Omar asked Radwan to help him carry the body to Marwa's room, and there they shrouded her on the bed by covering her with a woollen blanket. A few people arrived, among them Hajja Radia and Uncle Selim, who seemed unmoved. He sat at the head of the corpse, opened the Quran, and recited the Sura Al Baqara and some other short *suur*. He distributed parts of the Quran to Hajja Radia, Maryam and the neighbours who had come to extend their condolences in words that no longer meant anything to me. I stayed in my room. Zahra hugged me and we wept a little and then fell silent, only to start crying again; I hadn't realized what a pleasure it was until now. I listened to the murmuring voices reciting the whole Quran to calm her soul. In the morning Omar brought his workmen in to help him with the preparations for the burial, which was carried out quickly; he refused to wait for my brother Humam and father to arrive from Beirut. I tried to raise the woollen blanket from her face, but couldn't. I snatched a glance at her when Marwa arrived, accompanied only by Sheikh Abbas, her father-in-law, who sat beside Sheikh Daghstani in the house. I only noticed him after they returned from the tomb.

My mother's death was a banal occurrence, not worthy of much notice in a city where more than three hundred mourning ceremonies were held that day alone for the victims of the desert prison. Death had lost its prestige. They buried her beside my grandmother and left an empty place in the tomb, which I guessed was for Hossam. It provoked a protest from my father when he arrived from Lebanon in the evening to receive condolences. He sat next to Omar, despite their bickering over whether or not Hossam would be buried in my father's family tomb; Omar accused my father of neglecting his family and told him he was in no position to hand out orders. I thought it was idiotic of them to fight over an absent corpse. After the condolences were over, my father left my brother

Humam with us and returned to Beirut, cursing Bakr. He held him responsible for the murder of his son and the death of his wife. My little brother didn't understand what was happening, nor why women were hugging him, playing with his hair, declaring that he was an orphan, and teasing him about his funny Lebanese accent. He was a child of ten, mad about joining Bakr's children in rigging up a swing in the branches of the lemon tree and flying through the air.

Everything was silent in the house and the rest of the summer passed miserably. We could no longer absorb the surprises and catastrophes raining down on our heads. It seemed absurd that I should go to sit my exams; I looked at the textbooks as if they belonged to someone else. Zahra and Maryam encouraged me to go, even if just to the first one. I thought that leaving the house might bring me some slight relief; I didn't care about the destination. One day, after many visits to my mother's grave, I left Maryam, Zahra and Humam to be led there by Radwan and instead went by myself to the Umayyad Mosque. I sat alone and felt a humility I had almost forgotten. I prayed without performing any *ruk'at*, and I wished Rabia Adawiya would return to save me from the cesspool I had been drowning in for days. I spent a long time looking at the decorations in the Umayyad Mosque and inhaling the scents of the splendid prayer mats. A woman came to pray next to me, then flung a piece of paper at me and left quickly before I could see her face. I opened up the note; the wording was short and clear, and warned me against going to the house of any woman known to belong to the group. It asked me to wait for instructions, and finished with some curt and belated words of condolence. I no longer cared that Hossam was described as a martyr. I tore up the paper, flushed it down the toilet, and left the mosque.

I dawdled in the streets and raised the cover over my face; I saw my reflection in the window of a shoe shop, and I looked worn out and depressed, lacking in either youth or vitality. I felt my body beneath my heavy coat; my breasts were shrivelled, and had lost all memory of my fingers' caresses. I wandered back to the Armenian restaurant and collapsed, exhausted, on to the same chair where Hossam had sat with me and tried to smile without managing to. I asked for some food I then left untouched, and for a cup of tea I took two sips from. To any customers watching, I exhibited all the symptoms of a girl pining away with unrequited love. I paid the bill and ignored the sympathetic waiter who asked me if I was waiting for someone.

After the afternoon prayer I was still tired. I sat in another café and sipped a glass of juice, ignoring the laughter of the young men and women at the crowded tables. I felt unwanted there, but I didn't move; I stayed, taking up two chairs, and confusing them all by ordering several glasses of juice I didn't drink, and by the generous tip I left. I needed to be among crowds. I was surprised by my neutrality towards the young men infatuated with the flirt-atious girls. I wanted to stay out of the house for as long as possible, so I walked in the park, enjoying the autumn breezes.

But when it started to get dark, I wanted to get home to bed straight away. Jalloum's streets were deserted, even though it wasn't yet eight o'clock. I walked faster when I sensed someone following me. I took out my key and unlocked the door. A patrol of the Mukhabarat was waiting for me just inside. Two men were holding back Radwan, Humam, Omar, Maryam and Zahra in my room. One of the Mukhabarat seized me roughly by the arms and handcuffed me, but I didn't utter a word as I was taken away. My gaze clung to the window where they all gathered, to Omar's familiar, quiet, beloved face, as those around him reached out their hands, willing me not to die.

# PART III

# THE SCENT OF SPICES

I have to get used to life without spices,' I told myself; in my determination to stay alive, I had to come to terms with losing the pleasures I had been addicted to. For the first time, I thought hard about those moments of sweetness whose loss seemed an unbearable anguish. I remembered Maryam scolding me whenever I leaned over the saucepan and inhaled the scent of the spices like a drug addict. I would lift my head in rapture from the smell, which hit the back of my throat with a burst of flavour, and tickled my nose. The family had all grown accustomed to my quirky behaviour. I wanted to cling to something strange. I was so enamoured of spices that I would sprinkle them even on slices of raw carrot and devour these with relish.

Now, I had to reconsider my life and learn to exist in a narrow cell whose floor was cracked and cold. It was like a kennel fit only for an unloved dog caught by scavengers who kept it captive among the revolting detritus of the rubbish tip. A deliberately neglected animal, its skin grew blotchy, torn apart by fungal infections, but still it didn't whine. I was that dog whose jailers were on tenter-hooks for her to howl, so that they might better relish her pain and the wounds which wouldn't heal. The scars from their whips, electrodes and cigarettes would remain as tattoos, which even henna patterns couldn't hide. In later years, when-ever I uncovered them and stood in front of the mirror I realized that hatred was worthy of praise, as it lives within us exactly as love does. It grows moment by moment in order to settle finally in our souls, and we don't want to escape it even when it causes us pain.

For more than a hundred days, I was kept in solitary confinement. As I fought against the grave dangers facing me, I thought about the sea which I had once been content just to look at, rather than dive into. The few times I had seen it, I had been astonished by its awesome pres-ence. I needed its sublime power in order to avoid the image of my dead mother and the memory of my father's cruel gaze, as if he were accusing me of her murder. I was haunted by the sight of her cold face, staring into oblivion. I wondered why the dead loved oblivion to such a degree that they grew to depend upon it so immediately. I imagined my mother floating naked through open space, silently searching for Hossam. A living corpse thrown amongst us for a short time, she couldn't bear our incessant chatter and left us without apology so we would learn the meaning of her silence, and her passion for the space which she missed so much. There, the dead wandered uncurbed in an oblivion which was their own, in a time which was their own; they toyed with their memories and mocked their sanctity, letting them fall away from their skin like the repulsive sweat, which they had also rid themselves of. I imagined her throne in Heaven, overcome with the desire to decorate it with birds singing sweetly, and my mother smiling in apology for her deafness.

A picture of my dead mother; the sea whose depths I longed for. I lost track of time and began to calculate it according to the patrols and the sound of the guards' quick footsteps in the dark passages, lit only by a lamp which flickered plaintively in the damp. Its light seemed so weak, a lament for a strange world I could never have imagined until I tasted its pain and knew how barbaric people could be; the animal was still inside them.

I came close to death in the first days of my imprisonment. I saw its many hues, clearly defined, peaceful and quiet, leading each living being into God's kingdom and along the path stretching like a single line between Hell and Heaven; I was sure the latter would be my eternal home since I was a mujahida as described in the group's literature. Those pamphlets were full of long stories about my great faith and my heroic deeds, which I had no recollection of. My eyes didn't gleam with pride when an interrogator put one in front of me; they had published my photo next to those of some other girls, most of whom I knew, and some young men. I felt a stirring of sympathy for one of them, and I looked at his mocking smile for as long as I was allowed. It occurred to me for a moment that I loved life more than the title of 'exemplary martyr'. I no longer cared about anything other than getting out alive from the torturer's acid pit. My confidence was faked, as was my wish for the courage befitting one of *God's beloveds*, as we were described by the organization, in a writing style I grew to hate. This hyperbole distanced me from those things whose truth I was now to ponder, as if time and solitude were diminishing me even though I had spent most of the past years alone among my aunts.

In my cramped cell, my aunts were transformed into swans swimming on a calm river; Radwan was leading their chorus and gathering the spray from their wings, a lover content with his blind gaze towards the rustling of their feathers. At that moment the image fragmented, returning me to my jumble of memories. I thought of my pillow which had lured me towards the thousands of dreams I had then drawn in an attempt to master my fear of the nights spent in my grandfather's vast house; I thought of all that silence and space which had been bequeathed to us, as we moved through the house, feverishly seeking out the rustle of our ancestors' souls. Maryam was sure they lived alongside us, but when we in turn became just photographs she forgot about them and cried for us instead. She took charge of Zahra and Bakr's children and my brother Humam so she wouldn't be left alone with the cobwebs and Radwan's sighs, which she feared would bring back dreams of absent children. In my cell I couldn't escape from her kind and affectionate, even compassionate, face. I remembered how Maryam had brought out some henna from Mecca so she could send her beloved sister to the grave with her hair braided and coloured, just as my grandmother had done for her daughter when she was a young bride, so she could hand her over to be grasped by the strong hand of my father, and led away through the labyrinths of life that had determined her end.

My mother hadn't been able to find a better solution than death. For me, choosing death seemed the same as choosing life when the Mukhabarat men jeered at me as I staggered up the steps to their building. To Aleppans, this was a place of terror and inevitable death; even in the best-case scenario, it meant certain ruin. The commander was himself a symbol of the devastation that had settled over the country. He loved hearing about the torture of the detainees. He interfered in all matters relating to Aleppo, which had been glorious once, before he accepted it as a reward in return for betraying his fellow conspirators during an attempted coup, and sending them one by one to the basement gallows in a dank military barracks from which he alone would return. He took control of all the smuggling routes for members of his family, who abandoned goat-herding and were transformed overnight into businessmen. The sight of them in their loud suits provoked covert laughter, and pity for their utter lack of taste.

Silence was best when face to face with our enemies. My handcuffs hurt and the powerful odour of decay bored into me, overwhelming in the cell into which I was thrown by powerful, rough hands. Terrible dizziness caused me to drop to the ground. I saw the death that I had avoided contemplating when it stretched out beside me like a man whose breath I could inhale. He teased me, and I leaned away from him; he flirted with me, so I cursed him with an inner voice he nevertheless heard perfectly – but still he wouldn't leave me. 'I have to ask for mercy,' I thought, and I surrendered to the protracted time I knew would pass before I could return to the possessions which I had neglected. It was strange that thoughts of them returned to me now. I was rebuked by the soft bedcover; by the tablecloth prepared specially for the medical student and Radwan's singing companion I used to be; by my warm bed and by the small carpet hanging like an eternal icon. I pushed away these details so I wouldn't drown in my tears in this cellar full of prison cells. Feeble voices leaked out of them, begging for air or a single drop of water.

No one spoke to me for three days; a hand of which I saw no more than the coarse fingers would occasionally toss me a bowl of mouldy, unspiced food. In that place I had nothing but my memories, but I soon avoided reviewing them: I realized that suppressing memories was the only solution to their test of my ability not to lose my mind. It was like my request that they speak to me, even that they curse me, rather than leave me to the void of my unacknowledged whimpers. How cruel do people have to be before you wish to hear the voices of your executioners, just to be sure that you are not alone? I remembered Marwa looking at us with contempt, raising her chains as proof of her love for Nadhir. At that moment, I swore to kiss her feet so she would forgive me. This vow stayed with me for a long time. I imagined the scene a thousand times; I traced it until it became something tangible, impossible to disengage from.

On the fourth day (or so I estimated) a man took me by the arm, blindfolded, to an interrogation room. After a few words I was taken to another room nearby, and I went there with the submission of a lamb to the slaughter. I lay on the ground and the whips rained down on my body. I swam in a murky kingdom where rough voices were raised, cursing a murdered woman who was my mother, and extolling the praises of their leader. The darkness intensified; Rabia Adawiya fluttered like a white bird and I clung to her. Bats surrounded me with their scythe-shaped wings. Spices floated over me but I couldn't catch hold of them or sniff their scent. Deafness became a divine blessing. Whenever I took Rabia Adawiya's hand, the fingernails leapt up and tore my body to shreds, which were thrown to the wolves. These wolves didn't resemble the ones whose pointy muzzles and mean eyes I had adored. In the beginning, they only want to control your body, then they want your eyes, and finally even your breath, in that murky kingdom of darkness you have entered, where everything takes on new meaning. I lost consciousness. I couldn't feel the feet kicking me in my side in order to set my weeping wounds on fire again. I squeezed out the pus once and tried to taste it; I had to learn to love it like I loved my pain, in order to stay alive, to hold on to the ability to regain at some point the cohesion I had surrendered for a while to the charm of dissolution.

Sulafa closed her eyes. 'Stroke my hair; make me your toy,' she said. Her voice rang out as if it were coming from a time before she was as good as dead, from the outside, whose existence we tried to ignore so we could erect our kingdoms on a mountain of salt and clay. I was as surprised by her request as if she had just told me what was in my endless daydreams. I knelt down and she surrendered to my fingers which soothed the dryness of her scalp. Um Mamdouh usually woke up at night. She looked for a long time at the other sleeping women who had become used to crowding their bodies into a few centimetres; to suppressing their never-ending moans, and their desire to escape to spacious beds which would allow their skin to breathe freely and quiver in the presence of a man. Um Mamdouh looked at us, smiled, and joined me in twining Sulafa's braids to finish off the game.

In this new shared cell I had been moved to, there were several of my former associates; but I was often silent and didn't join in with the girls who were involved in endless debates on the fatwas of prayers relevant to these circumstances, as they tried to convince girls from other political parties of the necessity of returning to God. Each side would come out with passionate speeches, but it all ended in mutual recriminations. At night they were quieter; only their whimpers rose up, along with the smell of festering wounds. I put my head on Um Mamdouh's knee and also enjoyed being someone's doll; Sulafa and I were both in need of a mother. We repeated the game several times, and I didn't care about Hajja Souad's rebukes, or her description of us as 'abnormal'.

After the first year, the executioners no longer tortured us to the brink of death during interrogations as a matter of routine. We had confessed to everything they wanted us to; we didn't care any more. I decided to recreate my past all over again, as if I were only now slipping from my mother's womb and crawling over the cold ground. I decided to believe this lie so I would live with a recklessness I did not believe I possessed, with a frivolity I hadn't known before. I regretted my excessive gravity and convinced myself that I was in this hell so I would love my aunts more. I refused the little help available from our organization conveyed to us, despite the obstacles, through visitors to the criminals who spent a few days in our midst. Prostitutes in particular created an atmosphere of intimacy with their lewd talk and relaxed tone when describing their clients. They were aware that they were only passing through and seemed sorry for us, and then they would cheerfully leave us for other parts of the prison while letting out rumbling trills, and kissing me warmly.

A lack of understanding between Hajja Souad and me led at first to a cooling in our relationship, and then to a state of total and mutual disregard. This gave me the freedom to sit with Sulafa and Um Mamdouh, whom Sulafa and I began to call mother. If someone had told me two years earlier that Sulafa would become a lifelong friend, I would have thought them deluded. Now our conversation was unceasing; we each reshaped our past so that the memories were no longer the preserve of an individual, but could belong to both of us together. Thus we shared my room and sang Radwan's poetry, and we lit a lamp on the night of the Prophet's *mawlid*. We swam naked in the sea at

Latakia, and then stretched out rapturously on the white sand, drinking juice beneath the single palm on the beach at Samra. We wandered through forests and got lost on sinuous country roads. We welcomed the dawn as it touched the cacti on Mount Ben Younis, then we stood in front of my grandfather's shops like customers looking for the carpet upon which Scheherazade had sat in order to redeem women of their gender with a thousand and one stories. What did it matter that we were stuck in a narrow cell which was no more than a hair's breadth wider than our two bodies? I thought for a moment that everything that had happened was a game which would soon be over, and the losers would go home with a sigh, bewailing their bad luck.

I told Sulafa that it was her turn to lead the game, and that she should wake me when she was ready to tell me its new direction. She kicked me and leaned backwards, then covered her head with a heavy rug that smelled of the farts of the conscripts and prisoners who had preceded us and about whom we knew nothing. I knew that the night was halfway over: the hour of Mudar's arrival had come. Every night at this time, Sulafa fled to her solitude. She created a little tent from some ancient sheets, and she would leave a little gap, just as she used to leave the door of her room open for Mudar so he could slink in through the dark into her arms. She recalled her earlier life with all the conviction of a woman who

337

couldn't believe that the fig trees in her family home overlooking the distant sea had become but a dream and a memory. I watched Sulafa; with her I relived Mudar's arrival, his boisterous movements and vigour, his heavy tread. Like a lookout, I monitored the others, biting my nails and softly crooning sections of the Um Kulthoum song 'Days Have Gone By', which I now knew by heart because it had been repeated around me so many times. What did it mean when a man divided himself between two women, a lady and a servant? Between a wife and an unseen mistress? Whenever Sulafa unrolled her tent I composed an image of Mudar. I brought him into my room in that welcoming house which had never witnessed an unmarried man sleeping with any of its women.

I laughed when I remembered Abdullah sleeping alone in a cold room, surrounded by the hospitable splendour appropriate to the reputation of our ancestors, who had left a virgin to uphold their glories. She ordered a carded-wool bed weighing fifteen ratals to be brought down and took out the best bedding, along with cushions (which reminded me of nothing more than peacocks displaying to a blind crowd) and a special satin quilt from Istanbul bought for the guests whom the family had awaited so long, and who never came. Abdullah got into bed, surrounded by this opulence, while Safaa sighed next to Marwa; she didn't dare go to him out of fear of Maryam, who kept awake, circling around the courtyard all night like she was guarding our vaginas and very breath. Abdullah's dignity prevented him from returning Safaa's salacious winks. Whenever he visited Aleppo, he was forced to rent a separate house if he wanted to drown in her feminine warmth until morning. Later, he lodged at grand hotels in order not to arouse suspicion – he pretended to be like any businessman from the Gulf, laden with projects, while in fact selling Paradise to anyone who supported jihad in Afghanistan against the Soviet infidels. His enthusiasm, his tender expressions, his long history of failures and successes – all of this had made me miss him that day in the prison. I imagined him as a father to me, or as a husband who remained sleepless till morning so that the night wouldn't steal his breath from me. Now, as I guarded Sulafa's tent, I contemplated the futility of sharing one's memories of a man with a friend, while hiding our secrets from our surrogate mother; as we received her affectionate scolds, we would exchange glances like naughty children.

We wasted so many days. We surrendered to indolence and time stretched out, uncounted and desolate, over our bodies. One day Sulafa told me, 'It's raining now.' She laughed, and concluded, 'It must be raining now; Mudar has passed in front of my window where there's no light on, and he's crying.' I loved this image of a man, a lover, crying in the rain as he waited for a light to come on in his sweetheart's room. Sulafa and I seemed like old friends who had met by chance on a slow train journey which wasn't anywhere near long enough for them to exchange all their news, so they rushed to the nearest coffee house so they could finish what they had started. Sulafa neatly described Mudar's eyelashes, fluttering nervously over black eyes like swallows, and she pressed my hand when I turned my face away. I apologized tenderly and thought for a long time about the shape of those eyes which so resembled swallows. In a passionate whisper she recalled his tall frame, and how his lips tasted of strawberry and awakened in her a desire to drown in burning kisses she had thought would never end.

They had met by chance, and he entered her life when she was relatively secure. But she defended him at the trial convened by her organization to call her to account. She wouldn't surrender to her comrades' pleas and her girlfriends' contempt; they were furious she had broken the vow she had sworn to the underground Marxist party. She asked them to acknowledge him and they refused, and they asked her to recruit him to their party and she was silent. Desire for him was burning her up, and every night she left her door unlocked, indifferent to the stares of the curious neighbours. He would quietly cross Bab Tuma and detour past the Al Bakry hammam, to that ancient house whose rooms were shared by four students and two nurses (who took it in turns to use their only bed). The four students kept a lookout for her, and thereby ensured Mudar's safe passage to her room. They helped her convince the landlady that the night visitor didn't exist, despite the recurring sounds of Sulafa's pleasure, which she didn't try to hide. The students reacted to it shyly at first, and then eavesdropped eagerly.

Those girls had taken turns in guarding her. Now, I guarded the illusion which we shared, just as we shared everything willingly. She bewildered me when she cheerfully told me about the moment of her birth and her mother's joy at the arrival of a daughter after four sons. The umbilical cord had wrapped itself around Sulafa's neck and had almost strangled her; the midwives managed to revive her only with great difficulty. After Sulafa as a toddler fell into the well and emerged from it without a scratch, her mother became still more convinced that she had been formed for life. I tried to picture my own birth, but was assailed by my mother's dead, silent face.

The guards' faces were no longer obscured, and they became a part of our daily life. We coveted these faces sometimes, just to feel that our lives would continue after our detention; we would meet them one day, and call them to account for their oppression. We would ask them, 'Won't you die like us?' We would go out to them in their dreams; we would penetrate their memories, and

341

corrupt moments of harmony as they tried to enjoy their peaceful old age by playing backgammon and giving piggybacks to their grandchildren who played contentedly with their beards. Sulafa and I imagined various court settings: we were wearing judicial robes and holding the gavel, and then we began to interrogate them. 'Why do you find pleasure in masturbating over a woman when she is tied up and electrodes are burning her breasts?' Someone, known to his associates as Abi Ali, answered, 'I was serving my master and my homeland.' The word 'homeland' made me laugh. Everyone used it with veneration and respect, from members of my group to the torturers.

I was astonished at the breadth of scope contained within such a basic concept amidst the giddiness of all its various meanings. We wanted our 'homeland' to be Islamic. Sulafa and her group wanted it to be Marxist. The executioners wanted it to be their own private realm, where they could carry on masturbating and hanging on to power, heedless of anyone else as long as they still had armies and prisons. When I asked Sulafa, 'How could the country be Marxist?' she replied, with tepid enthusiasm, 'Red and no other colour.' To my own question I replied, 'We want it green.' Everyone wanted the country to be their own particular colour, like that of those three judicial robes in front of which I stood two years after first being imprisoned. My dreams of spices had grown trivial and pointless beside those of the others, who worried about their husbands, fathers and children.

One day, after two years in prison, I, along with nine others from our organization, was taken from the cell in chains and thrown into a secure van. They didn't allow us the briefest pause to look up at the overcast sky. The van crossed Damascus; we heard car horns; I exchanged long looks with Hajja Souad, whose fear I could sense, as if we were meeting for the last time. In front of the door to the court I tried to touch her hand to encourage her. The handcuffs prevented me, but she noticed my gesture and closed her eyes and murmured. I felt her contentment, which I needed along with the prayers of Um Mamdouh who had bid me goodbye like I was a child going to school with all her dreams in front of her. She kissed me and smoothed down the collar of my only shirt (which so long ago Maryam's fingers had touched when she blessed me, aware of what it meant that I was leaving with all those strangers).

The judges' dais gleamed and the courtroom was warm. A picture of the president hung oppressively in every corner. The judges' faces seemed bored as if they had had to leave unfinished their cups of coffee in order to come here and defend their many privileges, which ranged from luxury apartments and cars to foreign currency and shares. The organization's girls had given in, having already lost hope. There was emptiness in their glances, their spirit extinguished as if they no longer cared about anything. We had forgotten the smell of clean sheets; we had surrendered to our squalid cells. We no longer dreamed of marriage and enjoying family tiffs over the breakfast table. Our files on the desk revealed that we were now a collection of pages written by informers and interrogators. We had responded in turn to their idiotic questions about particular secrets, in the face of their ready-made accusations, which began with our honour and progressed all the way to an attempted coup on the ruling regime.

The interrogators had all been infatuated with my cellmate Suhayr's eyes. Her gaze was like an axe as she repeated to them violently, 'Yes. I wanted to overthrow the regime and kill the other sect: they are my enemies.' With a determination that infuriated them, she praised the virility of her ravishingly handsome husband, younger than her by three years and whose chest she had weighed down with charms to keep him from falling into the path of the evil eye. They were furious that she could praise him in this way in their presence. They couldn't resist the appeal of her haggard body. Her passion tyrannized even the most senior of the interrogators. She knocked his coffee cup to the ground and spat in his face after he gleefully informed her that her husband had been executed in one the periodic purges of prisoners, who were led to the gallows in a courtyard of the desert prison. She returned to her cell and stood there like a queen lamenting her kingdom. Staring distractedly, she said curtly, 'I am now the widow of a martyr, one of God's beloveds; the father of my son who is growing in my belly. I am the widow of Sobhi Al Janadi.' The bereaved queen went quiet and girls from our group rushed over with their condolences. They trilled and fired up my enthusiasm, but I discovered that I didn't know how to complete the trill, which was shaking the entire country. I cried, as did Hajja Souad. Um Mamdouh joined her, along with all our girls in the cells, and the Marxists rushed to eulogize the beloved of this haughty woman.

We got no sleep that night. They dragged us one after another to that chair which we had begun to know the way to, and which allowed the torturer total freedom to toy with our skin, breasts and stomach, opening up our wounds again before they could heal properly. Terror haunted the guards when calls of 'Allahu Akbar!' were raised from the neighbouring cells, from the men whose breath we used to feel on our necks. There was a pact between us: whenever they called out to alert us that one of their number was being taken off to be tortured, we trilled out our support for him; they in turn released full-throated roars whenever one of the women was led away. Suhayr had joined us seven months earlier; in recent days the sight of her had become thrilling, and her face covered with freckles. Her pregnancy filled us with enthusiasm and occupied us all as if we were sharing the coming child. We picked bits of potato for her out of the bowls of squalid food and dried them out to pretend to her that they were slices of peach, in an attempt to calm her cravings.

Rasha, the only one in our cell to receive visits, bossily ordered her family to bring enough balls of coloured wool to make blankets and other things for the baby. A battle ensued with the head of the Mukhabarat unit; he sometimes made allowances for Rasha in deference to the high status of her family, who were disheartened by their daughter's Marxist dreams. More than once, they tried to convince her to abandon her stance so they could get her out of this hellhole, but she was obdurate and threatened to refuse their visits. They were ashamed of her hatred for the luxuries of her home. As a child, she'd come under the influence of a distant family member, who had once fought in the International Brigade in the Spanish Civil War. He drew the hammer and sickle logo for her, and sang her the songs of the Brigade. Uncle Muti told her about imaginary battles and distant countries. She looked after him when she grew older, grateful to him for teaching her how to hate every religious sect and to sing the hymns of the International Brigade, which had gathered all humanity under its standard.

Rasha's mediation was successful. Her family brought us wool and knitting needles and we dedicated ourselves to our coming child, making clothes for an unborn baby known already by a variety of pet names. Rasha said to our cellmate Hoda what none of the rest of us dared: very simply, she told her that we knew she was informing on us, and that she didn't deserve to have anything to do with our child, and Hajja Souad did the same with one of the girls from our organization. We pushed aside any qualms and isolated them so they became like two corpses wishing for escape; it didn't take long until they were transferred to the central women's prison. We were all waiting to be moved there in order to escape from the smell of our torturers' shit; to humiliate us they would force us to clean it up after having smeared it liberally all over the walls and ceiling of the toilet.

We all took turns with the knitting needles. We made two tops and a blanket for our imminent baby, which Suhayr obediently shared with us. We needed it to ease the pressure of our sentences and to keep some perspective on the dream of eventually leaving this place. I had become accustomed to my daily life, and I entered my third year without any illusions. I kissed Hajja Souad's hand and head so she would forgive me for my cold glances, my closeness to Sulafa, and my lack of participation in the prayer and Quran sessions she convened every evening. Some of the girls rejected my apology and accused me of abandoning the dreams of our group, and of a lack of interest in the extreme punishments meted out to our men. Images of Hossam and my mother rose in front of me as I defended myself. I had an overwhelming longing to cry out for her embrace; to start everything again from its first innocence, from the colours which had once been clear. Hajja Souad smiled. She stopped the girls from harassing me whenever they made sure I could hear their whispers hinting at my relationship with the other sect, and cursing Marwa, her husband and all of my formerly respected family, of which only Bakr retained their admiration.

I asked Sulafa, 'Will our son come for a long or short time?' She gave herself up to playing her role in the game. 'Is it true that everything that has happened was an illusion, and everything that will happen will be an even bigger illusion?' We watched Suhayr, whose labour pains had started. All the prisoners woke up, all twenty-two of us, and we began to bang on the door with all the strength we possessed, announcing our devotion to the life of our child. The guards' fingers rushed to their triggers, ready to open fire. Um Mamdouh lay Suhayr down and ordered the girls to cover her with blankets. Rasha started to demand an ambulance. She babbled angrily and then left with the guards to negotiate. Suhayr resisted the contractions; she snatched a few gasps of air and did her best not to die. Rasha returned quickly and helped move Suhayr to a ground-floor guard-room, accompanied by four other women she ordered about. The voices of the prisoners in the adjoining cells were raised in a strange prayer we had never heard before. We needed their melodious voices to calm our worry and fear, as if their words had been extracted straight from the chants of the pilgrims during their circling of the Kaaba. A sweet voice recited lines and a chorus repeated them after him, defying the bemused guards as they stood in the corridor. Bewilderment reigned as if our child had overturned their rules, and the silence settling over them for a few moments was an indication of the compassion they very rarely liked to show in the absence of their master, who arrived later as our child's screams filled the world. Um Mamdouh trilled as she took on the role of midwife, assisted by Layla and Tuhama the mute, with a skill she had mastered in a city whose women wouldn't reveal their private parts to a male doctor.

Um Mamdouh's faint signal reached us and we exchanged cautious smiles. Those three hours of Suhayr's labour had seemed very long, filled with the hope we had lost. The male prisoners recited verses from Sura Maryam and sent congratulations we barely made out.

But the commander of the unit did not approve of the behaviour of the guards on duty. He spat in Rasha's face and accused her of adhering to our sect and abandoning her own. He put her into solitary confinement after an orgy of torture in which Rasha screamed in pain, spat on her torturers and cursed them. Um Mamdouh wept;

she kissed the officer's shoes so he would allow her to sit next to Suhayr who was submerged in pain and joy at regaining her beloved's face through our son, whom we passed around between us. We kissed him with relish after making space for Suhayr, who wasn't allowed to remain outside the cell. We took turns in carrying the child so he stayed close to the small window which overlooked the narrow passage, saturated with the smell of rot and urine from the adjacent toilet. It was like we were begging him for some air to save us from suffocating.

It was difficult to describe the colour of our child's eyes. He vanquished our boredom and the endless discussions, which the shadows of that depressing place made appear more like an exchange of curses heralding an escalation in hatred. We hadn't expected that religious opponents and ideological enemies could ever share the same space, but we were forced to share that air and pain, and break dry bread together. We belonged to Suhayr's child the moment we all felt the futility of words and the power of life. It took only a few moments to reconsider everything. I watched myself and the hatred I had loved; I remembered my father's agitated face, his violent words in defence of the other sect as he asked me not to hold them responsible for the persecution of our sect. He quoted dozens of examples of torturers and corrupt statesmen who belonged to our sect and, in contrast, of men from the other sect who had defended our right to speak the truth. He wanted to save me, or save the country, for which he saw no future other than one dominant ideology, be it red or green, which would extend to include everyone.

I thought about my father suddenly. I wished I could see him, if only for a moment. I hadn't understood the meaning of his move to Beirut, or when his voice got lost among our din and the flood of our emotions. Memories submerged me and distanced me from our child who began to grow day by day. The sound of his chirping and of his first hand clap transported us into ecstasies of adoration. We kissed his feet and abandoned everything just to watch him crawl and wave his hands. We waited for any new gesture from him, in order to reward it with inexhaustible love.

Rasha returned from solitary confinement a week after his birth. Weeping, she seized the child's tiny hands and kissed them as if we weren't there. They allowed Suhayr half an hour in the yard a day, which she spent under the guard of corrupt soldiers to whom we paid what little money we still had so that Suhayr would have a carton of milk, costing five times its original price. In addition, the few visits allowed to the ordinary criminals passing through the prison ensured a little extra food, which we surrendered to Suhayr so she could breastfeed. Our minds devised strange means of keeping death away from our beloved baby. Thana, a girl from our group, sang

'The Heart Loves All Beauty' for him in a surprisingly sweet voice. We repeated it after her, though fearful that the guards would drag us once again to that terrifying room where the whips would rain down on our naked bodies. Thana was revealed to us as a singer who had memorized odes from the Jahiliyya, and now she repeated the old songs of Mohammed Khairy, Najah Salam and Um Kulthoum with a sensitivity which made us believe, just for a few moments, that we were outside these repulsive walls. Intoxicated, we formed a ring around her – she had overcome her shyness all at once and was included as another sister; we were all Um Mamdouh's daughters, and I continued to call myself one until my release. Um Mamdouh would relate to every transient criminal the story of Hama, the city which had been destroyed and whose corpses had been thrown in the streets to rot.

We needed our child to help us endure. We discovered how wonderful it was to watch a human being grow within a prison cell with joy and defiance. Our torturers couldn't understand it – in his first days they willed him to die, but later they just regarded him as a strange creature. They couldn't stay silent and revealed the secret to their wives during nights full of worry, and when they tried to describe him they found that they couldn't. I told myself, 'It's wonderful that this baby now has twenty-two mothers.'

★   ★   ★

It occurred to me in my third year to be afraid of death; I was terrified when I was laid up with a high fever. The unit doctor confirmed it wasn't infectious, but I could feel that my cellmates were afraid even to look at me in case I passed it on to them. I pleaded with the doctor to put me into quarantine, even if it meant I had to be parted from them. He kicked me and threw me a few pills, which I refused to take in an attempt to kill myself.

With the severity of a real mother, Um Mamdouh ordered me to pull myself together. Didn't I want to return to the medical college and wear a white coat, and enjoy the streets of Aleppo once more? I saw them in front of me again. While I was in the grip of the fever all sorts of images mixed and overlapped in my mind. I discovered the glory of surrendering to long daydreams I didn't want to end. I wanted a child like our child. I wanted to escape from the lie that he belonged to all of us. Our child wasn't really *our* child. Um Mamdouh, the 'mother' who looked at us reprovingly to make us behave more decorously whenever Sulafa pinched me and we burst into loud peals of laughter, wasn't our mother. Mudar, Sulafa's lover, wasn't standing crying under my window, begging me to open it and throw myself into his arms so he could press my lips to his with a force which drove me mad.

The hatred which I had defended as the only truth was shattered entirely. The early questions surrounding the truth of belonging and existence came back to me, as I swam in confusion. My life was a collection of allegories that belonged to others. How hard it is to spend all your time believing what others want you to believe; they choose a name for you which you then have to love and defend, just as they choose the God you will worship, killing whoever opposes their version of His beauty, the people you call 'infidels'. Then a hail of bullets is released, which makes death into fact.

A slow, dilapidated train was travelling over the plains. Its wheels squeaking in pain, it advanced to pick up the dead who were awaiting burial with vacant eyes, looking up at the sky as if it were a dream. All along the train's path the dead signalled to the blind driver to stop by using their stench. The train let out a powerful whistle to greet the transient beings. The driver descended through the meadows and searched among the flowers for the bodies, piled up like forgotten sacks of lentils which had rotted in the rain. The blind driver carried the corpses lightly and skilfully and lined them up inside the cold iron carriages; the dead don't care about the niceties of the living. He climbed up to his cab and the invisible train moved off. The expanse of the driver's smiling face was brushed by the cool breezes and his imagination blazed. He traced pictures of the corpses piled up in the last carriage. He inveigled himself into their dreams as if he were their only guarantee that they wouldn't be left abandoned in a cold alley like empty paper bags.

I saw the train, quiet and unnoticed as it moved through the streets of a city I recognized; I believed it to be Aleppo. It really was Aleppo – its narrow alleys and squares filled with tanks, soldiers and corpses. No one thought of stopping this dread-inducing machine from which an old, blind man descended. He took up his cargo and left silently, without uttering a single question or grumbling about the weight. Hossam's corpse was fidgety, looking for someone to tickle him and make him laugh. The train reached another town; there were waterwheels nearby – Um Mamdouh saw them and screamed, 'It's Hama!' She asked the driver to stop for a moment, so she could examine the faces of her sons and neighbours, and of whoever else had been left by the birds of prey which had scorned thousands of corpses. The blind driver halted the train and drank some tea with soldiers, who would also bid goodbye to their lives, cut down at street corners. The driver stopped for a long time: he wanted more corpses. I thought that the train had nearly reached me. I saw its yellow lights approaching; I was delighted, like anyone wanting to see the plains and inhale the clean air of Paradise, as I moved among the white lambs which guarded it. Their melodic bleating was like divine music, which polluted humankind couldn't hope to enjoy.

I was frightened of becoming that train driver and I passed out. Multiple images clashed and my shadow laid siege to me, blinding me for a few moments. I surrendered to it totally. I asked Sulafa, 'Where is your hand?' She held out her hand and I pressed it for a few minutes, and a strange warmth overwhelmed me. It returned sight to me – opaque at first, then completely clear. I had been feverish for three months, and had enjoyed the delirium. I saw myself lying naked in a green meadow. I imagined passing men who raped me, or lovers who I only wished would leave me alone. I remembered Ghada, from whom I always tried to flee. I convinced myself that her grave was always decorated with narcissi.

The illness left its legacy on my face like one more hallmark of my time in that place. The stress we were under made us fight even over apple peel with the tenacity of normal women fighting for their lives. How much had our images of ourselves changed over the last couple of years? How much had we mocked ourselves? We carried our claims to superiority only in sanitized dreams. We wanted to remain like ripe peaches, but aridity reached our very core. When I finally got back on my feet, I was sure that my illness had been necessary to dispel the last of my illusions. I was ashamed of my face, which Sulafa tried to convince me was still beautiful and that the scars would soon fade. I thought how trivial it was to worry, in this place, of how my sunken cheeks looked. Everything inside me had become pale, and everything around me had become boring. I was possessed by everything I had fled from. I no longer watched our child or applauded warmly when he tried to stand on his own feet or waved his hands about. The air was no longer enough for me; I heard my pulse ringing in my ears like a strong hammer or the ticking of a huge clock in an abandoned city.

I was bored by the daily discussions, in which I participated only in a quiet voice, swiftly lost within the noisy uproar of others' certainty. The only thing on which we agreed was to ignore that the other sect was the reason for the conflict. The others in my group no longer called me to account for my friendship with the Marxist Sulafa. They tried to approach her and lean on her shoulder when Thana sang the final section of Um Kalthoum's 'Renew Your Love For Me', and they generously gave her some of the cold tea which they saved from the afternoon meal to have late at night.

It is difficult to be a woman in prison when all your guards are men. You listen to their footsteps in the corridor, you catch their scent, and it awakens desire; then you remember they are enemies who kick you brutally and wish you would die so they can devote themselves entirely to the card games which every soldier needs from time to time, to feel that everything is as it should be.

★　　★　　★

The death squad commander kicked open the door to the cabinet office, and marched in to bang his fist on the ancient walnut table and demand his portion of the country. The frightened ministers signed his orders without demur, aware that the dignity they enjoyed was dependent on his dignity; some of them identified with him publicly, while others left for quieter climes where they could write their memoirs and curse him, after yielding up more than half of the state's funds to him. He stashed it all in European and American banks, which conspired with him in their greed for the copious amounts of money he had accumulated as the price for murdering our group members, bombing unarmed prisoners, and destroying a city which loved eating *ghazal banat* and cheese pastries more than it loved death. Myths grew up about the commander, and his supporters hung up pictures of him in which he seemed to be a powerful man who loved life, smiling and raising his fist as if he were liberating Jerusalem – rather than the gang leader who ruled through his lieutenants and milked the country, a spoiled little boy everyone avoided upsetting, so that he wouldn't ruin the party for them all. He and his associates seemed like old childhood friends who had gathered to celebrate their reunion by murdering the head-master and plundering all the equipment from the school sports hall.

The commander became the symbol of the death squad, and the country began to buckle under its pressure. News of his scandalous behaviour with women leaked out, as of his officers' abduction of girls as they walked along formerly safe streets. If the gaze of one of his guards fell upon a figure graceful like a gazelle, they would drag the girl to one of his houses scattered throughout all the affluent districts of Damascus. They would hold the girls prisoner, gang-rape them, and then throw them out like dogs, leaving them to an unknown fate. Articles on the commander's corruption were published in foreign newspapers, so foreign newspapers were banned and anyone caught reading them was punished. There were suspicious disappearances among any of his trading partners who tried to muscle in on the profits. One who had not been lucky enough to flee abroad with some money had his accounts and assets frozen and recovered, and he himself was liquidated in cold blood. Another business associate was thrown from the seventh floor on to a chilly pavement – a grand funeral was held for him the following day, and a large wreath of roses was presented in the name of the death squad commander. He offered a mourning ceremony to the man's sons, who thanked him politely, abandoning their family honour and denying rumours that their father had been murdered; his death was transformed into a mere accident, as might befall anyone who happened to lose his balance on his seventh-floor balcony, while leaning out to look for the full moon.

★   ★   ★

Nadhir stood in front of the head of the death squad. He let his hands drop and steeled himself for the bullet which might come suddenly from behind the curtains of that grand office. Without looking at him, the commander asked, 'Weren't we in the same class once?' Nadhir answered curtly, 'Yes.' The commander followed this with a question which sounded vaguely conciliatory: 'Why did you betray me?' Nadhir fidgeted while trying to select the appropriate words which wouldn't anger him. 'I didn't betray you, sir. I tried to follow our code of honour by not attacking unarmed prisoners.' The silence seemed very long before the commander rose from behind his desk, looking straight at him. 'Don't you believe they were criminals, and that they wanted to kill our sect?' The words *our sect* rang out like a clap of thunder.

Hundreds of old images came to Nadhir's mind: one was of two young students trying to find shelter from the heavy winter rain under a tarpaulin, laughing like any friends would when they were faced with the likelihood of ending up looking like drowned rats. It was an idealized picture which helped him to gather up his courage all at once and say clearly, 'Where do you want to take the country?' He followed this with a plea, addressing the commander by his first name, without his title: 'Why do you want to destroy the sect and charge it with crimes it hasn't committed? Do what you want, and leave the sect alone. You can still carry on your rackets, and it will be the poor who pay the heavy price.' The commander seemed calm as he fingered his revolver, but then and there he ended the meeting, gesturing to his associates to show Nadhir out. As Nadhir was leaving the building, a young officer politely asked for the keys to his house and second car, and told him to await further instructions. Nadhir felt tense but when he opened the boot of the car to empty it, he saw, to his astonishment, that the young officer was smiling at him. Nadhir carried the cases of butterflies carefully over to the small van and driver he had hired earlier and set off for his house, which was no longer his. There he quickly reassured Marwa and gathered up a few belongings. He left behind all his uniforms, leaving a message for a childhood friend who has drowned in a lake of blood, bequeathing his family only thousands of corpses pierced with bullets whose curse would follow them for ever.

On the way to Nadhir's village, Marwa stroked his hands in an attempt to break the heavy silence which had settled over them like a portent of misfortune. When they arrived, Sheikh Abbas and Nadhir spoke together for a short time while his sister helped Marwa unpack. Nadhir gave his father an account of his meeting; he thought that the only thing that had piqued the head of the death squad was that he wasn't in a position to shoot Nadhir himself – he was afraid that his popularity among the troops and younger officers would make him into a martyr and a symbol for resistance. The commander was striving to avoid dissent within the sect, while he plotted to replace the president and consolidated his grip on power.

A document bearing the seal of the chiefs of staff relieved Nadhir of all his duties and allocated him a pension. It was delivered to him by a junior officer who saluted him for the last time and left quickly without answering any questions. The paper, which Nadhir promptly tore up, was enough to put an end to his dreams; all the same, he started speaking about when exactly he needed to spray the orange trees. He ate his breakfast before dawn with gusto, like a *fellah* with lots to do; the farm needed much work after Sheikh Abbas's three children had left it and headed for the distant cities. When much later I saw him again, on his first visit to me with Maryam, Omar and Marwa, his appearance seemed different from that of the officer who had been imprisoned by the butterflies of the woman he loved, and who had freed her from Bakr's chains. His laughter was kinder as he encouraged me to smile and go back to college, which I no longer thought of as being anything other than a vague dream, as if I had never started my studies. We had both lost our dreams. We had to piece them back together as if they were the threads of a carpet whose weave had come apart.

It was the fragility of dreams I was thinking about as the secure van transferred us to the central women's prison in Damascus – after four years in the Mukhabarat cells, we were a pitiful sight. We were delighted with our new prison, where we were allowed to spend two whole hours a day outside and look at the sky: a coveted image of the salvation we were no longer preoccupied with. In our former hell we had looked for the smallest comfort, it was so much part of us that we almost jumped in terror when we heard the cars and the sirens in the streets on our journey over. Sulafa had preceded me to the new prison by two weeks. I threw myself on her chest and wept bitterly, a missing part of her soul. She was bright-faced, cleaner and happier; the place was almost spacious and we could breathe in the cells, as air circulated through the open bars; the ghost of suffocation moved away from us. We were allocated to the various dormitories. Sulafa had reserved a place for me next to her. For the first time in four years I stretched my body out fully, and had the space to turn over as many times as I liked before plunging into a deep sleep.

The place we had dreamed of was however still a prison with reinforced-steel doors and guards stationed at intervals all along its high walls. The warders showed no respect for the taste of the Ottoman *wali* who had had it built, in what were then peach orchards outside Damascus, as a place where he could take pleasure with his Circassian wife every Thursday night. We had heard plenty of stories about him. The *wali* was fearful of other men's eyes, and jealous of the Circassian's beauty which had already destroyed the life of the Damascene trader, Muhyi Al Din, who had married her and then almost immediately started to complain to his friend the *wali* about all her caprices. The *wali* set eyes on her for the first time when she asked to see him with a petition, like any woman who might appeal to a *wali* renowned for his generosity in dealing with his city's inhabitants, for his deep-rooted lineage, and for his friendship with her husband. He didn't listen to a word she said. His gaze clung to her delicate waist, to the breasts hidden by the fabric which reached up to her shimmering white throat. He tried to lower his eyes and listen to her request, which came out suddenly: 'I want to divorce Muhyi Al Din.' She added, 'He doesn't fulfil me, and his friend the judge won't meet me or listen to me!' The *wali* contemplated her quietly, rubbed his chin and asked her to marry him, as if they were in one of Scheherazade's tales.

She returned to see the *wali* after three days which he had spent sleepless and miserable. She asked again for her divorce, and her brother, who had come from the village of Dadin, granted her the military pension arising from his service in the Topkapi Palace as her dowry. The two of them appeared to be concluding a strange sort of bargain that would eventually turn Muhyi Al Din into a brigand and an alcoholic. He swore to kill them both after the judge, under the threat of her brother's sword, divorced them *in absentia*. (Muhyi Al Din eventually forgot his vow and was killed by a stray bullet on the road to his family's plantation in Zabadany.)

Everything went off according to the *wali*'s plans. He then accompanied the judge on his Hajj pilgrimage in order to atone for his sins. They stood as partners at the gates of the Kaaba to thank God for His blessings, asked for forgiveness and returned to Syria cleansed. The judge, who saw the Circassian only once during their journey, hinted to the *wali* that he should hide her away from the gaze of others, and acquainted him with an architect, Abu Hind, who stood in front of Damascus's Umayyad Mosque every morning to point at the wide gates and the square minarets. He would criticize its engineer, Walid bin Abdel Malik, for the error which had made the mosque oblong-shaped, accusing him of not having read Pythagoras and enumerating the advantages of the circle as an architectural form more suited for that sacred place.

Abu Hind sat in front of the *wali* and without any inhibition chattered away about how awful it was architects were being deported from the Levant to Astana so that they might be kept as ignorant artisans who didn't even know the difference between white and yellow stone. The *wali* listened to his ramblings, regarding this as a necessary part of the process of convincing him to design a palace for a man who loved a woman

365

to the point of infatuation, and feared for her safety even from the summer wind. The *wali* did not object to the circular form so venerated by the architect, and acquiesced to all his conditions. Abu Hind worked tirelessly for three years so the *wali* could move there with his Circassian wife; she had awoken in him feelings of deep regret for all the years he had wasted in avoiding the pleasures of the flesh, and other material preoccupations, such as accumulating wealth or leaving a brilliant reputation as a legacy to his seven children. The serving women disclosed the secrets of the wild nights shared by the *wali* and the Circassian to the storytellers who wove a tale – substituting other names – about a sober man whose prestige was ruined by a Circassian woman before she committed suicide next to the garden fountain, leaving a short letter informing him that love had not taken root in her heart. She could no longer bear to lie down in that magnificent building designed by an awkward man as a prison, and not as a palace for lovers. Her blood had flowed over the edge of the fountain and mingled with its waters.

The storytellers went further. They said that the Circassian was in fact in love with her husband's son, who had seduced her at the instigation of his mother whom the *wali* had turned out. They also added that the *wali* abandoned Abu Hind's palace, as it became known in their yellowed records which told stories about the place where even the damp made us happy. We recreated its full glory in our imaginations and became like its Circassian owner who had bequeathed it to us, and we celebrated the blessing of being saved from the moods of the commander of the Mukhabarat unit. He seemed almost in tears that we were leaving his cells still breathing. We relaxed in the first days in the Damascus prison because our guards, ordinary policemen this time rather than Mukhabarat, seemed more sympathetic to our status as women.

I couldn't regain the power of my dreams. I used to draw them in confirmation of my passion for living, but I told Sulafa, 'Joy has escaped me, and my dreams have paled.' I warned her against forgetting Mudar but she shook her head and said, 'I can't forget him, but of course he's forgotten me; he's left me for another woman.' I realized that the letters we had written on the foil of cigarette packets, and smuggled out via Sulafa's family as soon as they were allowed to visit, had not reached him. Mudar had told her he didn't have a proper address, that he moved about. All Sulafa had had to prop up a dream which never paled was her shabby little room, as elegant as she could make it given her modest means. She had dyed some cheap material, from which she'd made curtains and the tablecloth they used every morning as Mudar drank his coffee unhurriedly: a man worshipped by a woman who laughed from the heart, as she lay down by his side and buried her dreams in his chest.

Her family visited her often and they brought food. Despite their poverty, they bribed the guards to allow us to have cotton pyjamas; we had forgotten how soft they were against our bodies, to which we believed that a man's touch would never return, even in our imagination. Sulafa's sister tried to reassure her that she would soon find Mudar and bring a letter from him with her next time she came, but she was worried by Sulafa's unceasing urgency. Eventually she had to tell her briefly and quickly that Mudar had refused Sulafa's letters and even denied all knowledge of her. She added that he had married a Mukhabarat officer's daughter who had pursued him and now led him off to a different destiny, as he had begun to work in the father's smuggling operation. But Sulafa wasn't the only forsaken woman. Thana's husband had sent her divorce papers. He hadn't waited for her to come out of prison, despite her lack of protest at his marriage to a woman twenty years his junior. He adorned his wife with Thana's bracelets and expelled all sign of her from the house to which she had expected to return, as befitted a long-awaited wife.

In some ways we hated the visits which were allowed once every three months for us, and once a month for the Marxists. The outside world came back to us and removed our delusions, without granting us the luxury of absorbing ourselves in petty day-to-day worries. Maryam never missed a visit. She had grown old and exhausted; she wouldn't explain anything, and I sensed she was making things up when she couldn't quite carry off the deception. I needed her to reassure me about Radwan. I was surprised by the strength of his presence within me, as if he were a frivolous reflection of myself in the life I neglected. She lavished clothes on me (most of which were stolen by the warders) and food which she had spent days making, and which she flavoured with all types of spices, bringing back all my old pleasure at that sharp taste which scraped the back of my throat. I was delighted and recovered a past I didn't want to die, so I wouldn't feel my very real orphanhood. I reverted to my old illusions as a source of comfort, and to combat thoughts of suicide, which I resisted after Hajja Souad reminded us of the birds of paradise fluttering over our heads. I had forgotten about them; now, they found us all together with our other cellmates: Marxists and criminals, all accused of prostitution, all enjoying songs.

It was a long time before my father visited me. I had longed to see him and look boldly into his sad eyes for the first time. He smiled at me encouragingly and tried to reach my fingers to touch them and warmly extend kinship to me. I forgot everything I had wanted to tell him and which I had spent five years memorizing; I now saw again the smile which relaxed his narrow lips, and I put out of my mind how Maryam had described him as an alcoholic who wanted to marry an Armenian from Beirut. 'And after a girl of your mother's breeding!' she had said disapprovingly, which made me laugh. I was astonished at my laughter, by which Maryam understood that I agreed with his new direction in life. I almost asked him about his new wife, and suggested that he bring her with him, but he never visited again, and I didn't blame him. That night, I stayed awake till dawn and made the girls laugh as I mimicked the prison governor who called us *daughters* when he was in a good mood, and *whores* when he wasn't, and whose face had begun to resemble a mouldy melon. Yes, I was happy with my father's visit. I had needed to acknowledge him and my kinship with him.

Sulafa's mental state worsened. She seemed vacant most of the time and took no notice when we spoke; she didn't even hear us. I never left her side and fought everyone who tried to mock her; I defended my friend. I would take on her share of the chores we all had to do. At night I listened to her moans, her ravings about Mudar. I felt like she was my young daughter who was terrified of the outside world and yet longed for it. After three months she no longer remembered Mudar's name, as if it were her that had left him. I drew her attention to the blossom on the peach tree, and then came the only evidence that she remembered where she was: she told me, 'Yes, they blossomed. I told you they would.' Then she buttoned up her woollen jacket, seeking protection from the cold spring breeze which made us all optimistic. We weren't sure why spring should make us so optimistic; to us, it meant flowers in the prison courtyard. Each spring, we picked the peach blossoms; we couldn't wait until they turned into fruit. We carried the branches to our dormitories and improvised vases, celebrating with flowers like any women, to prove to ourselves that we had mastered the wait.

The new prison had lost its novelty. Now we begged for images of the outside and cared for the details of the lives we had left behind, seemingly so neglected. We wanted to recover the passion which still lived inside us. We all turned back to our dreams as a means of overcoming the corruption of the security services, and to create the expectation of a pardon from the authorities and their Party. We circulated rumours that pardons surely must be inevitable. We never believed this again after they dragged Tuhama the mute out to a noose in the courtyard. They took us to see her dangling; in her eyes there was a look of reproach and apology. The scene was a shock to us and made us think about our fate again. They had demanded a retrial after accusing her of blowing up an armoured car in Hama, and a doctor ruled that she was feigning her dumbness to escape responsibility. Tuhama had shared our bed and our dreams, and her corpse, as it hung like a lamp, reminded us that she was just like us: corpses dangling in the breeze.

Tuhama had been nothing more than a girl who

had lost the power of speech after carrying the corpses of her three brothers through the streets, looking for two square metres of earth to bury them in. The sight of her, as Um Mamdouh described it, was like an actress moving in an abandoned theatre. The hail of bullets that besieged her from all sides didn't stop her from persevering and going on each errand with each corpse as if she were performing a role in a Greek tragedy. She buried the three of them on the banks of the Orontes, prayed over them, and when she tried to recite the Sura Fatiha she discovered that she had been struck dumb. It didn't bother her; she had spent the previous two nights with her brothers' bodies amid the sound of shooting, while helicopters hovered over the city and paratroopers sprang from them like arrogant rain.

Tuhama had become a corpse whose presence among us dazed us. Um Mamdouh tried to rush towards the gallows to hug the corpse which reminded us that the same fate was awaiting us. It was awful to see someone whom I had shared coffee with only the day before now hanging from a noose whose image would haunt us for ever. I said to Sulafa that Tuhama had been sacrificed as an example to terrify us, and she didn't reply. She didn't respond to the group's prayers for Tuhama's soul. Hajja Souad led us – we needed an imam so our prayers would be dignified, so we would appear as respectable mourners for the girl whose blankets and clothes we would now divide between us. A drug addict had left them to her after passing through our world one day.

Our child had long begun to walk properly. He trotted alongside Rasha who took great care of him. He lisped some prison vocabulary, and was so used to the place he could have lived out the rest of his life there without any feeling of regret. I thought that he had the advantage over us as I watched him, trying to trace any resemblance between him and Hossam or Mudar, so I could adore him like Rasha. She would chase him through the dormitories so he would not get lost, convincing herself that it was possible to lose him even in this place where yesterdays meant nothing more to us than unbearable misery. The peach tree lost its gleam; it seemed wretched and sickly. Fights among ourselves increasingly added spice to our mornings. We wanted to forget ourselves, as the best way of enduring was to forget one's memories. 'Leave your past at the door,' I thought in an attempt to steel myself for the loss of Sulafa, who had been ordered to prepare for her imminent release. Everything here happened without adequate notice: death, birth, freedom, fights, tears, and the dancing which so enraptured us that we drowned in it. We began to specialize in exhibiting our charms to the rhythm of saucepans and Thana's voice. She recreated Aleppo and the secret songs of its women, which Orientalists had tried to dig up over the centuries, and which seemed so intractable and obscure. The celebration was held for no particular reason, and remained unhampered by the protests of some prisoners from our group who were immersed again in memorizing the Quran and repeating it for the fifth time. They circulated the only book among themselves; it had been given to them by the prison governor that day, delighted at the birth of his first grandchild.

Not long after, one morning, we were ordered into the courtyard where a security man then read out a list of people who would be transferred immediately to a Mukhabarat unit to process their release. Turmoil gripped us. I thought for a moment of the order to take a look at Tuhama's dangling body. It wasn't like ours; despite everything, ours were still breathing and could still feel pain. The list of nine girls included three from our organization whose entire guilt consisted of being the sisters of wanted men who had been able to flee abroad. The girls who were being released started crying; my tongue went rigid and I couldn't join in with the chorus of trills which sprang up spontaneously. The guards rushed the girls out; we couldn't say goodbye as one should to companions who had shared such suffering and nights of torture. I embraced Sulafa without looking into her eyes, which were fixed on me like she was racked with pain. The departing girls waved; depression hovered over those left behind, something we had grown used to after any release. I tried to immerse myself in sleep; after I woke up, I was alone, and I needed sympathy.

Safaa's sudden visit saved me from depression. A gust of perfume wafting from her took me straight back to our shared past, as she distributed money liberally to the guards so they would look the other way. Maryam sat nearby absorbed in her long *misbaha*, and I thought that she now looked like my grandmother. She wanted to remind me that I wasn't a little child any more. Twenty-five years was long enough for me to feel my membership of the world of women, with all its joy and grief. There was no possibility of Safaa drowning in pre-destined tears; I contemplated the smoothness of her face, as serene as a queen's from a painting of the Nahda era. Her elegance was worthy of a princess. I sat beside her, stinking of the prison; I was like an orphan servant girl she had taken off the street, not her former companion of night revels when we had enjoyed the coolness of the fountain and lying on the damp ground in the scorching heat of summer.

Safaa slipped a small piece of paper under my shirt as she showed me photos of her son Amir, standing on a chair and frowning in concentration as he aimed a toy gun at an imaginary target. Safaa stirred up an atmosphere of mirth, aiming to be my clown for a few minutes. I noticed her swift glances at my face which took note of my pallor and confusion. She convinced the guards, who had never seen such a glorious creature in all their lives, that she had indeed come from the world of *A Thousand and One Nights* and proved it by her largesse – for the cup of coffee they offered her, she paid an amount equal to the governor's monthly salary. We spoke at length, and the private visit that I hadn't even dreamed of stretched out for more than two hours. I could smell her perfume the entire time. The heat of her hands scorched me, and they didn't leave mine for a moment. I reminisced about how she spoiled me when I was a child, and she said a prayer for my mother and intimated that Abdullah remembered me and prayed to God to end my captivity, as she winked and pointed to the letter she had concealed in my clothes. It was difficult for me to describe adequately the last six years in two hours. Before the end of the visit, I asked her if I could see my brother and Radwan, whom Safaa had told me was overjoyed at her presence. In a low voice, she described Maryam's fury at their warm relationship; her suspicion increased in proportion to her loneliness. She stayed in the old house for an entire week, causing laughter and sincere tears when she said goodbye. Safaa inhaled me as if she would never see me again. She didn't tell me that she was anxious, and that her insistence that I had only a short time left in detention was a lie to help me sleep.

I tried to speed up the time which still remained until I could return home and join in Radwan's singing. Safaa left me money which I gave to Hajja Souad, who blessed me and lent me the Quran for an additional hour every day. That evening I made sure I was alone in the bathroom, so that I was unobserved when I opened the delicate, carefully folded letter. I began to read what Abdullah had written especially for me: 'My dear, patient daughter, may God grant her long life. Know how proud I am when I speak about you to the councils of mujahideen. Know, my daughter, that I and the mujahideen believers in Afghanistan will avenge your pain, and the pain of all the Muslims. God bless you.' There was no signature.

I read the message again eagerly, ignoring the increasingly violent banging on the door. I hid it in my clothes and left without realizing how pale my face was, as Hajja Souad told me when she tried to draw me into the prayer circle memorizing the Quran. I needed to be on my own to review Abdullah's words. I didn't understand why he had taken the risk of sending a letter to a prisoner which contained information about his activities in Afghanistan. Terrified, I claimed I had stomach cramps so I could go back to the bathroom, and the girls who were waiting let me go first. I closed the door and tore the letter up, threw it into the hole, and flushed it away. I wasn't happy until the last scrap of paper had disappeared along with the filthy water. I felt strange that night. I reproached myself harshly for being so negligent with the words of a man as discreet as Abdullah.

He hadn't forgotten my loyalty, and was encouraging me to withstand the depression and the enormous injustice weighing down so heavily on me.

I thought of Abdullah, covered by the dust of Afghanistan's mountain paths as he transported supplies on mangy mules and donkeys, moving steadily over the rugged terrain. For many years now he had been taking medicine, food and money to be distributed among the mujahideen fighting to topple the Communist government, which the Soviets kept supplied with soldiers for its defence. Abdullah had found a new project to keep him awake at nights: devising ingenious new strategies with the 'Arab-Afghans' who had flooded into the dusty and windswept city of Peshawar. Its people were poor, content to exist outside time, and happy with a lifestyle that allowed them to lounge around enjoying endless cups of strong tea, while the dusty tape recorder in the corner played the same tape for the thousandth time.

Everything in Peshawar had indicated that it was an ideal place to put to use the donations from Muslims who considered the Afghan issue to be their own. The words of Sheikh Nadim Al Salaty during the Hajj shook them, and the Afghan pilgrims would never in their lives forget the sight of their brothers in Mecca scrambling towards them to bless their jihad. The pilgrims threw millions of dollars into the green wooden collecting boxes. Sheikh Nadim kept back for his good causes several millions, as the fee for his influential presence at the councils of various princes – they would give him the seat of honour and accede to all his requests so that he would bless them. The money was immediately transferred to his accountants who distributed it wherever he ordered.

One autumn day some years earlier, Abdullah arrived in Peshawar from Islamabad, exhausted from the journey and a long night spent in discussions with his friend Philip Anderson. They had both quickly left off the small-talk and their conversation began to exhibit clear signs of mutual mistrust, due to the nature of their mission. This didn't, however, prevent them from exchanging some small luxury gifts. That night was long. They had so much to discuss that they didn't find time to eat until after the morning prayer; Abdullah performed it with great humility, which caught the notice of Anderson. He had found it difficult to answer his superiors' questions about whether Abdullah – whose past was tainted with Marxist and Guevaran episodes and who was currently obsessed by expelling his former comrades from Kabul – was a mercenary or a special sort of Soviet agent. He was very impressive as he raised his finger to say the *shahada*; then he got up quickly, speaking in a playful tone and fluent English. He used it only rarely with Anderson, whenever he invited him to convert to Islam. They finally ate their breakfast after agreeing on the routes for the transfer of weapons to the Afghan mujahideen in the Kandahar mountains. Abdullah had bought them from American arms dealers who wandered through hotel bars in holiday wear, asking about the carpet souk and transport to Kashmir just like any other tourists. Anderson had arranged for them to complete the deals and benefit from the sizable commissions.

After their meeting, Abdullah had wandered through the markets of Islamabad before taking a taxi to Peshawar. Next to him on the back seat was a bearded young local who tried to sell him a blackbird he claimed sang in Arabic. The Yemeni liked the gestures of the cheerful young man. He inspected the blackbird, and haggled over the price – the man wanted three dollars and wouldn't budge. Abdullah bought the blackbird and immediately released it out of the car window as it sped along the pot-holed road, much to the astonishment of the young Pakistani who told him it would die after a few metres. He told Abdullah of other blackbirds born in captivity that died as soon as tourists bought them and set them free.

Sheikh Nadim Al Salaty was waiting for Abdullah in his Peshawar hostel, which was crammed with volunteers who had arrived that afternoon from Algeria, Egypt and Saudi Arabia. Among them was a young man of no more than seventeen; Abdullah scrutinized him as he reached politely for the simple food in front of him. He wasn't surprised at the presence of a young man who wore jeans and long hair, just like the friends he had left to their fun in faraway tea houses. Sheikh Nadim Al Salaty proudly introduced the newcomer as 'the famous Wasim Al Halawany, son of the famous neurogurgeon Samir Al Halawany'. Abdullah nodded and smiled, warmly shook the boy's hand and encouraged him to join in the fight. 'I know you well, my son.' He left the boy suddenly and continued to his room. The following morning, Sheikh Nadim didn't even wait for Abdullah to finish drinking his coffee (prepared with heavy cardamom to treat the bad headache he had suffered from all night) before voicing his fears and his irritation at Abdullah's modus operandi; he criticized him for handing donated money over to arms dealers, and distributing the rest unevenly among the various Afghan factions.

Years later, Abdullah would lean on the arm of Wasim Al Halawany (whose beard, to his own great satisfaction, had by now grown long and thick, rather increasing his charm) as they walked at Sheikh Nadim Al Salaty's funeral, recalling that distant morning in Peshawar, and the emotion of Sheikh Nadim who had come to offer his assistance to the poverty-stricken Afghan orphans and widows, not to fight alongside them. His voice had rumbled through the Grand Mosque, asking for funds to buy food for the starving children and wool for the destitute women whose husbands had gone to the mountains, or had been sent by the Afghan secret police to detention camps in Kabul and Moscow: the funds were not intended to arm the warring factions.

That morning, Abdullah did not listen very closely to the man who loved and respected him, and who had once laughed heartily at Abdullah's tales of the eccentricities of the Russian women he had known. Zeina, Abdullah's first wife, had even named their young son Nadim, whom the sheikh blessed as he sat on his knee. He took Nadim on a pilgrimage to the Kaaba, causing the sons of princes and princesses to cast jealous glances at Zeina; she didn't hide her happiness that day, just as she didn't hide her grief at the recent death of that majestic man. She recited a lament for him, a Nabataean ode, without declaring her identity – she dreaded being forced to sing laments at the almost daily princely funerals, now so frequent because the royal family had become so hugely extended that the palaces had become too small to contain all its members. She recited the ode in the salons of princesses who tried to convince her to write it down, or at least allow it to be recorded so their husbands could listen to it; the princes were desperately curious to hear the lines that 'made even stones weep', as the wives said when they attempted to remember some of them. Eventually a royal decree was issued to Zeina. She wrote the ode down in plain *ruq'a* script, added some decoration, signed it in small letters and then presented it to the king. He granted her the horse she had requested from the royal stable; she had fallen in love with him when she saw him in the annual race through the Najd Desert.

When Safaa came to Aleppo, she described the stallion to Omar in great detail and awoke his longing for horses, only for this to lose itself in the forgetfulness which then clung to him for three months, after Safaa went to Afghanistan to join her husband, and the Arab fighters transformed themselves from saviours of the poor and messengers of love into just one more faction in the conflict. They carried weapons and dreamed of the Islamic caliphate that would shine again amidst the vast plains planted with poppies, whose petals gleamed beneath the spring sunshine in an omen of imminent destruction.

During her only visit to me in prison, Safaa hadn't told me she was travelling to Afghanistan. When I found out some time later, I started to recall the words of Abdullah's letter. For long nights, I was besieged by Abdullah and his ever-cheerful face; he was secure in the certainty he had been granted, and which he had grasped with both hands, like a child who doesn't want to give up a bar of chocolate and continues squeezing it until it melts and is wasted. When Abdullah took Safaa to Riyadh Airport for her flight to Syria, he told her to wait for a letter which would give her the details of where they would next live. He handed her that letter for me, kissed Amir as if for the last time, and gave her enough money to live like a princess anywhere in the world. Our family was worried at Safaa's sudden arrival alone in Aleppo. She wasn't expecting anyone to meet her at Damascus Airport, so hired a car and driver; she thought that she needed a stretch of road to think about her future and the future of her son; Zeina had refused to leave the small palace she had shared for so long with Safaa like a close friend.

The affliction of love bound them both to a man in the grip of a dream. Abdullah wept bitterly when he returned from Sheikh Nadim Al Salaty's funeral, remembering how the sheikh had once said to him, 'You have to know where you are going before you leave your house; know your travelling companion, and *be wary of him*.' He was referring to Abdullah's long-standing association with Anderson, which had led to his dealing also with an American ambassador in the region. The latter would meet with Abdullah every so often for a few hours; he would extend greetings from the American president, and convey his pride in his allies' achievements at driving out the Soviets and the Communists from Kabul. Then, in a decisive tone, the ambassador would relay the president's orders relating to the Afghan groups who deserved to share in the victory. It didn't occur to the Americans that the Arab volunteers had also begun to have a hold over parts of the country. The ambassador equivocated in his replies to questions about the future position of the 'Arab-Afghans' in a strict Islamic state, but displayed more enthusiasm as soon as the conversation swung away from this towards demands not to disband the warring factions.

Abdullah tried to make good use of all his experience; he felt burdened by the countless faces of the people he had dealt with, and all the plotting which had almost killed him more than once. He recalled conversations with Bakr during their carefree wanderings to find furnishings for the palace Prince Shehab El Din was building to reclaim the warmth of his mother's womb. He remembered their discussions about power and its allure. He thought of the last time he had seen Sheikh Nadim Al Salaty. The sheikh had bid him goodbye as if he were a troublesome friend, and Abdullah asked that Wasim Al Halawany accompany him and promised not to leave his side. A hasty consultation was held with Wasim, who seemed like a shy young girl receiving her fate from her elders' commands, and the two of them left Sheikh Nadim's hostel in Peshawar for the last time. The mule caravan was waiting for them on the outskirts of the city, led by a silent, turbaned Afghani who knew his task well. They crossed the border at night, and in the darkness Abdullah started to tell Wasim about his friendship with his father Samir, now a renowned surgeon, with whom he had shared a desk at the English School in Cairo for three years. Wasim was astonished at this tale of his family, from whose opulent wealth and aristocratic heritage he had fled, to this filthy place in which the wolves found nothing to eat but their own young.

When Ülfet Hanim, a pasha's daughter, attended school, four Nubian guards waited for her in front of the door to accompany her home. Abdullah kept watch for his friend Samir, who would wait around so he could catch a glimpse of her. 'He looked just like you,' said Abdullah in fluent English, looking at the boy who kept his gaze averted out of respect for Abdullah's reputation. His name had often resounded in prayers in recent days as a role model and mujahid who had exploited the unbelievers' faults; his articles inciting jihad in Afghanistan were published by the Jama'a Islamiyya in Egypt and widely distributed. They were the reason why Wasim had given up drinking beer and chasing girls whose mothers had complained about his recklessness and foul language. He was aware that his new teacher was testing his English and replied in a few words to reassure Abdullah that he spoke it like a native. He asked Abdullah to finish his story, expecting to be told that his father was its chief protagonist. His father was busy earning money from all over the world so that Ülfet Hanim could spend it on the shoes she accumulated with an astonishingly thrilling madness, until everyone who knew her believed that humanity, in her view, equalled shoes. Abdullah spent long nights with his new secretary and jihad associate, speaking to him about his past as if he had at last found someone to whom he could entrust his story, who could preserve it after the death whose breath he could already feel.

The pictures I drew amidst the rot of the cells were soon erased. The spring sun, which I tried to forget just like all prisoners do, besieged us again and made us depressed and disposed to silence. At last, we agreed on something we could all share – the frustrations of celibacy. We ate in silence and got into bed quietly after making sure that lice hadn't settled in the bedding. We felt reassured that our deprived bodies were still capable of dreaming, like the bodies of any normal women, with predatory lust.

The seventh winter of my imprisonment had passed. Seven was our holy number, highly regarded in our Quran. Over the course of time, much had changed in the building we pretended to ourselves wasn't really a jail. But terror returned with the installation of a new prison governor, whose hobby was pinning medals to his chest and cursing us. He loved the guard dogs which wandered at night through our cells with their handlers. He spoiled them obscenely, laughing like an idiotic actor who has found an arena in which to show off his backstage compulsions. We were his urinal which he never left dry. He even slept in the prison and left it only at the instigation of his superiors, who would summon him to a meeting so they could divide up the bribes and the money extorted from us and our families. Everything had a price, as if we were an open market. The criminals, who were used to paying bribes, threw us morsels of the food their pimps, smuggling partners and fellow murderers regularly brought them from grand hotels in Damascus, along with the sumptuous clothing they would wear in order to seduce the warders and governor. He would drink tea with them in their cells while eavesdropping on us, women who had been isolated for years.

We exchanged wry glances about, and occasionally laughed at, Um Nadal, the prostitute in her fifties who had been in and out of this place more than fifteen times. She used to wear a revealing top which smelled of cheap perfume, and taught us her rules about not getting addicted to anything that might run out. Um Nadal would ask permission to see the governor; she would strut over to his office, cursing the country which didn't appreciate her talents, and threatening someone called Asmahan with ripping her in two. Um Nadal would return half drunk, and to the drug addicts it was obvious how much and what sort of hashish she had been smoking. She displayed infinite generosity towards us, which was unsurprising from a woman who seemed so alone, and she wept like a child when even a single finger of ours was scratched.

'Spring is dull this year,' I said to Suhayr as we

walked around the small courtyard, utterly bored, even knowing how many ants were in each hole. She didn't reply, as usual during the exercise hour. Suhayr was my only friend after Sulafa left. Sulafa had come back to visit me on one occasion – she had bribed the governor's wife to be allowed to see me for just five minutes, pleading that after all she would be back in the prison. I saw her in the governor's office, and he emphasized the secrecy of the visit and that it was against the rules. I laughed at the fear which had turned him into someone who spoke about *rules*. I first saw her face through the open door, and I was afraid they would rearrest her. She took me in her arms and we burst out crying before I left, pulled away roughly. We said only a few words to each other, which I had prepared thousands of times. I opened the small package from her which they allowed me to keep. I unrolled a simple blue dress, and its details revealed that she had sewn it for me herself. One of the girls in my group relayed an order from Hajja Souad not to wear it; I didn't argue with her, as had become usual recently. In the bundle I also found a small bag I hadn't noticed at first, and it smelled of spices. I knew they were from our kitchen. I recalled Sulafa's few words; I now knew that she had visited my home, like I had insisted. She had stood behind Radwan singing stanzas like the chorus I had once been.

That night, I wore the blue dress. I slipped it on carefully and kept all the buttons done up, so my breasts wouldn't be on show to the guards. Hajja Souad didn't object further. It was a sort of agreement between us which we tacitly respected; she sent me orders only through an intermediary and she didn't interfere in my relationship with the criminals, who kept me so entertained with their fantastic stories which might very well have been made up, but in which I believed passionately. I laughed from my belly at their anecdotes. I still remember Sana, accused of smuggling hash across the border with Lebanon, who convinced us that she was indeed Lebanese and the only daughter of a well-known diamond seller whose surname resembled hers; he owned a string of jewellery shops, the most famous of which was on the Rue Hamra in Beirut.

'We have to believe lies so we won't die,' I told myself as I watched the ceiling, which I had watched thousands of times. I couldn't find my star which I imagined hanging from a damp spot in the ancient plaster, and I tried to convince myself that I was sleeping in the same place as had stood the bed where the Circassian, in silk garments, had given up the splendour of her white flesh and the firmness of her seductive breasts to the enamoured *wali*. I felt the touch of my clothes on my naked body. The dress's fabric excited my skin. I almost went mad with lust; I imagined the faces of men I had seen, including Radwan, students from the medical college, and the warders. I wept from burning lust. How wretched I was;

how wretched we all were. This spring was so slow in passing. 'It's difficult to kill a woman's desire,' I thought. I imagined Sulafa sleeping in my bed; she embraced me, and we shared Mudar. We forgave him for abandoning us. We returned to play with delicious illusions which had delighted us once, a long time ago, and which I couldn't recall properly any more. It was as if, for the first time, I had become interested in ordering my memories of prison. Summoning them up, I was saved by remembering the faces of people it was impossible for me to reach from prison. The power of the place made us feel our weakness. Without our permission, we were colonized by hatred we couldn't escape, and love we couldn't live out.

Our child grew taller. He called us by our names, and we taught him to read and write, and a few words of English which we were delighted to hear him repeat. He stood in front of us gesturing like a public speaker to a non-existent crowd in an unlit hall. I was less charmed than the other prisoners by his games. I sometimes joined Suhayr in sewing clothes for him out of scraps of cloth, using tidy stitches so he wouldn't look like a beggar, or even his true self: a fatherless child, begging for sympathy from mothers who were getting tired of him bleating like a lost lamb. We all looked for something which could save us from feeling that time lay heavily on us, that our lives were stuck in an inescapable rut. We had to appear brave, as if we weren't afraid of the torture or the narrow, crushing walls, so we wouldn't be destroyed by our fellow inmates' glances, which might accuse us of weakness. These cruel looks made us wish for death. They laid bare the weakness we desperately tried to conceal. In the time which we scattered like worthless sand, I thought many things over; I thought of the executioners, whose roaring laughter we could hear as they left in the evening, carrying home vegetables and bread for their children like any normal person. I thought of the victims from both sides who had fallen so that an idea could be realized.

Dalal was a Marxist, driven away by her comrades for wearing a veil and praying humbly behind Hajja Souad as a means of atoning for her collapse during interrogation, when she had revealed the location of her Party's files. She reminded me of a girl from my group who had tried to flee to Saudi Arabia. A quick trial was convened, without any proper defence, so that it seemed more like a bit of fun than anything else. Dalal's trial was no different from our own trial of Suzanne, who later had thrown herself to the floor and grabbed the Mukhabarat unit leader by the feet to plead for release. She had written more than a thousand letters to the President asking him to pardon her and save her from her sentence. She wept and begged for forgiveness from our group which only increased its cruelty, and kept her from our table like she was a mangy bitch. We didn't even let her use the communal toilet. How cruel it is, when a secure existence within a group is your only safe-guard for breathing foul air inside cells whose inhabitants aren't even allowed to lie down on the cold floor. I didn't dare console the sweet-natured Suzanne, or approach her after all these years, or apologize for sitting in judgement next to Hajja Souad as we had coldly sentenced her to this further level of imprisonment within the prison, and prevented her from holding our child, as we had done with the informer Hoda. All this was more lies in which we believed absolutely.

Prison taught you the rules of staying alive. No one who hasn't been in jail can understand what it is like to be deprived of looking at the sun whenever you feel like it. Habits that had been trivial outside gained new meaning in prison. In that darkness, the euphemisms which we had sheltered behind withered away. We spat on our enemies. '"Life" is a difficult metaphor,' I thought, 'like "love", "betrayal"; even a light-hearted game in a lettuce field.' I laughed at the memory of lettuce which I hadn't seen for seven years. I missed its freshness; I imagined it covered in spices, crisp and delicious in my mouth.

In our house, lettuce used to be synonymous with Safaa, just as butterflies were with Marwa. Safaa would wash its succulent leaves and nibble at it with excessive relish, pretending to be a rabbit. I used to laugh when Maryam scolded her. Safaa would seek out such silliness as a means of resisting her fate, from which the only escape was into another life no less odd – from Aleppo to Saudi Arabia and finally to Afghanistan, that land which meant death or madness. The princess who had visited me in prison felt that all that was left of me was ice-cold, that I was a piece of sugar whose sweetness had faded. She had pressed my hand and gone off to an unknown destiny.

This idea of destiny obsessed me, and I felt great comfort that that mythical ship would carry me off to my fate. When our destiny is not in our control, there is nothing left but this suffocation I felt to be delicious. I pushed on more deeply into it, so I could surrender my will entirely. 'I'm so tired, Mama, so tired,' I said to myself. I imagined her sitting silently in front of me, smiling shyly as she skilfully cleaned a fish my father had caught and fried it for us before it went bad. My brothers and I hated fish; we constantly tried to escape from the rancid smell of my father's hands. Hossam and I pretended to chew it like good children, but Humam ate it with a gluttony we found astonishing. I forgot to ask him about this on his first visit, when Omar brought him. I hugged Humam over-enthusiastically – I wanted to hide my astonishment at seeing him as a young man with a thin, timid moustache. He was the only presence in my life which didn't require some sort of deceptive embellishment to give me a feeling of security, like calling Sulafa 'my sister', or Um Mamdouh 'my mother'. He really was my brother; there was no illusion involved. I was allowed to keep a photo of him. The other prisoners passed it around, and I heard their comments with the glee of a sister who knew the truth about that handsome face whose narrow lips they craved.

In my eighth year, as my sentence neared its end, I thought how I would soon be leaving this place. 'It will be difficult to go back to my room . . .' I thought as I lay in bed, surrendering to the fear which grew inside me like ivy, just as they wanted. I remembered the rounds of torture in the Mukhabarat unit, and the pus, the ulcers, the lice which attacked us and which we were afraid of admitting were in our cells. I had had recurrent bouts of illness that scarred me and kept the others well away from me – but there was no time for reproaches here, just as there was no time for living. We had to keep our bodies intact, as we still might need them some day. We kept breathing to reassure ourselves of the soundness of our lungs and arteries, which still boomed with blood like the rush of a waterfall. There is nothing quite like a prisoner's mindset; it made us perfectly capable of considering our limbs just as if they had come out of a dream.

Our craving for compassion made us praise those warders who overlooked little misdemeanours, such as dawdling on the way to the dormitories, or laughing too loudly. It made us tolerant of everything we used to condemn in our enemies, when we were on the outside. This enmity began to seem worthless; we remembered it, and thanked prison which made images of our old life beautiful. I looked for a sympathetic prisoner so I could tell her all about the dreams I had once drawn in the notebooks now taken from me, along with sheets of paper on which I had copied Prophetic *ahadith* and excerpts from books by Sayyid Qutb, Al Ghazali, and the fatwas of Ibn Baz; I had believed them all, just as I had believed the lie of hatred and praised it.

The daily inspections were the most futile acts in this forsaken place, given that we were surrounded by guards and iron doors. They counted us, sometimes making do with us calling out our numbers, at other times requiring us to stand up so they could confirm our presence. One by one we would slink to the other wall where we waited for the warders' moods to be revealed – we never knew where they would lead us. The governor walked in front of us, proud of his virility and his carefully clipped moustache. He strutted in front of women whose desires had died and whose skins bloomed with poison. His deputy would spend hours 'inspecting the inspection', which was repeated as if they too were afraid of being alone and needed us to entertain them with what remained of the pertness of our breasts and our dishevelled hair. The deputy-deputy never wasted an opportunity to speak to us about morals, just like a preacher. He would curse us and then describe us as *whores*, all as if he were addressing crowds hanging on his every word. In a quiet voice, he praised himself, his leader, his Party and his Islam, and then began to give us advice, his words growing increasingly tender as he called us his *sisters* and *daughters*. He drew on examples of moral rectitude taken from his own respectable household and his method of bringing up his four daughters. We began to know their names and the names of their husbands, the colour of their hair, the smell of the perfume they loved. Once Sulafa kicked me to get my attention and whispered sarcastically, 'Ask him about his daughter Mona.' I just laughed inwardly as I stared at his paunch and his feeble attempts to hide his repulsive baldness.

How many of those men came to us in our cells without asking our leave, when it used to be so difficult for anyone to enter a woman's bedroom without permission? We were so humiliated; repressed conscripts spied on us, and we could hear them masturbating on the other side of the doors to the cells. The fear of being raped made us cautious all the time, even when we were in the toilet. This fear clung to us for a long time; we wished that we could close up our vaginas and padlock them to keep the little that was still ours.

Buthayna's leg was broken twice, they plucked out an eye, and they cut off a finger, but still she didn't reveal the hiding place of the printing press she ran for our Party. During the three years she spent in solitary confinement near to us, we could hear her voice raised in cursing them. Her presence so close to us was vital in making us feel, in the first days, that our pain was meaningless. We heard her moaning like a wounded lioness, screaming after the numbness went from her limbs and she regained consciousness after the torture sessions we couldn't keep count of. They put her in with us after we'd been two years in the women's prison; we welcomed her with kisses, trills and the song 'The White Moon Rose Over Us'. She smiled, exhausted, grateful to the Marxists who cherished her courage and sang our hymns with us. We echoed the beauty of their compassion when we were joined by Helena, one of their girls, who had the slight build and face of a rabbit. The Mukhabarat unit let her be transferred only in the hope of breaking the knot in her tongue which wouldn't stop screaming at them, 'Dogs and traitors!' The woman's resilience oppressed the torturers, and they credited her with their own masculinity. They called Helena by a man's name and avoided her, even though she was in a cage. The strength of the malevolence in her heart terrified them, and made them regret that they hadn't included her in the earlier execution sprees which had harvested thousands of men and women. No one knew where these corpses had gone.

Helena and Buthayna were both sentenced to twenty years in prison. They relaxed when sitting together, and they chose a corner where they could sleep next to each other after fighting about God, Marx, Lenin, sex, children and songs. They celebrated their differences of opinion. Their long isolation in solitary confinement had made them hard, and they were dismissive of our transient pain; we didn't defend ourselves against their attacks of 'how spoiled' we were, nor their derision at our wish to return to our homes, and our defence of those who couldn't withstand the torture and revealed everything they knew. Isn't cruelty measureless, when someone asks you to be heroic, but the only resource you have to draw on is deference to the opinion of other prisoners that you are, indeed, a heroine? At first I was close to Buthayna, but I grew to hate her. I couldn't bear how she slandered Bakr and described him as a traitor. I respected her for tormenting our captors, but hated her overbearing behaviour, and the fact that Hajja Souad was afraid of her. I could hear Buthayna snoring in her troubled sleep as she tried to expel an insect from her nose. She tossed and turned like any worried woman. When she had been in solitary confinement, away from us, she was a legend. Myths grew up about her daring during battle; moving tributes circulated among members of our group who raised her to the status of a blessed female saint. But it is hard to come face to face with your heroine, breathing like any other woman, fighting for an additional slice of bread and a little of the bean soup brimming with dead flies. Insults created a being of hatred and let it out to play.

Ten days before my release, I celebrated my twenty-sixth birthday without much fuss. The girls who knew the date stayed close to me with the affection of friends who were to bid me goodbye soon. They hastily prepared the candle hidden away for such occasions, which had fallen into their hands two years earlier, when Rasha insisted on it to mark our child's fourth birthday. She had a cake smuggled in and we greedily gobbled small slices of it as we sang for him and helped him to blow out his candle; he looked at us, astonished at discovering that the act of blowing out a candle necessitated all this uproar. Rasha had since left but her candle stayed behind as a memory for us. We would light it for a few seconds so it could be blown out by a woman who needed to feel that she was a year older. We wished out loud for our freedom – what else would a prisoner wish for? I blew out the candle in turn and some of the girls clapped and kissed me. Um Mamdouh hugged me and cried: I was her daughter, who would no longer sit and eat with her after Buthayna and I had fought over whose turn it was for the bathroom. I kissed her hand and assured her that I wouldn't leave her side during the remaining ten days, and I would return to being her daughter.

In that time, I vowed to fast and perform fifteen

*ruk'at* every day. The girls from my group were surprised at this humility, as I had left off praying three years earlier. Um Mamdouh defended me when Buthayna commented that God didn't accept the prayers of infidels. 'I can be silent for ten days,' I thought, worried that they would change their minds and continue to hold me in the Mukhabarat unit, as had happened with many girls who had returned to hell and were still waiting for their release from day to day. I left it to God, and observed the prisoners who had accompanied me on this hellish journey. Hajja Souad had invented a unique way of keeping track of time. Every day, she sewed a stitch of black thread in her only shirt, which she only took off to wash every three months. She counted the stitches every day; the girls laughed when one of them tried to help her and reduced the total by two or three days. Hajja Souad recounted them as if she were mocking the time that hung on the edge of her blouse, a stitch of black thread acting as witness to her misery and the curtailment of her passion for beautiful fabrics. A woman who had loved elegance and cleanliness, her surrender to filthy clothes affected us; it gave us to understand that she had surrendered to death, and believed it inevitable.

However, two years after leaving prison, I knocked on Hajja Souad's door in the Sabil district of Aleppo and I almost didn't recognize her, she was so excessively elegant. She had covered her arms with real gold bracelets as Aleppans usually did when they wanted to boast of their wealth. She hugged me cheerfully and kissed Sulafa warmly. The daughters of the *wali*'s palace, as we still called the prison, moved feverishly and longed perpetually for fun and sumptuous banquets. I kissed them all as they arrived and registered their disturbance at the fact that my face was now unveiled, although they didn't comment on it. It was the last time I saw the Hajja before I heard that she had surrounded herself with the pomp of a mujahida, and now used her story to strike advantageous bargains with trading families who were sympathetic to our group. (Some time later, I went to visit Um Mamdouh in Hama, who resented Hajja Souad's standing.) That day, we laughed with joy at being free, delighted with the plates of kebab and other skilfully prepared food. My position as a medical student and my uncles' ascendancy in the carpet trade had prevented the trial which I expected from Hajja Souad, who had nothing more than her past to protect her. I felt that I still loved her when I saw her prison clothes, sewn with tokens of her wretchedness, hanging in her living room: a sacred amulet, testimony that the executioners had left us alive, although they were beasts whom we would never forgive.

I spent the last ten days in prison in great anxiety. Fasting calmed me and made me seem lighter, as befitted a woman about to leave Hell for all the minutiae of the outside world she had waited for so ardently. I had a few odds and ends which I gave to whoever wanted them, and left Um Mamdouh the task of distributing the rest. I closed my eyes and dreamed of a never-ending flight; from above, I could see rivers and countries, and I climbed over mountains as lightly as a butterfly. I hovered around Marwa's house so she would notice me, before revealing to her that I was that young girl she had known, who was now returning to her notebooks, and sitting Marwa's son down beside her. I had kept his picture inside my clothes, but I gave it to Layla after seeing her rush over and kiss it as if he were her own child, whom she had left with an old, half-blind mother. They lived in a house which was partly destroyed by a mortar shell. Layla had just left the bedroom to make coffee for her new husband; she went back in, and saw him in pieces. Our child slept in Layla's embrace. I told him stories and tried to recall the ones about a fox, even though he didn't know what it looked like. He only liked Rasha's stories, so we tried to copy the alluring way she narrated them, and failed. She would tell him how the fox Abu Ali spoke to the dog Abi Mandhar, and our child would laugh and imagine the story coming to life in front of him, including in it the warders, whom he knew as well as they knew him. I offered to take him with me, as had everyone else who had been released, but Suhayr never agreed. She wanted an additional witness to her story. These witnesses had now grown into a crowd which came every night to hear snippets of a myth where legend mingled with reality.

I didn't sleep at all on the last night. I was terrified that my name would be overlooked. In the morning, I kissed everyone and we all cried as we had never cried before. We released trills, which we called our twenty-one-gun salute to a guest of this large palace. In the office, I signed papers I didn't read; I didn't shake hands with the captors whose gaze still assessed the magnitude of the hatred I had borne and hidden inside me. I went outside with the guards who had come to effect my transfer. I got into the Peugeot estate; I carefully put my hands into the cuffs which a member of the Mukhabarat held up. We drove out of the prison. Omar and Maryam had been stationed in front of the main gate since dawn, but the only thing they saw of me was my hand-cuffed hands, waving from the car. I saw Maryam through the haze of my tears, and she looked like a scarecrow. The Mukhabarat officer refused my plea to stop for a moment so I could take her hand and reassure her. I saw the sky and it made me dizzy. The car went through Bab Masalla on its way to the Mukhabarat building. Seeing life passing by this simply and easily made me feel faint. I wanted to throw up; I couldn't understand this rush of feeling. I could see Omar's car in the rear-view mirror, and Maryam was leaning out as if she wanted to say something to me and couldn't wait any longer.

The unit's guards, interrogators and officers were all three and a half years older, and I was three and a half centuries older. I saw that Abu Jamil was going very grey; he welcomed me mockingly, as if deriding my wish to leave prison. He used to openly state his sectarianism and praise the desert-prison massacre in front of us, concluding his speeches with expressions of revenge on our group. I had often remembered him when I was ordering my enemies in my head: he was the officer who had fallen in love with Suhayr. When we heard the news that he had lung cancer, we all set up a trill and Suhayr danced, carrying her child in her arms. He was now weak and feeble, and I looked at him pityingly. I almost kicked him, because I didn't need anyone to lead me along the corridor to the cells. It was as if I were returning to a house I knew well. I waited in silence for four more months, sifting the gravel from a bowl of bulgur wheat with a skill we had all perfected, before they summoned me and led me to the commander's office. His health had improved a little after the government dispatched him to a French hospital. He told me to sit, so I sat, and forgot my dream of leaving. He spoke at length about the good will of the compassionate leader, and I nodded. He concluded with a wish that the past few years had guided me on to the right path and convinced me that my group was criminal, and that they

405

themselves were patriots who wanted nothing more than to safeguard the country. I didn't open my mouth. When he got up and handed me the piece of paper which authorized my release, he reached out to shake my hand, so I reached out to transfer the poison of my hatred. I shook the hand of my enemy and looked into his eyes, and I knew that he was dead.

# TRANSLATOR'S NOTE

While translating this novel in the second half of 2011, I experienced one of those rather neatly choreographed moments that rarely occur in real life. It would open a writer to the heinous crime of a 'contrived device' if it were to be included at a pivotal point of their plot. Towards the middle of *In Praise of Hatred* you will read a description of the ruling regime's systematic cleansing of Aleppo's university, and the arrest, interrogation and exile of those professors who were deemed to be insufficiently loyal. On the day I translated that particular passage, I turned on the news to hear the headlines – the second news item of the day was a story about Bashar Al Assad's methodical purge of Aleppo University, complete with enforced resignations and the arrest and subsequent 'disappearance' of several members of staff. It was a grim reminder that, although the players may have changed, little else about Syria's rulers has.

Readers may remember that before the current uprising against Bashar Al Assad, there was also an uprising against his father, Hafez, and it is this period of unrest that forms the focus of the novel. In the mid seventies Syria witnessed a marked increase in hard-line Sunni fundamentalism in response to the totalitarian excesses of the ruling elite, comprised mainly of individuals from the Alawite sect, a branch of Shia Islam. As the majority of Syria's Muslims are Sunni, widespread resentment at this monopoly of power was a useful ally for Islamist groups such as the Muslim Brotherhood, who harboured ambitions of over-throwing Alawite rule and instituting a state under *sharia'* law, of which they would naturally be leaders. After a series of increasingly violent attacks and reprisals by both the government and the Islamists, the city of Hama eventually declared open war on the Assad regime on 3 February 1982; in response to this challenge, Hafez gave his brother, then head of his security apparatus, *carte blanche* to deal with the insurgency as he saw fit. The result was the systematic destruction of one of Syria's most beautiful cities, and the massacre of tens of thousands of its inhabitants. Aleppo was not immune to crackdowns during these years after an increase in violent activities and assassinations. A regular target for the authorities, the trauma it suffered from was a drawn-out and relentless affair, documented closely by the novel.

It is vital to remember that *In Praise of Hatred* is not a historical record, but a representation of a particularly painful episode of Syria's history. Nevertheless, events draw heavily on real life and none of the atrocities committed by either side are fabricated; although no names of contemporary Syrian figures or organizations have been given, readers may recognize the oblique references to events and people from that time.

It is worth mentioning for those who don't read Arabic that the English edition looks quite different to the original text. After consideration, the publishers have decided to make some editorial changes, taken in consultation with the author, and the result is a novel that ends differently from the original.

At the time of writing, the current uprising has passed its first anniversary. The Assad regime has been shelling the Baba Amru suburb of Homs; even the most conservative estimates of casualties are still numbered in the many thousands and Syrians live in terror of arbitrary arrest and imprisonment, where torture and murder are rife. In contrast to the uprising central to the novel, this insurgency does not have a stronghold in any particular political ideology; it is another manifestation of the wave of discontent that has swept the Middle East, where the populace has had enough of the dictators draining their countries dry. When Bashar assumed power in 2000 it was hoped that he would reform the draconian rule instituted by his father, but any hopes for a more open and democratic government had been dashed long before this brutal crushing of dissent. It is difficult to know what direction events in Syria will take, but readers may see that the Assads have always been willing to go to extreme lengths to retain their grip on power, and the mindless sacrifice of innumerable Syrian citizens is a price they are more than content to pay.

*In Praise of Hatred* is a study of the absence of love and understanding in a nation historically famed for its tolerance. Khaled Khalifa has said before that the novel does not espouse any political ideology, but was written as a plea on behalf of the Syrian people for tolerance and peace. At the present time Syria's future is uncertain, and somewhat bleak. Nevertheless, as long as there are voices like Khalifa's raised against hatred and championing humanity, there must still be a ray of hope for this beautiful, blighted country.

I would like to thank Elias Saba for very kindly providing a translation and background information for the poetry by Mutanabbi on p. 46. And of course, many thanks are due to the author for his constant patience and good humour, both when dealing with my questions, and in general.

Leri Price
March 2012